PRAISE FOR THE NOVELS OF *NEW YORK TIMES* BESTSELLING AUTHOR *DALE BROWN*

"Dale Brown is a superb storyteller."
W.E.B. Griffin, *Washington Post*

"[Brown] gives us quite a ride."
New York Times Book Review

"The novels of Dale Brown brim with violent action, detailed descriptions of sophisticated weaponry, and political intrigue. . . . His ability to bring technical weaponry to life is amazing."
San Francisco Chronicle

"A master at creating a sweeping epic and making it seem real."
Clive Cussler

"His knowledge of world politics and possible military alliances is stunning. . . . He writes about weapons beyond a mere mortal's imagination."
Tulsa World

"Nobody does it better."
Kirkus Reviews

"Brown puts readers right into the middle of the inferno."
Larry Bond

Also in the Dreamland Series

(with Jim DeFelice)
Raven Strike
Black Wolf
Whiplash
Revolution
Retribution
End Game
Satan's Tail
Strike Zone
Razor's Edge
Nerve Center
Dreamland

Titles by Dale Brown

Tiger's Claw • A Time for Patriots
Executive Intent • Rogue Forces
Shadow Command • Strike Force
Edge of Battle • Act of War
Plan of Attack • Air Battle Force
Wings of Fire • Warrior Class
Battle Born • The Tin Man
Fatal Terrain • Shadow of Steel
Storming Heaven • Chains of Command
Night of the Hawk • Sky Masters
Hammerheads • Day of the Cheetah
Silver Tower • Flight of the Old Dog

DALE BROWN

AND

JIM DeFELICE

COLLATERAL DAMAGE

A Dreamland Thriller

HARPER

An Imprint of HarperCollins*Publishers*

This is a work of fiction. Names, characters, places, and incidents are products of the authors' imagination or are used fictitiously and are not to be construed as real. Any resemblance to actual events, locales, organizations, or persons, living or dead, is entirely coincidental.

HARPER
An Imprint of HarperCollins*Publishers*
10 East 53rd Street
New York, New York 10022-5299

ISBN 978-0-06-171303-3

First Harper premium printing: December 2012

Printed in the United States of America

Visit Harper paperbacks on the World Wide Web at
www.harpercollins.com

10 9 8 7 6 5 4 3 2 1

Dreamland: Duty Roster

Setting

Libya, Sicily (Italy)

Key Players

Americans

Breanna Stockard, director DoD Office of Special Technology (Whiplash supervisor)

Jonathon Reid, special assistant to CIA deputy director (Whiplash supervisor)

Colonel Danny Freah, commander, Whiplash

Captain Turk Mako, U.S. Air Force pilot, assigned to Office Special Technology/Whiplash

Chief Master Sergeant Ben "Boston" Rockland, senior NCO, Whiplash

Ray Rubeo, president and CEO, Applied Intelligence, key contractor to the Office of Special Technology

Colonel Ginella Ernesto, commander A–10E squadron "Shooters"

President Christine Todd

Senator Jeff "Zen" Stockard

The Rebels

Princess Idris al-Nussoi, leader of the rebel alliance

Others

Foma Mitreski, Russian chief of station, Libya and northern Africa

Neil Kharon, freelance technical operative employed by Russians

COLLATERAL DAMAGE

MALFUNCTION

1

Over Libya

THE VISION UNFOLDING BEFORE TURK MAKO'S EYES was one part natural beauty and one part high-tech phenomenon. Flying over central Libya at just under the speed of sound, he had a 360-degree view of the desert and scrubland that made up the country's interior. He could see every detail—leaves on low bushes starting to droop from the lack of water as the season turned dry, tumbled rocks that had been placed thousands of millennia ago by tectonic displacement, the parched side of an irrigation ditch abandoned to nature.

There were other things as well—the hull of an antiaircraft gun abandoned two years before, the picked bones of a body—not human—at the edge of a paved road that seemingly ran for miles to nowhere.

That was the ground. Turk had a similarly long and clear view of the sky as well—light blue, freckled with white in the distance, black retreating above as the sun edged upward in the east.

Turk saw all these things on a visor in his

helmet. Though the images looked absolutely real, what he saw was actually synthesized from six different optical cameras placed around the fuselage of his aircraft. The image was supplemented by other sensors—infrared, radar—and augmented by interpretations from the computer that helped him fly the Tigershark II. The computer could provide useful information instantly, whether it was simply identifying captions for the aircraft flying with him—four small unmanned fighter-bombers known as Sabres—or analysis of objects that could be weapons.

For Turk, an Air Force test pilot assigned to the CIA–Department of Defense Office of Special Projects, the synthesized reality portrayed in his helmet was real. It was what war looked like.

He checked his instruments—an old-school habit for the young pilot, still in his early twenties. The computer would alert him to the slightest problem in the plane, or in his escorts.

Everything was "in the green"—operating at prime spec.

The planes he was guiding were two minutes from the start of their bombing run. Turk gestured with his hand, and instantly had a visual of the target.

"Zoom," he told the computer.

As the screen began to change, a warning blared in his ears.

"Four aircraft, taking off from government airfield marked as A–3," declared the computer. "Located at Ghat."

Turk's first thought was that it was a false alarm.

He'd been flying the Tigershark and its accompanying Sabre unmanned attack planes over Libya for more than a week. Never in that time had he even gotten any indications of ground radar, let alone airplanes being scrambled. The alliance helping the rebel forces had established a strict no-fly zone in the northern portion of the country, and a challenge area in the rest of the country. The Libyan government air force had responded by keeping its planes on the ground practically everywhere, fearing they would be shot down.

When he realized it wasn't a mistake, Turk's next thought was that the planes weren't coming for him—the Tigershark and the four UAVs she was guiding were relatively stealthy aircraft, difficult to detect even with the most modern radar. The Libyan government, which had inherited most of its equipment from Muammar Gaddafi's regime, mostly relied on gear two decades old.

But the long-range scan in his helmet visor showed that the four Mirages taking off from the airfield were in fact headed in his direction.

All presumed hostile, declared the computer. It had automatically queried the planes' friend or foe ID system and failed to find friendly matches. But even if that information hadn't been available, it didn't take much silicon to guess whose side they were on.

"Weapons ID on Bandits One through Four," said Turk.

"All bandit aircraft similarly configured," declared the computer. "Carrying four Matra Super 530F antiair radar missiles. Carrying two Sidewinder missiles. Sidewinder type not identified. Computing."

The Matra Super missiles were medium-range, radar-guided antiaircraft weapons; while it wouldn't be fair to call them impotent, they were many years old. Similar to American Sparrows, the missiles used a semiactive radar system, taking their initial target data from their launch ship. The missiles would then continue to home in on the reflected signal, following the radar to the kill.

There were several limitations with such a system, starting with the fact that the launch ship had to lock on its target and then stay in a flight pattern that would keep it illuminated for a fair amount of time. The latter often meant that it was making itself a target.

There was no indication yet that the enemy planes even knew the Tigershark and her four escorts were there. Finding the planes, let alone locking them up for missiles, was not easy. The Tigershark and the Sabres had radar profiles smaller than an F–35. In fact, Turk had a hard time believing that the Mirages even knew his flight was in the air—right up until the moment he got a missile launch warning.

He double-checked with the computer. The Mirages had not locked onto the Tigershark or any of the four attack planes flying with him. Nonetheless, the four missiles—one from each Mirage—were all heading in their direction.

While ostensibly under his control, the four robot aircraft took evasive maneuvers without waiting for him to react. They dove toward the ground, making it even harder for the enemy to track them. They also altered course slightly, further diminishing the radar profile the enemy might see.

While each Sabre had ECM capabilities—electronic countermeasures that could be used to confuse the enemy missiles—these remained off. Under some circumstances, using the ECMs would be counterproductive, tipping an opponent off to their presence and even showing him where the target aircraft was.

The Tigershark's computer, meanwhile, began suggesting strategy for countering the attack. For Turk, this was the most annoying and intrusive aspect of the advanced flight system. He felt he was being lectured on what to do.

The fact that the computer was inevitably right only heightened the pain.

The computer suggested that he take a hard right turn, snapping onto a flight vector that would put his aircraft at a right angle to the incoming fighters. It then suggested another hard turn into them, where he would fire four AMRAAM-pluses. Missiles away, he would head back toward the UAVs.

He couldn't have drawn it up better himself.

But was he allowed to shoot them down? His ROEs—rules for engagement—directed that he not fire until he found himself or other nearby allies "in imminent danger."

Did this situation meet that standard?

If these guys couldn't hit the broadside of a barn, would any situation ever meet that standard?

Turk called in to the air controller aboard an

AWACS over the Mediterranean. He was handed off immediately to his supervisor, the acting "air boss" for the allied command.

"Four hostile aircraft, they have fired," said Turk. "Am I cleared to engage?"

"Cleared hot," the controller replied. "We see the launch—you are in imminent danger."

"Roger. Copy. Tigershark engaging."

While keeping the missiles in mind, Turk cut west to begin his attack on the planes. The Mirages split into two groups, one staying close to the original course north and the other vectoring about thirty degrees farther east.

Turk told the controller that he was ready to fire. Before the man could answer, the Mirages suddenly accelerated and fired more missiles.

"No lock," added the computer, telling him that the missiles had been fired. Turk guessed that the pilots in the Libyan jets had only a vague idea where he was, and were trying to bluff him away—a foolish strategy, though not entirely without precedent.

"Cleared hot to engage," reiterated the controller, just in case Turk had any doubts.

He did—he'd never shot down a real plane before—but that concern was far from his mind. His training had taken hold.

"Lock targets Three and Four," Turk told the computer. "Lock enemy missile one. Compute target course. Prepare to fire."

"Targets are locked." Red boxes closed in around each of the enemy aircraft depicted in his helmet. "Ready to fire."

Lined up on Mirage Three, Turk pressed the trigger. Within a nanosecond the Tigershark's rail gun threw a bolt at the lead Mirage.

The weapon emitted a high-pitched *vwoop* as it fired, and the aircraft shook like a platform when a high-speed train shot by. As soon as the shot was away, Turk moved the aircraft slightly, hitting the next mark lined up on his targeting screen, which was playing in the pseudo-HUD at the center of his helmet visor.

Vwoop!

He had to turn for the missile, but it was still an easy shot.

Vwoop!

All three shots were bull's-eyes; the projectiles hit their targets with less than .0003 percent deviation.

The projectile fired by the gun was relatively small, with a mass of only .7 kilograms—approximately a pound and a half. But the gun accelerated it at something in excess of 5,000 meters per second, giving the tungsten slug an enormous amount of kinetic energy—more than enough, in fact, to whip through the armor of a main battle tank.

In a conventional air battle, the pilot of a targeted jet might have many seconds and even minutes to react to a missile shot. He might employ a range of evasive maneuvers and countermeasures to ward off the incoming blow. In a head-on encounter at high speed, he would have the added advantage of a wide margin of error—in other words, even luck would be on his side.

In this case, luck wasn't part of the equation. The pilots had no warning that the weapon had been fired; there was no signal from the Tigershark or the missile for the Mirages to detect. Traveling at close to two miles per second, the projectile reached the closest plane in a little more than ten seconds.

In a conventional air fight, a pilot hit by a missile would generally have several seconds to react and eject; under the best circumstances, he might even have time to try and wrestle some sort of control over the aircraft. But the rail gun's bullet took that away. Under optimum conditions, which these were, the targeting computer fired at the most sensitive part of the airplane—the pilot himself.

Turk's first shot struck through the canopy, went through the pilot, his ejection seat, and the floor of the jet.

The second plane was dealt a similar blow. The missile was hit head-on as well, igniting it.

Turk had no time to celebrate, and in fact was only vaguely aware of the cues that showed his bullets had hit home. Aiming for the two surviving Mirages, he corrected his course twenty-eight degrees, following the dotted line marked on the display. This took him another eight seconds, an eternity in combat, but he knew from training that the key was to move as gently and deliberately as possible; rushing to the firing solution often made things take far longer.

He got a tone and saw the red boxes closing around the two Mirages. He was shooting these from behind, though the gun computer was still able to aim at the canopies and pilots because he had an altitude advantage.

"Lock targets One and Two," he told the computer.

"Targets locked."

He pushed his trigger for target One. The gun flashed. The rail gun generated enormous heat, and its dissipation presented a number of engineering problems for the men and women who had designed the Tigershark. These were complicated problems of math and physics, so complex that the solutions were still being refined and perfected—the rail gun could only be fired a limited number of times before it needed to be stripped down and overhauled.

Turk's presence here was part of the shakedown process. As part of the safety protocol, he was only allowed to fire the weapon two dozen times within a five-minute interval, and the safety precautions built into the weapon overrode any commands he might give.

The protocols weren't a problem now. He lined up for his second shot, and pressed the trigger.

Turk felt a twinge of regret for his opponents. In the absence of evidence to the contrary, he assumed they were brave men and skilled pilots; they had no idea what kind of power and enemy they were facing. From their perspective, the sky ahead was clear. Then suddenly their companions exploded. Before they could react, their own worlds turned painfully black.

"All enemy aircraft destroyed."

In the space of some forty-eight seconds, Turk had shot down four enemy planes, and a missile for good measure. Few if any pilots could make a claim even close.

Not bad for his first encounter with manned planes, ever.

He had a few seconds to savor the victory. Then three different voices began talking over one another in his radio, all asking essentially the same thing—what was the situation?

The voices belonged to the AWACS controller, the flight boss, and the French leader of an interceptor squadron charged with providing air cover for any airplanes in the sector.

The flight boss took precedence, though Turk in effect addressed them all, calmly giving his perspective on what had happened. The French flight, which had been vectored to meet the threat, changed course and flew toward the airfield the Mirages had launched from, just in case any other planes came up to avenge their comrades.

An Italian flight of Harrier jump jets was diverted from another mission farther west and tasked to bomb the control tower and hangars at the airfield, partly in retaliation and partly to make it more difficult for other jets to join the fray. Lastly, the controller ordered an American Predator and a British reconnaissance flight to attempt to locate any survivors of the planes Turk had just shot out of the sky.

Turk asked the AWACS controller if he knew why the Mirages had scrambled in the first place. The controller's supervisor, an American squadron leader who had rotated into the position from the combat line, indicated that the aircraft might have been spotted visually as they came south, something that had happened often in the very first week of the war. It was also possible they had been seen by a radar at sea, or by a supposedly neutral ship—the Russians had several in the Mediterranean that weren't really neutral at all.

It was also possible, he added, that it was just bad luck—the planes took off, then happened to see an enemy.

Turk had his own theory: spies were watching the Sicily base and sending information back to Libya when different planes took off. It wouldn't be too much more difficult for a spy to infiltrate the allied command responsible for targeting or scheduling the aircraft.

He had other worries at the moment. While he was engaging the Mirages, the Sabres had begun their programmed attack. Unlike older UAVs such as Predators and Raptors, or even the Dreamland-designed Flighthawks, the Sabres featured what the geeks called "distributed autonomous intelligence." That actually involved two different features: first, the Sabres pooled resources ("distributed"), sharing not only their sensor data but their processing power; second, the Sabres were allowed to make their own battle decisions ("autonomous"). Not only did they decide the best route to battle, but they could pick their own targets.

This was highly controversial, even within the military. Robots were used all the time in battle, but a man ultimately pulled the trigger. While the aircraft were under Turk's command and he could override at any point, they were every bit as capable a human pilot of fighting on their own.

The aircraft were targeting a government tank formation near Wadi al-Hayat. Located at the north side of a small cluster of hills, the camp looked out over a wide expanse of desert. There were several towns and villages in the area. These were claimed as loyal to the government, but that status was in doubt. If recent history was a guide, the inhabitants would join the rebels as soon as a sizable force got close. And that would happen once the tanks were destroyed.

The primary targets were T–72s, venerable Russian-made armor equipped with 125mm main guns. The tanks had not been used in either this war or the 2011 conflict, but were nonetheless operational; they had moved up to their present position only a few days before. The Libyan government had recently obtained a shipment of ammunition on the black market.

The attack plan was simple. The UAVs carried four antiarmor Hellfire missiles each, had been given four tanks as targets, and would attack much as a group of manned attack planes. The autonomous programming in the UAVs allowed them to do this without human guidance or input, though Turk could intervene and redirect the attack if he wished.

Turk had run a half-dozen missions along these very same lines, and with the exception of the Mirages, this looked to be as routine as all the others. Using a hand gesture—his flight suit was specially wired to interpret gestures in conjunction with the command context, or the screen displayed on his visor—he pulled up the overall sitrep map. This was a large area plot that superimposed the positions of all four Sabres as well as the Tigershark on a satellite image. The real-time sitrep showed the four UAVs coming in exactly as programmed, flying at about fifty feet over the sand dunes just northwest of the encampment.

That made it difficult for the mobile SA–6 antiaircraft battery protecting the camp to spot them, let alone target them. A pair of ZSU–23 four-barreled mobile antiaircraft weapons were parked in their path, but the radar-equipped weapons had apparently not found them either; all was quiet as the small UAVs approached.

Turk had taken the Tigershark some one hundred miles to the southwest as he engaged the Mirages. He now swung back to get a view of the attack. He was still about fifty miles away—well beyond the range even of the high-powered optical cameras the Tigershark carried—as the first aircraft reached its attack point.

"Visual preset two," he told the computer. "Image screen B Sabre One."

The command opened a new window on his virtual cockpit screen, displaying the feed from Sabre One.

Turk watched the aircraft launch a pair of missiles at the command and control vans for the SA–6 site. Launched from approximately five miles away, the Sabre's missiles used an optical guidance system to find their targets: the small sensors in their head essentially looked at the terrain, identified their targets based on preprogrammed profiles—photos, in this case—and flew at them. This meant that there was no signal from the missiles or their launch planes to alert the defenses to their presence; the first thing the Libyans knew of the attack were the explosions, which occurred almost simultaneously.

The destruction of the two vans rendered the missile battery useless, but the enemy's SA–6 missiles themselves were still relatively high-value targets, and as soon as the destruction was recorded, Sabre One's combat computer pushed the plane into a second wave attack on the launchers, two tanklike chassis sporting three missiles instead of a turret.

The first strike created an enormous secondary explosion, shrapnel and powder shooting across the complex. The Sabre's second missile disappeared into a cloud of smoke; a bright burst of flame confirmed that it, too, had hit its target.

Turk switched over to Sabre Two, which was aiming at one of the ZSU antiaircraft guns. It fired two missiles. Both hit. Still on the same approach, the aircraft dished out another pair of projectiles, this time at separate targets, having used the success of the first launch to decide it could go with just one shot per tank.

Meanwhile, Sabre Three initiated its own attack on the second ZSU gun and the nearby tanks. Using the data from Sabre One, it computed that one missile was all it needed to eliminate each target. It dished one at the gun, then fired three more in rapid succession, each aimed at a different tank.

By now Turk was close enough to see the battlefield through his own optical sensors. He closed the feed and expanded his screen, which duplicated in extremely high definition what he would have seen if the sleek Tigershark had a real canopy. Six plumes of black and gray smoke rose from the encampment, stark contrasts against the light blue sky and the gaudy yellow of the sand in the distance.

As he approached, Turk turned to get in line with a highway that ran through the area. The annual rains and an underground water supply combined to make the foothills suitable for agriculture, and a patchwork of tiny farm fields appeared under his nose. The squares were groves of citrus and olive trees, planted and tended by families that had lived here for generations. A little farther out were circles of green, round patches fed by pivot irrigation systems.

There was a flash of red in the far right corner of Turk's screen. He pointed his hand and told the computer to magnify.

It was a house, suddenly burning in a hamlet about four miles from the tank base. A black shadow passed overhead.

Sabre Four.

"What the hell?" sputtered Turk.

He watched in disbelief as a missile was launched from under the wing of the aircraft. The missile flew level for a few hundred feet, then dove down into the roof of what looked like a large barn. The building imploded immediately, setting up a huge cloud of dust and debris.

"Abort, abort, abort!" said Turk. "Sabre command computer, abort all attacks. Return immediately to base. Repeat, abort!"

"Authorize?" Direct command confirmation was necessary to override the preset attack plan.

"Authorization Captain Turk Mako."

Turk added a stream of curses even as the planes complied. He saw Sabre Four pull up and continue south, away from the settlement. Farther west, two other UAVs rose from their attack runs, missiles still clinging to their wings. The synthesized image included small tags under each, showing their IDs: SABRE 2 and SABRE 3.

He couldn't see the other plane. Where was it?

"Sabre One, status," said Turk.

"Optimal status," responded the computer. "Responding to abort command."

"Locate visually."

"Grid A6."

Turk glanced at the sitrep map in the left-hand corner of his screen. The aircraft was flying to the south.

"Sabre One, wingman mode," Turk ordered, telling the aircraft to shadow the Tigershark.

"Sabre One acknowledges," replied the computer.

He turned his attention back to Sabre Four, the aircraft that had fired its missiles on the village. The plane was rising in a wide arc to his south.

"Sabre Four, wingman mode," Turk told the computer, making absolutely positive it was responding.

"Sabre Four acknowledges."

Turk started to climb.

I hope to hell it doesn't decide to take a shot at me, he thought. It's a long walk home.

2

Sicily

SENATOR JEFF "ZEN" STOCKARD WHEELED HIMSELF past the row of parked F-35As, admiring the creative nose art employed by the RAF. No traditional shark mouth or tiger jaws for them—the first, on an aircraft nicknamed, "Show Time," featured a woman suggestively riding a bomb into battle, and they got less politically correct from there.

Zen was amused—though he also couldn't help but think about his young daughter. She was still in grammar school, but the images convinced him she wouldn't be allowed to date anyone from Great Britain until she was forty.

Pilots were completely out of bounds.

Zen pushed himself toward a pair of parked Gripen two-seat fighters. Their paint schemes were austere to a fault: the very respectable light gray at the nose faded to a slightly darker but still eminently respectable darker gray.

His interest was drawn to the forward canards, flexible winglets that increased the aircraft's lift at takeoff and landing speeds, as well as increasing its payload. The airplanes had only just arrived on the island as part of the multination peacekeeping force; they had not seen combat yet.

"Peacekeeping" was something of a misnomer in practice, though the alliance was trying to get both sides to the negotiating table. A month before, several European nations had acted together to condemn attacks by the Libyan government on civilians, and in essence begun supporting the rebellion. The U.S. had been asked to assist. Publicly, its role was limited to support assets, more or less what it had said during the 2011 war to oust Gaddafi. And just like that conflict a few years before, the U.S. was heavily involved behind the scenes, providing the unmanned aircraft and sensors that were doing much of the work.

As Zen stared at the fighters, he was hailed by a short man in jeans and a leather flight jacket. Few people spotting the man on the runway would give him a second glance, but Zen immediately recognized him as Du Zongchen, formerly one of the most accomplished pilots in the Chinese air force.

Zongchen was a native of Shanghai, but spoke English with an accent somewhere between Hong Kong and Sydney, Australia.

"Senator Stockard, once more I meet you on a tarmac," said Zongchen with a laugh. "I think perhaps you are considering flying one yourself."

"Du! Not a chance with any of these," said Zen brightly. "Though I wouldn't mind sitting in the backseat of one of those Gripens. I've never been up in one."

"Perhaps the UN can arrange for an inspection."

"You'd pull strings for me?"

"For the greatest fighter pilot of all modern history, nothing would be too good."

Zen smirked. Upon retiring as a general, Zongchen had entered government service as a representative to the United Nations. He had recently been asked by the UN General Assembly to inspect the allied air operation. As a neutral observer, Zongchen had considerable influence with just about everyone.

"If I were going to fly an airplane," the retired general confessed, "I would ask to try one of those."

He pointed across the way to a pair of F–22Gs, recently enhanced and updated versions of the original F–22 Raptor. The aircraft were single-seat fighters, which made it highly unlikely that Zongchen would get a chance to fly one—the Air Force wasn't likely to entrust what remained the world's most advanced interceptor to a member of a foreign government that still had occasions to act hostile toward the U.S.

"As soon as they get a two-seat version, I'll personally recommend you get a flight," said Zen.

"And then I will fly you in the backseat of a J–20," laughed Zongchen. Not yet operational, the J–20 was a Chinese stealth aircraft, more bomber than fighter. It, too, was a single-seat only plane, at least as far as Zen knew.

"How goes your inspection tour?" he asked.

"Very interesting," said Zongchen. "Much talk. Pilots are the same the world over, no matter who they fly for." He smiled. "Very full of themselves."

"Present company excepted."

"You are not. I am another story," said Zongchen. "I still think I am the best pilot in the world, no?" He patted his midsection, which though not fat was not as taut as it would have been a decade before. "The years affect us all. And the fine cooking. That is one thing I will say for NATO—good cooking. I hardly miss home."

"This isn't quite NATO," said Zen. It was a sensitive issue, since for all intents and purposes it *was* NATO—NATO countries, NATO command structures, the squadrons NATO would call on in an emergency. But the complicated politics required that the countries use a separate command structure called the "alliance," rather than admitting they were NATO.

"If you want to keep up the facade, that is fine with me," said Zongchen. "But other than that, the air forces are very professional."

"As good as Chinese pilots?"

"Chinese pilots are very good."

"I can attest to that."

"Senator?"

Zen turned and saw his aide, Jason Black, trotting toward him. Jason was his all-around assistant, in some ways more a son or nephew than a political aide.

"I think I'm being called back to work," he told Zongchen.

"Senator, I hate to interrupt you, but, uh, your wife was looking to talk to you," said Jason, huffing from the long run from the terminal buildings. "She has a limited time window. Your phone must be off."

"Guilty," said Zen. "Talk to you later, General."

He turned and started wheeling himself toward the building with Jason. When they were out of earshot, his aide whispered to him, "It's not Breanna. I'm sorry for lying. It was the only thing I could think of."

"Not a problem," Zen told the young man. "What's up?"

"There's been an accident with the Sabres. You need to talk to Colonel Freah."

Zen wheeled a little faster toward the building.

Ten minutes later, after negotiating the difficult bumps at the rear entrance to the building and then to the main corridor leading inside, the senator and former lead pilot for Dreamland entered a secure communications suite that had been set up for the American teams supporting the alliance. The room was literally a room inside a room inside a room—a massive sheet of copper sat between two sections of wallboard, which in turn were isolated from the regular walls of the Italian building. The space between the original room and the American inset was filled with nitrogen. Outside, an array of jamming and detection devices made it even more difficult to eavesdrop.

Two rows of what looked like ordinary workstations sat inside the room. All were connected to a secure communications system back in the States. Despite the high-level encryption, the system was so fast that the users experienced no lag at all.

There were drawbacks, however. Despite two small portable air-conditioning units, the room was at least ten degrees hotter than the rest of the building, and Zen felt sweat starting to roll down his neck practically as soon as he wheeled himself in front of the far terminal.

Seconds later Danny Freah's worried face appeared on the screen.

"Hey, buddy," said Zen. "What's up?"

"One of the Sabre unmanned aircraft went crazy," said Danny.

" 'Crazy' in what way?"

"It attacked civilians."

"What?"

"I know, I know." Danny looked grave. He was aboard an aircraft; Zen guessed he was on his way over from the States. "We're still gathering the details. Turk Mako is due to land in about twenty minutes."

Zen had helped develop the original Flighthawks some two decades before at Dreamland. It was another lifetime ago, though he still felt somewhat paternal toward the aircraft.

"You lost the aircraft?" he asked.

"Negative," said Freah. "At least we have it to pull apart."

"How is it possible?"

"I don't know." Danny shook his head. "We have an incident team already being assembled.

There's going to be a media shit storm. I figured you'd want a personal heads-up, especially since you're in Sicily."

"I appreciate that." Zen was planning to leave in the morning for Rome, but the heads-up would at least help alleviate some embarrassment.

"I was also wondering . . ." Danny's voice trailed off.

"What?" asked Zen.

"Could you meet Turk when he lands? I talked to him a few minutes ago over the Whiplash satellite system. He's a little shook up."

"Sure."

"I already talked to the White House," Danny added. "They suggested it."

"All right."

"I know it puts you in an awkward position. I know you're not there in an official capacity."

"It's not a problem."

"I've seen some footage of the attack from the Sabre," added Danny. "It's not pretty."

"I'll bet."

"There's more out," he said. "Posted on YouTube within the last few minutes. Supposedly by an outraged citizen."

"Supposedly?" asked Zen.

"Well, it was put up awful quick if you ask me. But it was definitely taken with a cell phone, so I guess it wasn't a setup. We're going to figure out what the hell happened, I promise." Danny took a deep breath. His face looked tired, but intent. "The Tigershark and the Sabres will be grounded until we're absolutely sure what happened. And until it's fixed. We will fix it. We absolutely will."

3

New Mexico

WAR HAD ALWAYS BEEN A COMPLEX CALCULATION FOR Ray Rubeo, one more difficult to compute than the most complicated calculus.

Rubeo had devoted himself to science from the time he was twelve, precocious and full of excitement over the possibilities knowledge offered. He had indulged his various interests, from computers to electronics, from biology to aerodynamics, for most of his life, first as an employee, then as a contractor, and finally as a businessman. Directly and indirectly, he had worked for various arms of the government, starting with DARPA—the Defense Department's research arm—then the Air Force at Dreamland, then the NSA and, briefly, the CIA. For the past decade he had run his own private company, with the government and its various agencies its primary customers.

The arrangements had allowed him to do a great deal. Unlike many scientists, he was able to turn the results of his pure research into practical things—computer systems, artificial intelligence programs, aircraft. Weapons.

And unlike many scientists, his work had made him an extremely rich man. Though he professed to have little use for wealth, he was not a fool. While science remained his passion, he was also very much an entrepreneur, and had no trouble reconciling capitalism with the supposedly more lofty goals of science that involved knowledge and mankind's quest to better itself.

Nor did he feel that there was an inherent conflict between science and war; he knew from history that the two pursuits were often necessary collaborators. Da Vinci was a pertinent model, but then so were the scientists who had unleashed the power of the atom on the world, saving hundreds of thousands of lives while killing many others.

Ray Rubeo could be cynical and hardheaded. More than one of his former employees would certainly swear that he was heartless. And in many ways he was and had always been a loner—a fact attested to by his home on a ranch of several thousand acres in the remote high plains of New Mexico.

But Rubeo also believed that science was, ultimately, a force for good. He had seen evil many times over the years, and in his heart he believed that science must fight against it. Not only in the vague sense of defeating the confusion and chaos of the unknown, but directly and immediately: if science was a product of man's better nature, then surely it found its greatest calling in fighting man's worst nature.

That was, for him, the simple reason that science and war coexisted: science opposed evil.

It was true, he conceded, that occasionally science was misused. Such things were inevitable. But they did not negate the fact that he counted himself among the good. He was not a religious man—at least from a conventional point of view he was arguably the opposite—but he was nonetheless moral.

And so, looking at the images he had just been sent, he felt his stomach turn.

It was not the destruction, or even the body of the child burned so badly that it was barely recognizable as human.

It was the fact that this destruction had been caused by his own invention, the intelligence system that guided the Sabre UM/F–9S.

Rubeo reacted to the video uncharacteristically—he deleted it. Then he flipped his tablet computer onto the table, got up and walked across the kitchen to the coffee machine. As it began brewing a fresh pot, he went out on the patio behind his house.

The sun was just rising over the hills. It was a brilliant sunrise, casting a pink glow on the clouds. The landscape in front of the rays brightened, the rocks and tall trees popping out as if they had been painted.

Rubeo walked to the far end of the patio, breathing in the air. He thought of the many people he'd known over the years, thought of the campaigns he'd been involved in, thought of the few people he regarded as friends.

Faces of those who were gone came at him. Jennifer Gleason, his assistant, his protégée—the only scientist who was truly smarter than he was, one of the few he'd turn to for advice on a difficult problem.

Gone, way before her time.

Too much nostalgia. Nostalgia was a useless sentimentality, a waste of time.

Back inside the house, Rubeo went down to his workout room and went through his morning routine quickly. The phones were ringing—his encrypted satellite phone, the work line, the private house line, and even the cell phone no one supposedly knew about.

He showered.

In the kitchen, he picked up the tablet and was glad to see that he hadn't broken it. He brought up his messaging program and retrieved the deleted file. He forced himself to look at it again. Finally, he took his private cell phone from the counter and called Levon Jons.

"Pack," he told him. "I need to leave in an hour."

"Uh, OK," said the former Marine.

Jons headed security for Rubeo's wholly owned company, Applied Intelligence, doubling as his personal bodyguard overseas. Rubeo knew that Jons was barely awake, but that was immaterial.

"What kinda clothes and how long?" asked Jons.

"It will be a few days at least," said Rubeo. He tapped the face of the tablet and got a weather report for Sicily. "It'll be warm during the day, cool at night. Thirty Celsius, down to twelve."

"English?"

"You are looking for Fahrenheit, Levon," said Rubeo dryly. "Roughly 85 degrees down to 54."

"OK. Where are we going?"

"Sicily, for starters."

4

Sicily

AFTER A SEEMINGLY ENDLESS SERIES OF DEBRIEFS AND interviews with intelligence officers and command, Turk was "released," in the words of the German colonel who was the chief of staff to the head operations officer, General Bernard Talekson. The colonel was not particularly adept at English, but the word choice struck Turk as unfortunately appropriate. More sessions were scheduled for the next day, and they would undoubtedly be more "rigorous"—another word used by the colonel with understated precision.

Turk was surprised when he left the headquarters building that it was only early afternoon; it felt as if he had been inside forever. Buses ran in a continuous loop between the various administrative buildings and the hangar areas. He hopped one and rode over to the area where the Tigershark and Sabres were kept. This was a secure area within the base; only personnel directly related to the mission were allowed beyond the cordon set up by the Italian security police.

All of the aircraft had been taken inside the

hangars. The Tigershark sat alone, parked almost dead center in the wide-open expanse of Hangar AC–84a. The Tigershark was a small aircraft—it would have fit inside the wings of an F–35. It looked even smaller inside the hangar, which had been built to shelter a C–5A cargo aircraft. So small, in fact, that even Turk wondered how he fit in the damn thing.

Chahel Ratha, one of the lead engineers on the Sabre team, was kneeling under the belly of the plane, shaking his head and mumbling to himself.

"Hey Rath, what's up?" asked Turk.

Ratha bolted upright so quickly Turk thought he was going to jump onto the plane.

"Didn't mean to scare you," said Turk.

"Then you should not sneak up on peoples!" said the engineer sharply. Even though he was American—born and bred outside Chicago—Ratha spoke with an Indian accent when he was excited. He blamed this on his parents, both naturalized citizens.

"Sorry," said Turk.

"Yeah, sorry, sorry. Yeah. Sorry."

Ratha waved his hand dismissively, then walked away, heading toward one of the benches at the far side of the office.

"Jeez," said Turk.

"Hasn't had his herbal tea today," said Gene Hurley, another of the maintainers. "Don't take it personally."

An Air Force contract worker, Hurley headed the maintenance team. Because of the advanced nature of the aircraft, the technical people were a mix of regular Air Force and private workers. Hurley had actually worked in the service for over twenty years before retiring. He claimed to be doing essentially what he had always done—but now got paid twice as much.

"He's freaking about the investigation," said Hurley. "And on top of that, all the janitors are on strike. Toilets are backed up and there's no one around to fix them."

"Really?"

"Italians are always on strike." Hurley shook his head. "Even the ones from Africa. If you gotta use the john, your best bet is hiking all the way over to the admin building. Or taking your chances behind the hangar."

"That sucks."

Hurley shrugged. "Third strike since we got here. I don't know why. The service people are always changing. And they're pretty incompetent to begin with. But at least the toilets worked."

"I just came by to see if you guys needed me," said Turk.

"No, we're good for now. Maybe tomorrow after we finish benchmarking everything we'll get down to some tests."

"Any clue what happened?"

Hurley shook his head. "I wouldn't want to guess," he said. "But if I did, I would start by saying that it almost surely didn't have anything to do with the Tigershark. But, you know—if I could guess about things, I'd be making a fortune betting on baseball."

"I'm going to knock off. Probably go back to

the hotel," Turk told him. "You need me, hit my sat phone."

"Sure thing."

Turk started away.

"We'll get it eventually, Captain," added Hurley. "We'll get you back in the air. Eventually."

EVENTUALLY.

The word stuck in Turk's consciousness as he rode the bus back toward the admin buildings. In his experience, "eventually" meant one of two things: never, and the day after never.

It was sick how quickly everything had turned sour. By all rights he should be celebrating right now—he had kicked ass and shot down *four* enemy aircraft in quick succession.

Four. He was still tingling about it.

Or should be. He could hardly even think about it.

The shoot-downs had been almost entirely glossed over in the debriefs. All anyone wanted to know about was the Sabre screwup.

Naturally. Stinking robot planes were the curse of the world. UAVs were taking over military aviation. The Predator, Reaper, Global Hawk, Flighthawks, now the Sabres—in four or five years there wouldn't be a manned combat plane in the sky.

The Tigershark was supposed to show that man was still needed. He was supposed to show that man was still needed.

And this accident showed . . .

Nothing, as far as Turk was concerned. Maybe

it would demonstrate why UAVs were not to be trusted, but somehow he didn't think that was going to happen. There was too much momentum, and too much money, for that to happen.

The bus stopped near the buildings used by the Italian base hosts, pausing for a few minutes because it was slightly ahead of schedule. Feeling antsy, Turk decided to get off and walk over to the lot where he had parked his car. It was a decent walk—about twenty minutes if he didn't dally too much—but it was just the sort of thing he needed to clear his head.

"*Ciao*," he told the driver, pretty much exhausting his store of Italian as he clambered down the steps.

They were miles from the sea, but the air was heavy with it today. The sun peeked in and out of the clouds, keeping the temperature pleasant. Sicily could be brutally hot, even in March.

Turk cut through the maze of admin buildings, zigging toward the lot. As he did, he heard something he'd rarely if ever heard on a military air base before—the sound of children playing. Curious, he took a sharp right between a pair of buildings and found himself at the back of a building used as a day care center by the Italian staff. A low chain-link fence separated a paved play area from the roadway.

A group of ten-year-olds playing a vigorous game of soccer caught Turk's eye and he stopped to watch. The kids were good. He had played soccer himself through high school, making all-county at midfield. He admired the way the kids handled the ball, able to move up not only through a line of defenders but across dips and cracks in the pavement without tripping or looking down at the ball.

Suddenly, the ball shot over the fence. Turk leapt up and grabbed it, goalkeeper style, as it was about to sail over his head. He hammed it up, clutching the ball to his chest and then waving it, as if he'd just caught a penalty kick at the World Cup.

The kids stared at him. There wasn't so much as a half smile among them.

"Here ya go," he yelled, tossing it back.

The player closest to it ran over, tapped it up with his knee, then headed it back over the fence. This was a challenge Turk couldn't turn down—he met it with his forehead, bouncing it back.

He was out of practice—the ball sailed far to the left rather than going back in the direction of the kid who had butted it to him. Another child caught it on his chest, let it drop and then booted a missile.

Turk jumped and caught it. He motioned with a mock angry face, pretended he was going to haul it back in the child's direction, then meekly lobbed it over toward the kid who had headed it earlier.

The boy caught it on his knee, flipped it behind him, and tried juggling it on the heel of his foot. But that was too much, even for the little soccer star in the making: the ball dribbled away. One of his teammates grabbed it and flicked it back to

Turk, who kicked it and managed to get it over to the kid who'd launched the missile earlier.

The back-and-forth continued for a while longer, and in fact might never have ended except for a van that pulled up at the head of the alleyway.

"Is that you, Turk?" called the man in the passenger seat.

It was Zen Stockard.

Turk bounced the ball back to the children and gave them a wave, then trotted over to the van.

"Bravo, il Americano," yelled the kids. *"Bravo!"*

"You have a fan club," said Zen.

"Just little kids—you see how good they are at soccer?"

"They look pretty good."

"I wish I was half that good now, let alone at their age."

"You seem to be holding up well," Zen told him. "You want a lift to your hotel?"

"I have a car in the lot."

"Rental?"

"There's like a pool at the hotel. You sign for it. Some days there's no cars, some days you have your pick."

"Hop in, we'll give you a ride."

Turk reached to the rear passenger door and slid it open. Jason Black was behind the wheel.

"I'm not supposed to say anything to you," Turk said. "Just, uh, just so you know."

"Colonel Freah told you that?"

"No, uh, General Dalce, the Frenchman."

"The intelligence chief, right?"

"Yes, sir."

Zen chuckled at some private joke.

"Thanks for meeting my plane, Senator," said Turk. "I appreciate it."

"Not a problem. I've been there."

Turk liked Zen—a lot—and he liked his wife, Breanna Stockard, who as head of the Office of Special Technology was his ultimate boss. But he wasn't entirely sure what he could or should say. Zen had been friendly and reassuring when he landed, but Turk hadn't been in the mood to talk. And now the questions the investigators asked made him suspicious that they were going to try and find some way of blaming him for the accident.

If there was an inquiry, Congress would probably eventually get involved. Anything he said now might come back to haunt him.

"You flying tomorrow?" asked Zen.

"Planes are grounded. I don't know—I'm sure I'll have to answer a lot of questions."

Zen was quiet for a moment. "I always tried to get right back in the air as soon as I could. Take a milk run or anything."

"Yes, sir." His options were pretty damn limited, Turk thought, but he didn't say that.

"I can mention that you're available, if you want," said Zen. "I know General Pierce pretty well."

"Sure." Pierce was the head of the American flying contingent. He was a two-star general; Turk had met him exactly once, in a reception line.

"Nice flying in that encounter," Zen continued.

"Four shoot-downs in the space of what? Two minutes."

"I think it might have been a little less, actually."

"Damn good. Damn good."

"Thanks."

It was high praise coming from Zen, who had pioneered remote combat piloting with the Flighthawks and had several dozen kills to his credit.

"I just kind of, you know, hit my marks," added Turk.

"I'm sure it was more than that."

"Well. It's what I did."

Turk wanted to say something more, but wasn't sure exactly what it should be. And so the conversation died.

Turk directed the driver to the car, which was near the front of the lot.

"Thanks for the ride," he told Zen as he got out.

"Any time," replied Zen. "You have the rest of the day off?"

"Oh yeah. I figure I'll catch something to eat. Maybe do some sightseeing or something later on. I'll be around, though."

"If you need anything, you should let me know."

"Yes, sir. Thanks."

ZEN WATCHED THE YOUNG OFFICER WALK TO HIS CAR. He couldn't blame Turk for being angry, even if he did hide it fairly well. The storm clouds were already thick and getting thicker. The Libyan government had picked up the images off You-

Tube and was circulating them far and wide. The casualty reports ranged from three to three dozen. A bevy of international journalists were en route, as evidenced by their Twitter feeds.

A tsunami of condemnation was sure to follow. Zen suspected that the matter would be brought before the UN General Assembly within twenty-four hours.

The only question was what effect it would have on the Western powers. Already there were rumors of a "pause" in the air campaign.

He turned to Jason. "We might as well go over to our hotel."

"He's pretty down," said Jason.

"Yeah, I don't blame him."

"All hell's going to break loose, huh?"

"Hopefully not on him," said Zen. "He seems like a good kid."

"Did he screw up?"

"Hard to say for sure, but I doubt it. Complicated systems."

"Yeah."

"He's practically a modern ace. He got those shoot-downs. Nobody's going to give him credit, though. They'll think the computer did it."

"But he was flying the plane."

"Yeah, but they won't think about that."

As Zen knew from his own experience, there was a sometimes bitter divide between "traditional" pilots and remote pilots. Turk actually fit into neither camp, as he did both.

In fact, it wasn't even easy to say where Turk fit in administratively. Technically, he was a test pilot assigned to the Office of Special Projects, doing temporary duty assigned to the allied flight command as part of a project to test the Sabres. He wasn't even an official part of Whiplash—the DoD and CIA joint command, which temporarily "owned" the Sabre UAVs on behalf of Special Projects.

"I'm just glad I'm not in the middle of it," said Zen. "What's the latest on Rome?"

"Flight is still on tomorrow for ten," said Jason. "You'll get there just in time for the opening speeches."

"Can't arrange to miss that bit, huh?"

"I thought—"

"Just teasing. Come on, let's go grab some dinner."

"Did you call your wife?"

Zen answered by pulling out his cell phone. Breanna had sent him a text earlier that he'd forgotten to return.

"Well, speak of the devil," she said, coming on the line.

"I'm the devil now? You must have been talking to the President."

"She doesn't think you're the devil. Just not a dependable vote."

"I wouldn't want to be dependable.

Zen followed Jason toward the rented van. It didn't have a lift; he had to crawl and climb into the front seat. It was undignified, but much preferable to being lifted, in his opinion at least.

"Danny told me you met Turk when he landed," said Breanna.

"I did, but Air Force security shooed me away,"

said Zen. "I tried to pull rank, but they said they were under orders from the Pentagon."

"I didn't issue any orders."

"I wasn't insulted," said Zen. "I imagine you're pretty busy, huh?"

"Up to my ears."

"Are you all right?"

"I'm fine. We have some people heading out to see what happened. Ray Rubeo is going, too."

"Ray himself?"

"He's really concerned."

Zen's relationship with the scientist was a complicated one. While he admired his intelligence and his work, he found Ray an extremely difficult man to get to know, and an even harder one to like. He certainly wasn't the type to hang out at the bar after work and have a few beers with.

"Congressman Swall is already calling for an inquiry," continued Breanna. "He wants to know if U.S. assets were involved."

"Well that's pretty damn easy to answer."

"Except that the general perception is that we're not involved in this war at all. So it'll be a firestorm one way or another."

Breanna seemed worn-out. Zen wished he was there.

"Teri says hi," she added, changing the subject. Her voice lifted a little. "You want to talk to her?"

"I thought you were at work."

"I am. We're having a video call. You want to talk to her?"

"Sure."

Breanna punched some buttons, and Zen

found himself on the line talking to his daughter.

"Why aren't you in school?"

"Superintendent conference."

"What is that?"

"Day off," said Breanna.

"Cousin Julie is babysitting," Teri told him. "I'm doing my homework."

She was having a little difficulty with triangles. They talked about them for a bit, then Breanna cut back in, muting their daughter.

"I'm afraid I have to get going here," she said. "Are you still heading for Rome?"

"In the morning. Why don't you meet me there?"

"Oh yeah, right."

"Come on. You're not doing anything."

"*Jeff.*"

Zen smiled. If he had a nickel for every time he had heard his name with that particular inflection, he would be a rich man.

"All right. See you next weekend, then," he told his wife.

"Love you."

"*Anche Io.*"

"Huh?"

"Italian for me, too. At least that's what they tell me."

AN HOUR LATER ZEN WAS MIDWAY THROUGH A DISH OF grilled baby octopus when he was approached by Du Zongchen, the Chinese UN advisor, who happened to be staying in the same hotel.

"Pull up a chair," said Zen. He gestured to his aide. "Jason, flag down a waiter and get General Zongchen a seat, would you?"

"Oh, no, no, thank you, Senator. Thank you very much."

"Have a seat," said Zen.

"I can only stay for a minute. I am on my way to an appointment. Very formal."

Zen nodded at Jason, who pushed over his chair for Zongchen then went to get another.

"All of this business with the airplanes, I know you have heard of it," he said to Zen. "What are your opinions?"

"No opinions." Zen shifted uncomfortably in his wheelchair. "I don't have all the facts."

"Very wise." Zongchen nodded. "I wonder, Senator—would you participate in an investigation?"

"I don't understand."

"Members of the General Assembly want me to investigate this matter personally. There will be a resolution tomorrow."

"I see."

"It will require an international presence. You were the first I thought of."

"I don't know." Zen wasn't sure how much Zongchen knew about what had happened—the news reports did not yet identify the aircraft as an American UAV, but there were certain to be rumors.

"You would bring integrity to the process," said Zongchen. "And expertise."

"What if my government or its allies are involved?" Zen asked. "That might be embarrassing."

"I would have to assume that if the event occurred, then one or more allied planes is involved." Zongchen nodded. "And I have heard many rumors that an American plane was the one there."

"I am fairly certain it was," admitted Zen. He saw no reason to lie to Zongchen, or even hold back basic information that would soon be common knowledge.

Zongchen bowed his head slightly, clearly appreciating his candor.

"To have a respected American aviator who is an expert, this would help the investigation a great deal," said the Chinese general. "We would be most enlightened. And things would be done in a cooperative manner."

That was the Chinese way—investigations were cooperative, not antagonistic. But the world Zen operated in was much more the latter.

"Do not answer now. Think about it, please." Zongchen rose. "It would add a great deal of integrity to the process."

"What was that about?" asked Jason, returning with the now superfluous chair when Zongchen had left.

"He wants me to join the investigation."

"Really? How would that work?"

"I doubt very well," said Zen, picking at his octopus.

TWO HOURS LATER ZEN WAS GETTING READY TO SPEND the rest of the evening in bed watching whatever Sicilian television had to offer when his cell phone rang. He picked it up and saw that the exchange was a familiar one.

He slid his thumb across the screen and said hello to the President's operator.

"Please stand by for the President, Senator Stockard."

Zen considered a joke about his inability to stand, but decided the poor secretary had enough to do without fending off his humor. President Christine Todd came on the line a few moments later.

"How is the weather in Italy, Jeff?" the President asked.

"Weather's fine. How's Washington?"

"Stormy as ever."

While they were members of the same political party, Zen and the President had never gotten along particularly well. Their relationship had always been a bit of a puzzle, not just to them but to those around them; philosophically, they weren't all that different, and certainly on the gravest national issues they thought very similarly. But their styles clashed—Zen was laid back and easygoing; the President was all calculation.

At least in his view.

"Let me get to the point," said Todd. "I know you've been briefed on the accident in Libya today."

"Somewhat."

"The UN General Assembly is going to call for an investigation. They're going to name a former Chinese air force general to head it."

"Zongchen," answered Zen. "Yes, I know him quite well."

"Good." The president paused. "I'd like you to be on the committee."

"Won't that be a little awkward?"

"How so?"

"For one thing, it involved airplanes that are under my wife's department."

"Actually, no," said the President. "They were assigned to the Air Force. In fact, your wife is not at all involved in the chain of command there."

Zen leaned his head back in his chair. What exactly was she up to?

"I think most people would see my involvement as a conflict of interest," he said finally. "I mean, Whiplash—"

"First of all, I'd prefer that Whiplash not be mentioned if at all possible. And secondly, I want a full investigation by someone I trust to give me all of the facts. If we did this, and it does look like we're the ones responsible, there's no sense denying it. Therefore, I want someone who knows what he's talking about giving me advice on how to fix it."

"Still, some people might expect a cover-up," said Zen. "People inside the government would know—"

"This isn't a cover-up. On the contrary—we'll have full disclosure. I'm going to give a press conference in a few hours. I want a thorough investigation. I want someone I can trust to do the right thing on the committee."

"The right thing?"

"Make sure that the committee is telling the truth," said the President, her voice even blunter than usual. "You know this is going to be a propaganda bonanza, Jeff. At least if you're there, I can trust some of the findings."

"Or be criticized for trying to hide them," said Zen.

"No. People have a high opinion of you. Other leaders. And the general public. As well as myself."

"I'm sure there's someone better."

"I'm not."

"Let me think it over," said Zen, fully intending on putting her off.

His voice must have made that obvious.

"Jeff, I know we've had a few personal difficulties in the past. I consider you my loyal opposition—and I mean that in a good sense. You've done our country, and this administration, a world of good. I know it's a lot to ask. But I think we need someone of your caliber on the oversight committee. You weren't involved in the operation, but you know as much about unmanned fighters as anyone in the world who's not directly involved."

"I know a lot about the Flighthawks," he told her. "Sabres are different beasts."

"Think it over. Please, Senator."

"I will."

"Best to your family."

Zen had no sooner hung up than there was a knock at his door.

"Come on in," he said, thinking it was Jason.

The second knock told him that it wasn't—Jason had a key. But now he had announced that he was there, and couldn't pretend not to be there.

"Who is it?" Zen asked.

"Mina Toumi, from al Jazeera news service," answered a woman. "I would like to ask a few questions, Senator."

"I'm in my pajamas."

"It will only take a minute. And I don't have a camera, only a voice recorder."

Al Jazeera—the Islamic news service based in the Middle East—had been generally favorable to the uprising. But he knew that didn't make any difference now. He didn't know what she wanted to talk about, but he could easily guess.

Was there a way to duck out?

"Give me a second to get my robe."

Zen fussed with his robe, pulling it tight. Then he realized that he really ought to have a witness—he sent a text to Jason and told him to come over to his room ASAP.

He rolled to the door, unlocked it, then moved back in the corridor.

"It's open," he said.

A young woman pushed open the door shyly. She was pretty—and young.

"I am sorry to bother you, Senator Stockard. I wanted a few questions about the incident."

"Is that a French accent?" asked Zen.

"My mother was from Lyon," she said. She was standing in the doorway.

"Tell you what—maybe I should get dressed and we can go somewhere a little more comfortable downstairs," said Zen, feeling very awkward in his robe.

"Oh."

"Could you just wait in the hall a moment? It won't take too long."

She stepped back. Zen rolled himself inside and grabbed his clothes. A few minutes later Jason knocked on the door.

"Senator?"

"Hang tight, Jay. Say hello to Ms.—"

"Toumi," she said.

Zen dressed as quickly as he could. When he came out of the room, Jason and Mina Toumi were standing awkwardly on opposite walls, staring down at the carpet. For just a moment Zen forgot that the woman was a reporter—they looked like they would make a fine couple.

"Senator Stockard, thank you for your time," said Toumi. She pulled out a voice recorder and held it toward him.

"Let's go downstairs where we can have a little more privacy. And you can sit down." He started wheeling himself toward the elevator.

"I didn't know . . ."

Zen glanced at her and guessed what the problem was.

"You didn't know I was in a wheelchair?" he asked.

"No."

"Yup. For a long time." He spun himself around and hit the button for the car. "It was during a flight accident. A plane went left when it was supposed to go right. They tell me I'm lucky to be alive."

"But, I heard you were an ace—"

"An ace?" He laughed. "Oh. Yes, I guess I am."

"An ace pilot," she said. "That you had been, before you were elected."

"Senator Stockard *is* an ace," said Jason, finally finding his voice, albeit a little awkwardly. "Certified."

"Jason's my flack," joked Zen, using an old term for a press agent.

She didn't understand. "You need a nurse?"

"I'm not a nurse," blurted Jason. "I'm his assistant."

Mina flushed. So did Jason.

Zen laughed. Clearly he was going to have to coach Jason a bit on how to deal with reporters . . . and women.

When they arrived at the lobby floor, the door opened on a small crowd. Zen felt a flicker of trepidation—were all these people waiting to talk to him? But it was a tour group, queuing to get up to their rooms after dinner. He rolled around them, heading down the corridor to a small conference room. Meanwhile, Jason went over and found a hotel employee.

The man unlocked the door. It was set up for a small talk, with four dozen chairs facing a podium at the front. Zen rolled down the center aisle to the open space near the podium and turned around.

"Grab a chair and fire away," he told Toumi.

She hesitated a moment—his slang had temporarily baffled her. Then she took her voice recorder out and began asking questions.

"So, you know about the accident?"

"I don't know much about it at all," said Zen. "I heard earlier that there was a bombing incident in Libya, and there are reports that civilians were hurt. This would be a tragedy, if true."

"If true?"

"I don't know whether it is true or not," said Zen, trying not to sound defensive. "Certainly if it is true, it would be terrible. Anytime anyone is killed or even hurt in war, it's tragic. Civilians especially."

"Should the perpetrators be punished?"

"I doubt it was deliberate," said Zen.

"But even mistakes should be punished, no?"

"I don't know the facts, so we'll have to see."

"In your experience," boomed a loud voice in American English from the back of the room, "are robot planes more apt to make this kind of mistake?"

Zen looked up. The man who had asked the question was wearing a sport coat and tie. Someone with a video camera was right behind him.

Several other people crowded in behind the two men as they came up the aisle.

"Are robot aircraft more prone to this sort of mistake?" repeated the reporter.

"I'm sorry, I don't know you," said Zen.

"Tomas Renta, CNN." The man stuck out his hand. "Pleasure to meet you, Senator."

I'm sure, thought Zen as he shook the man's hand.

"First of all, I haven't received any official word on what sort of planes were or weren't involved," Zen told the man.

It was an obvious fudge, and the reporter called him on it before Zen could continue.

"I'm sure you've heard the rumors and saw the YouTube tape," said Renta. "Everyone is saying it was a UAV."

"Well, theoretically speaking, unmanned planes are no more likely to have accidents than any other aircraft," said Zen. "The statistics are pretty close. Frankly, since people have been flying for so long, UAVs look a little better. Statistically."

The reporter drew a breath, seemingly gearing up for another question. Zen decided to beat him to the punch.

"But that doesn't meant that they can't have accidents," he said, looking directly into the camera. "It has to be investigated, obviously. I'm sure it will be. Speaking as a civilian—"

"And former pilot," said another journalist.

"And former pilot, yes." He gestured toward his useless legs. "My perception is, accidents can happen at any time. And they may be terrible ones. But I don't know what happened here, and I don't know that it would be of much value for anyone to pass judgment on anything until all of the facts are known."

"Should the U.S. compensate victims?" said the journalist. Zen thought he remembered him from a conference somewhere—he was an American representing AP overseas.

"I don't even know if it was a U.S. aircraft."

"Does this delegitimize the entire coalition involvement?" asked a short, dark-haired woman who'd just joined the group.

"How would it do that?" asked Zen.

"So killing civilians is its goal?"

She was obviously trying to bait him, but Zen had plenty of practice dealing with that sort of thing. He simply ignored her, turning back to the reporter for CNN.

"I think the coalition has a lot of good people here," he said. "I'm sure they'll figure out what happened and fix it. If it needs to be fixed."

"General Zongchen said that he wanted you on the investigating commission," said the AP reporter. "Are you going to join it?"

"I don't know."

"Why wouldn't you?" asked Toumi.

Mousetrapped. There was nothing else to do now but to sidestep, a maneuver best performed with a smile and a bit of a wink. Zen told them that he'd have to see what happened.

He proceeded to answer different variations of the same questions for the next ten minutes or so, until the reporters finally concluded that he wasn't going to change what he was saying. The man from CNN thanked him, and the others promptly turned around and headed away to file their stories.

"Well, that went over well," Zen said sarcastically to Jason. Following his aide's glance, he saw that Mina Toumi was standing on the other side of him.

"I'm sorry—you were trying for an exclusive," said Zen. "I didn't mean to ruin it."

"It's OK," she said.

"Did you get everything you needed?"

"I'm OK. Thanks." She gave him a tight smile, then left the room.

"Tongue back in your mouth," Zen said to Jason, who was staring after her.

"I wasn't—I didn't . . ."

"Relax, Jay. If it was any more obvious I'd have to hose you down. Did you get her phone number at least?"

"E-mail."

"You're on your own," Zen told him, wheeling from the room.

5

Benghazi, northern Libya

ALONE AS THE DOORS CLOSED, NEIL KHARON STEPPED back against the wall of the elevator and took a long, slow breath as he emptied his mind. Talking to the rebel princess required a complete suspension of ethics and opinion. Idris al-Nussoi was a despicable creature, ignorant and willful.

But perhaps that's why she had become the de facto head of the resistance.

Of course, it could be worse: he could be talking to the Libyan government officials.

His chest expanded slowly as he filled his lungs. He felt his muscles pushing outward, stretching the carbon-fiber vest he wore beneath his sweater as protection against a double cross. The vest would stop a Magnum round, and had even survived, intact, against a WinMag bullet in testing; otherwise he would not have put up with its constrictions. Kharon did not like to be constrained in any way. Tight spaces, like elevator cars, filled him with fear.

He could deal with it, as long as there was plenty of light. He had learned several tricks over the years.

He held his breath for a moment. The yoga guru he had learned the technique from emphasized the vibration one felt at this point, claiming that it put the adept practitioner in contact with the basic life force of the universe. Kharon had long ago dismissed this as bunk, but he savored the sensation nonetheless: a slight tingle through the muscles, relaxing against the nerve endings they intersected with.

A moment of calm preparation for the job ahead.

The elevator doors opened. Kharon stepped out and held up his arms as two men in tracksuits approached. They were bodyguards, though he wondered why anyone in their right mind would trust them. Disheveled, they smelled of fish and Moroccan hashish. They were several inches shorter than Kharon, and considerably heavier.

The one on the right frisked him quickly—it was so inefficient, Kharon could have smuggled an MP–5 in his pants—and then stepped back. The other growled in an indecipherable language—it wasn't Arabic, Berber, English, or Italian, all languages Kharon could converse in. But he knew from experience it meant he could go.

He walked down the hall toward a pair of men dressed in faded army fatigues. Their clothes were old, but the AK–74s they flashed as a challenge were brand new. These had been supplied by Kharon's sometime partner, a Russian spy-cum-arms dealer. The two men had been working together on and off now for several years, the Russian for profit, Kharon for something more satisfying and considerably darker.

The guards eyed him suspiciously even though they had just watched him being searched. Kharon ignored them as best he could, staring straight ahead at the door he was aiming for.

It opened before he reached it. His approach had been watched on a closed circuit television camera.

But there were no other sensors or bugs. A thin wire sensor in his shirt acted as an antenna, ferreting out transmissions. It would have buzzed gently to warn him.

"So, you have arrived. And on time," said the short, fat man who appeared behind the door. He was Oscar Sifontes, a Venezuelan advisor to the rebels, the princess specifically. In theory he was independent, though everyone knew he was paid by Petróleos de Venezuela, S.A., the state oil company. He had a cigar in his left hand and he waved it expansively, as if he was happy to see Kharon.

In reality, Sifontes considered him a tool of the Russians, and therefore a rival for influence. He had tried to persuade the princess to have nothing to do with him—something Kharon would have suspected even if he had not bugged the suite.

The Venezuelan's designer jeans were at least two sizes too small; with his white shirt, he looked like an ice cream cone, with a moustache on top.

And a very smelly cigar.

"We are having fine weather, do you not think?" said Sifontes, by way of making conversation. "It is more pleasant here than Sicily. The weather there was cloudy. In Libya, there is only sun."

"Weather is too random to consider," said Kharon.

While Sifontes struggled to translate the words into Spanish and then make some sense of them, Kharon strode from the small foyer into a large common room. The princess was sitting on a couch at the far end, watching a video feed on an iPad and talking on a cell phone at the same time. The iPad was a constant companion. It had been given to her by the Americans some months before as a present. It wasn't bugged—there had been numerous checks, including Kharon's own. Nonetheless, he suspected that the accounts it connected to were constantly monitored. The Americans never gave gifts without strings attached.

Kharon bowed slightly. It was an unnecessary flourish that the princess loved. She smiled, then in Arabic told whoever was on the phone that she would call back.

Her long black dress was baggy by Western standards, though here would be considered modern. The silk scarf that had slid back on her head had bright blue and green stripes on the deep black field, another straddle of old and new.

"Your trip back from Sicily was enjoyable?" Kharon asked in English. He preferred the language to Arabic because it was harder for her underlings to understand.

"Airplanes are not my favorite thing. But we made it in one piece."

"They treated you well?"

"Always." She dropped the iPad on the couch with a dramatic flourish. "But now we see that the Americans have bombed a city. That will set us back weeks."

"I don't think so," said Kharon.

"Eh, always an optimist," said the Venezuelan. He took a long pull from his cigar and exhaled. "You are good with science, but not with people's opinions, I think."

"Perhaps," said Kharon. "You have the key for me?"

The princess rose from her couch and walked to the settee across the room. She was a *real* princess, the daughter of a tribal leader whose claim to some sort of local royalty extended back several centuries. But that claim aside, the real attraction for the rebels following her were her looks. At thirty-five, she had the body of a woman ten years younger. But assuming that she was just a pretty face being used by others would have been a dangerous underestimation. The presence of the Venezuelan was proof of that. He was clearly a counterbalance to the Europeans and especially the Americans, who strongly suspected that his government was trying to curry favor with the eventual winners of the power struggle here.

They were right, of course.

The princess returned with a small thumb drive. Kharon gave it only a precursory glance as he took it.

"The man who delivered it was very scruffy," she said. "You really should deal with a better class of people."

Kharon ignored the comment. "The rest of the money will be in the accounts by this evening," he told her. "I appreciate your help."

"Maybe you should stay until then," suggested the Venezuelan.

Kharon turned his head and looked at the short, fat man.

"Señor Sifontes, are you suggesting I would cheat the princess?" he said coldly in Spanish.

"Oh, no, no, you misunderstand." Sifontes smiled weakly and turned to the princess. "He's worried that I think he's going to cheat you."

"Are you?" she asked Kharon.

"My integrity should be beyond doubt."

"When you deal with Russians, one wonders."

"The Russians have their pluses and minuses," said Kharon. He put the thumb drive in his pocket.

"I had heard that there were government planes near the city that was attacked," she said.

"I have heard that as well," said Kharon. "Do you think they made the attack, or the allies?"

"It would be convenient if they did. But from what I have heard, this was not the case."

"I see."

"I was wondering if you knew why the government chose that time to attack." The princess stared at him. "They have not flown their airplanes for several weeks, and now yesterday they come up. Perhaps they made the allied planes miss."

"I wouldn't put it past them," said Kharon.

"You have many contacts." The princess sat down on the couch, folding one of her legs beneath her. "I'm told you were south just recently."

"Who said that? The Russians?"

"I hear things." She waved her hand.

It had to be the Russian, he thought. Or had the Americans realized what he was doing?

Impossible. He would be dead by now. The fact that he could move around freely proved that they didn't know he existed.

"I do my share of traveling," Kharon told her.

"To both sides."

"As I've said several times, I don't care for either cause. Whatever advances my own goals are all I care about."

"Some people think you're a spy," said the Venezuelan.

"Who?" Kharon glared at Sifontes.

"Some people," said Sifontes. "I don't doubt that you are loyal."

"I am loyal to myself. That, I freely admit. In this case, our goals were similar."

"Stealing information from the Americans did not necessarily help my people," said the princess.

"But the money did."

"Yes." She smiled at him.

"I will stay if you wish."

"Oh, it's not necessary. Your payments have always arrived in the past."

"This one will as well. Until we have the pleasure of seeing each other again, Princess."

He nodded, smiled as evilly as possible at the Venezuelan, then left the suite.

ALONE IN THE ELEVATOR, KHARON TOOK THE SMALL USB key from his pocket. It looked like the right device, but he would not put it past the princess—or the Venezuelan—to try and cheat him somehow.

He smiled as he left the building, giving the surveillance cameras a big, toothy grin.

The princess was wrong. He was not trying to steal information about the American weapons. On the contrary. The USB key was one that his agents had used against them.

The Russian agents, to be more specific. Kharon didn't trust them to dispose of it on their own and had insisted that he get it back. The princess had saved him the trip to Sicily—a necessary precaution, as he didn't want to be linked to the "accident" in any way.

Not yet.

He crossed the street to a second hotel, the Awahi Sahara. Aimed primarily at businesspeople, the hotel had fallen on hard times since the start of the second revolution; it was less than a quarter full, and room rates had been slashed to thirty euros a night, nearly a tenth of what they had been before the war.

But Kharon hadn't come for a room. He went straight to the business center at the rear of the lobby, slipped a key card into the door lock and went inside. An older Italian gentleman sat at the computer at the far end of the row, flipping slowly through e-mail.

Kharon pulled the chair out in front of a computer. He moved the mouse to bring up the system screen, then took the USB drive from his pocket. With a glance toward the old Italian—he appeared absorbed in his work—Kharon pushed the key into the USB slot at the rear of the CPU.

The key didn't register as a drive.

So far so good.

He brought up the browser and typed the general address of Twitter. Entering an account name and password he had composed more or less at random, he did a search for #revoltinLibya.

The Tweet he needed was three screens deep. He copied the characters, then pasted them into the browser. That brought him to a Web page filled with numbers.

It was a self-test page, allowing him to ping the USB disk. A set of numbers appeared on the screen. He looked at the last seven: 8–23–1956.

Ray Rubeo's birthday. It was the right key.

He backed out, then moved the mouse to the Windows icon at the lower left of the screen. He went to the search line and typed *run*, adding the address of a small program he had installed on the computer several days before.

When he was finished, the unedited video of

the Sabre bombing mission had been uploaded to half a dozen sites.

AFTER HIS MOTHER DIED, NEIL KHARON HAD GONE east to live with an aunt and uncle. They were older, and not particularly warm people. Alone and isolated, he had concentrated on his schoolwork. It was an inverse acting out—his way of rebelling was to study harder and learn everything he could.

He soaked up knowledge. He loved math and science. Though not rich, his guardians had enough sense to get him into MIT for undergraduate work, and then, with the help of another relative, to Cambridge. From there, he studied on his own, making connections to labs in France, Germany, and Russia.

Russia especially. There, still barely twenty-one, he had been hired to work with a state research lab. At first he didn't know, or at least could pretend that he didn't know, that his real paymasters were officials in the Sluzhba Vneshney Razvedki, or SVR. Within a few months it was obvious. By then he no longer cared.

He was a star for them, a hired gun capable of anything. He learned to steal, to sabotage, and to live in the shadows. Always with one goal—someday he would know enough to ruin the man he blamed for his mother's death.

The Russians had been most helpful, paying him extremely well and, for the most part, allowing him to work where and when he wanted. They, too, were interested in Rubeo's inventions, though obviously for different reasons. An entire team had been set up to target them. Kharon had largely abandoned the team once the Sabres were discovered headed for Libya; the Russians did not particularly like his independence, but he was too important to be crossed. They treated him as a petulant child to be indulged—a particularly useful attitude for Kharon.

Over the past several weeks the dream he'd had for years morphed into something practical. Bits and pieces were still being formed in his head, but the overall shape had been set years before.

Ray Rubeo would be disgraced, ruined, and finally killed.

A COOL, MOIST BREEZE WAS BLOWING IN OFF THE Mediterranean, promising rain: a brief shower, surely, just a touch to take away the heat and keep the green spots of the city green.

Those spots were few and far between. The city had not yet recovered from the scars it had received during the first Libyan civil war, let alone the one it was fighting now. As he came out of the hotel, Kharon dodged a poorly laid asphalt patch on the sidewalk where a shell had fallen a month before, just as the uprising began.

War was a constant in mankind's history, more so in the areas that could least afford it. When he was a young man, Kharon had contemplated such thoughts for days on end. Though trained as both an engineer and a scientist, his mind had a philosophical bent, and on his own he read all of the great Western philosophers, from Plato and

Aristotle to Derrida and Julia Kristeva. But in all that reading, he had failed to find an answer to the most basic questions of life and death. Or at least find one that satisfied him.

Now he had little use for philosophy, at least in so much as it related to the question of war. War was useful to him; that was as far as he needed to ponder.

Kharon walked to the end of the block, passing the car he had used to get here, and continued across the street. There, he turned right and walked down an alley to a small shop that once rented bicycles to tourists, but now eked out a living repairing and selling them.

Ten euros bought a Chinese bike only a few years old. Kharon pedaled a bit uncertainly as he started, his balance wobbly. But before going a hundred yards he had mastered it, and joined the light traffic heading toward the sea.

A few minutes of pedaling brought him to the big lot at the base of the harbor. He rode the bike to one of the old-fashioned light poles, then hopped off gingerly. Propping it against the post, he walked between the cement benches toward the water.

The beachfront had been restored after the first war. But it was empty today, as on most days, its austere beauty a reproach to the haphazard and dirty city behind it.

Kharon stared at the water as if he were a tourist or perhaps a poet, contemplating his place in the universe. He turned to his right and began walking parallel to the water lapping against the stones. Glancing casually to his right, he made sure he hadn't been followed. Then he stopped again, and dropped the USB memory key on the ground.

He stooped to pick it up, started to rise, then stooped down again to tie his shoe. As he did, he ground the key under his heel, breaking it in two.

Rising with the device in his hand, he ripped it apart, exposing the chip. He snapped the memory chip from the rest of the device and walked closer to the water.

Over the rail, he went down onto the scrabble of rocks and sand and walked to the edge of the water. He bent, picked up a flat stone, then skipped it and the chip out across the surface of the nearby sea. The stone popped against the water, rose, flew farther, popped again, then plunked down with a tiny splash.

The chip had gone only halfway to the first large wave, but it was far enough. The saltwater would quickly deteriorate it.

Satisfied, Kharon turned and walked back to the promenade that lined the water. He glanced at his watch. Things had gone well, but he was behind schedule. He needed to leave for Tripoli as soon as possible.

6

Sicily

TURK RESTED HIS ELBOWS ON THE TABLE AT THE CENTER of the ready room, then cradled his face, reviewing in his mind what had happened. He was starting to think he should get a lawyer.

"I went to intercept the fighters," he told the three men who'd been interviewing him since 0600 that morning. "That's why I was off-course. I wasn't off-course at all," he added, realizing that he had inadvertently used his interrogator's language. "I set my own course. The course that was programmed into the Tigershark's computer was my plan. Plans change."

He raised his face, letting the whiskers of his unshaven chin scrape against his fingertips. His interviewers were French, Greek, and British, left to right, all members of their respective countries' air forces. They had been talking to him now for over three hours.

"When you change your course from the program," asked the Frenchman, "this then reprograms the fighters?"

"It doesn't necessarily affect them," said Turk. He glanced to his right toward Major Redstone, an Air Force security officer who was supposed to prevent any classified information from being discussed. Redstone said nothing, nor had he said anything the entire time they'd been in the room. "The UM/F–9Ss are autonomous until overridden. As I said before, they control themselves."

"Explain how that works," said the British RAF officer.

"I don't think I can."

"Because it is classified?"

"Because I don't know exactly how things work on that level," said Turk. "I'm not a programmer or an engineer. I'm a pilot. I fly the plane. I'm trained to be able to deal with the UAVs, but without the system itself, I would have no idea how they work."

The Frenchman leaned toward the others and whispered something. Turk turned to Redstone. "I'd really like some coffee."

"Let's take a break," suggested Redstone, finally finding his voice.

"A few more questions and we'll be done for the day," said the Greek.

"Let's get some coffee first," said Turk, who'd heard the "few more questions" line a half hour before.

"The captain should remain sequestered while we get the coffee," said the Frenchman. "No offense."

"Fine," said Turk.

Redstone nodded. "Black, no sugar for me."

Just as the Frenchman reached for the door, a tall, thin man opened it and came in. Turk recognized him immediately—it was Ray Rubeo, the scientist who headed the team that had developed the artificial intelligence controlling the Sabres. Rubeo looked at the foreign air force officers—it was more a glare than a greeting—then stood against the wall.

"Excuse me, chap," said the RAF officer. "Who are you?"

"Dr. Rubeo. I am reviewing the incident."

"We're conducting an interview."

"I understand," said Rubeo.

The men seemed puzzled by his answer, but didn't follow up. Rubeo remained, silent, standing against the wall. Turk thought he was full of contempt toward the foreign officers, yet if the pilot had been pressed to explain where this impression came from, he would have been at a loss. It was in his posture, his stance, his silence—subtle and evident, though somehow inscrutable.

Redstone came back and the officers began questioning Turk again, starting off with the most basic questions.

"You are twenty-three years old?" asked the Greek.

"Uh, yeah."

"And already an accomplished test pilot."

"I was in the right place at the right time," said Turk.

"But also very good, no?" The Greek smiled. Obviously the others had designated him Mr. Nice Guy, peppering Turk with softball questions.

Yes, said Turk, he had done well throughout his career. Part of the explanation for his young age was the fact that he'd gone to college two years earlier than most people, and graduated in three. But yes, he had been very lucky to be blessed with good instructors, and above all hand-eye coordination that was off the charts.

Not that it mattered so much when flying a remote plane.

And then he had been assigned to Dreamland?

Actually, he worked at Dreamland for only a short period. Some of his work, as a test pilot, was highly classified.

He needn't supply the details. Just give a general impression.

The Brit took over. How was the mission planned, who had authority to call it off, at what point had he known there was a problem?

Turk tried to answer the questions patiently, though he'd answered them all several times, including twice now for the men in the room.

"The autonomous control," said the Frenchman, finally returning to the point they really wanted to know. "How does it work?"

"Specifically, I don't know."

"In a general way."

"The computer works to achieve goals that have been laid out," said Turk.

"Always?"

"It has certain parameters that it can work within. In this case, let's say there's twenty tanks or whatever it was. It has priorities to hit certain tanks. But if a more important target is discovered, or let's say one of the tanks turns out to be fake, the computer can reprogram itself. The units communicate back and forth, and the priority is set."

"So the computer selects the target?" said the RAF officer.

"Yes and no. It works just the way I described it."

"How can that be?" asked the Greek. "The computer can decide."

"It works precisely as the captain has described,"

said Rubeo. "I'm sure you have used a common map program to find directions to a destination. Think of that as a metaphor."

"Excuse me," snapped the Frenchman. "We are questioning the captain."

Rubeo took a step away from the wall. His face looked drawn, even more severe than usual—and that was saying quite a bit in his case. "I'm sure the mission tapes can be reviewed. The pilot is blameless. You're wasting his time. There's no sense persecuting him like this."

Though appreciative, Turk was surprised by Rubeo's defense. Not because it wasn't true—it absolutely was—but because it was the opposite of what he expected. While he had no experience in any sort of high level investigation, let alone something as grave as this, he'd been in the military long enough to know that the number one rule in any controversial situation was CYA—cover your ass.

The others were baffled as well, though for different reasons. The RAF officer asked Rubeo how he knew all this.

"The team that designed the computer system worked for me," said Rubeo. "And much of the work is based on my own personal efforts. The distributed intelligence system, specifically." He looked over at Redstone. "I don't believe the exact details are necessary to the investigation."

"Uh, no," said Redstone. He sounded a little like a student caught napping in class. "Specifics would be classified."

"Precisely." Rubeo turned back to Turk. "The

aircraft responded to verbal commands once you overrode, didn't they, Captain?"

"Yes, sir."

"And there was no indication that there was a malfunction, either while you were dealing with the government planes or later on, was there?"

"No, sir."

"At no point did you give an order to the planes to deviate from their mission, or their programming, did you?"

"No, sir."

"You can ask if he took any aggressive actions following the shoot-down of the Mirages," Rubeo told the other officers. "But I don't think you'll get any more useful information from the pilot. As I said, he's quite correct—he had nothing to do with the malfunction."

"It was a malfunction?" asked the RAF officer.

"You don't think the aircraft are programmed to kill civilians, do you?" snapped Rubeo.

Judging from their frowns, Turk wasn't entirely sure that they didn't.

7

Sicily

"THE CONCEPT OF CONFLICT OF INTEREST—IT IS A very American idea," Du Zongchen told Zen.

"The fact that you are familiar with the program for many reasons—that is why I requested you. I am sure no one would object."

"People will object to anything," replied Zen. He glanced around the large suite room; two of Zongchen's assistants were speaking into cell phones in a quiet hush at the side. Another was working in one of the bedrooms, which had temporarily been converted into an office. "That's one thing that I've learned the hard way. They always object."

"But you will help me," said Zongchen happily. "You will assist."

"I will, but I want you to know that it's likely to be—that there may be controversy. Other members of the committee may object."

"I have spoken with them. They are all impressed and wish your assistance."

"Even so, the general public—"

Zongchen waved his hand. Zen wondered if Chinese officials were really so far removed from popular opinion and criticism that they didn't have to worry about accusations that they had unfairly influenced events.

If so, he was envious.

"Our first order of business," said Zongchen, "after the others join us, is to arrange for an inspection of the area. I am to speak to the government officials by videophone at the half hour. Do you wish to join me?"

"Sure."

"And then, to be balanced, we speak to the rebels. This is a more difficult project."

Zongchen rose from the chair. It was a boxy, stylish affair, but it didn't look particularly comfortable. The Chinese general walked over to the small console table and poured tea into a small porcelain cup.

"Are you sure you would not like tea or coffee, Senator?"

"No, thanks."

"In China, there would be scandal if people knew that I poured my own tea," said Zongchen. "It is customary for aides to do everything. To hire more people—in a big country such as mine, everyone must work."

"Sure."

"The little jobs. Important to the people who do them." Zongchen glanced toward his aides at the side of the room, then came back over to the chair where he had been sitting. The suite was decorated in an updated Pop Modern style, a Sicilian decorator's take on what the 1960s should have looked like. "These rebel groups—there are simply too many of them."

"There are a lot," said Zen.

"Some of them." Zongchen shook his head. "I do not like the government, but some of these rebels are many times worse. This woman, Idris al-Nussoi."

Zongchen made an exasperated gesture with his hand. Idris al-Nussoi—generally known as "the princess" because of her allegedly royal roots—was the figurehead of the largest rebel group, but she was by no means the only rebel they had to speak with. Zongchen hoped to get an agreement for safe passage of the investigators. This was not necessarily the same thing as a guarantee for their safety, but it was the best they could do.

"Coordinating the air campaign with the rebels must be a matter of great difficulty," said Zongchen.

"I don't know," said Zen truthfully. "But I imagine it must be."

"Shall we call for some lunch?"

"Sure."

THEIR FOOD HAD ONLY JUST ARRIVED WHEN THE CONference call with the government began. By now several more members of the international committee assigned by the UN to investigate the matter had joined them in the suite. They included an Egyptian army general, a Thai bureaucrat, and an Iranian named Ali Jafari. As a former member of the Republican Guard, Ali Jafari was not particularly inclined to view Zen or any American with anything approaching favor. But he was nonetheless polite, telling Zen how very grateful he was for his decision to join the committee.

Which of course made Zen doubly suspicious.

The video connection was made through Skype, the commercial video service. As such, they all assumed it was insecure, being monitored in capitals around the globe—and probably by the rebels as well. But this suited Zongchen's purposes. He wanted everyone to know exactly what the committee was doing.

Beamed wirelessly from one of the aide's laptops onto the suite's large television, the feed looked slightly washed out. But the connection was good.

The deputy interior minister was speaking for the government. Zen saw that this annoyed Zongchen; he had clearly expected a higher ranking official, most likely the minister himself. The mood worsened when the deputy minister began with a ten minute harangue about how the allies were being allowed to murder innocent Libyan people.

Zen watched Zongchen struggle to be patient. It didn't help that the deputy minister's English, though fluent, was heavily accented, making it hard for the Chinese general to understand. Zongchen turned occasionally to two aides for translations into Chinese. The men, too, were struggling with the accent, asking Zen several times for clarifications.

Finally, the Libyan allowed Zongchen to tell him that the commission wanted to inspect the sites.

"This will be arranged," replied the deputy minister. "We will need identities—we do not want any spies."

"We expect safe conduct for the entire party," said Zongchen. "And we will choose our own personnel."

"You will submit the names."

"We will not," insisted Zongchen. It was a small point, thought Zen—surely giving the names was not a big deal—but the general was holding his ground for larger reasons, establishing his independence. "We are operating under the authority of the United Nations to investigate this matter, and we will be granted safe passage. If you do not wish us to investigate it under those terms, you may say so."

The deputy minister frowned. "No Americans," he said.

"There will be Americans," said Zongchen. His voice was calm but firm. "There will be whomever I decide I need to accompany me. This investigation is in your interests. But you will not dictate the terms. We will undertake it on our terms, within the precepts of international law, or we will not undertake it at all."

The Libyan finally conceded.

"I will make the arrangements," he told Zongchen. "But you had best get safe conduct from the criminals as well. We cannot guarantee your safety with those apes."

"We will deal with them on the same terms we have dealt with you," said Zongchen.

The feed died before Zongchen finished. The Chinese general glanced around the room.

"I believe that went well," he said, with the barest hint of a smile. "And now, let us talk to the rebels."

8

Sicily

TURK WANTED TO THANK RUBEO FOR COMING TO HIS aid during the interview, but the scientist left the room before he got a chance; he was gone when he reached the hall.

He went over to the hangars and found out that the Tigershark and Sabres were still grounded, and would be for the foreseeable future. Unsure what else to do, Turk headed toward the base cafeteria to find something to eat.

Cafeterias on American military installations typically provided a wide variety of food; while the quality might vary somewhat, there was almost always plenty to choose from. The host kitchen here, run by the Italian air force, operated under a different philosophy. There were only two entrées.

On the other hand, either one could have been served in a first-class restaurant. The dishes looked so good, in fact, that Turk couldn't decide between them.

"I would try the sautéed sea bass with the *arancine* and *aubergine*," said a woman in an American uniform behind him. She was an Air Force colonel. "Or get both."

"I think I will. *Due*," he told the man. "Two?"

"*Entrambi?*" asked the server. "*Si?*"

"I don't—"

"Yes, he wants both," said the colonel with a

bright smile. Turk couldn't remember seeing her before. "Tell him, Captain."

The server smirked, but dished up two plates, one with the bass, the other with quail.

Turk took his plates and went into the next room. The tables were of varying sizes and shapes, round and square, with from four to twelve chairs. They were covered with thick white tablecloths—another thing you wouldn't typically find in a base cafeteria.

He picked a small table near the window and sat down. The window looked out over the airfield, and while he couldn't quite see the tarmac or taxiing area, he had a decent view of aircraft as they took off. A flight of RAF Tornados rose, each of the planes heavily laden with bombs—probably going to finish off the airfield the government planes had used the day before.

No one wanted to talk about *that* encounter, Turk thought to himself. The briefing had been little more than an afterthought.

Oh, you shot down four aircraft. Very nice. So tell us about this massive screwup.

By rights, Turk thought, he ought to be the toast of the base—he had shot down four enemy aircraft, after all.

"I see why you took two meals," said the woman who'd been behind him in the line. "Hungry, huh?"

Turk glanced down at his plate. He was nearly three-fourths of the way through—he'd been eating tremendously fast.

"I didn't have breakfast," he said apologetically.

"Or dinner yesterday, I'll bet. Mind if I join?"

"No, no, go ahead. Please," said Turk. He rose in his chair, suddenly embarrassed by his poor manners.

She smiled at him, bemused.

"You don't remember me, do you?" she asked, sitting.

"I, uh—no. I'm sorry."

"Ginella Ernesto."

"I'm Turk . . . Turk Mako."

He extended his hand awkwardly. Ginella shook it.

"You were involved in the A–10E program at Dreamland," she said. "You briefed us. My squadron took the planes over."

"Oh."

"Still think the Hogs should be flown by remote control?"

"Uh, well, actually I like the way they fly."

Ginella laughed. The A–10Es were specially modified versions of the venerable Thunderbolt A–10, far better known to all as "Warthogs," or usually simply "Hogs." The aircraft had begun as A–10s, then received considerable improvements to emerge as A–10Cs shortly after the dawn of the twenty-first century.

The A–10Es were a special group of eight aircraft with an avionics suite that allowed them to be flown remotely. There were other improvements as well, including uprated engines.

"We had met before," added Ginella. "I waxed your fanny at Red Flag last fall."

"You did?"

"You were checking out a Tigershark. I was flying a Raptor. Masked Marauder."

Turk had been at a Red Flag, but as far as he could remember, no one had gotten close to shooting him down—which was what Ginella's slang implied. But she didn't seem to be bragging and he let it slide.

Besides, though a good ten years older than he was, she was very easy on the eyes.

"How do you like Italy?" she asked.

"I haven't seen that much of it."

"You've been here a couple of weeks, haven't you?"

"Yeah, but I've been pretty, uh, I've had a lot to do."

"You should have time coming now with four kills, huh?"

Turk felt his cheeks redden. "Not exactly."

"No? See now, if you were in my squadron, I'd make sure you had down time—and maybe a free stay at a fancy hotel of your choice."

"Maybe I should ask for a transfer," he blurted.

Ginella smiled, and started eating. Turk had lost his appetite and felt awkward and out of sorts, as if he'd just blown some major opportunity.

Suddenly he felt very thirsty.

"I'm going to go grab something to drink," he told Ginella. "You want something?"

"Sure."

"Uh, what?"

"Well, that wine would be nice, but since I have

to fly later, just some of that sparkling water. The Ferrarelle. It's the one in the green bottle that's not Pellegrino."

"Gotcha."

Turk went back to the serving area and got two bottles of water, along with some glasses. When he returned, Ginella was texting something on her BlackBerry. He opened one of the bottles and poured some water for her, then filled his own. The water was fizzy, and a little heavy with minerals.

"Flu," said Ginella, looking up from her phone. "Half my squadron is down with it."

"What's your squadron?"

"The 129th, Shooter Squadron."

"That would be A–10Es."

"You got it. Still flown by people."

"It's a great aircraft," said Turk. "I was just, you know—"

"The hired monkey."

It was a put-down he'd heard many times: Most of Turk's work had been to sit in the cockpit while the remote control concept was tested. But he had done a lot more than that.

"It's all right," continued Ginella. "We staved off the geeks for now. We still have people in the cockpit."

"The machines flew OK," said Turk. "But, uh, it's too nice a place not to have a man at the stick."

"Or a woman."

"Right." He felt his cheeks redden at the faux pas, and hurriedly changed the subject. "When did you get here?"

"Yesterday."

"The way you were talking, with the food and the water, I thought you'd been around."

"With a name like Ernesto, you don't think I've ever been to Sicily before?"

"I just . . . I don't know."

"Mako—that's Italian?"

"My great-grandfather shortened it from Makolowejeski. This is the first time I've ever been in Italy."

"Sicilians think they're from a different country," said Ginella. She started telling him a little about the island and Italy in general. Her great-grandparents had come from different parts of the "mainland," as she called it. She still had some relatives living there.

Turk kept waiting for her to turn the conversation to the "incident," but she didn't. Instead, she regaled him with a veritable travelogue, detailing the beauties of Siena and Bologna, her two favorite cities in the whole world. Turk had never had much interest in visiting Italy, but now felt guilty about that.

"You don't like to travel, do you?" she said to him finally. Then she got an impish grin. "Are you afraid of flying?"

"Very funny."

"You should do more sightseeing."

"Maybe I will. I guess you've probably heard about the, uh, accident."

Her face became serious again. "Yes, I'm sorry. It must be a real ordeal."

"It is," said Turk. "It's—the whole thing was weird. But . . . I'm not supposed to talk about it."

"So don't." She smiled, and took a sip of her water. "You know, this is naturally carbonated. Other waters have carbon dioxide pumped into them, like seltzer. Yuck."

"I kinda like seltzer."

"Oh, excuse me, Captain." She laughed. "I didn't mean to insult you."

Before Turk could answer, they were interrupted by two pilots in flight suits, bellowing across the room as they entered.

"Hey, Colonel, how's it hanging?" said the taller one.

"Colonel, Colonel, we are here to brighten your day," said the other man, much shorter—he looked perhaps five-four—and so broad-shouldered that Turk thought he must have a hard time fitting into the cockpit.

"Private party?" asked the taller pilot when they were closer.

"Turk Mako," Ginella said, "let me introduce two of the worst pilots on the face of the earth. How they manage to stay off that face of the earth is beyond me. Captain Johnny Paulson." The taller man bowed. "And Grizzly."

"That's Captain Grizzly to you," said Grizzly, putting his plate down.

"I'm Turk Mako."

"No shit." Paulson grinned. "Are we allowed to sit at the superstar's table?"

"Careful, Pauly boy," said Grizzly. "He's liable to vaporize you with a death ray."

"Don't take them seriously, Captain," said Ginella. "No one else does."

"Because we are bad boys," said Grizzly. "That's why we fly Hogs."

"As did Turk," said Ginella. "He's the guy who ran all the A–10E tests."

"The monkey who sat in the seat for the geeks, right?" said Paulson after sitting down. "What do you think, Dreamland? Do we look like remote controllers?"

"I was just saying it's such a great plane to fly that it would be a shame to do it by remote control."

"Got that straight."

"Excuse me, gentlemen. I'm going to get some dessert." Ginella rose. "Captain, would you like something?"

"I'm good. Thanks."

"We hear you're better than good," said Grizzly as the colonel walked toward the serving area. "You fried four planes yesterday."

"They kinda got in my way," said Turk.

"Ha, that's a good one," said Grizzly, across the table. "What do you think of the Hog?"

"It's good," said Turk.

"You were a passenger," said Paulson.

"No. I pretty much flew every day a couple of hours at least. The remotes tests were just a part of it."

"How long?"

"Couple of months. It's better than the A–10C, thanks to the engines, and the—"

"Thank God they didn't go ahead and put remote controls in it," said Paulson. "Then we'd all be working for Dreamland. Like you."

"I don't work for them. But what's wrong with Dreamland?"

"Oh, Dreamland," said Grizzly. Smiling, he jumped off his chair and fell to his knees. He extended his arms and lowered them as if worshipping Turk. Paulson followed suit.

"Good, you got them on their knees," said Ginella, returning. "It's a position they're used to."

"Only for our dominatrix leader," said Grizzly in a loud stage whisper. "For her, anything."

"Don't look now," said Paulson, "but here comes the Beast."

"Oh, God," said Grizzly.

"Are you degenerates eating off the floor again?" growled a black pilot, strolling over. He was tall and well-built, a linebacker in a flight suit. His smile changed to a frown as he turned to Ginella and in a mock-serious tone said, "I'm sorry you have to see this, Colonel. Perversion in the ranks."

"We're just worshipping at the altar of Dreamland," said Grizzly, rising. "This is Turk Mako."

"No shit." Beast held out his hand. Turk rose to shake it. "Pleased to meet you, Captain."

"Turk."

"There room for me here?" joked Beast. His name tag declared his last name was Robinson. "Or is this a segregated table?"

"It's segregated all right," said Grizzly. "Pauly boy was just leaving."

"Hahaha."

"Actually, I'm done," said Turk, getting up. "You can have my place."

"Don't let them chase you away," said Ginella.

"We can move to a larger table," said Grizzly.

"No, I got some stuff I gotta do."

"Look, I'm grabbing a chair and pulling it over," said Beast.

"I gotta check my plane and do a million little things," said Turk.

"Colonel, given that Turk here has flown Hogs," said Grizzly, "maybe we can get him on board as a backup. We need subs."

"That might not be a bad idea," said Ginella. "What do you think, Captain?"

"Well, uh—"

"I understand your aircraft is grounded until they figure out what happened to the Sabres."

"Something like that."

"I am short of pilots," said Ginella. "You want me to talk to your command?"

Turk hesitated. He *did* want to fly. Even Zen had suggested he should. He liked the A–10E, a predictable, steady aircraft. But it had been nearly a year since he'd been in a Hog cockpit.

"Does Dreamland have the stuff to be a Hog driver?" asked Paulson mockingly. "It's a come-down from his sleek beast."

"I could handle it," said Turk.

"I'll talk to some people," said Ginella.

Turk shrugged. "Sure."

BACK AT THE TIGERSHARK AND SABRE HANGARS, TURK discovered that the guard had been doubled. The men were visibly tense, and not only asked for his ID card but examined it carefully.

"Hey, Billy, what's up with all this?" Turk asked one of the security people he'd grown friendly with.

"Big honchos from D.C. are tearing apart the airplane," said the sergeant. "How you holding up, Cap?"

"I'm good. What honchos?"

"Pinhead types." The sergeant shrugged.

"Dr. Rubeo?"

"Couldn't tell you. They drove up in a couple of SUVs, had attaché cases—kinda like the *Men in Black* movie. You ever see that?"

"Not in a long time."

"We're not supposed to go inside even because of the security."

"No shit?"

The sergeant shook his head. "I don't know. Maybe they think we'll see that it's put together with rubber bands."

"It's actually paper clips," said Turk.

Inside AC–84a, the Tigershark had been stripped of much of the top of her skin. A large scaffolding ladder sat over her nose, and two mobile platforms extended over her wings. Several other ladders, ranging from four to sixteen feet, were arrayed next to various parts of the aircraft.

Gear was spread all around her. Men dressed in white suits dotted the aircraft. They looked like surgeons. Several others, wearing blue suits similar to the scrubs a hospital surgical team would use, manned a portable computer and other sensor screens at three different workbenches set up on the far side of the plane.

Another group of men and women were standing at the side of the hangar behind a velvet rope, as if the Tigershark were a nightclub and they were waiting to get in.

"Captain Mako," said Ray Rubeo, walking over to him from behind the plane. He was wearing blue scrubs. "What can we do for you?"

"I just thought I'd see if the Tigershark was ready to fly."

"It will be a few days," said Rubeo. "I'm sorry, Captain. As I told the investigators this morning, this has nothing to do with you, or anything you did."

"Thanks for that," said Turk.

Rubeo stared at him.

"I just wanted to make sure the plane is OK," said Turk.

"So do we," said Rubeo.

"What do you think happened?"

Rubeo sighed. It was a loud sigh—Turk had heard it described by Breanna and others as a horse sigh.

"I cannot speculate," said the scientist. "Even if I was given to speculation, which I am not, in this case, I simply can't."

"You think it was the Tigershark?"

"It must be ruled out."

"Guess I'll go take a nap," he told Rubeo.

TURK WASN'T ABOUT TO TAKE A NAP, THOUGH IN TRUTH he wasn't really sure what to do with himself. He headed toward the headquarters building, thinking he might at least check in with the duty officer and see if there was an assignment he could rouse up. If not, maybe he would follow Ginella's suggestion and check out some of Italy. She made it sound pretty alluring.

Maybe a nice tour of the country would divert him. Even better, maybe he'd find a nice Italian girl, one who'd whisper some sort of Italian come-on in his ear.

Ciao. Bene.

He was nearly at the building when he was flagged down by one of General Talekson's aides. Talekson, an RAF officer, headed operations for the coalition; he was giving a briefing to the squadron leaders and wanted to know if Turk could detail his encounter with the four Mirages.

"Be glad to," said Turk, happy to finally have something to do.

The session had already started by the time they got there. The general sat at the front of the large conference room, frowning. An RAF major on his staff—the intel officer, whom Turk had met only once—was giving an overall situation report. He flailed at a map projected on the large screen in front of him, waving his laser pointer around as he spoke of the government concentrations. The rebellion had started in the area of Benghazi, northern Libya, and slowly spread west and south. The government forces had done a good job moving their equipment down, and clearly had more of it ready to use than had been suspected.

"The airfields marked A3, A6, A7, and A8 have been hit this morning," said the major. He used the laser pointer in his hand in a highly impressionistic way, barely pausing at the spots he referred to. A3 was the airfield at Ghat, where the Mirages had launched from the day before.

"The fields are only marginally usable. This is a double-edge sword," added the major. "It means we will be delayed from making them usable when the rebels take them over."

"Quite," said the general.

The intelligence officer continued, saying that he didn't believe the government could launch any more aircraft, as they were only in possession of two more airfields, neither of which was long enough for the fighters still in their possession. Nonetheless, the allies would have to be mindful, as he put it. The Libyan government still had upward of eighty fighters.

"Most are obsolete Mirages and older MiG–23s, –25s, and –27s," said the general, interrupting. "But there are MiG–29s, and we have heard rumors of at least six Sukhoi Su–35s. We have not located them. Which frankly is more than a little worrisome. If they exist."

The intel major smirked, and a few of the squadron leaders did as well. Clearly, they didn't think the planes would materialize.

The general looked over at Turk.

"Captain Mako is here. Perhaps he can tell us about the Mirages he encountered."

"Glad to." Turk glanced around. "I don't have the gun video—I'm kinda doing this off the top of my head. But there really wasn't much to it, I guess."

He ran through the encounter. It seemed pretty simple now that he recounted it.

Line 'em up and shoot 'em down.

Turk didn't say that, but he certainly thought it. The squadron leaders asked about his aircraft and the weapon. The questions were mostly technical: how much was automated, how far away was he when the engagement began and ended. But one, from a German *oberst*, or colonel, completely surprised him.

"What did you feel when you shot the planes down?" asked the Luftwaffe commander.

"I don't know that I felt anything," said Turk truthfully. "I just, you know, went with my training."

"Ah." The officer was a member of Jagdgeshwader 73, the 73rd fighter wing, and headed a four-ship group of Eurofighters. The fighters had not yet been in combat. "So you feel nothing?"

"I just, uh, just didn't think about it really."

Even as the words came out of his mouth, Turk thought that it was the wrong thing to say. Everyone seemed to stare at him.

He felt . . . good about getting the kills. He felt triumphant. Wasn't that what he was supposed to feel? It was a win—a big one, four of them in fact. And each one of those bastards was trying to kill him.

Damn, of course he felt good. What else was he supposed to feel?

Bad because he'd won? That made no sense.

And then the Sabre had gone off course. How did he feel about that?

That was the real question, and the truth was, he couldn't really answer.

It was terrible that the plane had gone off course and struck the wrong target. He felt bad that people had died. But there wasn't anything he could do about that.

And there was a limit to how much he could feel. He didn't cry or get sick or anything like that. Was that what was supposed to happen?

He certainly didn't feel guilty—he hadn't been responsible. Truly, it wasn't his fault.

So he felt bad, but clearly not bad enough, as far as anyone seemed to think he should.

The briefing continued. Turk felt out of place, but it seemed too awkward to leave. The commanders recounted some of the basic protocols, some of the SAR arrangements in case things went wrong, and reiterated the need to call in for permission to blow your nose . . .

That got a laugh, at least.

As the briefing broke up, Turk slipped out of the room. He was halfway down the corridor when Ginella called after him.

"Hey, Turk, why are you running away?"

"Running?" Turk stopped and waited for her. "I was just walking."

"That was a weird question." Ginella started walking with him toward the door at the end of the hallway.

"What?"

"How did you feel about gunning down four fighters trying to kill you?" said Ginella, paraphrasing the German's remark. "That was a weird question to ask."

"Yeah. I guess."

"I would have said 'kick-ass.'"

"Well, uh—"

"Isn't that how you felt?"

"Kinda," he admitted.

"You feel bad because of the accident," said Ginella. "We all get that. But that has nothing to do with the dogfight. You nailed those bastards. You oughta be proud of that."

"Thanks," said Turk.

"So you really want to drive Hogs, huh?"

"Well, I like them—"

"They're a lot different than that pretty li'l thing you've been tooling around in," she told him. "Stick and rudder. Meat and potatoes."

"I remember," said Turk.

They reached the door. Turk reached to open it, but Ginella got there first, slapping her hand on the crash bar and holding it for him in a reversal of etiquette, chivalry, and rank.

"I need another check pilot for a flight this afternoon," she told him. "You're welcome to apply. We'll see how good you are."

"You'll let me fly?"

"If you won't break it."

"Well, I—"

"It's already cleared."

"Really? But I'd be bumping somebody—"

"I told you, three-quarters of my people are

down with the flu," said Ginella. "You saw who I have left at lunch. If I use their hours for the check flights, we won't be able to take a mission. At least not if I obey the alliance flight rules."

"Hell, I'd love to do it," said Turk.

"Report to Hangar B–7 at 1600 hours," she said, her voice suddenly all business.

"I will," said Turk.

She smacked his back. "See you then, Captain."

9

Washington, D.C.

WHEN SHE WAS RUNNING FOR PRESIDENT, CHRISTINE Mary Todd was asked how she would respond if woken up at 6:00 A.M. for a national emergency. She had responded that anyone looking for her at 6:00 A.M. would find her at her desk.

Or in this case, in the secure conference room in the White House basement, where she'd arrived to review the situation in Libya with her national security team.

"Good morning, Mr. Blitz," she said to the National Security Advisor. She nodded to the secretary of state, Alistair Newhaven. "Mr. Newhaven."

The chairman of the Joint Chiefs of Staff, along with several Air Force officers, were at the Pentagon, displayed on the large video screen at the front of the room. Breanna Stockard, who headed the Defense Department's Office of Special Projects, was also participating via a link to her office on the CIA campus. NATO liaison General Daniel Yourish and Air Force Special Warfare Command Chief of Staff James Branson were in Belgium and Florida, respectively.

"I assume that you have all read the latest bulletins," said the President. "The preliminary reports that I've seen indicate that the aircraft made the attack on its own."

"It's pretty clear that the pilot did not initiate it," said Breanna. She had been working much of the night, and didn't seem to have bothered much with makeup beyond a small dab of lipstick. Yet she looked as well put together as ever.

The President admired that. Smart, good-looking, virtually unflappable—Breanna would do well in politics. Except of course that her husband had that covered.

Todd would have preferred Breanna to Zen, actually. He was a crucial ally, but often a difficult one.

"There are two problems here," continued Todd. "One obviously is the media fallout. But just as important, in my mind, is the implication of the technology failure. What went wrong?"

"We have to find that out," said Breanna. "That obviously is our focus here. Ray Rubeo has already volunteered to go personally and assist in the examination."

"How close is this to Raven?" asked the National Security Director. The loss of the Raven drone two months before had caused considerable consternation—and an attempt on the President's life.

"We don't believe it's related at all," said Breanna. "The UAVs use a different protocol, different systems entirely. They are unrelated."

"The Sabres are autonomous as well, though," said Branson. "They make their own decisions."

"I think we want to keep that under wraps as much as possible," said Blitz. "As a matter of national security."

And as an important public relations measure, the President thought. It wouldn't do to have stories to the effect that U.S. robots were killing people on their own.

Yet, that was what they were doing. The technology employed in the UAVs, now used for the first time in combat, allowed the machines to decide who their enemies were. There were a large number of parameters, but in the end the decision was the computer's.

Was it a remarkable and necessary extension of a weapon? Or was it the beginning of the end for the human race?

It was a question straight out of a 1950s sci-fi flick, and yet one Todd had wrestled with carefully before authorizing the deployment of the Sabres to Libya.

There were plenty of precedents for computers being involved in the decision-making process. The Navy's Aegis system, far back in the 1980s, computed firing solutions on its own—

though these were always under the supervision of crew. The Flighthawks developed by Dreamland in the mid- and late 1990s chose their own course and tactics when dealing with enemy fighters.

From one perspective, the Sabre missions were hardly different. The targets were specified by humans, and the feeds from the sensors aboard the aircraft could be constantly monitored.

Could be, not were.

That was one difference. Another was the fact that the Sabres plotted their own courses, and chose their own strategies for approaching targets. They didn't need humans at all. They were capable of switching off prime targets, and even secondary targets. They could decide how to handle threats.

They'd done an excellent job in all the tests so far. They seemed ready for the next step.

And now this. A humanitarian disaster.

"Taking people out of the loop was a definite mistake," said Branson, who though he had welcomed the Sabres was now clearly having second thoughts. "I was under the impression that they would be controlled by the Tigershark pilot at all times. I'd like to review why he diverted."

"He diverted because he came under fire," said Breanna.

"I think we're drifting into an area of debate that will be unfruitful at the moment," said Blitz. "We all know the issues involved long-term. The ability of robots on the battlefield is something to be discussed another day."

"You prejudice the argument by using the word 'ability,' " countered the general.

"Dr. Blitz is right," interrupted the President. "This will be a valuable discussion for another time. Right now, we need to sequester those aircraft and find out what went wrong."

"We're working on that," said Breanna.

"Good. Now, for the diplomatic fallout. I assume you've all seen the gun camera video."

"We're working on who leaked that," said Yourish. "Unfortunately, there's a large list of people who had access."

"Why?" asked the President.

"Well, the investigation . . ."

There was no satisfactory answer. Well over a hundred staffers had access to the computers where the information was being gathered for review, and dossiers had been prepared for all the members in the alliance. There were any number of people who wouldn't mind embarrassing the United States, or perhaps making a little extra money by selling the video.

President Todd assumed that the investigation would go on for months without coming to any real conclusion.

In a sense it didn't matter. The gun tape wasn't particularly revealing: a building targeted, the missile launch, then on to the next target before the missile hit. The images on the ground were much more devastating, in terms of public relations.

But they did mean blame couldn't be shifted away from the Sabre project, if anyone was so inclined.

The President was not. She had already directed a statement to be issued with the bare facts—the attack had been misdirected and was under investigation. The U.S. deeply regretted the loss of life. The victims would be compensated in accordance with past precedent.

"What do we do when people ask how it happened?" asked General Yourish, returning to a question that had been nagging at them since the incident first occurred.

"The truth," said Blitz. "It's still being investigated. We don't want to prejudice the investigation. And we don't know."

"I think Senator Stockard's presence on the committee has helped defer some of the questions," said General Branson. "I just hope it doesn't backfire."

"I talked to the senator personally," said Ms. Todd. "I think he'll do an excellent job."

"For us," added Blitz.

"For everyone."

The President glanced at Breanna. She had a vaguely worried look on her face.

"I don't expect Jeff to mince any words," the President added. "I know that he'll be a straight shooter. But really, that's the best we can hope for. And we will fix the problem."

"We will," said Breanna.

"All right, very good," she told them, rising. "We all have a lot to do. Keep me up to date on this."

The deputy chief of staff was waiting in the hall with her news briefing as she went out.

"How are the reports?" she asked.

"You want the good ones or the bad ones?"

"Good ones first."

"There's a headline from the New York *Post*: American killer drone wipes out village."

"That's a good one?"

"Wait to you see what al Jazeera has."

"I think I'll save that for after lunch," said Todd, stepping into the elevator.

10

Sicily

TO KNOW WHY SOMETHING HAD FAILED, ONE FIRST HAD to know exactly what had happened.

This was not necessarily easy. In the case of the Sabre UAV, for example, hundreds of subsystems contributed to the aircraft's flight behavior, and while the main focus was on the flight computers and AI sections, the systems that it interacted with had to be investigated on their own. It was a laborious and time-consuming project.

Despite a well-earned reputation for being exacting to the point of overbearing, Ray Rubeo no longer had the patience to oversee the myriad mundane details that needed to be attended to as the investigation proceeded. Instead, he turned to Robert Marcum, the vice president of his main

American company, Applied Intelligence, tapping him to head the investigation. Marcum was among the most anal retentive people he employed.

Which was saying quite a lot.

Traveling from Paris, where he had been overseeing another project, Marcum arrived in Sicily shortly after Rubeo, but already had an impressive investigative team in place. They were given a small facility at the air base, and rented much larger quarters about five miles away. These quarters consisted of the top three floors of an eight-story building perched above a series of hills that cascaded down toward the seacoast some ten miles away.

The executive suite on the eastern side of the top floor had a gorgeous view, and even Rubeo had a difficult time concentrating on the video projection as Marcum briefed him on what was known so far about the accident.

"Pilot action from the Tigershark can now be one hundred percent ruled out," said Marcum. He had worked as an engineer for many years before going into administration. "The flight records have been carefully reviewed. He gave no command that altered their flight."

"You've looked at the logs yourself?" asked Rubeo. The two men were alone in the large, sparsely furnished room. Levon Jons had gone into town to arrange for more transportation and backup, in case they went to Africa.

"Of course," said Marcum. "The pilot was Captain Mako. He's been flying for Special Projects for a few months. I don't know too much about him personally. I'm told he's an excellent pilot. Young."

"Very young, yes," said Rubeo.

"Additionally, we are fifty-eight percent through with our checks on the Tigershark. It would appear unlikely that it was involved in any way."

"I wonder if it's a coincidence that the fighters were scrambled," said Rubeo.

"In what way?"

Rubeo folded his arms. The office chairs that had come with the rooms were deep leather contraptions that would be very easy to fall asleep in. This would have to be fixed.

"I understand that the government hasn't flown against allied coalition planes until this mission," said Rubeo.

Marcum shook his head. "An exaggeration. This is what I mean when I say there has been much misinformation about the entire intervention. I don't blame anyone, not even the media. It's a very difficult situation, and NATO command has been less than forthcoming with them. We have already identified half a dozen flights by the government in the past five days. This was the largest, and the only time they engaged a plane. My bet is they won't be doing that again anytime soon."

"Nonetheless, it is an interesting coincidence," said Rubeo. "If it were significant, how so?"

Marcum frowned. Engineers didn't believe in coincidences. But then again neither did Rubeo.

"The pilot would not be paying attention to the Sabres, not fully," said Marcum. "He admits this."

"Yes."

"But the government would have to know about the attack in advance. A possibility not yet ruled out, but a far-fetched one."

Rubeo wasn't so sure. His attention drifted as Marcum continued, reviewing the preliminary data from the Sabres.

"All of the system profiles are absolutely within spec," said Marcum. "There are no anomalies. Sabre Four believes it struck the coordinates it was told to strike."

"But it didn't."

"No. Exactly."

"The visual ID package should have checked off," said Rubeo, referring to a section of the system that compared the preflight target data with information gathered by the aircraft before it fired. "It should have seen that it wasn't hitting the proper target."

"One of our problems. Or mysteries, I should say."

Marcum went through a few slides, showing the designated target and then the village that had been hit. The devastation was fairly awful, as would be expected.

"Were the coordinates entered incorrectly?" asked Rubeo.

"If they were incorrect, how are they right now?"

"Hmmmph."

"We are checking, of course, for viruses and

the like. But at this point we have nothing firm."

"Understood."

Marcum turned to administrative matters, briefing Rubeo on the different team members he wanted and the procedures he would follow as he proceeded. NATO and the Air Force were conducting their own investigations; there was also to be a UN probe. Marcum had assigned liaisons to all, but expected little in the way of real cooperation. These were more like spies to tell him what the others were thinking.

Rubeo listened as attentively as he could, but his mind was racing miles away. He was thinking of what the attack would have looked like from the ground.

There would have been no warning until the first missile was nearly at the ground. A person nearby would hear a high whistle—Rubeo had heard it himself on the test range—and then what would seem like a rush of air.

Then nothing. If you were within the fatal range of the explosion, the warhead would kill you before the sound got to you.

That would be merciful. If you could consider any death merciful.

"Brad Keeler is on his way from the States," said Marcum. Keeler had headed the team that developed the control software. "Once he's here, we should be able to move quickly."

"Good," said Rubeo, still thinking of the missile strike. He saw the fires and the explosions. Bodies were pulled from the wreckage before his eyes.

Was I responsible for all that?

My inventions make war more precise, so that innocent people aren't killed. But there is always some chance of error, however small that chance is.

Little consolation if you're the victim.

"Something wrong?" asked Marcum.

Rubeo looked over at him. Marcum had turned off the projector.

"Just tired," Rubeo told him. "Keep at it."

11

Sicily

ANY AIRCRAFT WOULD HAVE FELT A LITTLE STRANGE TO Turk after the Tigershark, but the A–10 was nearly as far removed from the F–40 as a warplane got.

The A–10A Thunderbolt had been something of a poor stepchild to the Air Force from the day of its conception. With straight wings and a cannon in its nose, the aircraft was the antithesis of the go-fast, push-button philosophy that ruled the U.S. Air Force in the late 1960s—and in fact, still largely ruled it today.

The Hog was born out of a need for a close-in, ground attack aircraft. While the country at the time was fighting in Vietnam, the perceived enemy was the Soviet Union, and the early design specs anticipated an aircraft that could be used to stop a massive tank invasion across the European plains. The plane was inspired partly by the success of the A–1 Skyraider—a highly effective throwback used to great effect in Vietnam, despite its alleged obsolescence. The "Spad," as the A–1 was often nicknamed, was powered by a piston engine. Its primary asset—beyond the tough resourcefulness and skill of its pilots—was its ability to carry a large variety of ordnance under its wings. Clean, the Spad was comparatively fast for a piston-powered plane, but it was slow compared to jets. As a ground support aircraft, however, the lack of speed was something of an asset. In the days before complicated sensors and constantly updating satellite imagery, ground support relied heavily on the so-called Mk–1 Eyeball. Human pilots flying low and slow had a much better chance of putting the era's unguided ordnance on target than fast-movers rocketing over the terrain.

The A-X project produced two aircraft sharing the same philosophy, both designed essentially around an armor-pounding, 30mm Gatling. The A–10 by Republic eventually won out. (The loser, the YA–9 built by Northrop, became the answer to a trivia question rarely asked of anyone, including plane buffs.)

The A–10 was designed and built in an era of tight budgets, and some say that the penny pinching hurt the plane from the very beginning. It was strictly a daytime, good-weather aircraft, with effectively no ability to fight at night: a critical oversight given the evolution of war-fighting doctrine in the years that followed, not to mention the fact that war generally takes place in all sorts of weather. And many critics pointed out that its engines were somewhat underpowered from the beginning. This was important not so much because it lowered the aircraft's speed—speed wasn't a real factor for the A–10A—but because the power of the engines limited the weight it could carry into the sky and the endurance of the aircraft.

A series of improvements in the last decade addressed the first set of drawbacks, adding enough modern sensors to the A–10A airframe that the planes had been redesignated the A–10C by the Air Force. While the plane remained essentially the same from the outside, inside the pilot's "office" there were new displays and a data link that gave the Hog driver access to real-time combat information. The updated Hogs could also carry more modern "smart" weapons, including JDAM, or Joint Direct Attack Munitions.

Ginella's eight planes were a further evolution. The upgraded avionics systems were tied to smart helmets, which functioned similarly to Turk's—the pilots could use those helmets rather than the glass cockpit. There were certain subtle improvements—there was now a full-blown autopilot, separate from the remote link—and more obvious ones: uprated power plants that allowed the planes to carry even heavier bomb loads. The Hogs were still subsonic, but they had noticeably more giddy-up when accelerating. According to the stats, they had approximately forty percent more power, but used about a third less fuel under normal conditions.

The stats reminded Turk of EPA estimates on cars—always to be taken with a grain of salt—but there was no denying that the A–10E was a more powerful beast than its cousins.

At the same time, the plane remained an easy aircraft to fly. She just loved being in the air.

Sitting at the end of the runway, Turk got clearance and ramped the engine. The Hog galloped forward, gently rising off the concrete after he had gone only 1,200 feet—a better rollout than most other aircraft he'd flown.

He cleaned his landing gear, then following the controller's directions, flew north over the Mediterranean to an airspace cleared of traffic.

Turk's A–10E helmet duplicated the glass cockpit a pilot saw in an A–10C, and though it didn't have quite the customization he was used to, it was nonetheless easy to deal with. The center of the board had the familiar attitude indicator, a large floating ball that told the pilot where his wings were in relation to the world—not always something that came intuitively, especially in battle. The heading indicator just below showed where the nose was going—again, an all-important check for the senses. To their right and slightly above, the climb indicator and altimeter did the obvious; a row of clock-style gauges at the lower right showed the aircraft's vitals.

Ironically, the least familiar parts of the pseudocockpit for Turk were the most modern.

The multiuse displays had a number of different modes, which he stumbled through slowly as he made sure he was familiar with the aircraft. The data transfer system, the embedded GPS navigation, and even the status page—a computer screen detailing system problems—were far different than what he was used to in the Tigershark. He had only to say a few words to get a response in the sleek F–40; here, he had to punch buttons *and* think about what he was doing.

But even hitting those buttons and occasionally pausing over the screens couldn't detract from the solid feel of the aircraft around him.

Planes had a definite soul, basic flight characteristics that they seemed to come back to no matter the circumstances. The Tigershark moved quickly. She turned quickly, and she went forward quickly. Given her head, she accelerated. This could certainly get her in trouble—a quick flick of the wrist on the stick, and the plane could pull more g's than Turk could stand.

The Hog's nature was completely different. She was more a solid middle linebacker than a fleet receiver. Not to say she wasn't nimble: she could dance back and forth, even sideways, as a few minutes of experimentation with her rudder pedals showed him. But her true nature was stability. Beat her into a turn, abuse her into a dive, jab her into a sharp climb—shc camc back gentle and solid.

The original A–10s were designed to be reliable, predictable weapons platforms, and the changes had left that completely alone. Try as Turk did to abuse it, the plane kept coming back for more. It went exactly where he pointed it, never overreacting to his control inputs.

In fact, Turk had so much fun putting the aircraft through its basic paces that he felt almost disappointed when it was time to land. The only consolation was that another Hog was sitting on the tarmac near the hangar waiting for him.

"All your controls solid, Captain?" asked Ginella, who walked over to the plane as he descended the ladder.

"They were kick-ass," he told her, hopping down.

"Good. Don't break this next one. They had a little trouble with the indicators on the starboard engine," she added, her voice instantly serious. "Be gentle, all right? We don't want to give the SAR people too much work this afternoon."

"Gentle is my middle name," he told her.

"I'll bet you say that to all the women," bellowed Beast, who walked over from behind the plane.

"Play nice now," said Ginella. "Captain Mako, Beast is going to check out Shooter Four while you're in Six. Don't let him trip you up."

"I'll try to stay out of his way," said Turk.

A FEW HOURS LATER TURK TESTED THE ENGINES ON the ramp, his brakes set to hold him in place. If there had been an actual problem with the jet, there was no sign of it now. The instruments said the power plants were smooth and ready, and his gut agreed.

With Beast following in his trail, Turk took the aircraft skyward. All of the indicators were pegged at showroom stats, systems as green as green could be.

When they reached their testing area, Turk took a long circle around his airspace. He told Beast to stand by, then spooled the starboard engine down. The Hog didn't entirely welcome flying on one engine, but she complied, reacting like a calm, indulgent workhorse. The plane jumped a bit when he brought the engine back on line, but there was no drama, no emergency. Nor did anything untoward happen when he flew on only the starboard motor.

"I think we're good," he told Beast.

"Hey yeah, roger that," replied the other pilot. "How do you like the Hog?"

"It's nice. I like it a lot."

"As good as that little go-cart you fly?"

"The Tigershark is a special plane," said Turk.

Beast laughed. "Fly with us enough and you'll think the Hog is, too."

"Shooter Four, Shooter Six, be advised you have two aircraft heading toward Box Area Three," said the controller, alerting them to an approaching flight. "Call sign is Provence."

A few seconds later Provence leader checked in. The planes were a pair of Rafale C multirole fighters. The Frenchmen had just arrived in Sicily.

"What are you up to, Provence leader?" asked Beast.

"Just getting some flight time and checking our systems," responded the flight leader.

Turk saw the two planes approaching from the southwest. The Rafales were delta-wing fighters, developed by France in the late 1980s and early 1990s. Originally conceived as air superiority fighters, they had retained those genes as they matured to handle a variety of other roles. While the aircraft might not match American F–22s, they were nonetheless extremely capable dogfighters. In fact, in a close-range knife fight against a Raptor, the smart money would be on the Frenchmen; much smaller than the F–22, they could turn tighter and fly extremely slow: a little appreciated value in an old-fashioned fur ball.

Of course, any Raptor pilot worth his salt would have shot them down at beyond-visual range, but where was the fun in that?

"You boys looking for a little practice?" asked Beast.

"*Pardon? Excusez?*" said the French leader. "What is it you are asking?"

"Let's see what you can do," said Beast. He pushed his throttle and pointed the nose of the A–10E upward, in effect daring the Rafale to follow.

An "ordinary" Hog would have more than a little difficulty going nose up in the sky, but the enhanced power plants in Shooter Four brought her into a ninety degree climb almost instantly. Turk watched as the Rafales swung over to follow. Though caught a little flat-footed—a challenge from the ungainly Hogs must have been the last thing they expected—the two French fighters soon began to catch up, angling toward the A–10's path. Then, just as it looked as if they would complete an intercept and put themselves in a position to wax Beast's fanny, the Hog fell off hard to the right, diving down toward the purple-blue of the ocean.

Again the Frenchmen were caught off-guard. By the time they started to react, cutting off the climb and circling to the east, Beast had recovered and was looping underneath them.

From where Turk was flying, it was hard for him to see if Beast ended up on one of the Frenchman's tails, but Beast's laughter over the radio sure made it seem as if he had.

"Ya gotta watch out," he told the Frenchman. "This is not your daddy's Warthog."

Turk turned his plane toward the others, waiting as the Rafales broke away. There was no way Beast could keep up, and so he didn't, climbing merrily and then circling back to the south as they spun away.

The two French fighters regrouped at the north end of the box they had been given to fly in, then banked back toward the Warthog in a coordinated attack. The truth was, a radar missile at this range would have meant the end of the Hog and its guffawing pilot, but that wasn't in keeping with the spirit of the encounter. As the Rafales moved in, they separated nicely, one high, one low, one to the east and one to the west, basically positioning themselves to cover anything Beast tried to do.

But that left the trailing wingman vulnerable to Turk, assuming he could accelerate quickly enough to make an attack. A "stock"

A–10A couldn't have managed it, but with the uprated engines, the refurbished Warthog had just enough giddy-up to pull it off. Turk jammed his throttle and pointed the A–10E's nose at the Rafale's tail, pulling close enough to have spit a dozen pellets of depleted uranium into the Frenchman's backside before Provence Two realized where he was.

The Armée de l'Air pilot's first reaction was to try to turn—he was hoping to throw the Warthog in front of him, essentially turning the tables. But the Hog was at least as good at slow-speed flying as the Rafale was, and Turk was able to dial back his gas just enough to stay behind the other plane. Only when the Rafale put the pedal to the metal and accelerated was he able to shake his sticky antagonist.

Beast was having a bit of difficulty shaking the other pilot, who wisely kept just enough distance to shadow the Hog without getting too close. The front canards on the Rafale—small winglets that added greatly to its maneuverability—worked overtime as the French flight leader remained figuratively on Beast's shoulder. The two planes' speed dropped down toward 100 knots—extremely slow, even for the straight-winged Hog. Still, the French-built fighter was able to hang in the air, a tribute both to the man at the stick and the gentlemen who had designed her.

Turk cut in their direction, making sure to clear over them by several thousand feet. A few touches on his trigger and the Frenchman would have had his *pain* buttered.

"OK, OK," said the French flight leader. "Knock it off."

"You owe us drinks," laughed Beast.

The Frenchmen were good sports, promising that they would pay off at their earliest opportunity. They also added that they would have beaten the two Americans in anything approaching a fair fight.

"That's your first mistake," said Beast. "Never, ever fight fair."

GINELLA WAS WAITING FOR THEM AT THEIR PARKING area when they returned.

She was not happy.

"What the hell did you think you were doing?" she said to Beast as he stepped onto the tarmac. "Where do you think you were, kindergarten? That action was dangerous and unauthorized. It was completely against regulations and, damn it, common sense!"

"I, uh—"

"Don't speak," she snapped. She turned to Turk. "And you—you! You're a test pilot. An engineer."

"Well, no, I—"

"Is this what they teach you at Dreamland? I'm really disappointed in you, Captain. Really disappointed. I've seen your record—you're supposed to be a mature pilot with a good set of decision-making skills. Quote, end quote."

Turk wanted to shrink into the macadam below his feet. She was absolutely right to bawl him out, and he knew it. He kept his eyes fixed on the ground as she continued, giving him one of the sternest lectures he had ever received.

"What do you have to say for yourself?" she asked finally.

"I was stupid," he said. "I lost my head and acted like a jerk."

"Get out of here before I do something rash," she said. "Report to the maintenance officer."

Beast took a step to leave. Ginella whirled toward him. "You and I are not done."

"Yes, ma'am," said Beast softly.

Turk didn't hang around to hear the rest. He practically ran to get out of his flight gear, then quickly made his way to the squadron's offices.

"Colonel talked to you?" asked the major sitting at the desk when he came in.

Turk nodded.

"I assume the plane checked out."

"Yes."

They went over the flight quickly. Turk wanted to finish as quickly as possible, hoping to avoid seeing Ginella again.

No such luck, though. She was standing in the doorway when he finished.

"Give us a minute, Major?" she snapped. It wasn't a question.

"Wanted to grab a coffee," said the officer, who quickly slipped past her.

"I'm sorry," said Turk, sitting back in his seat. "I know I was out of line. I know it."

She frowned, but the quick admission of guilt

seemed to take a little of her anger away. She went over to the desk the major had been using and sat behind it.

"I realize that I run things a little loose at times," she told him. "On the ground. Yes. But that doesn't mean it's OK to act like a cowboy in my squadron. In the air, we are all business. Do you understand that?"

"I know. I was totally out of line."

She stared at him. Her eyes were a light blue with small wrinkles of brown in them, as if the blue were tiny pages of a book arranged one on top of the other around the pupil.

"You're a good pilot, at least," said Ginella finally.

"Thank you."

"I wouldn't grin."

"No." Turk shook his head.

"All right, Captain. You can go."

Turk rose and started to leave.

"Thank you for helping us," said Ginella.

Turk turned around.

"It was my pleasure," he said.

"Good."

He left the room chastened, but unbroken.

12

Sicily

"IT'S NOT POSSIBLE THAT THE SABRE DIDN'T KNOW where it was." Brad Keeler thumped his hand against the wall, tapping the map image projected there. "We have the GPS data all the way through."

"And it functioned optimally?" asked Rubeo. "You're positive of that?"

"As positive as we can be."

"Was there interference through the control channel?"

Keeler pursed his lips. The one vulnerability of all unmanned aircraft systems was their reliance on external radio signals, for control and navigation. Much progress had been made in the area over the past decade but it remained at least a theoretical vulnerability.

"We don't believe so," said Keeler, weighing his words. "It would fail-safe out. Even if it were done very well, we should have a trace somewhere in the system."

"The GPS?"

"GPS is trickier to track," admitted Keeler. The Sabre got reads on where it was by querying the global position satellite system. In theory, the system could be fooled or even infiltrated. But it was difficult to do technically.

"Harder to catch," noted Marcum.

"Absolutely," admitted Keeler. "But there should be some trace of that."

"Simple interference?" asked Rubeo.

"Again—it's theoretically possible. But if so, they're doing it in a way that we haven't seen before. And the NATO sensors didn't pick up any direct interference."

"They hardly know what to look for," said Rubeo. Interference in this case meant some sort of radio jamming, which generally was fairly obvious but could be done very selectively. In fact, Rubeo's companies were working on a system that jammed only select aircraft—in theory, one could confuse a single UAV in a flight, turning it against its fellows.

Only in theory, so far. The Libyans naturally would be unable to do this on their own. But there were plenty of people who might want to take the chance to test their systems in the field.

Rubeo couldn't control his agitation. He rose. "A virus?" he asked.

"So far, no trace. And it would have to be introduced physically. Which means by someone on the team."

"Or someone who has access to the hangar," said Rubeo. "Or the transports. Or one of the bases where they stopped. Or—"

"Point taken."

"I want to know exactly what happened," he said. "We need to know."

"We are working on it," said Marcum, rescuing Keeler. "We haven't been at it all that long. Barely twenty-four hours."

"I've been here less than twelve," said Keeler.

Rubeo pressed his hands together. "The government planes? What's the connection there?"

"At best, a diversion," said Marcum. "More likely a coincidence."

"Did they jam?"

"No," said Keeler. "No jamming was recorded by any of the aircraft, including the Tigershark."

"But there were ECMs," said Rubeo. "They might have covered it. That would explain why the government attacked in the first place."

Marcum looked as if he had just sucked a lemon.

"We've mapped all of the radars in the area," said Keeler. "It's possible there was another one. But if it was interfered with, we can't figure out what the interference form would have been."

"These are early days, Ray," said Marcum. "We will get there. We have to build up slowly."

"How well are you sleeping?" Rubeo snapped.

Marcum didn't answer.

"We all want to figure out what happened, Dr. Rubeo," said Keeler gently. "We will figure it out."

"I can't sleep at all," said Rubeo.

13

Sicily

THOUGH HE HEADED WHIPLASH, THE HIGH-TECH DEpartment of Defense and CIA's covert action team, Danny Freah was not in Sicily on a Whiplash mission per se. Officially, he was only here to work with the locals and Air Force and secure the Sabres and the Tigershark, which were Office of Technology assets on temporary "loan" to the alliance. He wasn't even supposed to provide actual security, just make sure that the people who were charged with doing that did it.

Unofficially, he was here to find out what the hell had happened and to make sure that no one associated with the Office of Technology got railroaded.

Politics was a wonderful thing, especially in the military.

Danny had brought his figurative right arm, Chief Master Sergeant Ben "Boston" Rockland, along with two troopers, John "Flash" Gordon and Chris "Shorty" Bradley. He had a pair of Ospreys as well—one had come over with him on the Whiplash M–17, and the other had been part of a demonstration that Flash and Bradley were conducting in Germany when Danny got the word to get over to Sicily in a hurry. The Ospreys were available as transportation in the unlikely event he had to go over to Libya.

He doubted he'd need them. Nor did he anticipate needing more people. Most of his team was in the States on a training mission with U.S. Special Operations Command, and he decided to let them be for the time being.

"Pretty island," said Boston, surveying the suite they'd been assigned at the NATO base. "Piece of shit command post, though. Barely fit a desk in either of these rooms."

Boston wasn't exaggerating. Space at the facility

was at a premium, as were simple auxiliary services like getting the floor washed—the ones in front of them were brutal.

"We'll have to make due," said Danny. "You sent Flash over to the security?"

"Yeah, he's talking to the NATO people now. They have our Air Force guys, an assigned team from DoD working for OT, and Eye-tralians." Boston had a smug grin as he mispronounced the word. "You going to call Nuri back from vay-kay?"

"I think we'll survive without him."

"Probably be help ordering dinner."

"We'll survive."

Nuri was Nuri Abaajmed Lupo, the lead CIA officer with Whiplash. As an Italian-American who'd spent part of his childhood in Italy, Nuri spoke excellent Italian. He also had a decent amount of experience in the Middle East. But he was on his first leave in two years, and Danny saw no need to interrupt it.

"Probably knows where all the hot babes are, too," added Boston.

"Find someone to clean the floor, Chief," growled Danny. "I have work to do."

14

Sicily

THE HIGH OF HIS A–10E FLIGHT HAVING BEEN PUNCtured by Ginella's scolding, Turk took his bruised ego back to his own small office on the base. He found it locked, with a guard in front of the door.

The Italian MP did not know what was going on or even why he was there, specifically. But he did know that his orders were that no one was to enter. And Turk fit the qualifications of "no one," even though his name was handwritten on the door.

He went over to the hangar where the team was working over the Tigershark and Sabres, but no one there seemed to know anything about it. Turk was on his way to General Talekson's office when his satellite phone rang; it was Colonel Freah.

"Colonel, am I glad you called," he said as the connection went through. "I've been locked out of my office."

"Yeah, it's routine," Danny told him. "Part of the investigation, Turk. Don't worry about it. How are you holding up?"

"OK, I guess."

"Did Colonel Ginella hook up with you?"

"Uh, yes sir. I, uh, checked out two planes for her."

"Two? Great."

"I didn't think to check with you. I—"

"No, no, it's fine." Technically, Danny wasn't in

Turk's chain of command anyway. "She talked to me about it, then went through channels. I think it's a good idea for you to be, uh, useful if you can. Assuming you want to be. Do you want to fly with her?"

"Yeah, I will. Good squadron. I don't know how short-handed they are."

"You're familiar with the planes?"

"Yes, sir. I flew them before they did, actually."

"Well, good. Keep checking with the team to see if they need you for testing, but otherwise, as far as I'm concerned, you're good to go."

"Thanks," Turk told him, even though he figured the odds of getting back into one of Ginella's planes were infinitesimal now. He was thankful that she hadn't told Danny what had happened.

Not yet, anyway.

Danny told him about his office, suggesting he stop by "once we've gotten some furniture and figured out where the restrooms are."

"I will."

"If you want time off—"

"Actually, I'd prefer to keep busy," said Turk.

TURK EVENTUALLY FOUND HIS WAY BACK TO THE HOTEL, exhausted from the day and in need of a serious change of scenery. Once again he thought of Ginella's travelogue. But arranging a trip to the mainland seemed like too much of a hassle.

He went down to the bar and bought two beers, then smuggled them back upstairs to his room, feeling more than a little like a felon, though all he was doing was cheating the self-pay refrigerator out of a sale.

He flipped through the channels for a while. Most of the programs were in Italian, naturally, though after a few spins he found a movie in English with Italian subtitles. It was one of the early Terminators, the first, he thought, with Arnold Schwarzenegger before he became governor material.

Turk hadn't seen the movie in years and years. It was nice how the storylines in movies were always so clear: good versus evil. Good did good. Evil did evil.

You might have one flip around, or in a complicated movie, two or three. But in the end, you knew who was good.

Real life was always trickier. You might be a hero one second, then literally in the middle of a disaster the next.

He couldn't help but think about the Sabre attack. He'd seen a few screwups in his time, a couple of crashes, though never with anyone getting hurt. One time he'd come close to having to bail out of an aircraft. Ironically, it was an F/A–18, not an Air Force jet—he had been taking it up for NASA on an instrument run, testing a recording device—they had a new instrument to measure vortices off the wings. He was out over the Pacific when one of the engines decided it didn't want to work for some reason. Then the other one quit.

Fortunately, he had plenty of altitude and options. Among them was trying for a miraculous restart, as he called it now—he got the first engine to relight somehow, then hung on long enough to get into Miramar, the Marine air station in San Diego.

On final approach the engine quit again.

That caused him a little consternation. He'd been a little high and fast in his approach, perhaps unconsciously thinking the engine would blow, and that helped. Still, he barely managed to get the wheels onto the edge of the strip.

A lucky day. He might have plunged into the bay.

Or really gone off, and hit houses in the city.

He hadn't thought about either possibility at the time. You didn't—you just flew the plane, went down your checklist. Do this, do this; try this, now this, now this. Contemplating consequences was a luxury you didn't have.

So much so that when people congratulated him later, Turk wasn't even sure what the hell they were talking about. As far as he was concerned, the incident was a tremendous pain. He had to find another way back to Nellis, where he'd started the flight. And talk to a dozen scientists, most of whom were actually interested in the instrument the plane had carried, not the engine system.

For some reason, he'd never drawn a NASA assignment again. Coincidence?

The Terminator ended—or didn't end, as it would go on to spawn a huge string of sequels. Turk went back to flipping through channels.

He stopped on the scene of a fire. He watched a row of houses burning, fascinated. They were in a small city. The sky behind them was dotted with black smoke, swirls rising like thick tree trunks in the distance.

Only gradually did he realize that he was watching an account of the Sabre accident. There were shots of ambulances coming and going. Then a close-up of a victim on a stretcher.

A woman, eyes closed, head covered with a bandage already soaked through with blood.

A small child, already dead . . .

He flipped the TV off and went to see what was in the minifridge.

15

Tripoli

KHARON NEVER CEASED TO BE AMAZED AT THE POWER of money. It was both corruptor and motivator, an incredible genie with almost unlimited ability. A hundred euros could influence a man to take incredible risks, like flying from the safety of Benghazi to the open city of Tripoli.

"Open" meant claimed by neither side, but not entirely neutral—it would lean to whomever had the most power nearby, which at the moment was the rebels. Nor did it mean completely without risk—gangs from both sides fought openly in the streets several nights out of the week, and occasionally at the airport as well. A portion of the terrain southwest of the city was held by government forces, which had repulsed several attempts by rebels to clear them away.

A hundred euros, plus the regular fees of fuel and airplane rental. That was all it took to enter the outer ring of hell.

Kharon was taking the same risks, flying through a war zone, in an area where theoretically anything flying could be shot down. The fact that the allied air forces had not yet fired on civilian planes did not necessarily mean they would continue to hold their fire.

But the risk was nothing for him, a necessary part of his plan: twenty minutes along the water, a beautiful flight in the dusk.

KHARON KNEW HE WOULD BE FOLLOWED FROM THE airport—everyone was—and so he went straight to a hotel, using the alias he had established two weeks before. The room he'd rented had been bugged by two different agencies. He gave it a quick look and saw that the bugs were still in place before changing and heading back downstairs.

Things were going well, but hubris was a killer. Kharon reminded himself of this as he walked down the steps to the Western-style lounge. He was a little early for his appointment, but this was as planned—he always liked to survey the environment at leisure.

It was a swamp. Besides the mixture of journalists—Kharon was masquerading as one himself—there was a thick mix of foreign agents and men who euphemistically referred to themselves as "businessmen." Most were arms dealers, eager to strike an arrangement with the rebels who did business in the open city, or arrange transport south to the government-held territory.

There were women businesspeople, too. Their business was older than war.

"There is my friend!" declared Foma Mitreski as he approached the long bar. "Tired from his long journey and in need of scotch."

"Foma."

Kharon was not particularly surprised to see the Russian spy; while this was not Foma's normal hangout, he often made the rounds of the hotel bars in the city. His presence was inconvenient, but Kharon knew he could not afford to alienate him. The Russians were important partners, and Foma personally oversaw much of the relationship.

"How is the reporting going?" asked Foma. He knew of course that Kharon was not a reporter, but then Kharon knew that Foma was something more than the lower level embassy employee Foma pretended to be.

"The usual pronouncements of victory from both sides." Kharon spoke just loud enough to be overheard. He pushed away the stool that was next to the Russian and leaned against the bar. He liked to move around easily, something that wasn't possible while perched on the stools here.

A few inches shorter than Kharon, the Russian was nearly twice as wide. He was a good decade and a half older, with hair so black, Kharon assumed it must have been dyed. He had a very red face, the sort associated with heavy drinking.

As always, Foma was dressed a little formally for Tripoli, with well-tailored trousers and a collared pullover shirt. His hands seemed too stubby for his body, thick, as if pumped with air or fluid. He had a small signet ring on his left pinky, and a larger black opal inset in gold on his ring finger.

A wedding ring as well. On the right hand, in the Eastern Orthodox tradition. But in the two years they had known each other, Foma had never spoken of his wife, or of any children. He did his best to present a blank slate to Kharon and the rest of the world.

"Scotch?" asked Foma. His English had a double accent—southern Russia and London, where according to his classified résumé he had both gone to school and served as a spy at the embassy. "They have some very old Glencadam," he said. "Here, we will share a few sips."

A few sips typically meant half a bottle. Kharon nodded indulgently, then waited as the bartender came over with a decanter of 1978 Sherry Cask Glencadam—a rarity even outside the Muslim world.

Foma took the glass after the whiskey was poured and held it to the light.

"Amber," he said in English. Then he said a few words in Russian that further defined the color. Though adequate, Kharon's Russian was not quite good enough to capture the nuances of the words.

"It never fails to surprise me that I am drinking scotch with a Russian," said Kharon, holding up the glass.

"*Za vas!*" said Foma, offering a toast.

"Your health as well."

Kharon drained the tumbler and returned it to the bar. Foma immediately asked for a refill. Kharon knew his own limits; he would sip from now on.

"So, a good scotch, yes?" asked Foma as they waited for the bartender.

"Good, yes," agreed Kharon. "Very good."

"It is complex." He took the refilled glass and held it up, knowing from experience that Kharon would not have another. "Someday they will have good vodka in Tripoli. Until then . . ."

He drank.

"So, you have had a successful trip?" asked the Russian after he drained his drink.

"It was interesting."

"Benghazi is peaceful?"

"More or less."

"The princess? She is back from Sicily?"

"Yes."

"I hope you gave her my regards."

Kharon hadn't told Foma that he was seeing the princess, but he merely shrugged.

"You see, my friend, I am always gathering little details," said Foma.

"I wouldn't worry too much about anything,"

said Kharon. "Eventually, you will get what you wanted."

"What has been paid for."

"Not in full. And you already have quite a lot of information, thanks to me."

Foma pushed his glass forward, silently requesting a refill from the bartender. "When will the delivery be made?"

"I'm working on it," said Kharon. "Soon."

"A man such as yourself with many contacts, back and forth—"

"I know where my best interests are," said Kharon.

"I heard that a Chinese man was looking for you."

Kharon didn't bother to answer. He would never do business with the Chinese—they were too apt to turn on their helpers. Say whatever else you wanted about the Russians, they honored their commitments.

"You're not drinking." Foma gestured at Kharon's glass, still half full, as his own glass was refilled once more. "You are going to have a way to catch up."

"I could never keep up with you, Foma."

The Russian smiled, as if this was a great compliment.

"You are going south?"

Kharon shrugged.

"I assume that is necessary, no?" said Foma. "But being on both sides is difficult for you."

"No more difficult for me than you," said Kharon.

Kharon saw his contact coming through the door. Their eyes met briefly. Then the man saw Foma and slipped to the left, going over to the other end of the bar.

"So, we will meet again very soon?" asked Foma, putting down his glass.

"I'll call."

"I must go. Much business today."

"Naturally."

"Enjoy your meeting."

Kharon smiled tightly. Foma left a pair of large bills on the counter to cover his drinks, then left.

FEZZAN BARELY LOOKED UP WHEN KHARON CAME OVER and sat down at his table. Though he was Muslim, Fezzan had two beers in front of him, both German Holstens.

"What did the fat Russian want?" asked Fezzan in Arabic as Kharon pulled the chair in. Between the local accent and Libyan idioms, Kharon sometimes had difficulty deciphering what the man said, but his disdain for Foma had always been obvious.

"He wanted to say hello," Kharon told him.

"You talked long for people exchanging greetings."

"It's polite to spend time with people who buy me drinks," he told the Libyan. "Including you, Ahmed."

Fezzan had used the name Ahmed when they first met. Kharon knew it was not his real name, but it was convenient to continue the fiction. In fact, it felt almost delicious to do so, a kind of proof to himself that he was far superior to the people he was dealing with.

Hubris is a killer, he reminded himself.

"You wish transport south again?" asked Fezzan.

"Yes."

"When?"

"As soon as it can be arranged."

"Tomorrow then. At four."

"In the morning?"

"Afternoon."

Kharon shook his head. "Too late. I want to be there before noon."

"Noon." Fezzan made a dismissive sound and picked up one of the beer bottles. He emptied it into his glass. "Who would even be awake then?"

"If you can't do it, I can find someone else."

Fezzan scowled at him. "I have other business."

"That's not my problem." Kharon started to get up. He noticed a young woman in a silk dress eyeing him at the end of the bar. She might be useful.

"All right." Fezzan thumped the empty bottle on the table. "You know, you are not always a welcome person behind the lines."

"No?" Kharon glanced over at the woman, studying her. It was difficult to tell her age in the bar. She could be anywhere from fourteen to thirty.

Most likely on the younger end of the scale, he decided.

Fezzan followed his gaze.

"You should be careful," warned the Libyan. "Some fruit has terrible surprises inside."

"Best pick it before it rots, then."

THE GIRL WAS GONE BY THE TIME KHARON FINISHED with Fezzan, but that was just as well; he had much work to do. He went upstairs and caught a taxi to the Tula, a tourist-class hotel on the ocean about a half mile away. The hotel had a spectacular view of the ocean, and a restaurant on the roof some thirty-five stories high. But for Kharon, the attraction was the computer in the alcove just off the lobby.

There were two there, generally used by patrons to confirm airline reservations and print out boarding passes. But the Internet connection was not limited to this, and within a few moments Kharon had disabled the timer as well.

He went to Yahoo News and did a quick recap of the stories on the bombing attacks on the government city.

Two hundred thirty-eight stories had been published in the past twelve hours. But none included the video he had uploaded the night before.

All of that work—not to mention expense—for nothing?

That was not true. The same man who procured the video had also introduced the worm; it was a package deal. But still, it was disappointing that the video had not been used.

Most of the stories were vague about what had happened. Kharon decided he would have to help things along. Choosing one at random, he went to the comments section. He created an account and then began typing:

THE VICIOUS ATTAK ON THE TOWN IN LIBYA WAS CONDUCTD BY A AMERICAN DRONE . . .

He liked the typos. They would stay.

Kharon wrote a few more lines, then posted it. After repeating the process on a dozen other news sites, he turned to his real work.

Opening the text editor, he began pounding the keys:

THE ATTACK THAT WENT WRONG IN THE LIBYAN CITY YESTERDAY WAS LAUNCHED BY AN AMERICAN UAV USING AUTONOMOUS SOFTWARE TO MAKE WAR DECISIONS. IT WAS DESIGNED BY RAY RUBEO, A PROMINENT AMERICAN SCIENTIST WHO CREATED DREAMLAND . . .

Kharon added the slight inaccuracies in Rubeo's biography—he did not create Dreamland, nor did he profit there, as Kharon wrote further down in his missive—out of design rather than spite; they would provoke questions about the scientist. The fact that Rubeo was no longer associated with Dreamland—the project was now under another arm of the Department of Defense—was immaterial. The press knew what Dreamland was. Saying the name gave them a bit of red meat to chew on.

Kharon signed the e-mail with the letter F, then sent it to the address of the *New York Times* national security reporter. He retrieved the text, made a few small changes, and sent it to the *Washington Post.*

He sent it three other newspapers, and to reporters at several blogs. Then he backed out, erased all of the local memory, and rebooted the computer.

Work done for the day, Kharon looked at his watch. It was well past midnight—too late to bother trying to sleep. He thought of the girl he had spotted earlier in the bar. Perhaps she would have returned by now.

He made sure the computer screen was back to the hotel's front page, then went out to find a taxi.

16

Sicily

TURK'S FOURTH BEER OF THE NIGHT FINALLY GOT HIM off to sleep. He dozed fitfully, curled up at the side of the king-size mattress, huddled around one of his pillows. His dreams were gnarled images that made no sense—an A–10, an F/A–18, Ginella, Zen, buildings, and endless sky.

His phone woke him up, buzzing incessantly.

He had no idea where it was, or where he was. He pushed around in the bed, disoriented. His head hurt and his legs were stiff.

The phone continued to ring. Its face blinked red.

"Turk," he said, finally grabbing it.

"Captain Mako, I'm sorry I woke you."

It was Ginella. Her voice was officious, almost quiet.

"Not a problem," Turk managed.

"I'm down two pilots, Grizzly and Turner. I'm told you're available, if you choose to volunteer."

"Yeah, uh, well uh—"

"I just spoke both with your Colonel Freah and Operations. It's entirely voluntary."

"When do you, uh—when do you need me there?"

"We'll be briefing the mission at 0600," she told him.

"Um, sure. I guess."

"That's a half hour from now, Captain. Can you make it?"

"Yeah, um, I'm at the hotel," he said.

Her voice softened a little. "I realize that, Captain. Would you like me to send a driver?"

"Man, if you could do that, it would be super."

"Be in the lobby in ten minutes," she told him. "He'll have coffee."

"Ten minutes?"

"He's already on the way. I knew you'd say yes."

17

Sicily

IT WAS ABSURD AND RIDICULOUS TO THINK THAT HE WAS responsible in any way for the dozen deaths and the other casualties at al-Hayat. And yet Ray Rubeo couldn't help it.

The images he had seen of the strike tortured him. The fact that his people had no luck finding what went wrong bothered him even more. Surely it wasn't just a mistake—the enemy must have done this for propaganda purposes. And yet his people found no evidence of that.

Something had gone wrong. But what?

Working over his secure laptop in his hotel room, Rubeo worked as he had never worked before. He pulled up schematics and data dumps, looked at past accidents and systems failures, reviewed the different aspects of the mission until he practically had it memorized. And still the cause remained as much a mystery to him as it did to his people.

There was nothing wrong with the system that he could tell. The systems in the Sabre that had made the attack were exactly the same as those in the others.

So the attack hadn't happened. It was all a bad dream.

Rubeo had presided over disasters before. He had stood in the Dreamland control center as the entire world fell apart. He'd never felt a twinge of guilt. Fear, yes—he worried that his people would be hurt, or perhaps that his ideas and inventions would fall short. But he never felt guilty about what he did.

And he didn't feel guilty now. Not exactly. He saw wars as a very regrettable but unfortunately necessary aspect of reality. This war was a righteous one, to stop the abuse of the people who were being persecuted by Gaddafi's heirs. It was justifiable.

Accidents happened in wars.

He knew all this. He had thought about these things, lived with all of these things, for his entire life. And yet now, for the first time, he was upended by them.

Rubeo worked for hours. If he could just figure out what had happened, then he would be able to deal with it. He could fix the machines—his people would fix the machines—and this sort of thing wouldn't happen again.

If it was a virus, how would it have worked? It would have had to be extremely sophisticated to erase itself.

Not necessarily, he thought. The aircraft recycled its memory when it transitioned off the mission. It had to do that so it had enough space for data.

But where would it be before you took off?

The only empty positions were the video memory.

Actually, you could easily slot it there—it would be erased naturally, as the aircraft engaged its targets and recorded what happened.

Impossible, though—who among his people would do this?

So interference from outside? A radar signal they couldn't track?

That NATO couldn't track. He could easily believe that. Certainly.

But it could interfere with just one aircraft, not the others? Did that make sense?

Need to know more about the source.

Need to know more . . .

I have to have this checked out. This and a dozen other things. A hundred . . .

Twelve lives. Was that all it took to unhinge him?

Weren't his contributions greater than that? Without being boastful, couldn't he say that he had done more for mankind than all of the people killed?

But it didn't work that way, did it? And guilt—or responsibility—were concepts that went beyond addition and subtraction.

He was focused on a virus because he didn't want to take responsibility. He didn't want it to be a mistake he had made.

Same with the interference.

Maybe he had just screwed up somewhere.

Rubeo pounded the keys furiously.

It *might* be possible to throw the mapping unit off by varying the current induced in the system . . .

Hitting another stone wall as his theory was shot down by the data, Rubeo slammed the cover of the computer down in disgust.

He was a fool, tired and empty.

But he had to solve this. More—he had to know why it bothered him so badly. It paralyzed him. He couldn't do anything else but this . . .

Rising from the hotel desk, the scientist paced the room anxiously. Finally, he took out his sat phone and called a number he dialed only two or three times a year, but one he knew by heart.

The phone was answered by the second ring.

"Yes?" said a deep voice. It was hollow and far away, the voice of a hermit, of a man deeply wounded.

"I am stumped," said Rubeo, trusting his listener would know what he was talking about. "It's just impossible."

"Someone once told me nothing is impossible."

"Using my words against me. Fair game, I suppose."

"There was a beautiful sunset tonight."

"It's night there," said Rubeo. "I'm sorry. I didn't mean to wake you up."

"You know I seldom sleep, Ray. I wasn't sleeping."

"The problem is . . . I . . . the thing is that I feel responsible. That something we overlooked—that I overlooked—caused this. And I have to fix it. But I don't know how."

"Maybe it wasn't anything you did. I don't really have many details, just what I saw on the news. I don't trust those lies."

"What they've reported was true enough, Colonel."

"They made me a general before they kicked me out."

"One day I'll get it right."

"I think it would sound strange coming from you, Ray." The other man laughed. "Besides, they did take that away. Along with everything else."

"I don't know what to do," confessed Rubeo.

"Go there. Go there and see it with your own eyes."

"I don't know about that."

"What other choice do you have?"

"It's not going to tell me what happened. The failure—or accident or attack, whatever it was—happened in the aircraft. Not on the ground. There may have been interference. It's possible—it is possible—but it's a real long shot. I think—"

"Ray, you're not going there to find out why it happened. You're going there to see. For yourself. So you can understand it, and deal with it. Otherwise, it will haunt you forever. Trust me."

Rubeo said nothing.

"You saw my daughter recently?" asked the other man.

"I spoke to her yesterday. She's in Washington. You should call her. Or better yet, visit. Let her visit."

"Thanks."

"You're very good at giving advice. If you were in my position—" Rubeo stopped, realizing he was wasting his breath. Dog—the former Colonel Tecumseh "Dog" Bastian—was in fact excellent at giving advice, perhaps the only person in the world that Ray Rubeo respected enough to take advice from. But Dog was terrible at following it, and there was no sense trying to push him; they had been over this ground many times.

"Your son-in-law is over here," Rubeo told him instead. "He's looking as fit as ever."

"Good," said Bastian, with evident affection. "Take care of yourself, Ray."

"I will."

"Take my advice."

"I wouldn't have called if I didn't intend to."

18

Over Libya

VISOR UP, TURK LEANED AGAINST HIS RESTRAINTS, peering through the A–10E's bubble canopy toward the ground. Dirty brown desert stretched before him, soft folds of a blanket thrown hastily over a bed. He could hear his own breathing in his oxygen mask, louder and faster than he wanted. Chatter from another flight played in the background of his radio, a distant distraction.

The target was a government tank depot near Murzuq. Eight tanks were concealed there beneath desert camouflage, netting and brown tarps. Shooter Squadron would take them out.

"Ten minutes," said Ginella in Shooter One. Paulson was her wingman, flying in Shooter Two.

"Roger that," said Beast in Shooter Three.

Turk acknowledged in turn. The planes were flying in a loose trail, slightly offset and strung out more or less behind one another. Turk was at the rear, flying wing for Beast.

He swiveled his head to check his six, then pulled the visor down, automatically activating his smart helmet.

Ginella directed them to take a course correction and then split into twos for the final run to the target. The first element—Shooter One and Two—would make their attack first. Beast and Turk would move to the north, watching for any signs of resistance from another camp about two miles in that direction. Depending on how well the initial attack on the tanks went, they would either finish the job or look for targets of opportunity before saddling up to go home.

Turk found the new heading, checked his six, then nudged his Warthog a little closer to Shooter Three as the lead plane ran through a cluster of clouds.

"Shooter Four, let's bring it below the clouds," said Beast. All laughs on the ground, he was nothing but business in the sky. "We need to be low enough to get an ID on anything we hit."

"You see something?" Turk asked.

"Negative. I just want to be ready."

Turk slid his hand forward on the stick. Thc threat radar began bleeping.

"We have an SA–6 battery," said Ginella calmly. "Beast, you see that?"

"Looking for it," said the pilot.

The detector had spotted the radar associated with the mobile missile launchers, and gave an approximate direction—south, just off the nose of Shooter Three. The radar had been switched on and off quickly—most likely to avoid being detected.

Turk hunted for the launcher, zooming the optical sensors. The center crosshair hovered over a gray and very empty desert.

"I see it," said Beast. He pushed his nose ten degrees east, cutting in Turk's direction as he gave him the location. Turk, nearly two miles behind Beast and a little higher, couldn't see it.

"Two launchers. One up farther east just getting into position," said Beast. "I'll take the one with the van—Turk, take the missiles."

"Roger that."

Turk didn't see the truck. In the Tigershark it would be labeled neatly for him, and the computer would prompt him if directed. But adapting wasn't a hardship—he took his cue from Beast's course and pushed toward the closer target.

He'd rehearsed the weapons procedures several times before taking off, and had of course used them many times during his earlier stint testing the A–10E. But as he closed in and got ready to pickle his weapons, his mind blanked. Fingers hovering over the buttons that controlled the Tactical Awareness Display, he momentarily couldn't recall how to set it up.

Just like the A–10C. Slew the target by using the control on the throttle.

The cursor started moving. He edged it into

position, "hooking" or zeroing in on the tanklike launcher on the ground.

Digital Weapons Stores. Move quickly. Let's go!

He brought up the screen on the display. Turk felt the sweat pouring down the sides of his neck. His hands were wet and sticky inside his gloves. He thought of taking them off but there was no time. Time in fact was disappearing, galloping away.

The firing cue was rock solid in the HUD.

Big breath, he reminded himself. Big, slow, very slow, breath.

Someone on the ground was firing at him with a machine gun. He could see tracers.

Far away. Ignore them.

Both the cue and the launcher seemed to shrink.

Shoot the bastard.

The target was dead on in his sights. Turk pressed the trigger, pickling an AGM–65E2/L laser-guided Maverick missile.

The missile popped off the A–10E's wing. The infrared seeker on the missile homed in on the laser target designated by the A–10. A little under four seconds later, 136 pounds of shaped explosive burrowed through the body of the middle SA–6, igniting inside the chassis of the launcher. A ball of fire leapt skyward. Turk shuddered involuntarily, banking to his right and starting to look for whatever had been firing at him earlier.

"There's another radar unit flashing on to the south," said Beast. "Straight Flush. Has to be pretty close."

The Straight Flush radar was used to control

the SA–6s. Turk pulled back on his stick and started to climb in Shooter Three's direction, covering his back while he hunted for the radar.

The radar flicked off.

Beast cursed.

"Still there somewhere," said Turk.

"They have an optical mode. Be careful."

The surface-to-air missiles could be launched and guided by camera. In that case the range was some eighteen miles.

"Gotta be down there behind that hill," said Beast. "On the right. See it?"

"Yeah, yeah."

"Probably just the radar. But watch yourself. We'll swing in from the south," added Beast, already starting to bank. He didn't want to come straight over the hill; if there was a launcher set up in its shadow, it could fire before he saw it.

Turk closed the gap with his leader as he came around north with him. A cluster of houses appeared off his right wing as he turned.

A lump grew in his throat.

"Oh yeah. I see him," said Beast. "All mine."

By the time Turk spotted the launcher, Beast had already fired. Turk watched the missile hit, a geyser of smoke, vapor, and pulverized metal erupting upward. A half second later there was a flash of white and then orange, then little flicks of red in a black cloud that seemed to materialize above the launcher.

"Scratch one SA–6 launcher," said Beast, recovering to the west. "You want to get that radar van?"

"I see it on my left," said Turk, finally spotting the telltale antennas.

"All yours."

Turk steered gently to his mark, fired on the truck, then came back to join Beast. The A–10E trucked along contentedly.

"Let's do a racetrack here," said Beast, suggesting that they circle in an orbit above the desert. "Come up to twelve thousand."

They were at 5,000 feet. The climb to twelve in a laden A–10A could take a while, but with the uprated engines it was easy for the A–10E. Turk spun upward while Beast called in the kills to both the controller and Ginella, who was still working with her wingman on the tanks.

Ginella and Paulson had discovered another group of tanks just to the south. She told Beast to stand by while they went and checked them out.

"We can be down there in a flash," said Beast.

"Just hold your horses. You've done enough for now."

"Got plenty of arrows left."

"Stand by."

"Roger that, boss lady."

Beast was now in an almost jaunty mood, his tone much more animated. The strike on the radar and missiles had been his first ever hits in combat. He called out the altitude markers as they rose, clearly enjoying himself.

"So did this feel as good as taking down those Mirages the other day?" he asked as they circled.

"It was OK."

"Just OK? I'd think better than this even."

"This was good. Doing a job. I'm a little unfamiliar with the plane," admitted Turk. "I kept thinking I was going to screw up the weapons system. So it was good to kind of get past that."

"Just about foolproof," said Beast. "But I bet it's easier in your Tiger, huh?"

"The Tigershark can target by voice," said Turk. "Or by pointing."

"See, that's not flying." Beast was almost gleeful. "That's push button. Don't even need a pilot. This is flying. This is fighting. Right?"

"They're both good."

Traffic on the channel spiked as another group of aircraft came nearby. Beast switched over to a different radio channel so they could talk plane-to-plane. The Hog pilots spun out a little wider to survey the area, making sure there were no further threats. Everything looked clean.

"I'll bet those Frenchies we met yesterday are eating their hearts out about now," said Beast. "We just made the skies safe for them."

"So I guess we're out of the doghouse, huh?"

"Oh, that's the thing with G. Her bark is worse than her bite. You take care of business, she'll give you a long leash."

"She was right. We kinda got carried away."

"Ah, don't let her fool you. I bet she was pleased as hell. Hearing that a pair of zipped-do-my-dah fancy French whiz jets got their fannies smacked by two of the ugliest planes in the Air Force? She loved it. Especially since one of 'em was flown by a nugget and the other by a retard? Ha."

"I guess I should be glad I'm not the retard, huh?"

"Oh, you'll like G eventually," said Beast, laughing. "She's a good leader."

A few minutes later Ginella hailed them on the main squadron frequency, telling them to come north.

"All tanks splashed," she added.

"We still got some missiles here," said Beast. "What do you want us to do with them?"

"Oh, I have something you could do with them," answered Paulson.

"Settle down, munchkins." Ginella called into their airborne controller, telling him that they had accomplished their task.

"If you have nothing for us, we're going to fly the prebriefed course home," she told him. "And per our brief, we'll strike any—"

"Standby Shooter One. Standby," interrupted the controller.

"That's a good sign," said Beast. "He's looking up some trouble for us in a hurry."

The controller came back a few seconds later, asking what their fuel and weapons situation was. Ginella had already given him that information, but she replied evenly; they had six missiles between them and a full store of gun ammo. The fuel was fine, with more than twenty minutes left before they would have to head home.

"Rebels are reporting a mortar crew working out of a pair of Hi Liners on Highway designated A3 on your maps," said the controller. "Can you check that out?"

"Roger that."

"Stand by for download."

Before the Hogs had been upgraded, the controller would have delivered what was known as a nine-line brief—the mission set in a nutshell, beginning with an IP or initial point for them to navigate to, elevation of the target, its description, and other related matter. Now the nine-line brief came to the plane digitally; the target was ID'ed on the Tactical Awareness Display. The moving map on the TAD gave a top view of the tactical situation, showing Turk's location in the center. An A–10C would have gotten this as well, but in the A–10E it came directly to Turk's helmet.

It wasn't the Tigershark, but it was a lot better than writing the instructions down on the Perspex canopy—the method used in the original A–10A.

The target area was roughly 150 miles due north. Cruising a few knots north of 300, it took roughly twenty-five minutes to get close. But because it was almost on their way home, they would have plenty of time to complete the mission without getting close to their fuel reserves.

Coming north took them past the town where the Sabre accident had occurred. It was some miles to the west, well out of sight, but Turk couldn't help glancing in that direction as they drew parallel.

The images from the news video came back. All of the action today—getting up, getting ready, flying, fighting—had made him temporarily forget the images. He tried not to think about them now but it was impossible. They were horrific, all the more so because they were unintentional accidents.

Killing an enemy wasn't a problem. Killing someone who was just there, in their own house . . .

"Shooter One to Three. Beast, can you see those trucks out ahead?"

"Yeah, copy. I'm eyes on."

"They have guns?"

"Stand by."

The trucks were on a side road almost directly ahead of Shooter Three. Turk watched as he tucked on his wing to lose altitude.

Damn, I'm his wingman, he thought to himself belatedly. He pushed down to follow.

The trucks were Toyotas, ubiquitous throughout the Middle East. They had four-door crew cabs. Whatever was in their beds was covered by tarps.

"Stay behind me," Beast told Turk. "I'm going to buzz them."

"I'm with you."

Beast took Shooter Three down to treetop level—or what would have been treetop level if there were any trees. The attack jet winged right next to them, flew out ahead, then rose suddenly. Turk, flying above as well as behind, tensed as he watched the trucks for a flash.

Nothing happened.

"Got something in the back, that's for sure," said Beast. "But I'd need X-ray eyes to tell you what's going on."

"All right. Let me talk to Penthouse," said Ginella, referring to the air controller by his call sign.

"We should just splash them on general principles," said Beast.

"Don't even kid around on an open circuit," snapped Paulson.

"Oh, Lordy, I got a hall monitor along with us today."

Paulson couldn't think of something witty enough to respond before Ginella told them she was going to take a run at the trucks to see if she could spot anything out of place.

"Otherwise they're clean and we have to let them go," she told them.

"I don't think so, Colonel," objected Beast.

"What you think does not count, Captain. Pauly, you're on my six."

"The place everyone wants to be," said Paulson.

Beast and Turk climbed and circled above while the squadron leader took another two passes at the trucks. The vehicles were moving slowly, but it couldn't be said suspiciously. They didn't react to either pass, not even shaking their fists.

As Turk turned in his orbit north, he saw a dust cloud in the distance.

"I'm going to get a better look," he told Beast.

"Go ahead, little brother. I'm right behind you."

Turk nudged the nose of the hog earthward. The more he flew the plane, the more he liked it. It was definitely more physical than the Tigershark. While the hydraulic controls had been augmented with electric motors to aid the radio-controlled mode, the plane still had an old school feel. He knew what older pilots meant when they talked about stick and rudder aircraft and working a plane. You got close to the Hog when you used your body. She was like another being, rather than a computer terminal.

The cloud of smoke separated into three distinct furls. They were made of dust, coming from the rear of a trio of pickups, speeding across the desert.

Now *that* seemed suspicious. Turk reported it.

"Weapons on them?" Ginella asked.

"Don't see anything."

Turk felt himself starting to sweat again as he got closer. He pushed the plane down closer to the ground, through 500 feet, then hesitated, looked at the altimeter clock to make sure he was right. The dial agreed with the HUD.

His airspeed had been bleeding off, and now he was dropping through 150 knots—very slow with weapons on the wings. But the Hog didn't object. She went exactly where he pointed her, nice and steady.

Turk came over the trucks at barely 200 feet. Sensing that he was pushing his luck, he gunned his engines, rising away.

"Nothing in the back, not even tarps," he told Ginella and the others.

His thumb had just left the mike button when a launch warning blared—someone had just fired a missile at him.

RUMORS OF REMORSE

1

Over Libya

TURK'S FIRST REACTION WAS: *ARE YOU KIDDING ME?*

He said it out loud, nearly insulted by the audacity of the enemy to fire at him.

Then learned instinct took over. He hit the flare release, pounded the throttle, and yanked the stick hard, all at the same time.

The decoys and sharp turn made it difficult for the missile to stay on his tail. At such low altitude, however, the harsh maneuver presented problems for him as well. In an instant his plane's nose veered toward the dirt and threatened to augur in. He pulled back again, his whole body throwing itself into the controls—not just his arms, not just his legs, but everything, straining against the restraints.

"Up, up, up," he urged.

The Hog stuttered in the air, momentarily confused by the different tugs. Finally the nose jerked up and he cleared the ground by perhaps a dozen feet.

"I have a launch warning," he told the others belatedly. "Missile in the air. I've evaded."

"We're on it," said Ginella. "Come south."

"The trucks—"

"Didn't come from the trucks," said Beast. "Came from that hamlet south. It was a shoulder-launched SAM."

Turk swung his head around, first trying to locate his wingman—he was off his left wing, up a few thousand feet—and then the hamlet he'd mentioned.

"Shit," he muttered to himself. He'd been ready to splash the trucks, blaming them for the missile.

He angled the Hog to get into position behind Beast. Ginella, meanwhile, called in the situation to the controller. The missile was shoulder-launched, surface-to-air, sometimes called a MANPAD, or man-portable air-defense system. While the exact type wasn't clear, more than likely it was an SA–7 or SA–14, Russian-made weapons that had been bought in bulk by the Gaddafi government.

The hamlet where the missile had been fired was the same one that had reported being attacked by mortars—a fact Ginella pointed out rather sharply when she got the controller back on the line.

"Is this a rebel village or a government village, Penthouse?" she demanded. "Are we being set up?"

"Stand by, Shooter."

"Screw standing by," said Beast. "I say we hose the bastards."

"Calm down, Beast." Ginella's voice was stern but in control. "Are you there, Penthouse?"

"Go ahead, Shooter One."

"We're going to overfly this village and find out what the hell is going on down there," she told the controller.

"Uh, negative, Shooter. Negative. Hold back. We're moving one of the, uh, Predator assets into the area to get a look."

"How long is that going to take?"

"Listen, Colonel, I can understand—"

"By the time you get a UAV down here, we'll be bingo fuel and the bastards will be gone," she told him. Bingo fuel was the point at which they had just enough fuel to get home. "I'm not sure they're not gone now."

It took nearly a half minute for the controller to respond. "Yeah, you're OK. Go ahead and take a look."

By that time Ginella had already swung toward the town. The Hogs spread out in a pair of twos, each element separated by roughly a mile.

Flying as tail-gun Charlie, Turk kept watch for sparkles—muzzle flashes—but saw nothing. A white car moved on the main street, but otherwise the place seemed deserted.

"What do you think about that car?" Beast asked as they cleared the settlement.

"Didn't look like much," said Turk. "All buttoned up."

The Hogs circled south, building altitude. The car left the village and headed for the highway. Beast suggested they buzz it, but Ginella vetoed the idea.

"Waste of time," she said.

"Probably has the bastards who shot at us," said Beast.

"Unless they're stupid enough to take another shot," said Ginella, "we'll never know. And we're almost at bingo," she added. "Time to go home."

2

Desert near Birak Airport

THREE YEARS BEFORE, MEMBERS OF THE COALITION OF rebels had chased Muammar Gaddafi progressively south. Now history was repeating itself, with the new government being pushed farther and farther from the coast. There were certainly differences this time around—different factions of the government had broken away from the main leaders and established strongholds in neighboring Algeria and Niger—but the parallels were upmost in Kharon's mind as Fezzan drove him south from Tripoli. It seemed some places were stuck in a cycle of doom, and would just continue spiraling toward hell until finally there was nothing more to be consumed.

Most of the journey south was boring, a long stretch of empty highway flanked by even more desolate sand and waste. Two checkpoints made it worth the money he paid Fezzan, however—clearing the barrier ten miles south of Tripoli, manned by rebels, and stopping at the gates to Birak to the south.

Getting past the first barrier just before dawn had been easy: Kharon slipped the first man who approached a few euros and they were waved around the bus that half blocked the highway.

The gate at Birak several hours later was another story.

Birak Airport was some 350 miles south of Tripoli. During Gaddafi's reign it had been a major air base, with a good portion of the Libyan air force stationed there. Though the planes had been moved, the airport remained a government bastion, with temporary quarters set up in the revetments where fighter-bombers were parked. These quarters consisted of RVs and tents, with a few larger trailers mixed in.

A civilian city had sprouted just south of the base. Populated by family members and "camp followers," as the age-old euphemism would have it, it was even more ragtag, with shanties and trailers clustered around tents and lean-tos that were more like lean-downs. The sun hit the white roofs of the trailers, creating a halo of light in the desert, a glow that made it look as if the settlement was in the process of exploding.

The road past the airport was a straight line of yellow concrete that ran through an undulating pasture of rock and sand. Grit and light sand covered everything, making the surface as slippery as ice. The path and nearby terrain were littered with vehicles. A few were burned-out hulks, set on fire during battles and skirmishes too insignificant to be remembered by anyone but the dead. Most were simply abandoned, either because they had run low on fuel or the keepers of the gate refused to allow the occupants to proceed with them.

Or proceed at all. Low mounds of sand not far off the road covered dozens of decayed and picked-at corpses. Hawks and other birds of prey circled nearby, drawn by the prospect of an easy meal.

The government forces had a "gate" on the highway, which they used ostensibly to keep rebels from coming south but in reality existed only to extract a toll—or bribe, depending on your perspective—from travelers. To reach the gate, a driver had to first weave past the abandoned vehicles, and then run the gamut of a de facto refugee camp populated by travelers who either couldn't pay the toll or were waiting for others to join them from the North.

The camp had swelled since Kharon's last visit, barely a week before. It had consisted then of no more than a hundred individuals, most of them living in their own vehicles under broad canvas cloths stretched for cover. Now it seemed to be ten times the size, extending from the shoulders to block the road itself.

Fezzan took their four-wheel-drive pickup off the road, moving west as they threaded through the ad hoc settlement. Kharon raised his Kedr PP–91 Russian submachine gun, making sure anyone looking toward the cab of the truck would see that he was armed. Fezzan had one hand on the wheel; the other gripped his own PP–91.

In truth, the pair would be easily outgunned in a battle here, if only by the sheer number of potential opponents. But brandishing the weapons made it clear they would not be casual victims, and that was enough to ward off most of their potential enemies.

A small group of children ran up to the truck, begging for money. Kharon waved them away, yelling at them in Arabic, though he was careful not to use or point the weapon—he feared inciting the parents.

They were in sight of the barrier to the west of the gate—a row of abandoned tractor trailers, augmented by the wrecked hulk of a Russian BMP and a tank that had lost its treads—when their pickup slid sideways in a loose pit of dirt and got stuck.

Fezzan tried rocking it back and forth, overrevving and making things worse. Jumping from the cab, Kharon sank to his knees in the loose sand. For a brief moment he felt a wave of fear take him; the unexpected hazard had left him temporarily without defenses.

He pushed his knee up, then shifted his weight to the right, wading through the sand to firmer ground.

By now a considerable audience had gathered, children in front, women in the middle, men to the rear. Most of the men were gray-haired and silent, glum-faced.

"Push us out," Kharon commanded. "Get to the rear. Five euros for each person who helps."

Five euros was a good sum, but no one moved.

Finally, two of the children ran toward the truck. A woman began scolding them, but as soon as Kharon took out a fist of bills, two women went over and put their hands to the rear of the vehicle. Soon the entire crowd was there, pushing amid a cloud of sand.

Fezzan managed to get the truck out with the help of the crowd. Kharon could have just hopped in and driven off—he suspected many would. But he expected to be passing through this way again, and welshing on his promise might gain him more enemies or at least more notice than he wanted. And so he walked over to a clear spot and began passing out cash. He gave the children ones—giving them the same as the adults would have caused consternation—then doled out fives to the women.

Six men had helped; four others joined the queue. To the men who had helped, he gave ten euros apiece. The others he waved a finger at.

When they began complaining, he put his money back in his pocket, then rested his hand on his gun. They moved back.

"I would not have paid anyone," said Fezzan when he climbed into the cab.

"Then most likely you would be food for the buzzards," said Kharon.

FEZZAN RECOGNIZED THE SERGEANT IN CHARGE OF THE men at the gate, and the "toll" was quickly negotiated down from fifty euros to twenty. Once clear of the gate, they sped down the highway to Sabha, an oasis city in the foothills about forty-five miles south.

They drove to Sabha's airport. Unlike Birak, the base here was still manned by the government's air force. MiG–21s were parked on the apron near the commercial terminal building, and batteries of antiair missiles and their associated control vans were stationed along the road into what had been the military side of the complex. There was no "gate" here, only a pair of bored soldiers who gave a cursory glance at the letter of admission Kharon carried before waving them on. Fezzan drove slowly through the complex, turning north toward the administrative building. Here another pair of guards blocked the road with a pickup truck and a fifty caliber machine gun. Kharon opened the door and got out.

"I will let you know where to meet me," he told Fezzan, banging on the roof of the truck after slamming the door closed. As the driver made a U-turn, Kharon walked to the guards, slinging the submachine gun on his shoulder and holding out his hands to show that he came in peace. They eyed the submachine gun suspiciously. Kharon had twice lost weapons at government checkpoints, more because the men wanted his gun than for security reasons. The Russian weapon, used mostly by policemen, was unfamiliar and required special bullets, making it less of a prize. Still, the soldiers made him remove the magazine before proceeding.

A second set of guards near the building were

not as lackadaisical; here he had to surrender the weapon, giving it over to the custody of a corporal who came barely to his chest. Kharon was given a tag in return; he interpreted this to mean that he might actually be able to liberate the weapon for a small bribe on the way out.

He resisted the urge to trot up the steps of the main hall of the building after he was admitted. Instead he made his way as leisurely as possible, walking slowly down the hall to large office overlooking the airfield, where he found Muhammad Benrali frowning over a desk covered with Arab-language newspapers.

General Benrali, the commander of the government's Second Air Wing, wore a tracksuit that appeared a size or two too small; his sleeves were rolled up his arms. The suit was a present from a Russian arms delegation the first week of the war; Kharon suspected it was the only thing Benrali had gotten out of the meeting.

"You are late," Benrali snarled as he entered.

"There were delays on the road."

"I lost four aircraft and men because of you."

"I warned you not to engage the aircraft," said Kharon calmly. "I told you only to get its attention and divert it over the vans."

"You said it was a reconnaissance plane." Benrali's Libyan-accented Arabic was curt. "Reconnaissance planes do not fire on others. They run away."

"I said it was *used* for reconnaissance. There is a difference. I warned you," added Kharon. "I was very explicit about the power of the forces you're facing. And by this point you should realize that."

Benrali frowned.

"Where are the trucks?" Kharon asked.

"Two miles from here. You have several things to do for us first."

"Several? I know of only one."

"You must fix the radar installation, and arrange for the Russians to resupply us with missiles."

"I'm prepared to fix the radar," said Kharon. "But as for missiles—that was not part of our deal."

Benrali rose from his desk. He had been an air force colonel under Gaddafi, joining the revolution only in its last weeks. In Kharon's mind that was why he was more objective than many of the others he had to deal with.

"We'll get something to eat and discuss it," said Benrali. He began rolling down his sleeves. Kharon noticed he was wearing fancy Italian shoes.

"We can talk, but any help with the Russians is separate from our agreement," warned Kharon. "I have no power with them."

"You have influence."

"Not at all."

"My people say you meet with them all the time."

"I meet with you. Would you say I can get you to do something you don't want to do?"

Benrali chuckled. His mirth was as explosive as his anger.

"You have a silver tongue," he told Kharon. "Come and let us eat."

A FEW HOURS LATER KHARON DROVE A BORROWED jeep through the low hills south of the city to a cluster of hills exactly one mile east of the power line that ran through the desert. He drove by GPS reading; there was no road here.

Two large tractor trailers sat on the southern side of the hill, seemingly abandoned. They had in fact been driven here immediately after the air raid on al-Hayat, having captured important telemetry for Kharon.

He wasn't sure how much Benrali understood, let alone if the Libyans had figured out what he was truly up to. They knew that the devices in the trucks were modified radar units; he'd had to request a trained crew and demonstrate a few areas where the radar differed from the Russian gear they were familiar with. They knew they were recording something, and they knew it must involve the Tigershark, which had been engaged by the fighters.

How much beyond that, who could say?

Kharon circled the two trailers, trying to see if anyone was lying in wait for him. In truth, it was impossible to be certain—a practiced assassin could easily hide himself in the sand. He knew that the Americans had such men; his only real protection against them was the fact that they didn't know what he was doing.

After two circuits, he drove over to the trailers. Leaving the engine running, he got out of the jeep with his submachine gun—it had cost him ten euros to retrieve—and walked quickly to the trailers.

His key jammed when he tried to open the padlock on the first trailer. He jiggled it back and forth, pulling and prodding, nearly despairing—the alternative would be to shoot through the chain, possibly damaging the gear inside.

Finally he got the key in and the lock clicked open. He pulled it apart and unlatched the door.

A thick loaf of warm, stale air greeted him. He lowered his head and pushed in as if he were a football player.

The trailer was the back of a Russian radar station, upgraded from the Soviet era, sold to Libya in the 1980s, and since then updated at least twice more, not counting the pieces Kharon had added himself. In a way it was a fascinating display of technological evolution, with bits and pieces remaining from each of its active periods.

Kharon wasn't here to admire it. He took a small LED flashlight from his pocket and moved quickly to a console at the far end of the trailer.

Two hard drive enclosures sat atop metal gridwork just below a radar console. The drives were held in place by a small plastic bracket at the side. He pushed the long handle in, swung the arm out of the way, and then picked up the first drive.

Wires at the back stopped him after a foot and a half. He undid the wires—the connections were the same as those used on Ethernet cables—then scooped out the second drive and did the same.

The trailer was extremely hot. So much sweat poured down his hands that he thought he was going to drop the two boxes. He went over to the door, leaning out to catch his breath. He dropped to his knees, resting for a few moments. Then he backed into the trailer, moving on all fours.

There was a small tool kit on the second console on the right side. He found it, removed it, then made his way to the back.

There was a CPU unit under the bench against the back wall. He couldn't see one of the bolts holding it to the floor and had to squirrel around with his hand to get the wrench on it. It took him nearly ten minutes to get the one bolt off. By the time he was done he felt like he couldn't breathe. He dragged the CPU out, yanking the cords out of the panel. They were superfluous at this point anyway.

He was so exhausted when he put the gear into the Jeep that he considered leaving the other drives in the second trailer. But he needed all the data, and so he pulled himself together. He went back to his vehicle and drank half of his bottle of water. Feeling a little better, he went to the other trailer.

This time the lock was easy. He pulled it off the latch, then jerked the door open. As he did, he turned and saw the eastern horizon had turned gray. White clouds furrowed above.

A sandstorm was approaching.

He pushed into the trailer and closed the door. A howl rose in the distance.

The drives were located in the opposite side in

the trailer, along with a small flash memory box he also needed to retrieve. He had them ready within a few minutes.

Back at the door, Kharon stopped when he heard what sounded like pebbles slapping against it. The storm had arrived, and it was a fierce one.

Going out in the sandstorm was not advisable. Kharon put the devices down and sat in the center aisle, listening to the wind as it whipped the sides of the trailer. He played the flashlight's narrow beam around the interior of the trailer, trying to trick himself into thinking it was massive.

HE HATED DARK, CONFINED PLACES. THEY REMINDED him of the closet he hid in the night they came to tell him that his mother had died.

His hands shook.

Kharon turned off the light and tucked his head down. He was well protected from the storm, and yet felt that it was enveloping him, as if he was its prisoner and there was no escape.

He'd known who they were and what they wanted. At nine years old, he was precocious in many ways. And it didn't take much to guess something was very wrong.

His mother never left him for long without calling. That night, she was already several hours late, without any word, without even a note.

Home from school, he had done his homework and waited. When it was an hour past dinner time, he fed himself a sandwich, the only thing he knew how to make. He watched the cartoon channel after that—a special privilege ordinarily reserved only for days like his birthday or holidays or times when he was sick.

Then he spent an hour at the window, his fears and worries becoming so strong he could no longer keep them away.

Another hour. Two more.

A dark blue sedan pulled up. Two men in uniform got out.

He ran to the closet, knowing what had happened, hoping that if he didn't let them in the house, everything would be all right.

But it wasn't. His mother had died, and there was nothing he could do about it.

Until now.

HUDDLED IN THE DARK, KHARON TRIED TO CLEAR HIS mind of the memories. He put his head down on his knees, eyes closed. He believed in science, not God, but even he felt the moment as something like a prayer—*let it stop.*

When it didn't, he thought of Ray Rubeo.

He saw Rubeo's thin face, his ascetic frame. He saw the sneer in his eyes—Kharon loathed that sneer.

I will do you in.

Whatever it takes. I will ruin you.

IT TOOK A HALF HOUR FOR THE STORM TO PASS. GRIT covered everything outside.

Kharon, back to himself, put the drives in the jeep and headed back to the city.

He called Fezzan and told him to have the car waiting near the Red Sand Hotel, a place where they had stayed before.

"You want to drive north tonight?" asked Fezzan. Clearly, he didn't want to.

"That would be ideal." Driving at night through the desert did entail some risk, but in Kharon's experience it wasn't much more than during the day.

"There are many reporters in town," said the Libyan idly. "They are all talking about going to al-Hayat tomorrow."

"Why?"

"The commission investigating the bombing accident will be there. They have experts coming along. Americans and French."

"Americans? Who?"

"I can ask. It didn't come up."

"Interesting," said Kharon.

"Should I get rooms?"

"I don't know that al-Hayat would be of any interest to me."

"Most reporters are going. If you want people to think you are a reporter—"

"Thank you, *Ahmed*. When I want your advice, I'll ask for it."

"Just a suggestion."

Of course he was right. There was no sense being pigheaded—this was an opportunity.

"Get the rooms," Kharon told Fezzan. "Two of them. Make sure you get a good rate."

"I'll be in the bar when you get back," said Fezzan.

Like a good Muslim, thought Kharon, hanging up.

3

Sicily

DANNY FREAH RUBBED HIS TIRED EYES, TRYING TO clear the fatigue away. "I don't think it's a good idea to go to Africa," he told Rubeo. "Nobody can guarantee your safety."

"People go back and forth between Libya all the time. Westerners generally aren't harmed." Rubeo rocked back and forth, as if he was having a hard time keeping himself contained in the small office. Danny couldn't remember seeing the scientist more animated. "I don't really need your permission, Colonel."

"I don't know about that. I am in charge of Whiplash," said Danny.

"Really, Colonel, you have no rank to pull over me. If you're not going to help me, I'll go on my own. I have Jons, and other people to call on. Really, Colonel, I have given this some thought. I need to see the crash site and the environs if I'm to figure out what happened."

"All right, listen. Give me a little time. I'll

figure something out, something that gives you some protection. Beyond your own team," Danny added. "It won't be until tomorrow at the earliest. I'll have to arrange an escort."

"I think it would be better to travel without the UN people."

"That's not what I'm talking about. We'll have more of our people here tomorrow," Danny said. "Right now, it's just me and Boston."

"I don't need an entourage."

"Two troopers and an Osprey to get you around quickly. You can't argue with that."

Rubeo looked as if he could, but he pressed his lips together and said nothing. Danny half expected him to ask for the Osprey now, but he had a ready answer—he had loaned both to the UN commission investigating the bomb strike.

"Do you really think you're the best one to go?" he asked Rubeo. "You have a dozen people over here looking into the incident—"

"Two dozen," corrected Rubeo. "Plus the team that was here to begin with. But yes, I do think it's a good use of my time. If one of your people had been involved in an accident or something similar, you'd want to investigate firsthand, wouldn't you?"

"I guess."

"I'm sure you would."

Conceding, Danny leaned back in the seat and changed the subject.

"You know, Doc, I think sometimes accidents like this—and even blue-on-blue incidents . . ." He stumbled for the right words. "These things are terrible, but you know, you have to put them in perspective."

"I'm trying to," said Rubeo, rising to leave.

4

al-Hayat

THE BLACK SCORCHES ON THE WALLS LOOKED AS IF they had been painted on, a kind of postmodern expressionism as interpreted by the god of fire.

The rubble in front of them was less poetic. What had once been a row of houses was now flattened stone, wood, and scraps of material too charred to recognize. The stench of death still hung in the air. The government could not have arranged a better scene if they had staged it.

Kharon was amazed at the damage the missiles had done. He had seen the results of the war firsthand before, but everything else paled compared to this.

The government said sixteen people had been killed and another twenty wounded. If anything, the number seemed miraculously low.

He curled his arms around his chest, suddenly cold. The slightest, very slightest, hint of grief poked at the very edge of his conscience. But it was more a rumor of remorse, less actual guilt or regret than an unease. It was easily ignored.

Two dozen reporters, most of them Western freelancers, had been admitted to the area by the government troops in anticipation of the special UN investigation commission's arrival. Kharon's phony credentials were more than enough to get him past the guards. They hadn't even bothered to search him, though he had thought it prudent to leave his weapon back with Fezzan in the truck at the edge of town.

He'd seen a few of the reporters in Tripoli. He nodded at anyone who said hello, but kept to himself as much as possible. There was always the possibility that someone might start asking too many questions about his credentials. If necessary, he could mention the German and the Australian Web sites which he had legitimately sold stories to, but anyone who really dug would come up with questions.

Even a simple one could be devastating: *What did you do before Libya?*

When he first arrived in Libya, he was surprised at how few of the reporters actually spoke Arabic. He was also surprised at how little they knew of the actual conflict. And he was stunned at how lazy most of them actually were. Not that they weren't willing to risk their lives—that, most had no trouble with. But nearly all settled for the first answer they got. And most would sooner walk barefoot in the desert than question the simple dichotomy they had arrived with: *rebels good, government bad.*

This story, at least, promised to make things a little more complicated.

The government had posted "facilitators" at different spots around the ruins. While their function was essentially that of press agents, Kharon suspected that they were high-ranking officers in the army or other government officials, well-trusted and dependable. He listened as one detailed the lives of the three people who had been killed in the building a few yards away. The man, a middle-aged Libyan, handed out glossy photos of the dead bodies with an enthusiasm that would have seemed more appropriate at a movie preview.

The government's interior minister was overseeing the press briefing, preening for the cameras as he talked about how the civilians were going about their everyday lives when the American plane struck.

Almost on cue, a pair of aircraft appeared in the distance. They sounded a bit like helicopters, but as Kharon stared he realized they were American V–22 Ospreys, tilt-rotor aircraft that flew like planes but landed like helicopters.

"The UN commission is arriving," said the minister in his heavily accented English. "They are going to land in the field across the way. Please give them room to arrive. We assume that they are unarmed."

Some of the reporters sniggered.

Kharon's heart began pumping hard in his chest. Some of the reports he had seen overnight indicated that the Americans had assigned technical experts to accompany the investigators.

Was Rubeo among them?

He thought it was very possible. The scientist

was a control freak. He would insist on seeing something like this firsthand.

If Rubeo came himself, Kharon would stay back and avoid the temptation to confront him. It would be difficult, though, extremely difficult.

Kharon wanted to see the pain on his face.

Then, he would kill him. But first he needed to know that he had suffered.

ZEN GLANCED AT ZONGCHEN AS THE OSPREY SETtled. The former Chinese air force general had seemed visibly nervous the entire flight. Now as the rotors swung upward and the aircraft descended he clutched the armrests at the side of his seat for dear life.

It was funny what made some people nervous.

"A little different than flying in a J–20, eh, General?" Zen asked as they gently touched down.

"Very different," said Zongchen, with evident relief. "There, I am in control. Here, very different."

As the crewmen headed for the door, Zen unstrapped his wheelchair and pushed it into the aisle. The maneuver into the seat was tricky, but Zongchen held the back of the wheelchair for him.

"You notice that my chair just fits down the aisle at the front," Zen told the general.

"Yes, very convenient."

"They did that especially for me."

It was a white lie, actually, but it amused the general. Zen rolled over to the door. A lift had been tasked to get him down; it rolled up, and after a bit of maneuvering and a few shouts back and forth, the plane crew turned him over to the lift operator.

Zen held himself steady as the ramp descended. It was the sort of thing workmen used while working on buildings, and it had only a single safety rail at the front. It moved down unsteadily—truly, it was scarier than almost anything he'd experienced in an airplane for quite a while.

"Do you get tired of being in a wheelchair?" Zongchen asked when they were both on the ground.

"Always," admitted Zen.

THE CROWD OF NEWS PEOPLE SEEMED TO HAVE TRIPLED since the Ospreys first appeared in the sky. Kharon wondered about the security—there were plenty of government soldiers around, but they seemed more focused on holding back the local villagers than watching the reporters.

Kharon slipped toward the front of the group. His heart thumped in his throat. He regretted leaving the gun.

Relax, he told himself. Just relax.

The UN team had brought security with them—a dozen soldiers, all with blue helmets, fanned out from the first Osprey, along with a few plainclothes agents. All of the dignitaries seemed to be in the second aircraft.

There was one in a wheelchair.

Kharon wasn't quite close enough to see his

face, but he guessed that it must be Jeff Stockard, the former Dreamland pilot who was now a United States senator.

Zen.

His mother had told him stories about Zen. He was "just" a star pilot then, before his accident and struggle turned him into something approaching a national hero.

A real hero, whom even Kharon admired. Not a phony legend like Rubeo.

A wave of damp sadness settled over Kharon. Zen had been at his mother's funeral. He remembered shaking the pilot's hand.

"We all loved your mom," he said.

Rubeo hadn't even spoken to him.

Kharon craned his neck, trying to see if the scientist was with the UN committee. He spotted someone of about the right height and moved up in the line, bumping against one of the armed guards before realizing that it wasn't Rubeo.

"Back," said the soldier. He was Pakistani, wearing his regular uniform below the blue helmet and armband.

"Sorry."

Kharon shifted back, joining the throng of reporters as they followed the commission walking up the road to the ruins. There was a light breeze; every so often a burst of wind would send grit in their faces.

AS A FIGHTER PILOT, ZEN HAD THE LUXURY OF DIStancing himself from the effects of ground war.

Rarely had he seen firsthand damage to anything other than an airplane.

Now it was all around him.

It was horrific. While the government guide was a bit heavy-handed, there was no question that the bombs sent by the Sabre had inflicted a terrible toll.

Zen reminded himself that the government, too, was to blame. It was inflicting a heavy toll on the populace, robbing and stealing from the people. In the roughly two years it had been in power, thousands of people were imprisoned without trial. The new leaders were repeating many of the outrages that had flourished under Gaddafi.

But that didn't make this any less tragic.

He wheeled slowly along, gradually falling behind the main pack as they moved along the sides of the battered buildings.

"Excuse me, are you Senator Stockard?" shouted one of the journalists trailing them.

The man had an American accent. Zen debated whether to ignore him, but finally decided it was better to speak.

"Yes, I am," Zen told him.

"I'm Greg Storey from AP. I'm interested, Senator—what's your impression?"

"It's terrible," said Zen. "A horrible accident."

"The government is claiming that it was done on purpose, as a terrorist act."

"That's clearly not what happened," said Zen.

"How do you know?"

Zen controlled his anger. He had enough experience with reporters to know that they often tried to provoke people to get an extreme reaction.

"NATO doesn't go around targeting civilians. We hope to get to the bottom of what happened, and then fix it so it doesn't happen again. That's the committee's aim."

Seeing that Zen was taking questions, the other reporters quickly gathered nearby and asked a few of their own. The government minder ran over, but by the time he arrived there were so many other people around that he had a difficult time pushing through the crowd and was in no position to reshape the conversation.

A few of the questions were things Zen couldn't answer in any detail—what exact aircraft had been in the raid was one he just ignored. But most were thoughtful, and he answered as fully and honestly as he could.

The U.S. was not controlling the investigation. He was an honorary member, willing to help as much as possible. Zongchen, a respected Chinese air force officer as well as diplomat, was a careful man and would sift through the evidence. It was unfortunate that the government of Libya had chosen to take a hard line against the rebels. There was room for a negotiated peace, if the sides would come to the negotiating table.

Zen admitted that he didn't know the exact ins and outs of the local politics, and would have to defer to others on specific grievances. He was interested in finding out why things had gone wrong with the air attack.

"Was it because the planes were UAVs?" asked the American reporter.

"Assuming that they were—I'm not sure that's one hundred percent yet—there's no reason to think the tragedy would have been avoided with a manned plane," said Zen.

"Really, Senator?"

"Obviously, we have to see the circumstances of the accident," he said. "But manned planes make mistakes, too. Unfortunately."

"UAVs seem more dangerous."

"Not really. UAVs have helped reduce casualties," Zen answered. "Now some people—pilots especially—long for what are thought of as the good ol' days, when every aircraft was manned. But remember, back in the very old days, collateral damage was a serious problem. World War Two saw horrendous civilian deaths. We've come a long way."

A voice from the back shouted a question. "Why are robots making the decisions now?"

Zen tried to ignore the question, turning to the right, but the reporter he glanced at asked the same thing.

"I don't know that they are," said Zen.

"There have been anonymous reports to that effect," said the first reporter. "Several news organizations have gotten leaks."

"I don't have information on that, so I guess I can't address it," said Zen.

"Are the UAVs acting on their own?" asked Storey.

"It's not a robot rebellion, if that's what you're asking," said Zen. "Men are in the loop."

"I've heard from sources that they are not," said the reporter in the back.

"I've given you pretty much the details I know and can give," said Zen. He noticed Zongchen standing nearby. "We're looking into everything. Probably the person you really want to talk to about the committee would be General Zongchen."

Zongchen gave him a look that said, *Thanks a lot.*

The reporters began peppering him with questions. Before Zongchen could answer, a rock sailed overhead. Zen looked up and saw several more flying from the direction of the ruins.

Suddenly, there were many rocks in the air.

THE RIOT TOOK KHARON BY SURPRISE. HE MOVED TO his left, looking for a way out of the crowd.

People surged from the edge of the ruins, pushing toward the thin line of UN soldiers. Clearly, the action had been planned by the government. A foolish, stupid move.

But then, what did they do that wasn't foolish?

The cameras shifted their aim from the dignitaries to the crowd. The people yelled about killers and murderers, and threw more rocks—they couldn't quite see the irony.

The journalists moved toward the rock throwers, most thinking they were immune to the violence. Kharon realized they were just as much the target as the dignitaries were—and they didn't have anyone to protect them.

It was time to leave.

He pocketed his ID and moved quickly back through the ruins, walking at first, then running back to his truck.

ZEN MADE IT TO THE OSPREY JUST AS THE UN soldiers fired warning shots into the air. He wheeled himself toward the platform but was intercepted by two of the plainclothes security people who had traveled with them but stayed in the background.

"Sorry, Senator. We're getting you out of here," said one of the men gruffly. He grabbed him under the arm.

Zen started to protest but realized it was too late—he was half carried, half thrown into the Osprey. The props were already spinning.

"My chair!" he yelled.

No one heard him in the confusion. The door closed and the aircraft veered upward.

Zen crawled to the nearest seat and pulled himself up. Someone helped him turn around.

It was Zongchen.

"This did not go as well as I hoped," said the Chinese general. He was sweating profusely. His pants were torn and his knee was bleeding.

"No, I would say it didn't go well at all," said Zen, wondering how long it would take to find a wheelchair as good as the one he had left behind.

5

Tripoli

THE FACT THAT THE GOVERNMENT THOUGHT STAGING A riot at al-Hayat would have any beneficial effect toward their cause showed just how far removed from reality the leaders were.

Kharon brooded about this on the drive back to the city, worried that the government would collapse before he was able to exact his revenge. If so, years of effort would have been wasted; he would have to begin fresh.

He was so distracted that when they arrived in Tripoli he agreed to pay Fezzan an extra hundred euros to help him carry the box of drives and CPUs up the stairs of the small house he had rented in the western quarter. Taped shut in a cardboard box that had held bags of cashews, the components were neither large nor particularly heavy. Fezzan left as happy as Kharon had ever seen him.

A few minutes after he left, Kharon took the devices from the box and put them in a large, padded suitcase. He went downstairs—he used the building only for his sporadic contacts with Fezzan and other locals—and found his small motorcycle in the alley at the back. He tied the suitcase to the rear fender with a pair of bungee cords, put on a helmet to obscure his face, then set out on a zigzag trail through the city.

His paranoia poked at him a few blocks later,

when he came to an intersection blocked by police vehicles. Officially neutral like the city, the Tripoli police were generally considered pro-rebel, though you could never tell whose side they were on. And given Kharon's situation, either could instantly decide he was their enemy.

But the police were investigating a routine traffic accident, and waved him past as he approached.

Kharon drove to the dense residential districts north of Third Ring Road. After making sure he wasn't being followed, he pulled down an alley and raced toward a building at the far end. Reaching into his pocket, he took out a garage door opener and pressed the button in the middle. Then he hit the brakes, skidding under the thick branches of several trees as he turned into a bay whose door was just opening. He took the turn so hard that he had to steady himself with his foot on the cement floor, half crashing to a halt.

He jerked his head back and forth, making sure he was alone. Then he hopped away from the bike and went to the empty workbench a few feet away. Reaching under it, he found a key taped to the underside. He used it to open the circuit breaker box above the bench just as the door opener's automatic lights turned off. With his fingers, he hunted until he found the switch at the very bottom of the panel. He threw it to off, and then, still in the dark, walked to the side of the room and found the light switch.

When the lights came on, he glanced to the

right, looking for the red light connected to his security system. The light stayed off. No one had been inside since his last visit.

Kharon went to the door to the garage and opened it. He glanced around the small room, making sure it was empty. Then he went back outside to the garage and the power panel, turned the breaker back on, and went inside.

The garage was the side end of a small workshop used as a sewing factory some years before. All of the machinery had been removed, a perfect place for Kharon to set up shop had he wanted. But he had decided it could be too easily surrounded; he used it only as a temporary staging area.

Inside the large room, he retrieved a touch-screen computer hidden in a small compartment beneath the tile floor. He activated it, then used it to interface with the security system, running a second check to make sure it had not been compromised. Satisfied, he pulled a large duffel bag from the compartment, replaced the tile, and went back to the garage, where he put the CPU drives in the bag. Then he locked down the building and went out through a side door.

AN HOUR LATER KHARON CARRIED THE DUFFEL BAG down the steps of a lab building at Tripoli University to the subbasement where the utilities were kept. He waited at the bottom of the stairs, listening to hear if anyone was following. Then he slipped a thin plastic shim into the doorjamb to get around the lock. He stepped into a corridor lined with large pipes. Closing the door, he found himself completely in the dark.

The confined space stoked his claustrophobia. His hand began to shake as he reached for the small flashlight in his pocket.

It's nothing, he told himself. Nothing.

But that didn't stop his hand from shaking. Kharon's fingers finally found the light. He switched it on and played it across the space in front of him.

Breathe.

He took a step forward, then turned back and made sure the door was locked. Lifting the duffel onto his shoulder, he walked swiftly to the end of the hall, where he found a set of steps leading off to his right. He went down cautiously, one hand tight on the rail. Then he ducked under another set of large pipes and electrical conduits and walked through an open space to another door. This one led to a second hallway, lit by a dull yellow light at the far end.

There was a door near the light, guarded by a combination lock. Kharon pounded the numbers quickly, pushing inside as the lock snapped open. Still breathing hard, he reached for the two switches to the left. One killed the light outside; the other turned on a set of daylight fluorescents that lined the ceiling.

The light helped him relax. He was inside a hidden lab complex that was once part of the Libyan effort to build a nuclear weapon. It had been abandoned for years when Kharon stumbled upon it.

He walked through what had been a large

security/reception area. There was a lab room at the far end, guarded by another coded lock. Inside, he found his two workstations in sleep mode just as he had left them.

After making sure that his security had not been breached, Kharon unpacked his boxes and began downloading the information from the hard drives into his native system. While the drives spun, he booted a third computer that was tied into the university's mainframes. He used it to get onto the Internet and scan the news relating to Libya.

Most of the stories about the riot either hinted that it had been staged or said so outright.

Idiot government.

The commission had returned to Tripoli. They said all the right things—the accident had been inexcusable, the loss of life was horrible.

And the questions he had asked about the autonomous drones?

Not even mentioned. The reporters were too stupid to understand what was going on.

Frustrated, Kharon began scanning stories from several days before, looking to see if the tips he'd planted had borne fruit. Rubio's name didn't even come up in the stories related to the incident.

Kharon leaned his elbow on the bench in front of the keyboard. He put his chin against his hand, then bit his index finger. He bit it so hard and so long that when he finally let go, his finger was white.

Embarrass Rubeo? Ruin him?

Hardly.

He was going to have to just kill him and be done with it.

6

Sicily

FOLLOWING THEIR RETURN TO BASE AND THE FORMAL debrief, Turk joined Shooter Squadron at their *second* ready room—the hotel lounge at the Sicilian Inn a few miles from the base. The seaside resort had been taken over by the allies, and the bar was filled with fliers from several member countries: Greece, France, a few Brits, and even some Germans. The pilots from Shooter Squadron commandeered a table on the terrace overlooking the beach and the sea. It was a brilliant night, with the stars twinkling and the moon so massive and yellow it looked as if it had been PhotoShopped in.

Grizzly and most of the others were still sick, but two pilots Turk had never met before came down to join them, Captain Frank Gordon from San Francisco, and the squadron's junior pilot, Lieutenant Li Pike, a woman who had joined the Hog squadron just a few weeks before.

There was plenty of the usual joking around, but there was also a serious conversation on the rebel movement and the role of the allies as well.

Pike, who had a degree in international relations, pointed out that this was the second time around for the allies—the first intervention, almost universally hailed when it ousted Gaddafi, had resulted in a terrible regime that was now itself being contested. In her opinion, intervention of any sort was futile; the locals should have been left to fend for themselves.

Paulson countered that just because things hadn't worked out in the first place, there was no reason to give up—try, try again was more or less his motto.

"Ah, waste 'em all," groused Beast, reaching for his beer. "Shoot 'em up and go home."

"Do you really feel that way?" asked Pike. She had a sweet, almost innocent face—pretty, thought Turk.

"That's how I feel, shit yeah. Doin' good? Almost got us killed today. Turk had to blow a missile off his back."

"Almost flew his Hog into the dirt," said Paulson. "That would have been embarrassing. Dreamland hotshot kicks in the desert because he oversticks his plane."

Turk was starting not to like Paulson very much, but he tried taking the ribbing good-naturedly. Objecting was the easiest way to guarantee it would continue.

"I have to say, the Hog goes where you point it," he told the others. "Very nice aircraft."

"Sure your muscles haven't atrophied?" asked Paulson.

"I can still make a fist," said Turk.

"I'm just jokin' with ya, Captain," sneered Paulson, getting up and heading toward the bar.

"Do you believe in intervention?" asked Pike.

"I haven't really thought about it, to be honest," Turk told her, grateful for the chance to change the subject.

"So what's the F–40 like?" asked Beast.

"It's interesting. Some days you forget you're really in an airplane. It's real smooth."

"I don't think I'd like that," said Li.

"You get used to it."

"They blame you for the accident?" asked Beast.

"No. That's one good thing about all the systems they have in place for monitoring everything. They can see exactly what I did."

"You think they'll figure it out?" asked Li. "Soon, I mean."

"I hope they don't," said Ginella, returning to the table after speaking with one of the French fliers. "Because it means we have our friend Turk here for a little bit."

"You're staying?" Li asked.

"Well . . ."

"Captain Mako can stay until we have our full complement back," said Ginella. "As far as I'm concerned, he can stay forever."

"I'm glad to be here," said Turk.

The mood lightened as Ginella told a story she'd just heard from the Frenchmen. Turk watched Li, whose expression remained serious the whole time.

The more he watched her, the more beautiful she seemed to become. Her light tan skin was smooth and exotic in the dim light of the club. Her eyes sparkled.

Turk looked away whenever he suspected she was going to turn in his direction. She caught him once and smiled.

He tried to smile back, but he was sure that he must have looked like a deer caught in the headlights of an oncoming car.

Paulson returned with a fresh round of drinks. He started bragging about how well he'd done in some Gunsmoke competition a year before. He seemed to be playing to Li, who sipped her drink coolly and avoided looking in his direction.

Turk got up and went over to the window, looking out at the sea. He was starting to feel tired. Everything that had happened over the past few days had worn him down. He decided he ought to find a ride back to his own hotel.

A pair of French pilots came over and introduced themselves. It turned out they'd been nearby when Turk shot down the Mirages, and asked him to recount the engagement. He did so gladly, using his hands to show the different paths the antagonists had taken.

"It was over in less than two minutes," he said. "I had to be lined up perfectly."

"He is quite a pilot, isn't he?" said Ginella, coming over. She threw her hand around his shoulder. "A real ace."

"Well, not so much an ace," said Turk.

"You need five planes to be an ace," said one of the Frenchmen, citing the traditional tally for the honor.

His companion mentioned Célestin Adolphe Pégoud, the French World War One pilot who had first earned the title. Turk confessed that while he had heard of the pilot, he didn't know much about him. The other man described him as an early test pilot—Pégoud had looped a Blériot monoplane before the war, by legend and common agreement the first man to do so.

As the Frenchmen spoke of some other early aces, Turk realized that Ginella's hand was lingering on his back. It felt warm, and reassuring.

And sexual, though she didn't do anything suggestive.

Eventually, the French pilots excused themselves, saying they had an early op. Turk turned to Ginella, whose hand was still on his back.

He hesitated a moment, not exactly sure what to do.

She leaned in and kissed him.

Her lips were lush, much warmer and more moist than he would have imagined. She pressed him gently toward her, her right hand coming up on his side.

He moved his lips to hers, tilting his head to meet hers. He felt her tongue against his teeth and opened his mouth to accept it.

A small part of his brain objected—he would have much preferred kissing Li—but every other cell in his body urged him on. He closed his eyes, enjoying the sweetness of the moment. It had been a long time since he'd had a kiss this passionate.

Finally, Ginella started to move back. Turk did

as well, sliding his hands down. She caught them, gripping tightly.

"Problem, Captain?"

"Um, uh, no. No. Not at all." He glanced behind her. The rest of the squadron had left. In fact, that bar was empty except for the two of them and the bartender.

"Maybe we should continue this upstairs," she suggested.

"Well, I—"

"Sshhh." She put her fingers on his lips. "Nothing."

"Well."

He was truly undecided. He wanted to go to bed with her, without a doubt. But there were reasons not to.

Like?

They didn't quite compute at the moment.

"Come on," she told him.

Turk opened his mouth to say yes, but before he could get a word out, she leaned in and kissed him again.

7

Sicily

THE VIDEO WAS VERY POOR QUALITY, AND EXPANDING IT to fill the fifty-five-inch screen in Zongchen's conference room further distorted it. But it wouldn't have been very pretty to look at under any circumstance.

Zen shook his head as the video continued, the camera running with the mob after the Osprey. He saw a glimpse of his wheelchair heading for the aircraft, then saw only the backs of heads and finally the ground. The last shot was the Osprey in the distance.

"They showed us," said Zen sarcastically. The two men were alone; except for an aide watching the phones, the rest of the staff had quit for the night.

"My government has filed a protest," said Zongchen. The Chinese general wore a deep frown. "This has been a great disgrace."

"We should have expected it," said Zen.

"We were assured complete security," said Zongchen.

Zen kept his answer to himself. The general was a military man, with high standards and expectations. Like military professionals the world over, he placed a great deal on personal integrity and honor.

Noble assets certainly, traits that Zen shared, and traits one could depend on in the military world, and often in the world at large.

But the world of politics—geopolitics included—was different. Lofty values often held you back. Zen had learned the hard way that the knife in the back from a friend was more common than the frontal assault from an enemy.

"We will pursue our investigation," said Zongchen. "We will continue."

"Good."

"The explanations of how the system works have been most useful," Zongchen added, nodding to Zen. "We appreciate your candor."

"And your discretion." True to his word, Zongchen had not pressed for the technical aspects of the system. Given the animosity between China and the United States, they were working together remarkably well. Part of it was certainly personal—the two old pilots respected each other—but perhaps it was an indication that the two great powers in the world, one young, one not quite so young, might find a way to cooperate going forward.

Careful, Zen warned himself, you're getting all touchy-feely. Next thing you know, we'll be sitting around the campfire singing "Kumbaya"—and then Zongchen will knife me in the back like a proper ally.

"The pilot is not at fault," said Zongchen. "This is clear. But from your discussion, the only possibility seems an error aboard the aircraft. Would you agree?"

"There's nothing that would contradict that," said Zen. "Perhaps with a little more work we can identify it. But the teams working on it haven't succeeded yet."

"Hmmm." The general seemed temporarily lost in thought.

One of the general's aides approached quietly. Zen noticed him first, and glanced in his direction. Zongchen looked, and apparently saw something in the young man's face that told him it was urgent.

"Excuse me, Senator."

"Of course."

Zongchen spoke to the aide in Chinese, then turned to Zen in surprise.

"A member of the Libyan government is on the phone and wishes to talk to me. He speaks English—which is good since Cho here does not speak Arabic." Zongchen smiled. "Come, you should listen as well."

Zen wheeled himself from the large room to Zongchen's suite office. He stopped a few feet away, waiting as the Chinese general put the call on speakerphone.

"I have another member of our committee here with me," Zongchen said before he even greeted the other man. "Senator Stockard, from the United States."

"The man in the wheelchair," said the Libyan. His English was good, with an accent somewhere between Tripoli and London.

"The senator lost the use of his legs in an air accident many years ago," said Zongchen, glancing at Zen. "But he has had quite a career since then. He was an excellent pilot."

"I am pleased to talk to him, or anyone else you designate. Allow me to properly introduce myself. I am Colonel Abdel Bouri, and a few hours ago I have been designated to head the military portfolio of our government."

"I am pleased to speak to you," said Zongchen.

"The security breakdown was deeply regrettable," said Bouri. "And a fault of the previous minister. Things have changed. The government has . . . reorganized. I have been asked . . . Let me find the proper words here."

He paused, speaking to someone else in the office in soft but quick Arabic.

"I have been authorized to speak of a peace arrangement," said the minister in English. "We are prepared to hold discussions with the rebels, if the proper conditions can be arranged. These talks would lead to a new government. Elections would be established."

Zongchen and Zen exchanged a glance.

"The president himself cannot make this statement," Bouri continued. "But I have full authority to conduct talks. This can only occur at the most confidential . . . under the most quiet circumstances."

"Pardon my skepticism," said Zen. "But given the events of yesterday, and much of what has been happening over the past week, how do we know that we can trust you?"

The minister began protesting, saying that he was a man of integrity and had not been involved with the leadership in the past. To Zen it seemed a clear case of someone protesting too much.

"We do want to trust you, but trust is something that is earned," Zen told him. "You should declare a cease-fire—"

"If we stop, the rebels will continue," said the new minister. "You have seen them. They are animals."

Not exactly the sort of opinion that was going to pave the way for peace.

"Perhaps your government could begin with a

very small gesture," said Zongchen. "Perhaps you could begin with apologizing for the attack on the committee yesterday. That costs you nothing, yet is rich in symbolism."

Bouri didn't answer.

"You have already apologized to me," said Zongchen.

"Yes, but you are asking for something different. The president would have to apologize."

"Since the government has already fired the defense minister, it's going to be clear that mistakes were made," said Zen. "A public statement won't cost you anything."

"And it will earn you a great deal," added Zongchen.

"It will cost much," said the Libyan. "But I will see what I can do. In the meantime, let us establish a proper procedure for these conversations. The talks between your committee and I. They will be strictest confidence, yes?"

"Of course," said Zongchen.

"We'll have to talk to others in order for our work to mean anything," added Zen. "We have to talk to the UN leaders, our government, and eventually the rebels."

"Carefully," said Bouri.

"Quietly, you mean?" asked Zen.

"Yes, both. Carefully and quietly."

Zongchen agreed that would be wise. The two men spoke for a few moments more, deciding how they would contact each other, and establishing a routine of "regular" calls twice per day.

After Bouri hung up, Zongchen turned to Zen.

"This is an interesting development. Perhaps our being attacked has had a positive result."

"Maybe," said Zen.

"You don't think this is genuine?"

Zen wheeled himself back a few feet. His substitute wheelchair was powered, something he didn't like. But it would do for now.

"I suppose our best option is to treat it as if it is genuine," he told Zongchen. "The question will be more the rest of government—does he speak for it? Hard to tell."

"Hmmm." The general was silent for a few moments, thinking. "It is very late, and we have not eaten. Let us go and find something. Deep thought is better on a full stomach."

He spoke to his aide in quick Chinese, then led Zen out into the hall.

"It is interesting," said Zongchen as they waited for the elevator. "Two former men of war negotiating a peace."

"Interesting, yes."

"But peace was also our aim," added the general, "even if not our profession."

8

Sicily

TURK FELL ASLEEP IN GINELLA'S BED AFTER THEY MADE love, but only for an hour. He slipped off the side onto the floor, trying to be quiet and not entirely sure what he was doing here. He hadn't forgotten what had happened; he just didn't believe it. Sleeping with another officer was one thing; sleeping with a colonel who was at least temporarily his boss . . .

Ginella lay with her head turned toward the wall, dozing peacefully. She had put on a T-shirt, but it was pulled halfway up her back, revealing her curved buttocks.

It was a nice curve. She was good in bed—a little more assertive than he was used to, but definitely a woman who knew how to please and be pleased.

But not quite his type. Older than he was.

And his boss.

What had he been thinking?

He hadn't been, was the answer. He grabbed his clothes and got dressed, then slipped out without waking her.

The bright lights of the hotel hallway stung his eyes. Turk walked quickly to the elevator, but as he pressed the button he realized someone might come out and see him waiting, or worse, be in the car when the doors opened. He didn't want to deal with any questions that might raise, so he used the stairs.

Outside, he realized it was too late to get a car. He had to go back to the desk and ask them to call a taxi.

By the time Turk got back to his own hotel, it was nearly three. He collapsed on the bed, even more tired than he had been the night before.

The next thing he knew, his phone was ringing. He had left it on the desk opposite the bed, and by the time he got there, the call had gone to voice mail.

It was Chahel Ratha.

"Didn't you get the text? We need you here by 0800. It's five minutes past."

TURK MADE IT TO THE SABRE HANGAR A FEW MINUTES before nine.

"Need some O_2?" asked one of the guards at the hangar. Pure oxygen was a common cure for a hangover among flight crews.

Turk shook his head and went inside. He found Ratha and one of the lead engineers fussing over a pot of coffee at the side bench.

"Sorry I'm late," he told them.

Ratha shook his head. "It's just static tests anyway."

Turk rushed to get into his gear. The Tigershark had been mostly placed back together. His job was to run the controls in a flight simulation mode while the technical people ran a bunch of tests on the interfaces with the Sabres. It was very routine, but it got his mind off the night before.

Some two hours of tests later, the engineers decided they had enough data and helped Turk from the cockpit.

"Figure it out?" he asked.

Ratha just shook his head. He didn't look particularly pleased.

"Just the man I'm looking for," said Danny Freah, coming into the hangar. "How are you, Turk?"

"I'm good, Colonel. Yourself?"

"Fine. Step into my office here a second." Freah motioned him to the side. Turk followed, bracing himself for questions about Ginella.

Deny, deny, deny, whispered a little voice.

Why? He'd done nothing wrong. It was Ginella who would get in trouble, if anyone was going to get in trouble.

Right.

"I heard you did really well yesterday with the A–10s," said Danny.

"Um, yeah."

"You really made an impression on Colonel Ginella," said Danny. "She was singing your praises this morning."

Turk felt himself flush.

"It was good of you to step up," said Danny.

"Thanks, I—"

"Colonel Ginella says you rate higher than most if not her whole squadron. She wants as much of you as she can get."

Turk struggled to find his tongue.

"Hard getting used to the Warthog after flying the Tigershark?" asked Danny.

"Just about night and day," said Turk.

Danny nodded. "You look like you had a rough night. You all right?"

"Oh, just a little . . . pilot stuff."

"All done here?"

"Yes, sir."

"All right. Don't get in any trouble, you hear?" Danny chucked his shoulder, then walked away.

THE ENGINEERS TOLD TURK HE WOULDN'T BE NEEDED now for several days. He got changed and caught the bus over to the cafeteria to get some lunch. But once inside the serving area, he decided he wasn't particularly hungry, a decision reinforced by hearing laughter in the seating area that sounded very much like some members of Shooter Squadron. He grabbed two large bottles of water and went back out the way he came.

A small field sat across the road at the back of the building. There were some picnic tables there. He walked over and sat on the top of a table—the benches themselves had inexplicably disappeared. He took a long pull from the water bottle, then leaned back, arms behind him, inhaling and exhaling in long, deep breaths.

A flight of Eurofighters took off with a loud rush, roaring into the air. Turk watched their bodies glow silver as they climbed, melting into a white light as they turned in the sky. Rising into the mid-morning sun, they turned black, vanishing into tiny daggers as they turned once more, this time toward Africa.

As the sound of the jet engines faded, he gradually became aware of the shouts of children. Remembering his soccer game the other day, he got up off the table, hopped the short fence, and walked in that direction.

The day care building was on the other side of the road, just beyond a low-slung barracks type building that was temporarily unused. The shouts were coming from a small group playing tag in the corner of the yard. Turk watched them for a few seconds, deciphering the rules, which seemed unusually free-flowing.

"You have children yourself?"

The woman's voice startled him. Turk turned abruptly and saw Captain Li Pike, the Warthog pilot from Shooter Squadron. In her arms was a cardboard box so big her chin barely rose above it.

"No, I don't have any kids," said Turk. "You?"

"Not yet."

"Oh."

He took that to mean that she was married, but when he glanced at her hand, she didn't have a ring.

"When my career gets under control," Li added. "Then maybe we'll see."

"What's your husband think?"

"I'm not married."

"Boyfriend?"

"I don't have a boyfriend. No time yet. Like I said, when my career gets under control."

"Makes sense."

She smiled, and he felt like a fool—it was the sort of indulgent smile you gave a simpleton.

"What's with the box?" he asked.

"Oh, we took up a little collection and got the kids a few puzzles and games," said Li. "It was the colonel's suggestion. They're on a limited budget."

"Really?"

"The shelves are kind of bare. They gave us a tour the first day—I think they saw women in the squadron and thought that's what we would be interested in. Italians."

Her smile was so beautiful it was almost a weapon.

"Let me help you with the box," he told her.

"Oh, it's not heavy."

Turk took it anyway, then followed her around to the side of the building. There was no one at the door or in the hallway; they went along to the first classroom. Li knocked tentatively, then inched in.

Some of the children spotted her peeking in and began to laugh. She pushed the door open wide, greeting the teacher and explaining, in English, that they had brought the things they had promised the other day. The colonel, she added, was sorry that she couldn't come herself.

The teacher's English was limited and heavily accented, but she greeted Li warmly, and told the children in Italian that the American pilots had brought them some presents. Turk, meanwhile, went over to a table near the front and put the box down.

"*Il Americano!*" said one of the children, running over. Within seconds Turk found himself surrounded by the soccer players, who were chattering in Italian.

"I don't understand a word you're saying," he told the boys.

"We will play," said one of the children. "Football."

"Soccer," said Turk.

"They were playing football with you the day two ago," said the teacher. "You are good, no?"

"No," said Turk. "They are very good."

"They want to play with you now. It is almost time for their, how do you say?"

"Game?"

"Yes, game. That is a good word."

Turk glanced at Li, who stood with her arms folded, a bemused expression on her face.

"You gonna play?" he asked her.

"I have work, Captain. I'm the maintenance officer. I'll see you later."

"Sure."

The boys had retrieved three soccer balls and were already urging him toward the door.

"Just a little while," he told them. "Five minutes."

"*Cinque minuti*," said the teacher. "*Cinque. Solamente.*"

"What she said," Turk told them. "Exactly."

9

Sicily

THE PILOT KHARON NORMALLY USED TO GET BACK AND forth in Libya didn't respond to his messages, and not wanting to wait, he booked on a commercial flight to Sicily, flying on Tunis Air, which was doing a booming business ferrying people in and out of the country. Kharon's final destination was on the east coast, near Catania, but getting a flight there involved no less than three transfers. Renting a car and driving from Palermo made more sense and gave him greater flexibility. It also meant he would be able to arrive armed.

He had determined that Rubeo was at the base by following the movements of his private company plane, whose registration was public. He wasn't yet sure where the scientist was staying—there were a half-dozen likely possibilities—but that was a solvable problem.

The more important question was how he would kill him.

Ironically, he had not planned the actual event. He had been so focused on the other aspects that he failed to map it out.

But murder was best executed on the spur of the moment. To plan that too carefully—certainly, he would leave clues that would be discovered and trip him up.

And after all, what had his planning otherwise

gotten him? Rubeo so far had not been touched by the disaster of his prideful invention.

Kharon was more than a little out of his element in the tough precincts of Palermo, and he knew that no amount of intellect could substitute for street savvy. But he wanted to obtain a gun, and he knew that this was the easiest place to do it, as long as he was willing to overpay.

He stopped first at a legitimate gun shop, where he had no luck; the owner told him that since he was not an Italian citizen, he could not obtain a license at the local police station, and therefore he could not buy the weapon. But at least Kharon learned what the actual procedure was.

It was not particularly onerous—one was required to register the gun at the local police station, a practice the gun dealer hinted was not always strictly followed. But it was impossible to register if you were a foreigner. Anyone even suspected of being from outside Italy—as Kharon's poor accent undoubtedly made clear—would be immediately asked for identification.

Armed with the information, he decided that the easiest approach would be to simply claim he was an Italian citizen, back to the country after spending many years in America. All he needed were documents that would prove he was Italian.

Such documents were valuable not only to new immigrants, but to legitimate citizens who wanted to avoid the hassle of getting official records from city hall. A web search of news sources showed that two years before there had been a raid on several tobacconists accused of selling these papers; the list was an obvious pointer on where he should go.

The first was closed. The second was in the lobby of an expensive looking hotel. The only clerk Kharon could find was a young man who gave him a befuddled look when he mentioned that he needed new documents. Kharon told him a story about having lost his driver's license—the story he had seen indicated that many of the customers of the phony docs bought them to escape the bureaucracy and fees involved in getting replacements. But the young man seemed indifferent.

Outside, Kharon was looking up the address of the next place on his smart phone when a man yelled to him.

"*Signor*—you need help, yes?"

The man had been in the shop, standing near the magazines. He was in his early twenties, dressed in new jeans and well-tailored sport coat. The odor of his cologne was strong enough to fight its way through the cloud of diesel smoke nearby.

"I need documents," said Kharon.

"Why?" asked the man.

He seemed too young to be a policeman. But Kharon hesitated. The man's English was very good, the accent more American than British.

Just the sort of slick operator he needed. If he trusted him.

Am I doing this?

Yes, finally. I am moving ahead after all these years of planning. It is time.

"I need to buy a gun," Kharon said.

"That's a very expensive problem," said the man.

"Not from what I've heard."

"Come on and have a coffee," said the man, pointing to an espresso bar across the street. "We will talk."

IN THE END, KHARON PURCHASED A GLOCK 17. THE pistol was an older version, the type before the accessory rail was added, but the gun itself was in excellent shape. Kharon field-stripped it for inspection in a small room at the back of the coffee shop the man had taken him to. Before he had it back together, his "friend" appeared with a driver's license and an EU passport. He took a photo, and within ten minutes Kharon was an Italian citizen.

Amazing what five thousand euros could do.

The gun didn't come with a holster, and Kharon knew better than to try and carry it bare in his belt. He went back to the legitimate gun store and purchased a holster. The whole time, he expected the clerk to say something, perhaps even refuse to deal with him, but the man didn't even indicate he knew him, or glance suspiciously at the wrapped-up bag Kharon carried with him.

He stopped at another store and bought himself a jacket for two hundred euros. It was a little big, and the shop owner gave him a hard time, insisting that he have it altered, a process that would take a few days. Kharon had to practically shout at the man to get him to sell it as it was.

It was easier to buy illegal documents and a gun in Italy than an ill-fitting jacket.

Better equipped, he filled the tank on the rental car, then set out on the autostrada for the eastern end of the island.

Soon, he thought to himself, he would see Rubeo.

10

Sicily

TURK'S FIVE MINUTES PLAYING WITH THE *I RAGAZZI* turned into roughly a half hour, and certainly would have lasted longer had the teacher not finally declared it was time for the children to eat lunch.

The kids demanded that he return. He promised he would come back in two days—a vow the teacher made a big deal of, even writing it on the class calendar.

The game vanquished Turk's hangover, or whatever physical funk he had been in. It also left him hungry, so he walked over to the cafeteria and got himself lunch—a warm octopus salad with red and blue potatoes and the mandatory side of pasta.

He was just about done when he realized he hadn't checked his phone for messages. There were a stack of them, including two from Ginella: Shooter Squadron was having a pilots' meeting at 1500, and she hoped he'd be available.

It *sounded* like a voluntary request, and while the military wasn't exactly known for volunteerism, Turk decided he would interpret it that way. He also decided he would head toward Catania, a city on the coast about eleven miles north of the base. He hadn't been there since arriving, and from what he'd heard, it would be the perfect place to let his mind wander while he took a mental breather.

A public bus ran from the base up to the city. Turk hopped on it, and after a confused negotiation with the driver—who finally made it clear that he didn't have to pay, *grazie*—he settled into a seat near the back and watched the countryside. Sicily was basically a volcano in the shallow Mediterranean, and the focal point of that volcano—Mount Etna—rose beyond the window as they rode. Despite the early spring heat, the top of the mountain was white-capped. A dim layer of mist rose from the peak; it was a benign presence this afternoon, barely hinting at its power to reshape the lives of the people in the area as well as the landscape.

Turk got out near the city square, or piazza. He walked around for a while, looking at the buildings and the people, his mind wandering. Finally he took a seat at an outdoor café at one side of the square, ordered a wine, then got the menu and had a plate of pasta and a second wine.

A succession of pretty women passed nearby en

route to the tourist spots or somewhere to shop. He started to think he might like the idea of touring the country alone.

Few people came close to him, though occasionally he got a smile when his eyes met a stranger's. Probably this was a function of the flight suit, he realized. He should have dressed in civilian clothes—he was the only serviceman around, American or otherwise, and it seemed to strike an odd note with the tourists who wandered by.

He was just about to pay his bill when his cell phone rang. Taking it from his pocket, he glanced at the number. It wasn't one he recognized, but he answered it anyway.

"Turk, are you making our meeting?" asked Ginella as he said hello.

"Oh, Colonel, hey," said Turk. "Meeting?"

"We're planning the next few sorties," she said. Her voice was pleasant but businesslike. There was no hint that they had been together the night before. "I was hoping to see you."

"I got stuck with a few things," he said. It wasn't a direct lie, he thought; more like a slight disarray of information. "I didn't think you guys needed me."

"The flu has knocked us down badly," she said. "I'd like to be able to count on you tomorrow."

"Well—"

"We'll brief the mission at 0600," she said, her voice growing more officious. "I am counting on you. I did speak to Operations. And to your colonel."

"Yes." Turk wasn't sure what to say. He did want

to fly—he was developing a definite taste for the Warthog. It was just the situation with Ginella that was awkward.

Maybe this was her way of removing that. She was being completely official—yes, he thought, she's trying to make it easy for me.

Great.

"If I'm not needed by the Tigershark people, I'll definitely be there," he told her.

"At 0600," she told him.

"Got it."

TURK SPENT THE REST OF THE AFTERNOON WALKING around the city. Around six he decided he would head back to the hotel and get changed before finding a place to eat. He thought it might be a good idea to find a dining companion.

Li came to mind. But he had no way of getting hold of her—he didn't know if she even had a phone.

Maybe, he thought, he could just call her hotel and have the desk connect him to her room.

He couldn't remember the name of her hotel. His description of it didn't help the concierge downstairs at his hotel.

"*Mi dispiace,* Captain," said the man. "But you have described nearly every hotel in Sicily. It even sounds a little like ours, though maybe not so close to the sea."

"True," agreed Turk. "How about a nice place for dinner, not too fancy?" he asked.

"I know just the place. Very quiet and out of the way."

Turk nearly jumped. Ginella had come up behind him. She placed her hand on his hip.

It felt good, tempting even. But . . .

"I didn't mean to startle you," she told him.

"I—I didn't know you were here."

"I was waiting. They said you were out."

She was in civilian clothes, a mid-thigh black skirt and a red top. Not quite see-through, the top gave a hint of lace beneath.

Which was pleasant.

He thought of objecting, but what could he say?

And why? Why object? Why not just . . . go with what felt good?

"I was—I kinda went for a walk to clear my head," said Turk. "After everything that's happened. You know?"

She nodded sympathetically, then leaned toward the concierge. "Can you make a reservation for two at il Bambino. Say in about an hour? No—make it an hour and a half."

"Il Bambino," said the concierge approvingly. "Very nice."

THEY MADE LOVE TWICE, ONCE IN A FRENZY BEFORE dinner, Turk still damp from his shower, then again afterward, this time with even more desperation. Ginella silently urged him on, pulling him toward her. The second time she dug her fingers into his back so hard as he climaxed that he found tiny traces of blood on his sheets in the morning when he woke.

She was gone by then. There was no sign that

she had been on the bed or even in the room. The scent of her perfume lingering in the sheets and on his chest was the only hint that she was there.

He called down for coffee, and took a shower for so long he was still inside when the coffee arrived. He got out, brought the tray inside, and showered again.

It wasn't pathological, he told himself. He had wanted to have sex. The memory of it as he showered threatened to arouse him again.

Turk shaved and dressed. He jogged down the stairs rather than taking the elevator, trotting out to the lot after scoring his pick of the car pool.

Heading to the base for the mission briefing, he began rehearsing different things he might say to her to break off the affair.

He wouldn't say them today, probably. But soon. Very, very soon.

11

Sicily

KHARON'S SEARCH FOR RUBEO'S HOTEL TURNED OUT to be much easier than he thought, though as always it was absurdly expensive. He called the man who had arranged to connect the USB device to the maintenance computers; the man called him back inside an hour, while he was still driving. For two thousand euros he learned the American civilians were staying at the Crown Prince, a fancy hotel a few miles from the base.

For another thousand euros he got the floor and room number.

Kharon reserved a room at the hotel without trouble. He studied the layout, and within a half hour had it memorized.

He walked through, placing a dozen miniature video cameras around, giving him a full view of anyone entering or leaving the hotel, and surveying each of the floors.

Sending the images directly to his laptop would have been too easy to trace, so Kharon routed the data through the hotel wireless out to the Internet, then through a set of servers, and had it post to a Web page hosted by a Polish provider. The page was encrypted, but it wouldn't take a hacker with half the expertise of Rubeo to track it down and eventually decrypt it. For that reason, Kharon resisted the temptation to put extra devices on Rubeo's floor, and didn't set up anything to watch specifically for the scientist.

Finished, Kharon went up to his room and took a shower. He decided he would rest—he hadn't slept for twenty-four hours at least—but once in bed flopped around, unable to sleep. In short order he rose and began stalking the room. Nothing on television interested him, and he was loath to use his laptop to connect to the in-hotel network. He finally decided he would work off some of his excess energy with a walk. Dressing, he went out to the hall and walked down to the elevator. He leaned on the button, then saw from the display above the door that the elevator was all the way downstairs in the lobby.

Better to walk, he decided.

The marble tiles that lined the hallway floor were old and worn, but there were no cracks in them that Kharon could see. This intrigued him—was the marble so thick or perfect that it couldn't break?

Or was it fake? The overhead lights were not particularly bright. He was tempted to drop down and examine the material.

Marble *always* cracked. The hotel had to be at least fifty years old. The floor looked original—scuffed and worn, yet no cracks.

The stair treads were made of thick stone, some sort of granite, he guessed.

Obsessing over odd matters was one sign of fatigue. Another was his eyes' reaction to the light—everything seemed brighter than it was.

There was no door on the stairway where it opened onto the floor above the lobby. Kharon shielded his eyes from the bright light reflected upward from the lobby chandeliers by the mirrored walls below. He started down the steps. Already he was tired—he'd walk once around the building outside, then return quickly and sleep.

He was three-quarters of the way to the bottom of the stairs before his eyes could fully focus. Two men were coming in from the main door to the right. One large and bulky, the other even taller but thinner.

Ray Rubeo.

RUBEO SAW THE FACE FLOAT ABOVE THE STEPS. IT transported him back some twenty years to his early days at Dreamland.

Alissa Kharon. A talented scientist who'd died in an idiotic lab fire.

It wasn't her—obviously—but the eyes, the cheeks, the nose: the face was almost exactly the same.

It was a man a little younger than she had been when she died, taller, but with the same coloring, the same expression.

Haunted.

Her son.

"Neil," said Rubeo loudly. "Neil Kharon."

He strode toward the stairs. The young man stared at him, confused.

"Neil Kharon. I'm Ray Rubeo. Do you remember me?"

"Uh, uh, yeah." The young man stuttered, then glanced awkwardly at the hand Rubeo thrust toward him.

"Your mother worked for me at Dreamland, back in the nineties. Do you remember me? I sent you an e-mail when you graduated from MIT. I know it's been years?"

Rubeo had done more than that. He had written a recommendation to help Kharon into a doctorate program in Europe—surreptitiously, with the help of the young man's teachers at MIT. He'd actually hoped to steer him to Stanford, though there was really no arguing about Cambridge.

Rubeo had lost track after that. It was a shame—the young man was brilliant, every bit as smart as his mother.

"What are you doing in Sicily?" Rubeo asked.

"I'm here—I was supposed to interview for a position at VGNet."

"With Rudd?" Rubeo touched his right ear, squeezing the post—an ancient habit, especially when holding his tongue.

Armain Rudd, who owned the company, had the ethical standards of a slug, and treated his employees little better than slaves. VGNet was active in the artificial intelligence field, handling cognitive interfaces—basically helping sensors "talk" to brains. Its work was solid, but not anywhere near as advanced or as interesting as Rubeo's work.

Surely young Kharon could do better than that.

"You're looking for a job?" Rubeo said. "Why didn't you ask me?"

"I—"

"Give me your contact information."

"Uh—"

"Forget what you've told them, or they've told you. They're not to be trusted anyway. We will easily meet their offer. Really, Neil, I'm disappointed you didn't think of us. You'll be a good fit for us—we have a lot of interesting projects. Tell me about your interests."

"I, uh, well—"

"You have a date tonight?"

"I was actually meeting, uh, a young lady," stuttered Kharon.

"Naturally. Unfortunately, I'm going to Africa tomorrow. Wait." Rubeo took out his wallet and retrieved a business card. It was a bit worn at the edges; he couldn't remember the last time he actually gave one out.

"Here," he told Kharon, handing him the card. "You are to send me an e-mail. Or call that number at the bottom. Call as soon as you get back to your room tonight. There'll be a secretary. Make an appointment."

Kharon took the card.

"The secretary may be a computer," added Rubeo. "Or maybe not. See if it passes the Turing Test."

KHARON SHOVED THE CARD IN HIS POCKET AND WALKED toward the lounge. His cheeks were burning; he felt unbalanced, small and weak. It was as if he was trapped again, back in the closet.

He went to the bar and ordered a beer. He took it from the bartender's hand and practically drained it, still feeling pressed in on all sides.

Undone by a chance meeting? What kind of coward are you?

What kind of sissy weakling are you?

You should have shot him dead right there. Killed the bodyguard, too.

He hadn't brought his gun. That was just one of his many mistakes.

"Are you all right?" asked the bartender in Italian.

"*Bene, bene.*" Kharon raised his head and looked at the bartender. Then he glanced at the bottle—it was nearly empty. "*Un altro, per favore,*" he said stiffly. "Please. Another."

The bartender smiled. "A woman, eh?"

"Yes. My mother."

"Ahhh," said the bartender knowingly. He went and got the beer. "I am sorry for your loss," he said, placing the bottle on the counter.

In a way, the man had drawn exactly the right conclusions, Kharon thought. He was still grieving.

UPSTAIRS, RUBEO LEFT LEVON JONS AND WENT INTO his room, checking the security first with his bug detector. The device mapped the room's electrical circuitry, and was sensitive enough to detect even the NSA's latest generation of nanopowered "flies"—a certification Rubeo was sure of since his company had worked on the technology employed in the microsized listening gear.

The room was clean. Rubeo sat down in the large chair opposite the television and turned the set on, flipping to the U.S. news stations.

Alissa Kharon's son working for VGNet. Good God!

The news program detailed a shake-up in the Libyan government's ruling body. A group of alleged moderates had taken over.

Since when did moderates take anything over? Rubeo wondered.

He changed the channel. CNN was carrying a discussion program. The host introduced a speech from a member of the Iranian government saying the American plane that had bombed the village was the spawn of the devil.

"I'm sure you're an expert on that," spat Rubeo.

He sat back on the bed, mind drifting. He thought of Alissa Kharon. He'd had a crush on her. She probably didn't even know. He'd certainly never acted on it: She was married and, though he was her supervisor, a few years older than he was.

Pretty woman. And very smart.

He closed his eyes and heard the alarms, smelled the fire, the aftermath. Alissa had died from suffocation in the lab bunker. The laser system she was working on had malfunctioned, and rather than leaving, she'd tried to put out the fire—a classic mistake, but like her in a way, insisting that she could shut down the systems and prevent more damage.

Rubeo knew exactly what she must have thought—all that work they'd done about to be ruined. The laser was connected to a hand-built targeting system that the team had spent two years perfecting. She had jumped from her station and run to it as the others began to leave.

The bunker had been equipped with a state-of-the-art fire suppression system. But state of the art in the early 1990s wasn't quite good enough to kill the chemical fire the laser unit spawned. The doors locked, and for some reason no one realized that she was still inside.

Rubeo, working upstairs on something else, distracted as he always was then, arrived to find one of her assistants screaming frantically.

"Where's Alissa?" she'd yelled. "Where's Alissa?"

He overrode the system, but when they opened the doors they were met with a wall of black smoke. He had to close the doors—he closed them himself, knowing she was already dead, lost somewhere behind the smoke.

The hazmat team arrived a few seconds later. Rubeo went and got himself a suit, and went in after them.

Her body, badly burned, was back near the unit. The main AI unit lay inches from her outstretched hand.

She was a beautiful woman, and smart, with a kid and a husband. The husband dissolved after her death. He died of cancer a year later, but he'd been a broken man, unable to pull himself back together.

By then the assistant who had screamed had committed suicide.

Not because of Alissa's death, or so the investigators said—she had marital problems, which were prominently mentioned in the note she left. But Rubeo remembered the last line of the suicide note:

I will see Alissa for you all.

So much pain. So much success and achievements, and all he could think of was the pain.

Rubeo glanced at the television. The talking heads were pontificating about the dangers of drones and the inevitability of "disasters."

"What about the decline in collateral damage brought on by smart weapons?" Rubeo asked the screen. "What about the ability to empirically correct problems in the machines, unlike intractable human error?"

He flipped the television off.

What sort of thing did VGNet want young Kharon to do for them? His graduate work, if Rubeo recalled correctly, had to do with systems integration relating to intelligence.

Or was he wrong?

He'd look it up in the morning. And check on VGNet—they had a lab in southern Italy, obviously, but where?

He really should pay more attention to his competitors and potential competitors. Now, though, he needed sleep. He had to leave for the airport at four, and it was already past one.

Two and a half hours of sleep. About his norm when traveling. Rubeo pulled off his clothes and climbed into bed.

12

Sicily

ZEN SAT IN THE SECURE COMMUNICATIONS ROOM, SIPping his coffee and thinking about his daughter, Teri. More than anything in the world, he wanted to talk to her about baseball, one of their morning routines.

An odd thing. A decade and a half ago, back at Dreamland, he never would have thought he would have preferred speaking to his little girl rather than the President of the United States.

"I'm sorry for the interruption, Zen," said the President, coming back to the video screen. "Some days the schedule just gets ahead of itself."

"I understand, Madam President."

"I think there's no downside in proceeding," said National Security Advisor Michael Blitz, who was sitting next to her in the secure communications center in the White House basement. "At least at this point. Naturally, down the road, it could all blow up in our face."

"I don't like the idea of nonprofessionals conducting these sorts of talks." Alistair Newhaven, the Secretary of State, shook his head as if he'd just come out of a pool and was getting rid of excess water. Zen didn't know Newhaven very well, and what he did know of him he didn't like. "This is a very sensitive and dangerous area."

"No offense intended for the senator, I'm sure," said the President, glancing toward the camera.

"None taken," said Zen. "The Secretary wasn't getting a Christmas card anyway."

Newhaven, who had exactly zero sense of humor, stared at the camera without comprehending.

"The committee is perfect," countered Blitz. "The allies have absolute deniability."

The President's aides debated back and forth

a few more minutes. Zen's mind drifted back to Teri. He wondered if Breanna had managed to take enough time off to take her to a ball game since he'd been gone.

"I think we've talked this to death," said the President finally. "Jeff—Senator—please proceed. You have my blessing. Obviously you can't guarantee anything, but I think it would be fair to say that you have my ear."

"Thank you, Madam President."

"And for the record," she added, "I think you're a hell of a negotiator. Having seen you operate from the other side of the table, I'm very glad to know you're working for us this time."

"I'm always working for America, Mrs. Todd," said Zen as he signed off.

13

Sicily

DANNY FREAH SHOOK HIS HEAD VEHEMENTLY.

"No way, doc. There is no way I am letting you go to Africa now. Not after what happened to the commission."

"The incident was staged." Rubeo folded his arms in front of his chest. "As you yourself have said. Three times now."

"Just because the government incited them

doesn't mean there's not a lot of anger out there. No American is safe. No Westerner. There is just no way you're going."

"You're exaggerating the danger . . ."

"Look Ray, I'm sorry. No way."

"I need to find out what happened, Colonel."

"You don't have to be there to do that. Come on, Ray—you're too valuable to be walking around in Africa. Crap—you're not twenty years old anymore."

"Nor am I an employee of the department of defense."

"Yeah, but come on."

Rubeo scowled and walked out of the room. He was determined to see what had happened for himself.

"I DON'T KNOW, BOSS. GETTING THERE IS NO PROBlem. Once we're there, though . . ." Jons shook his head.

"We'll hire people," Rubeo told him. "I need to examine the radar facilities near where the accident happened. And I want to look at the attack pattern."

"Why?"

"Because if this isn't fixed, everything will be flushed."

"I don't know. Getting there—"

"Hire a guide. It's easily done, I'm told."

"Yeah, but finding the right people . . ."

"That's your job."

Jons frowned.

"We are booked on a flight to Tripoli at three, using our alternative identities," said Rubeo. "I already have gear en route. So line the right people up quickly."

14

Over the Mediterranean

TODAY'S TARGET WAS LITERALLY DIALED IN—TURK AND the rest of the Hog drivers would drop satellite-guided smart bombs at artillery at the edge of a city under government control.

Fly in, fly down, fly home. Piece of cake.

Counting Turk, the squadron was up to eight active pilots, which let them split into two different groups and take on a pair of missions. Turk's group got the artillery; the other flight of A–10s would attack a motor depot where a variety of armored vehicles were parked.

Turk's flight of four Hogs was led by Paulson in Shooter One. Grizzly was his wingman. Beast had finally succumbed to the flu and was a late scratch. That made Turk, flying Shooter Three, the leader of the second two-plane element in the flight. His wingman was Lieutenant Cooper "Coop" Hadlemann in Shooter Four.

Ginella was leading another mission to a different part of Libya at roughly the same time. She'd been all business today, without any mention or even hint that they had hooked up.

Fortunately.

"Shooter flight, we're two minutes from IP," said Paulson as they neared their target. "Look alive."

Turk did a quick scan of his instruments. He was at 30,000 feet, moving a hair over 380 knots. It was a bright day, with no clouds within a few hundred miles.

The government forces had not scrambled any fighters since their encounter with Turk earlier in the week. Nonetheless, there was a heavy contingent of fighter coverage aloft. A two-ship of Eurofighters had flown down from the Med with the Warthogs, and were lingering overhead. A pair of Spanish F/A–18s were tasked right behind them. Technically, the Spanish versions were designated EF–18As, with the E meaning España; Spain. These variants were similar outwardly to the first generation of the Hornets produced by McDonnell-Douglas, but had upgraded avionics and other electronic gear.

The presence of the different aircraft types pointed out the different approaches to air warfare undertaken by the Americans and Europeans. While the air forces were much more similar than they were different, their varying needs and philosophies were expressed in the airframes they chose to build.

As a general rule, European aircraft were at least arguably better than their American peers when it came to sheer maneuverability. They were almost always better suited at taking off from short runways, even with decent loads. Their Achilles' heel tended to be their fuel capacity; they had "short legs" compared to Americans.

This wasn't surprising, considering the physical environments the respective air forces expected to be fighting in. The U.S. was always worried about distance, whether in its own country, the Pacific, or even the European and African theaters. In contrast, a French or Spanish pilot never had far to go to defend his borders. He might find it necessary, however, to do that from a highway rather than an airfield—and he could.

Americans would scoff at what they saw as incremental improvements in maneuverability. In their view, advanced electronics and weapons gave them a decided edge. To oversimplify, American strategy called for detecting the enemy before you were detected, and killing them well before they became a threat: an enemy pilot could maneuver all he wanted before he was shot down.

"Two minutes to IP," said Paulson, signaling that they were almost at the start of the attack. "Let's do it."

The flight split in two. Turk and his wingman cut twenty degrees farther south, lining up for the bomb run. As they closed to fifteen miles from target, Turk got the weapons screen up, triple-checking his position and markers. He was going to launch his JDAMs ten miles from the target.

"Four, how are you looking?" he radioed.

"We're good, Three. Coming up on sixty seconds."

"Yeah, roger that."

Turk checked the armament panel one more time, then took a slow breath. The targeting computer provided a cue for him as he approached—it wasn't the fancy color-coded box the Tigershark's computer drew, but it did the job. The system would automatically compensate for wind or any other unusual environmental factors.

"Firing," said Turk.

He pressed the trigger, releasing a pair of 500 pound bombs. Though unpowered, the bombs were steered toward their target by small electronic devices that shifted the positions of the fins at the rear. Checking themselves against satellites above, the miniature brains piloted the charges toward a howitzer parked between piles of sandbags near the main highway.

Turk pulled the Hog's stick up to increase separation as he let off the bombs. He quickly took the Hog toward its second release point, shifting in the sky to aim at an ammo dump about two miles north of the artillery emplacement. As the cue for the pickle appeared in Turk's screen, he released the bombs. This time the Hog jerked up quickly, as if the aircraft were glad to be free of the weight it had been carrying.

"Away, away," said Turk. Coop had already dropped his bombs and was moving back to the north. "Egressing north," said Turk. He checked his compass reading and gave Coop the heading, moving toward the rendezvous they had briefed.

He could hear the chatter of the other pilots over the squadron frequency, calling "good bombs" and "shack," indicating they had hit their targets. Fingers of smoke rose in the far distance—at least some of the bombs had hit their targets.

Primary mission complete, Paulson checked with the flight boss, making sure they had a clean screen—no enemy fighters—and then told the others that he was going to take a run over the target area.

"If I see anything else we can hit down there, we'll come back and grease them," said Paulson. "Grizzly, you're on my back."

"Copy."

The A–10s were relatively high, over 15,000 feet, which put them out of range of guns and light MANPADs, but also made it difficult to get a definitive read of anything on the ground. They crossed once at that altitude, then came back, dropping to about 7,000 as they ran past the site.

Paulson reported that there were two fires burning near the artillery emplacements, and that there seemed to be widespread destruction. A few moments later he added that the ammo dump had been obliterated.

"Only thing here is black smoke and red flames," he said, climbing out.

Deciding there were no targets worth taking a run at, the flight leader had them saddle up and head westward, aiming to get them back to Sicily by lunchtime. But they'd only gone a short way before they got an emergency call from a harried JTAC ground controller, requesting immediate assistance in a firefight that happened to be less than fifteen miles out of their way.

Out of habit, Turk punched the mike to acknowledge and ask for more details. Paulson overran his transmission with his own acknowledgment a moment later.

"Sorry," said Turk, clicking off. "My bad."

"Go ahead, Turner," Paulson said to the JTAC. The forward controller—JTAC stood for joint terminal attack controller, the formal military designation—was a Navy SEAL operating with a group of rebels caught in an ambush on the edge of a stream. The rebels were huddled around two disabled vehicles, under attack from both sides.

"What ordnance do you have?" asked the JTAC. Bullets were whizzing in the background as he spoke; Turk could make out two distinct heavy caliber machine guns. "Say again?"

"Turner, we have our thirty calibers and that's it," replied Paulson. "Give me a location."

"Shit." The controller was clearly looking for a big boom. Maybe he hadn't worked with a Hog before.

"Repeat?"

"At this time, I would like you to put down heavy fire to the southwest of my position," said the JTAC, calmer, though his voice was nearly drowned out by gunfire. "Restrictions are as follows. Make your heading east to west. We are near the two pickup trucks. The enemy is north and south of us. The heaviest— Shit."

There was an explosion in the background before the JTAC continued.

Pushing his wing down, Turk got his nose in the

direction of the southernmost grouping of enemy soldiers, figuring that Paulson would divide the group in two for the attack, and take the northern bunch himself, since he was closest to them. But instead Paulson called for them to all attack the northern group.

"I can get that southern gun," said Turk. He could already see it on his target screen. "Coop can follow me in."

"I'm in charge, Dreamland."

Turk blew a wad of air into his face mask in frustration. "Copy that," he said.

The Hogs ducked low. The first two aircraft tore up the terrain with long sprays of thirty caliber. Fire rose over the position.

Turk followed in, about two miles behind. But as they approached, his gear became confused by all the secondaries and smoke and he couldn't see well enough to get a specific target.

He told Coop to pull off. They rose, circling north.

"What the hell are you doing, Three?" radioed Paulson.

"I didn't have a definite target. Too close to the friendlies," said Turk.

"Picture's clean down low."

Bullshit, thought Turk. Stop giving me a hard time. But he said nothing.

Paulson told him and Coop to orbit north in a holding pattern.

"We can get that target south," said Turk.

"We're on it, Dreamland," snapped Paulson.

Turk did his best to keep his head clear, checking his instruments and making sure there were no threats in the immediate area. Paulson and Grizzly took two runs at the area. Finally the JTAC called to say they had stopped taking fire.

"We're good," said Paulson. "Heading home."

TURK SEETHED THE ENTIRE FLIGHT HOME, AND WAS IN A finely wrought lather by the time he touched down. Paulson managed to avoid so much as eye contact during the postmission briefing. He made no mention of their disagreement when he talked to Ginella, and was even complimentary toward Turk, whom he called Turk, not Dreamland.

Turk figured it was a show for the boss, and that made him even angrier. But there was nothing to be done short of knocking the asshole on his back—which he might have done had he managed to get out of the briefing room quickly. But he was waylaid by Ginella.

"Lunch?" she asked, putting her arm across the doorway. He was the last pilot in the room; they were alone together.

"A little late."

"It's never too late for some things."

"I gotta check with my guys," said Turk. He started to push against her arm.

"Turk." She put her hand on his chest.

A pilot from another squadron walked down the hall just then. He cleared his throat loudly. Ginella pulled her hand back. Turk took the opportunity to squeeze past into the hallway.

"I just gotta go," he told. "I'll talk to you."

Ginella rolled her eyes, then went back into the room.

15

Tripoli

KHARON SPENT THE NIGHT IN A SLEEPLESS STUPOR, unable to do anything but berate himself. He told himself he was a weakling and worse. He called himself a coward and a jerk and a fool. He punched his stomach with his fist until he collapsed in the bathroom, retching over the edge of the tub.

His life had led to that one moment, and he had failed.

He offered me a job!

The guilty fool!

And still I did nothing! Nothing! I could do nothing!

Kharon writhed on the floor of his hotel bathroom for hours, alternately beating and sobbing to himself. He was incapable of getting up, of moving.

Morning came. There was no epiphany, no conscious decision to reverse course. He simply rose, and in the still of the night fled the hotel, driving himself to the Aeroporto Fontanarossa Vincenzo Bellini, which was still taking civilian traffic, though largely given over to NATO operations. He found it surprisingly easy to find a flight off the island, and within a few hours had connected into Morocco, and from there bribed his way onto an Egyptian Air flight to Tripoli.

By the time he arrived, he had decided what he would do. His head felt like an empty space; the decision neither cheered nor frightened him. It seemed only preordained.

He found a cab and had the driver take him to Al-Fateh Tower, near the beach area. The government offices that had been located in the building were shuttered, as were most of the banks, but a few stalwart tenants remained, carrying on as best they could. Guards were posted on the bottom floor, but as far as they were concerned, Kharon was no threat: he was clearly a Westerner, and they let him pass after a brief look at his passport.

He took the elevator to the eighteenth floor, got out and took the stairs to the top floor, where the restaurant had been located. In the good days of the Gaddafi regime, Arab tourists and Western diplomats filled the revolving restaurant at the top of one of Tripoli's tallest buildings. Now, though, the place was vacant, shut since the start of the war. Iron gates blocked the way from the floor below. The locks probably could have been picked, but Kharon didn't have the equipment, or the will. Instead, he went down to the twenty-second floor and found his way into the maintenance section. There was a ladder leading up; he climbed it, and within a few minutes reached a ledge area below the main roof.

A fierce wind struck him as he stepped outside. It was so strong it pushed him back through the threshold, and slammed the door against his outstretched arm. He fell back into the corridor, stunned.

Kharon rose slowly, surprised by the pain. He went back to the door, and this time pushed out onto the white stone ledge.

The stones rimming the ledge were wide but slick, and he felt his feet starting to go out from under him. He put his hand up to grasp the wall but couldn't find his balance.

Down he went, down face-first, chest slamming against the stones.

He was still on the ledge.

The city screamed in front of him, the noise of its traffic rising above the wind. The ocean roared in the distance, and the sun looked down from on high.

Kharon crawled closer to the edge. Oblivion seemed to beckon. He was inches away from the end.

Something rose inside him then, a sense of rage—how unfair it was, for Rubeo to ruin not just his mother's life, but his life as well. To destroy him: Was he going to end things like that?

He pounded his fists on the stone. He was a coward. He had proven himself to be a coward, impotent and toothless.

Was that one moment all that defined him? Being caught off guard—taken by surprise, fooled by a man he knew was nothing short of a demon? A man who had insisted that his mother work in an unsafe lab, then stood idly by as she died?

Is this who he was?

I'm not the little boy who cowered in the closet, afraid to hear the truth. That isn't me. That isn't the way I am.

Kharon began to tremble.

He couldn't let Rubeo win. Not like this.

He pushed back slowly from the edge, then took a deep breath. As calmly as he could—slowly, to show himself that he was in charge—he rose. After three more very deep, slow breaths, he walked to the service door and went back inside.

FINDING FOMA MITRESKI PROVED MORE DIFFICULT than Kharon had anticipated. The Russian spy master made a regular tour of the city's bars and hotels, and was not in the more popular places where he looked first. He finally found the Russian having lunch in the bar of a hotel a few blocks from Tariq Square. Kharon made sure to nod, then went over to the bar and ordered himself a bourbon.

His mood had changed dramatically. In effect, he decided, he was already dead—so nothing that happened next mattered. It was a strange and liberating feeling.

The bar counter was made of old wood, and bore the marks of millions of glasses. Thick scrollwork hung down from the rafters directly above, holding a pair of mostly empty shelves. A quartet of American whiskey bottles were spaced out there; the mirror at the back of the bar was so old and the light so poor that the bottles were reflected only as oblique shadows.

While the hotel had been popular with European tourists looking for bargains before Gaddafi fell, its dated decor and cramped rooms upstairs made it an unlikely place for the generally stylish Foma to meet anyone. But that was very possibly its attraction—it was close to the last place anyone, even Kharon, would look.

Foma concluded his business in a few minutes, then got up with the others and left the bar. Kharon ordered another drink.

Twenty minutes later, glass empty, he wasn't sure whether to stay or not.

The bartender came over. Kharon nodded, accepting a refill. The bartender mumbled something Kharon couldn't understand; he gave a noncommittal grunt.

Halfway through the drink the Russian returned.

"Ah, I was worried that you would have gone," said Foma, speaking in Russian.

"I knew to wait."

"We can use English."

"Better Russian. Less chance of being understood."

"More mystery for others." Foma smiled at him, then ordered a scotch.

"Dalmore," said Foma. "Very good."

"I'm sure."

"What do you have there? Not scotch."

"American bourbon."

"Americans always think they know better."

They sat for a moment, Foma swirling his liquor in the glass before downing it in a gulp.

"I have a new proposition," said Kharon.

"More information?"

"No. Everything I promised. But I need extra help. I need someone to cause a diversion, and I can't be connected to it. So you're going to arrange it."

"Something too dangerous for you, but not for me?"

"Danger is all around us," said Kharon coldly.

Foma pushed his glass forward for a refill. "You are in a bad mood today."

"No. I'm in a good mood."

Foma's glass was refilled. Kharon waited for the bartender to leave. If the Russian wouldn't help him, he would find another way. Fezzan could certainly find someone. But for something like this, he trusted the Russian more.

"Well," said Foma finally, studying his drink. "Tell me what it is, and then I will tell you if it can be done."

16

Benghazi, northern Libya

AS MUCH AS HE TRIED, RUBEO FOUND IT IMPOSSIBLE to stay behind his bodyguard as they walked through the narrow streets filled with outdoor markets. Jons finally gave up trying to nudge him back and let him walk at his shoulder.

Jons had tried very hard to talk him out of coming along to meet Halit. But Rubeo was determined to see the man for himself in his own environment before they hired him. You could only learn so much from a sanitized meeting in an office or at the airport.

Both Rubeo and Jons were armed—Rubeo with a pistol hand made by a colleague at Dreamland years before, and Jons with a pair of weapons made by Rubeo's companies. Both guns employed so-called "smart bullets"—microprocessors inside the ammunition received target information from the aiming mechanism at the top of barrel, and could adjust the flight of the bullet via a muscle wire: actually a piece of metal that changed the bullet's shape and ballistic characteristics.

The bullets couldn't change direction, nor were they able to find their own target or do anything outrageously fancy. But the weapons simplified aiming, while at the same time increasing their lethality. The shooter pointed his gun at the largest part of his target—generally the torso. The finlike reader on the top of the gun automatically adjusted the aim for its target's face, and put the bullet there. Not only did this avoid the problem of bulletproof vests, it made even novice gunmen dangerous no matter what the situation.

Rubeo wasn't a novice—he had acquired a taste for hunting long ago—but he certainly wasn't combat-trained, and the weapon made it much easier for him to be sure that he would protect himself. Levon Jons, on the other hand, disliked the idea that the gun would aim on its own.

"What if I just want to wound someone?" he often complained to Rubeo.

This was an entirely theoretical complaint: Jons himself would be the first to admit that when his gun came out, it came out to be used, and when it was used, it was only with the intent to kill. But he didn't see the contradiction, and more often than not turned the smart technology off.

He had it on today. Benghazi was not a place to worry about purity.

"Left," suggested Jons. The bodyguard was listening to directions from his earpiece.

"Mmmm," said Rubeo. He kept walking, sensing that they were being watched. Like most of the Libyans on the street, they were wearing Western clothes; more traditional dress would have highlighted them rather than made them blend in.

Rubeo wore his thin protective vest beneath his shirt as well as a light jacket that concealed his pistol. Jons had a bulky sweater. The copper-boron web vests used a layer of glass filaments to reduce their thickness, but they restricted the wearer's body subtly, and even though his vest was tailored to his chest, Rubeo felt as if his arms were banded. His discomfort annoyed him, but at the same time it heightened his watchfulness, and as he continued past the street where they were supposed to turn, he picked out a small boy staring at them from across the way.

Rubeo stopped at the nearest stall, where a man

was selling leather goods. He picked up a wallet and glanced at the boy from the corner of his eye.

"Kid watching us," he told Jons.

"Probably a pickpocket."

"Maybe."

Rubeo gave the wallet back, then started walking again. The city was patrolled by members of the rebel militia, or at least men who claimed to be so. Most wore civilian clothes, but were identifiable by red bandannas on both arms. They were armed with rifles, AK–47s and AK–74s for the most part, though the one Rubeo saw at the end of the block had an M–4.

"Let's turn," he said.

He led the way through the thin crowd about halfway down the block, where he found a small store selling groceries. He pulled open the door, turning casually in the direction they had come. The boy was there, looking at them.

"Maybe he is with our friends, and maybe he is not," said Rubeo. "But let us find out."

"Your call," said Jons, in a tone that let Rubeo know he disagreed.

"There's a door in the back." Jons moved to check it out.

Rubeo rummaged through the front of the store, looking at the shelves of dusty canned goods, making sure the boy could see him. The store owner came over, delighted at having a Western customer. Rubeo nodded at him.

"This, very good one," said the man, stumbling in English.

"Nice."

"You like?"

"No."

"You buy this one, then?"

"No. I'm not buying anything," said Rubeo flatly.

The man went off, offended. Rubeo turned his attention back to the street. The boy saw him and started to back away—right into Jons's arms.

Rubeo came out of the store. The boy kicked and wiggled, but Jons held him firmly.

"How old are you?" Rubeo asked in English. "Eight? Nine?"

The boy didn't answer.

"I cannot speak Arabic well," said Rubeo. "But this device will translate for me."

He took out his phone and queued up a translation program. He pressed the large circle in the middle of the screen, scrolled through his most recent lines, and highlighted the questions. The machine repeated them in fluent Arabic.

"Go to the devil," said the boy.

Even Rubeo's Arabic was good enough to figure out what he had said without the program. He reached into his pocket and slipped out a ten euro note.

"Would this help?"

The boy grabbed at it.

Rubeo pulled it back. "Tell them I'm coming." He double-tapped his screen without looking; the machine gave the translation almost instantly. Then he handed the boy the money.

"I say he's a purse snatcher," said Jons as the boy ran off.

"That is why you are the brawn of the company, Levon." Rubeo flicked the app on his screen to the tracking display. While holding the kid, Jons had placed a small video fly on his shoulder. The fly transmitted his location, displaying it on an overhead map.

He ran straight to the alley where they were supposed to meet the men. Rubeo brought up another app, and images appeared on the screen.

"All right. I'm an asshole," said Jons glumly as he took the phone from his boss.

TEN MINUTES LATER RUBEO AND JONS CLIMBED OVER A short fence that ran behind the building where the boy had run. Jons knocked on the back door, then put his shoulder to it, breaking it off its hinges. Rubeo walked inside.

The three men the kid had reported to were still questioning him about Rubeo.

"Excuse my dramatic entrance," Rubeo told them. "I was somewhat disconcerted by the fact that you had a child shadowing me."

Jons held his gun on the men, but that was superfluous: they were all too surprised to react.

"Which one of you is Halit?" asked Rubeo. He had practiced the phrase several times, and said it smoothly.

A man in a white-and-blue striped sweater raised his hand.

"These are my brothers," said the man in English. "They have just been here with me, to keep company."

"I'll bet," said Jons. "Come here."

The squat Libyan tried to suck in his gut as he got up. He wore a gray warm-up jacket and black jeans, along with black shoes polished to a high shine.

"Spit," said Jons, holding out a small device with what looked like an air scoop on the edge. "Into it."

Halit did so. The device analyzed the DNA in the spit, uploading parts to a database back at Rubeo's company headquarters. It worked quickly, picking out only small parts of the complicated code, looking for signatures that would be compared to known agents, terrorists, or criminals in the federal database.

The system was not foolproof. From a scientific standpoint, there was too much potential for a bad match: about 122 chances out of 65,000; roughly the standards law enforcement had used for preliminary DNA matches with limited markers just a few years before. But it was fine for Rubeo's purposes.

The small screen on the device went green, indicating the sample was sufficient to be tested. A minute later the screen blanked, then flashed green, yellow, then green again. Halit was not a criminal or a known terrorist. Or anyone else in the U.S. data banks, for that matter.

A start, at least.

Rubeo reached into his pocket and took out a few euros. He threw them on the floor.

"Halit comes with us. The rest stay, or that money will be used for your funerals."

Rubeo looked at his phone, where the feed from the video fly was still operating. The boy was outside; the area was clear.

Jons took hold of Halit's elbow and they went out the front door. Rubeo, more relaxed, walked behind them, looking back and forth.

There was something invigorating in dealing with danger, he thought. He liked the way his heart pounded in his chest.

They brought Halit to the truck. After checking the monitoring system to make sure the vehicle had not been tampered with, Jons put Halit in the backseat.

Rubeo climbed in the front. He let Jons drive.

"Do you know the head of the guards at the gate below Tripoli?" Rubeo asked Halit.

"I know them, yes. Why do you treat me like a prisoner? I was told you need a guide. I am a guide, the best."

"I don't trust you," said Rubeo. "You used a child to spy on me."

"Only to see when you are coming. My son."

"He wasn't your son," snapped Rubeo. He hated being lied to.

"My son, yes."

Rubeo stared at him with contempt. The two couldn't appear more different. The boy had been rail thin, with light features and blue eyes; the man was dark and pudgy, very short, with curly hair where the boy's was straight.

Which was worse? The fact that he would lie on such a petty matter—or that he would think it OK to put his own son in danger?

Or any child, now that he thought of it.

Rubeo found most people venal and petty. A good number were stupid as well. Navigating around them was one thing; inevitably, though, there were situations where you had to count on them.

Jons had found three men capable of getting them south into the government-held areas. Halit was the most highly recommended.

Rubeo couldn't help but imagine how horrible the other two must be.

"Your job is to get us past the guards," he told the man as they drove. "You will stay with us at all times. If you say anything beyond what I ask you to say, if you attempt to leave us, if you do anything that puts us in danger, you will die."

"A lot of words," said the Libyan, holding his hands out. "I don't understand."

"Let me explain," said Jons. He pulled one of his pistols out and pointed it toward the backseat. "Fuck up and we kill you."

THEY DROVE BACK OVER TO THE AIRPORT. TWO ASSOCIATES were waiting, sitting on the front bumper of a large Ford 250. The diesel-powered pickup had been flown in only an hour before.

The taller of the two men sprang off the bumper as they approached. Rubeo had met him when he'd helped pull security for him during some travels in China. His name was Lawson, and he had been a Ranger in the Army. He was personable, a talker—rare for the profession, in Rubeo's experience.

The other man was Abas, an Iranian-American who had been a SEAL and done some work for the CIA before joining a private company Jons often called on for backup. Abas was silent to the point of being rocklike. He never smiled, and if he blinked his eyes or even closed them, Rubeo had never seen it.

"Boss, how's it going?" said Lawson, stalking over. He was tall and thin. His right knee had been torn up in Afghanistan. For some reason it didn't keep him from running, but he walked with the slightest of limps. The others sometimes called him "Igor" because of it.

"Where is everybody?" asked Jons.

"Siesta in the warehouse," said Lawson. "And Kimmy's out with the helucopper."

Lawson thought his mispronunciation was funny and began chuckling. The men in the warehouse were four Filipinos, trusted by Jons but unknown to Rubeo. Between them they had plenty of firepower, ranging up to a pair of automatic grenade launchers.

Unlike Rubeo and Jons, the team used commercial weapons and tactical gear. The only thing supplied by Rubeo's company were the com units—small ear sets with a pocket broadcast device. The units linked through a satellite connection and could share data; they worked solely by voice command.

"Go wake them up," said Jons. "When's Kimmy getting back?"

"Oughta be here any minute. She's just shay-uh-aching the chopper down."

Laughing again, Lawson turned and walked over to the warehouse to get the others.

"Are you sure we shouldn't just take the helicopter in?" Jons asked.

"It'll attract too much attention," said Rubeo. The helicopter was a backup, in case they needed to be extracted quickly. While it was tempting to fly directly in and out, the chopper brought its own risks. It would be a target not only for the government and the rebels, but the Western coalition as well. While Rubeo assumed they wouldn't shoot him down, he wanted to avoid telling them that he was here.

Jons took Halit over to the pickup and put him in the front seat. With Abas looking on, he showed him the GPS mapping system, which had a seven-inch screen mounted on a flexible arm between the driver and the front passenger.

The 250 cab had another row of seats in the back. Abas would drive; Jons and Rubeo would be in the back. Lawson and three of the Filipinos would be in the other truck. The last Filipino and Kimmy would stay back in the helicopter, on alert.

Rubeo turned his attention to the horizon. The desert was calm. There was no wind to speak of. A few pancake clouds sat on the horizon. The temperature was mild, considering where they were.

"Kimmy's about five minutes away," said Jons. "You want to wait for her, or should we hit the road?"

"There's no reason to wait."

"Let's go, then." Jons turned to the others.

"You want to hit the can, better do it now. We ain't stoppin' for nothing and nobody once we leave."

17

Sicily

WITH THE REST OF THE AFTERNOON OFF, TURK DEcided he would work out back at his hotel, then maybe go for a swim in the pool there. He hoped the activity would give his mind a break. He was almost at his car when his phone buzzed with a text message.

It was from Li Pike:

R U AROUND?

He answered yes.

COL WANTS TO KNOW—CAN U FLY TONIGHT? MISSION. IMPRTNT

ON MY WAY.

The briefing had already started by the time he got there. A French plane had gone down near a city held by the government in the southeast corner of the country, very close to the Chad border. The plane had apparently been lost to engine trouble; in any event, the government did not appear to know that it had crashed. A team of British SAS commandos was looking for the downed airman; the Hogs had been asked to join the second shift of air support tasked to aid the mission.

The A–10s would be equipped with Maverick missiles guided to their targets via laser designators; the bombs could be targeted either by the ground forces or the aircraft themselves.

All eight of Shooter Squadron's planes were tasked for the mission, but they would be divided into two groups to extend coverage.

The first flight, with Paulson as lead, would take off at 2200. The second group, led by Ginella, would come off the runway three hours later, at 0100.

The two flights would overlap for a brief period, but the general idea was that the first flight would be relieved by the second, which would operate until daylight.

"What happens if they don't find the guy by then?" asked Grizzly.

"Then he's not alive," said Ginella. She glanced at her watch. It was a little past 1900, or 7:00 P.M. "There's a little time to grab something to eat, but make it quick. Anyone that's too tired, I want that hand up now."

She looked at Turk. He wasn't about to admit fatigue.

Assigned to the second group, he would fly wing to Grizzly; Ginella explained that he had never flown at night with the special gear the Hogs used. Coop was flying as her wingman.

Li was in the first group as Paulson's wing.

"I'm sorry for you," Turk told her as they went over to get some dinner.

"For what?"

"Paulson can be a real prick."

"I think he's a pretty good pilot." Turk felt a little stab in his heart, until she added, "A class A jackass and a jerk besides, but he flies well."

While they ate, Grizzly regaled them with stories about his first nighttime refuel in a Hog—not particularly morale inducing, as he had fallen off the fuel probe not once, not twice, but three times, which the boomer—the crewman manning the refuel probe—had claimed was a new Hog record. Turk gathered that the difficulty of the refuel was the reason he'd been relegated to the back of the line.

"The boomer, though, claimed the worst pilots at night refuel are the F–22 jocks," said Grizzly.

That got a jealous laugh from the others, even though it was probably not true.

Turk hardly touched his food, spending most of his time watching Li instead. She had long slim fingers. They were expressive, even just holding a fork.

He wanted to ask her why and how she had become a pilot, but Grizzly started another story about how he'd spent "a year one week" flying Hog missions with a SEAL team.

His stories were too involved to be interrupted. The ops weren't the interesting part; the shenanigans, missteps, complications, and above all the nightly parties with members of the SEAL team, were the real point. According to Grizzly, they had gotten into a total of ten fights in six days, including one all-out brawl with members of a mixed martial-arts troupe.

True or not, it was a good yarn. Li, anxious to get ready for her flight, excused herself before it ended. Unable to find an excuse to accompany her that wouldn't sound overly corny, Turk watched her leave.

Even her walk was sexy.

He was glad that he didn't have to fly with Paulson, but the long wait before the sortie weighed heavily. He finally found a couch in a corner of the room next to the ready room and bedded down.

He started to drift off. He saw Li in his mind, starting to slip into unconsciousness. The image was pleasant, but almost immediately it morphed into Ginella. They started having sex.

Turk opened his eyes. Grizzly was shaking him.

God!

Turk practically jumped to the ceiling.

"Rise and shine, bro," laughed Grizzly, who fortunately had no idea of the dream he'd just woken him from. "We got some flyin' to do."

18

Libya

FOLLOWING HALIT'S ADVICE, RUBEO DECIDED TO AVOID the gate south of Tripoli, riding about twenty miles across open desert to reach a road that connected to the main highway south.

The road was barely discernible from the dirt, grit, and sand that washed over it. They drove up through a succession of hills. From a distance the terrain looked like the rumpled back of a giant sleeping facedown on the earth. Up close they were brown and almost featureless, bland nonentities that only slowed them down.

So much of life was like that, thought Rubeo. From a distance things looked remarkable. And then you got there and they were bland and boring.

Even his own life. For all his work in artificial intelligence systems, in related technologies, in the interface between man and machine—what accomplishments filled him with excitement?

The work that he was doing now on autonomous machines? On computers that really, truly, thought for themselves—not in the areas where they had been programmed to think, but in areas that they knew nothing about.

The Sabres were a small by-product of that work—a distant offshoot, really, because of course war had to be programmed into a machine.

And programmed out. The machine needed to

be taught limits so it would not turn on its master, as everyone who had ever picked up a scifi novel surely knew.

Had he not given the Sabres proper limits? Or was it a mechanical flaw?

Some combination, surely.

They had not yet ruled out direct action from the enemy. But that seemed to make little sense. Why do something to cause more casualties? The aim would be to have the plane destroy itself.

"What do you think of this?" asked Jons, handing him one of the team iPads. The device was equipped with a satellite modem in place of the usual cell and wireless connections; the com system used a series of anonymous servers to hide the identity and origins of the Web requests.

The screen showed a news story on the UAV incident. Labeled "Analysis," it recounted some of the popular theories on what had happened. Most were far off base or so vague that they could be describing a car accident.

But the paragraphs Jons had highlighted speculated that the attack had been made because of software problems. And it cited anonymous e-mails from "developers" indicating that the aircraft were making targeting decisions on their own.

In contrast to the rest of the piece, there was plenty of well-reasoned thought on the subject, enough to convince Rubeo that the source knew a great deal about the problems involved. He scrolled back to the top and reread the story carefully. Much of it was generic, so much so that he couldn't figure out whether the writer, as opposed to the source, actually knew what he was talking about.

"It's not very specific," said Rubeo, handing the iPad back. "This middle part is interesting, but I don't know that he has any real sources inside our organization. He might know someone at another company that's working on the problem."

"That's what I thought." Jons opened the browser to a new page. "But I did a couple of searches on some of the phrases just to be sure. Look at this list."

There were twenty-eight matches from bulletin boards and comment areas. All used similar language to describe the accident and the theory that the aircraft had been under their own autonomous control when the attack was made.

"These drones are being operated without human supervision," read one. "They decide who to kill and who to spare. The man who invented them, Ray Rubeo, thinks machines are better than people."

The latter was a rather common criticism, not just of Rubeo, but of practically any scientist who worked in the area. But the fact that it was being directed at one person, rather than a team, bothered Rubeo immensely. Coupled with the alleged e-mail, it looked as if someone either in his company or at least tangentially related was leaking information.

"What do you think?" asked Jons.

"Someone doesn't like AI," said Rubeo, handing the computer back.

"Or you. You're mentioned by name in these. My guess is that a bunch of organizations got the e-mail cited in that article," added Jons. "It looks like a campaign."

Rubeo said nothing. He had many competitors. Each one was an enemy, at least figuratively. And any number of people would benefit if the government stopped dealing with his firm; there would be a vast void to fill.

"No one seems to be taking them very seriously," he told Jons. "Or otherwise I'd have heard."

"Maybe. In any event, it's a potential security leak. It could definitely be a disgruntled employee. Anyone willing to put out this kind of information, add your name—they won't stop here."

"I don't think it's an employee. Or an ex-employee. They're paid too well."

"It's not always about money. Or science."

In Rubeo's experience, if it wasn't about science, then it was *always* about money. Or sex.

"Rerun our security checks," he told Jons.

"Oh, we're well into that."

"Good."

"It may be a contractor," suggested Jons. "We're checking that as well. I wonder if there's any disgruntled military. Maybe on the Whiplash side."

"We can certainly check. There aren't many of them."

"Not directly. Indirectly, you'd be surprised."

"Right." Rubeo settled back into the seat, as frustrated as ever.

HALIT PROVED HIS WORTH AT THE GATE, SPEAKING quickly to the guards. Jons, standing next to him, handed over a folded envelope, and they were through.

"One hundred euros," Jons told Rubeo, climbing back into the truck. "That is all it took to get us past the front line. The government doesn't have long."

Rubeo nodded but said nothing. Darkness had enveloped the desert.

They drove quickly, nearly missing the turn that would take them to the military site where the government's most powerful radar units were located. There were two sets here, general warning radars and radars that were connected with an SA–10 antiaircraft battery.

According to Rubeo's calculations, the latter were the only ones in the area capable of interfering with the Sabre telemetry. Supposedly, they had come on very briefly during the engagement. The allies, for reasons known only to them, had not yet gotten around to targeting the radars, possibly because there were civilians inside the complex where the units were located.

There were two ways to see if the units here could have interfered with the Sabre. One was to somehow turn back time and record everything they did. The second was to examine them very closely, which required being physically nearby and provoking, or at least attempting to provoke, a similar response.

The latter choice was only slightly less impossible than the former. But more likely twice as dangerous.

They stopped a mile outside the site, clearly visible on a slight rise, guarded by two armored personnel carriers and three sandbagged machine-gun emplacements.

"Guys in that post over there are sleeping," said Jons, looking through the night glasses.

"Go ahead and launch the Streamer."

Lawson had already taken the small aircraft out of its case. With a wingspan just under twenty-four inches, the robot aircraft was an electronic noise machine. Powered by a small kerosene-fueled engine, it would circle over the radar installation, broadcasting a signal that would make it seem as if NATO aircraft were approaching.

"Come on little birdie, time to start you up," said Lawson, half singing the last few words as if he were Mick Jagger singing "Start Me Up."

The motor didn't seem to be in a musical mood, or maybe it just didn't like rock 'n' roll. It refused to start. He reprimed it and pressed the starter, which used a spring and battery combination to spin it to life.

The engine spat, coughed, then finally spun into high speed.

Up close, the miniature power plant sounded like an HO-scale racing car, its high-pitched whir almost a whistle. The sound didn't carry very far, however; it was difficult to discern at a hundred feet, and would be easily covered by the hum of the electronics and cooling gear in the control vans at the base.

"Fly, my pretty," said Lawson, pushing the UAV into the air.

It launched like a paper plane, the wings struggling to find airflow as the motor revved. The nose dipped down, the plane gathered speed, then suddenly tilted up and soared skyward on a preprogrammed climb.

Lawson picked up the controller—it was a hobbyist's kit, with only slight modifications for security—and worked the plane up to two hundred feet. Then he put it into a wide circle above the base.

Rubeo was watching the screen on the detection processing unit, which was attached to a set of wire antennas. As the UAV circled, Lawson turned its broadcast system on.

The radar system on the ground believed it was looking at a Predator some twenty miles away—well inside the missile's effective range.

"They're just watching," said Lawson.

"Good. Phase two."

A second signature now appeared on the screens of the operators inside the van—F/A–18s approaching from a distance. The aircraft popped up, preparing to attack.

The engagement radar for the ground-to-air missiles came on. The operators had decided to take down the Predator, which they interpreted as scouting for the manned aircraft. But within seconds both radars shut down.

"They're afraid of antiradiation missiles," said Rubeo, looking at the screen over Lawson's shoulder.

"Yup."

The radars stayed off.

If the Libyans had a way of interfering with the UAV transmissions, Rubeo reasoned, they would have likely used it against the Predator, which after all looked as if it was bird-dogging for the other planes.

Still, he needed to be absolutely sure. The jamming unit might be "tuned" to the Sabres.

"Launch the Mapper."

"With pleasure," said Lawson.

The Mapper was a larger UAV, with a wingspan over twenty feet. The large size allowed it to carry a heavier payload—a device that would map the electronic layout of the camp. Every wire, every circuit, would be diagrammed.

Rubeo monitored the Streamer controls. If the radars suddenly turned on, the Mapper would be an easy target; it was not only bigger, but louder than the first UAV.

"It's on its own," said Lawson. The plane had been programmed to fly a very slow circuit over the compound. As it did, its sensors would map the electronic and magnetic fields and circuits below, giving Rubeo a picture of the installation, or at least its electronic components.

"They're going to hear it," said Jons. He was watching the machine-gun position through his glasses.

"Hopefully they won't," said Rubeo.

"Relying on luck? That's not like you, Ray."

Rubeo didn't answer. The data from the aircraft had to be recorded and then uploaded to his systems back in the States. They didn't have the equipment to analyze it in real time. Rubeo had calculated that they needed three circuits to get a sufficient image; he wanted at least six.

The plane was just completing the second when the radar came back up.

"Why the hell did they do that?" grumbled Lawson.

The Streamer pumped out fresh signals, making it seem as if the site was going to be attacked by the F/A–18s. This time it didn't work.

"They're running around like crazy men," said Jons.

A second later someone in one of the vehicles began firing a fifty caliber. The Mapper was way too close to be targeted by the missiles, but within easy reach of old-fashioned machine guns.

Red and orange tracers cascaded in the air, peppered here and there with bolts of black. The sound was oppressive, even from where they were.

"They're going to launch missiles," said Lawson. "Radar thinks it has a lock."

"Wonderful," said Rubeo sarcastically. He kept his eyes on the control screen, watching the Mapper UAV. It was about three-quarters of the way through its third turn over the complex, heading directly for the tracers. Rubeo could take over the flight program and divert it to safety, but that would mean the circuits would have to be repeated.

The odds were better to just keep it flying, he decided.

A few seconds later the screen on the control blanked. It had stopped transmitting. The Libyan gunfire had caught the aircraft.

There was a ground flare at the complex. For a brief moment Rubeo thought it was the aircraft crashing, but in fact it was an SA–10 missile launching. A second and then a third and fourth came off the ground in quick succession.

"It is time for us to leave," announced the scientist. "Pack quickly."

HESITATION

1

Over Libya

THE A–10E HELMET HAD A NIGHT VISION ATTACHMENT allowing the pilots to see in the dark. The combination was still lighter than the smart helmet, but it was awkward, tilting the helmet forward so the edges rubbed against Turk's cheekbones.

The glasses turned the world into a crisp collection of greens and blacks, an alternate universe that lived parallel to the real one. It was as if the pilot was an electronic ghost, slipping through the dark solids before him.

While the technology was different, the view itself was familiar to Turk from the smart helmet, where it was one of the preset defaults, designed to make the transition from older technology to new as seamless as possible. He felt it was superior to the view offered in F–35 helmets—another preset. There was a sharpness to it that the Lightning II view seemed to lack.

Turk took Shooter Four up from the south runway, moving into a gradual climb over the Mediterranean. The four-ship flight's first stop was a tanker track to the southwest; they would top off there before heading over Libya.

Turk listened as Ginella checked in with the AWACS, getting a picture of the situation over the country.

She was an odd case—professional to the point of cold indifference toward him in the squadron room, outrageously passionate in bed.

It confused the hell out of him.

Remembering Grizzly's tales of tanker woe, Turk approached the boom gently, easing in at a crawl. At any second he expected the boomer to squawk at him about how slow he was going. But all he got was an attaboy and a solid *clunk* as the probe was shoved into the nose of the Hog.

He held the aircraft steady as the JP–8 sloshed in. The cockpit filled with the heady scent of escaping kerosene. Turk tried to relax his shoulder and arm muscles, afraid that any twitch would jerk him off the straw. By the time the boomer called over to tell him to disconnect, his arms had cramped.

"Copy that. Thanks."

Turk slipped downward, dropping through several dozen feet before banking right and moving out and away from the tanker. The radio whispered hints of distant missions; it was a busy night over Libya, the allies keeping pressure on the government as the rebels continued with their offensive.

Grizzly had already tanked and was waiting for him.

"You did good, Turk," said the other pilot.

"Gonna make a real Hog driver out of you yet."

"I'm getting there."

"You gotta work on your grunts." Grizzly made a noise somewhat similar to the sound of a rooting hog. His voice lost an octave and became something a caveman would have been proud of. "Real Hog driver talk like this."

"All right, you two, knock it off," said Ginella. "Let's look sharp and keep our comments to business. Turk, how are your eyes?"

"I'm good."

"There's been no sign of our package south," she added. "Let's get there. You know the drill."

THIRTY MINUTES LATER THE FOUR HOGS APPROACHED an arbitrary point in the sky where they had been assigned to loiter. The other half of Shooter Squadron was to the southwest about seventy miles. The aircraft were flying at roughly 30,000 feet, high enough so they couldn't be seen or heard in the dark night sky.

The American planes were part of a massive search and rescue operation. Dozens of aircraft were strung out across the country, ready. All they needed was a downed pilot.

The wreck had been located in a ravine twenty miles south. But the pilot's locator beacon and radio had not been detected. Ground forces were conducting a search near the plane and in an area where computer simulations showed the man might have parachuted. Army Special Forces units had been inserted just after dusk, and had made contact with some rebels in the area who were helping with the search.

Turk didn't have a lot of experience with rescue operations, but it took little more than common sense to realize that if the pilot hadn't radioed in by now, the odds of finding him alive were extremely slim. But no one in the air wanted to mention that. It was too easy to put yourself in the downed man's place—you didn't want to think of giving up.

An hour passed. The other half of Shooter Squadron called it a night and headed home. Ginella led her group farther south, orbiting over two different spec op detachments.

Adrenaline drained, Turk found staying alert extremely difficult. He stretched his legs, rocked his shoulders back and forth—it was a constant battle, far more difficult than actually flying the plane.

One of the ground units reported that they were following a lead from the rebel guerrillas; the information was passed back down the line to the squadron. Turk felt his pulse jump. But when the lead failed to pan out, he found it even harder to keep his edge.

With dawn approaching, Ginella decided they would refuel so their patrol could be extended if needed. She split the group in two so they could continue to provide coverage. Grizzly and Turk went north to the tanker track while she and her wingman stayed south.

Mostly silent during their loops, Grizzly became animated as they approached the hookup.

He told Turk he had brought along an iPod and was listening to music as they flew.

"Got some old stuff I haven't heard in a while."

The music may have been old, but Turk hadn't heard any of it. It was country and country pop—Son Volt and Civil Wars and half a dozen other singers and groups completely off his radar.

"You gotta get out more," laughed Grizzly when Turk confessed he'd never heard of the groups. He began filling him in, keeping the patter up all the way to the Air Force 757s.

"What do you think of G?" asked Grizzly after they had finished tanking.

"Seems OK," said Turk as neutrally as possible.

"Real hardass sometimes. Good pilot, though. First woman commander I've ever had."

"First one?"

"Probably had a female in charge of one of the schools somewhere along the way," said Grizzly, referring to the different classes the officer would have attended. "But not, you know, like this."

"Uh-huh."

"Kinda different flying for a woman, you think?" said Grizzly.

It sounded somewhere between a statement and a question. Turk didn't know how to answer it either way. His boss—Breanna Stockard—was a woman, but he wasn't supposed to refer to Special Projects if possible, and he worried that mentioning her would inevitably point the conversation in that direction. It took him a few moments to think of something suitably neutral and bland to come back with.

"I haven't worked with an actual squadron in a while," he told the other pilot. "I'm pretty much a one-man shop."

"That's kind of cool."

"Yeah."

"Word is the Air Force is gonna phase us down," said Grizzly. "Turn all the electronics in these suckers on and let them fly themselves."

"I don't know about that," replied Turk.

"Probably replace us with laser jets, if not."

Both ideas were actually plausible. A few years before, that would have sounded like science fiction or maybe fantasy. But there were in fact plans to replace the A–10 squadrons with airborne laser planes. The aircraft, modified from civilian airliners and housing high-energy weapons, could fly at a safe distance and altitude yet make attacks with pinpoint precision. It was almost guaranteed that a fleet of the laser jets, as they were called, would replace the Air Force's small force of AC–130s in the next eighteen months.

"I think there's a real need for people in the loop," said Turk. "But, I don't know."

"I hear ya."

"Everything's going in the other direction," said Turk.

"You're part of it though, right? You're playing with those little dart jets? Pretty soon they won't need you either."

Grizzly was absolutely right. He didn't answer, though—because of his position, what would have been interpreted as a casual remark by any other person could be seen as a breach of security if he said it.

Maybe the accident would turn things back in the other direction. But it could just as easily be used as an argument against keeping a man in the loop—his being there, or being close, hadn't stopped the Sabre from making the mistake.

The accident had grounded the Sabres, but not the rest of the UAV fleet. That in itself was statement of how important they were. Right now at least three were operating in the rescue area. Two provided a continuous infrared picture of the ground to the controllers and the team hunting for the pilot. The other was sniffing for his radio and signal beacon.

WITH A FULL BELLY—OR MORE ACCURATELY, WING tanks—of fuel, Turk followed Grizzly in a loose trail south as the sun tiptoed toward the horizon. As the light strengthened, he removed the night goggles and left the augmented visor retracted, preferring to see the sky and aircraft as they truly were.

He had plenty of fuel, but this mission couldn't go on forever. Eventually, the pilots' fatigue would build to the point where they simply couldn't trust themselves. To use one of the more formal terms and measures, situational awareness would degrade severely.

That was a problem one never had with computers.

"Shooter One, this is Three," radioed Grizzly.

"One."

"We're about thirty minutes away. Anything?"

"Negative. Still on hold."

"What do you want to do, G?"

"We'll go tank when you're here," she told Grizzly. "Play it by ear from then."

"Understood."

"How's your wingman?"

"Still there every time I turn around."

"Four?" Ginella asked.

"Shooter Four is good," said Turk.

"A little boring for you?" asked Ginella. Her voice had a hint—but only just a hint—of the more familiar tone she used when they were alone.

"I'll survive."

"That's the spirit."

"We covering the pickup of the search units?" Grizzly asked.

"Not sure yet," answered Ginella. "Pickup has been delayed."

"That's a good thing."

"Don't jump to conclusions."

"Just saying."

The four Hogs joined up, flying in a large circular pattern above the desert. Ginella rebriefed Grizzly on contact frequencies and some of their protocols—all things Grizzly already knew. But he didn't complain.

"We'll be up and back as quickly as we can," she told them. "There's a flight of F–16s north for backup."

"Roger that. Have a good trip."

But before Ginella could check in with the controller, he radioed to tell them there was a flight of Blackhawk helicopters inbound. The IDs on the choppers belonged to the units tasked for the pilot's rescue pickup.

"Groundhog has located the beacon," explained the controller. "Stand by to cover a pickup."

"In that case, we'll hang down here," Ginella told her squadron. "We have plenty of fuel for now."

The A–10Es were vectored southwest, near a small settlement at the edge of a long, open square of desert. They waited until the helicopters were about five minutes away before going down to take a look; they didn't want to call attention to their presence until absolutely necessary.

Ginella contacted Groundhog for an update on their situation. From the accent of the radioman, Turk guessed that the ground unit was a British SAS commando squad, one of a number of special operations troops operating in the theater. His communiqués were terse, with quick acknowledgments when Ginella responded.

The commandos were in a village isolated from the highway by a narrow winding road through a series of sharp but narrow hills. The village had no more than two dozen houses, and was centered around a pair of unpaved streets that came together in a Y at roughly the center of the settlement. A small mosque and minaret stood near the intersection on the southernmost street.

The helicopters were directed to hold at a position roughly ten miles away from the village.

The SAS troopers had located a very weak

signal inside a building on the street north of the mosque. With all of their support elements in place, they were going to storm the building. If things went wrong, they wanted the Hogs in fast.

"Acknowledged, Groundhog," Ginella told him. "You can count on us."

Turk studied the image of the village in the multiuse screen. The nearby hills limited their attack approach to an east-west corridor above the main streets.

Once again Ginella split the flight into two elements, but kept both on the east side of the village. All the planes would fly in the same direction on the initial attack. After that, she and Coop would recover south while Grizzly and Turk would go north. The idea was that the two groups would be in position to attack anyone coming from the outside.

"We'll play it as it develops," she added.

Groundhog radioed that they were going in.

Turk felt his chest starting to tighten. Sweat began collecting under his gloves.

He told himself to relax, but his heart started thumping. His adrenaline level shot up—he was starting to feel a little jittery, as if he'd had a few pots of coffee. He knew he must be physically overtired, but his body seemed to be overcompensating.

Relax.

Relax, goddamn it.

The commandos used a special short-distance radio to talk among themselves; the Shooter aircraft couldn't hear what they were saying.

Five minutes passed. The planes circled in the sky, waiting.

"Shooter One, Groundhog here. We're moving south through the village."

"Groundhog, say status."

"We don't have him."

"Is he there? What's going on?"

"We recovered some gear. We're moving to the mosque."

"Groundhog, do you require assistance?" asked Ginella.

"Negative. Hold your position."

"Shooter One acknowledges. Holding position."

"We oughta take a 'low-and-slow' and see what's up," said Grizzly. "Just let them know we're here. At least shake 'em up a bit."

"Negative," snapped Ginella. "Just do what they want."

"I wasn't saying I was going to do it."

"Silent coms," she told him.

"Yes, ma'am."

"I have a vehicle on the road, two vehicles," said Coop. "You see these, Colonel?"

"Yes, roger that," said Ginella. "Groundhog, be advised we're seeing two pickup trucks with people in the truck beds. They're approaching the road to your village."

"Splash them."

"Negative, Groundhog. That's not in my ROEs."

The ROEs—rules of engagement—permitted the Hogs to shoot at a target only if it presented an imminent danger to friendly forces or themselves. In this case, the men in the trucks would have to be firing at the commandos to justify aggressive action.

"We don't need company," said Groundhog.

"Understood, Groundhog. But we're limited by our orders."

Turk expected the British soldier to tell them what they could do with their orders. But he didn't reply.

"Coop, follow me down," she said.

The two Hogs dove toward the roadway, dropping precipitously. They rode in over the pickup trucks, accelerating and jerking away.

Ginella's idea was clear—she was putting the fear of God, or rather Hogs, into them.

The trucks sped up, continuing past the turnoff for the village.

The two jets cleared north and came back around.

"I'm getting close to bingo," said Coop.

"Acknowledged," said Ginella. "Groundhog, what's your status?"

"Working toward the mosque," he replied.

"Do you have resistance?"

"Negative."

They took a few more turns. Finally, Ginella admitted the inevitable.

"Groundhog, my wingmate and I are going to refuel. I'm turning you over to Shooter Three and Shooter Four. You'll be in good hands."

"Affirmative. Thanks, mate."

Ten minutes later the SAS trooper radioed that

they were going inside the mosque. He asked the two planes to fly over "loud and low"—exactly the distraction Grizzly had thought of earlier.

"We're on the way," said Grizzly. "Ten seconds."

Turk came in off Grizzly's right wing, his head swiveling as he searched the ground for some sign of resistance, or even life. The small village seemed completely deserted, with no one on the streets. Ordinarily the small towns had goats, dogs, or other animals wandering about. He saw nothing.

The two planes circled left, pulling up around one of the small hills. As they did, Turk caught a glint off something to his right. He raised himself in the seat, looking back over his shoulder.

"Hey, I think we got those trucks coming back," he told Grizzly. "Got something on the road."

"What is it?"

"Turning."

Turk circled back to get a better look at the trucks. Grizzly contacted the airborne controller, trying to see if the Predator overhead could shift closer for an image. He then tried to contact Groundhog directly, to check on their status.

The Brits said only that they were "good." By then the trucks had gone off the main highway, moving in a direct line toward the road that led to the village.

"Those the same trucks as before?" Grizzly asked.

"Can't tell," said Turk. "What about the Predator?"

"The trucks are a little far from the road for

the Predator to spot. He has to stay eyes on the village."

"By the time they're in range they'll be in the hills." The geography would make it harder to watch the trucks there.

"Let's get in their faces," said Grizzly. "See if we can run them off like before. I'll come in first. They fire at me, light them up."

"Yeah, all right. Roger that."

Grizzly led him south before banking and pushing down, his nose angling toward the pickups. Turk waited, giving the other plane enough of a head start so he could react if he saw anything. He tucked down, pushing the Hog through 1,500 feet and picking up speed.

He was on the back of a sleek stallion. The engines rushed behind him, a steady whoosh. He edged his finger on the trigger of the gun, double-checking the panel to make sure the weapon was ready.

The two trucks were no more than thirty yards apart. The lead vehicle was just reaching the road to the village as Shooter Three came in ahead of him, low.

Something winked below Grizzly's A–10.

Gunfire?

Turk couldn't tell if it was a muzzle flash or just a reflection from the sun.

Another glint. A flash.

Weapon. Guns. MANPAD!

"Flares! Evade!" yelled Turk, warning the other plane even as he pressed the trigger to zero out the threat.

The big gun in the nose of the A–10 began rotating. The force of the cannon was so intense that it seemed to hold the Warthog up in the sky. The burst lasted not quite two seconds, but in that time, somewhere over one hundred rounds burst from the gun. Nearly every one hit the truck—or would have, if there was truck left there to hit. The heavy slugs tore the front of the truck in half, igniting a huge fireball and vaporizing a good portion of the vehicle.

"Missile in the air!" yelled Grizzly.

Turk's warning system was bleating as well, but he was too focused to pay attention. He leaned his body left and the jet followed, moving quickly as he lined up his second shot. He was a little too close to get more than a few slugs into the truck before he passed it, but they were more than enough to stop the vehicle.

Turk dished flares and turned hard right, himself a target now. Gravity hit him in the side of the face and chest. He felt the bladders in his flight gear pushing hard against his stomach and his legs. The Hog floated a bit, moving sideways as it struggled to sort out the conflicting demands of gravity and its pilot's will.

The peak of the hill loomed dead ahead, a jagged slag of red and brown.

"Power, baby," Turk said, his hand already slamming the throttle. "Power."

The Hog's nose pulled up and the aircraft lifted in the sky, almost hopping over the hilltop.

He felt weightless. He wasn't sure what had been launched at him. He was afraid it was on his tail.

"ECMs," he said, momentarily reacting as if

he were in the Tigershark. He recovered quickly, hitting the panel to activate the electronic countermeasures—a fancy name for a radar jammer.

The Hog continued to climb for a few more seconds before Turk realized that whatever had been launched had missed. Either it had been sucked off by the flares or was unguided to begin with, just a rocket-propelled grenade. He banked back around.

The first truck was hidden by steam and smoke. The second was sitting on the side of the road.

He had it on his nose. He glanced up, locating Shooter Three on his left wing at about ten o'clock, coming up from the south.

"I'm going in on that second truck," Turk called on the radio.

"Roger that."

"You OK?"

"Yeah, yeah, I'm good, I'm good. Go for it—I got your six."

The truck was fat in his windscreen. The men on the ground were firing at him—Turk could see their muzzles blinking.

One of his missiles would have wiped out all of the men, but he wanted to save them for the SAS unit. And in any event, he'd already made up his mind on how he was going to attack.

The truck grew large in his pipper. He pressed the trigger, spitting a steady stream of spent uranium into it.

The vehicle disappeared beneath a cloud of smoke. Turk cleared south.

"We're good, we're good," said Grizzly. "Hold south of the village."

"We need to move back east in case we have to run into the village," said Turk.

"Yeah, all right, you're right. Good—let's get there. Follow me."

As they pushed their aircraft back into a position that would make it easier to support the ground units, Groundhog checked in, asking what was going on.

"Just smoked two pickups that fired on us," reported Grizzly.

"Copy."

"What's your situation?"

"We're going through the building."

"You have subject?"

"Negative."

"We're standing by."

"Copy, Shooter."

The brief engagement had been more physical than Turk realized. His arms and upper body felt as if he'd been in a boxing or MMA fight, sore and drained.

But his breathing was calm. The action had relaxed him.

Groundhog reported that there were people on the street.

"A lot of watchers," said the British soldier.

"Threatening?" asked Grizzly.

"Negative. Just watchers. We're moving to your south."

A minute or two later he called back.

"We're on the street," said Groundhog. "Can you take a pass?"

"Stand by."

"I'm with you," Turk told Grizzly.

"Follow me through. Same game plan."

"Let's make it fast," said Turk. "We don't want to push our luck."

"No shit on that."

Turk dropped the Hog through four hundred feet as he came down. Grizzly was another hundred feet lower. He dropped to two hundred feet as they came over the village. Turk worried his wingman would plow into the buildings or the nearby hill, but he cleared them and rose south.

The flyover lasted only a few seconds, but each moment was a full day, weighted with tension. Turk looked left and right, heart pounding. He saw the broken edges of the roof tiles, a half-eroded garden wall on the largest house, a car that had lost its tires.

And he saw the tops of heads ducking, a bald man, two startled teenagers, a woman white with fear.

He punched the throttle, powering away.

"Wooo-hoo," said Grizzly as they climbed. "You see that crowd?"

"Copy."

"Weapons?"

Turk had to think about what he had seen. People moving, standing. Weapons?

None that he remembered. He tried processing it again.

"Negative. Not even rifles," he added.

"You sure?"

"I think so. You see something?"

"No." Grizzly sounded disappointed.

Groundhog began squawking. They were calling the helicopters in for a pickup.

"We're moving to the south side of town," said the SAS soldier. "Do you copy, Shogun Six?"

"Shogun Six copies."

"Point is marked as Landing Four on your map. It's behind a low wall."

"Affirmative. We copy."

Turk spotted the two helicopters flying from the north, crossing in a wide arc west of the hamlet. They were aiming at a field behind a large building.

"Got people in that building," said the helicopter pilot.

"Are they aggressive?" asked the controller. "Weapons?"

"I just see people."

A three-way conversation between the helicopters, the controller, and the ground unit ensued. The voices were quick and sharp as the men tried to determine whether the people in the building constituted a threat. No weapons had been spotted, and the ROEs declared that they be left alone. That seemed to be a relief to all concerned, especially the ground unit.

As a precaution, Turk noted the building. He could blast it with a missile if necessary.

The dozen members of Groundhog hopscotched down the street toward the landing point. Turk could see knots of people moving roughly parallel to the soldiers.

"A lot of people down here," said Groundhog.

"We want to keep them as far back from the helicopters as possible," said Shogun. "More Hog psyops."

The helicopters touched down. The Brits fell into a dead run.

They were still twenty or thirty yards away when one of the helicopters jerked upward.

"Gun! Gun!" yelled someone over the radio.

Turk, about a half mile east of the pickup area, strained to see what was going on.

Grizzly radioed Groundhog and Shogun but got no answer. Bits of smoke appeared in a line on the ground about a hundred yards from the pickup area, near the village.

"Shogun's firing," said Grizzly.

"Hold back," warned Turk. "Helicopter is circling."

Turk had to bank to give the chopper room. Smoke spread across the field. It looked like something from a smoke grenade rather than gunfire.

"Groundhog? Groundhog!" said Grizzly. "Say your situation. What the hell is going on?"

The first helicopter circled south, ramping upward. The second helicopter remained on the ground.

"I don't see any gunfire," said Turk.

"I can take out that building," said Grizzly.

"Negative, negative," said Turk. "There's nothing coming from there. Hold off."

The blades on the second helicopter began rotating furiously. The helicopter rose upward, cutting across a thick fist of smoke.

"We're good, we're good," Groundhog said. "All recovered."

Turk lost sight of the helicopter as it passed behind him, flying northeastward. He found Grizzly on his left and followed him upward, climbing away from the village.

Barely two minutes had passed since the ground element began running for the choppers. It had been a tangle of confusion, at least from Turk's point of view. He tried sorting it in his mind: the helicopter that lifted off had seen people coming and decided to hold them off with gunfire that missed but scared people away. The other chopper made the pickup, the trooper tossing smoke grenades behind to cover their retreat.

Simple. Assuming that was the way it went. It was hard to decipher even the most obvious action in combat.

The helicopters arced northward, getting away from the village. Turk started thinking about the long flight home—and how long he would sleep once he reached the hotel.

"This is Shogun Actual," called the helicopter commander. "All allied assets, be advised. We have two men still on the ground. They are moving through the field at the north side of the village. Mountain Three is coming for a pickup."

The men, providing an overwatch from the northern end of the village, had been separated as the units began exfiltrating. Confusion on the ground had sent the helicopters skyward before they reached the pickup point.

Damn.

The two SAS men on the ground were in radio contact with the controller. The men, using the call sign Rodent, were on the north side of the village. The helicopter pilot flying Mountain Three was closing in. He told them he would meet them wherever they wanted.

"Hell if necessary," added the man, who had the slight lilt of a Boston accent.

They told him they would go north and meet him in the flat desert area. No one was following them.

The air controller, meanwhile, tried to gather more information about the crowd that had been following. The SAS men said they hadn't seen any weapons, something Turk and Grizzly confirmed. But someone aboard the helicopter believed he had.

It was impossible to know the real facts. As a practical matter, the rules remained the same for the two A–10 pilots: they could watch, and buzz the crowd if necessary, but at the moment they couldn't fire.

How strange it must be on the ground, Turk thought. A civilian in the war zone was a voyeur, an observer, maybe reluctant, maybe against his or her will. Yet the fascination to find out what was going on must be incredible.

You'd be drawn to the strangeness, if not the danger. The danger might not even seem real, because the situation was so bizarre—men with guns running through your village, a nightmare in the middle of the day. But it was absolutely real, and a false move or a mistake could easily lead to your death—either from someone on the ground or someone in the sky.

Was that what it had been like in the village when the Sabre attacked? It must have been worse—hell simply broke open from the sky without warning, arriving on the nose of a fast-flying missile before the plane was close enough to make a noise.

A terrible, terrible mistake.

Not his, though. Not his.

The troopers on the ground moved around the backs of two houses, toward the Y intersection at the center of town. Turk used the zoom feature on the satellite image to check the path they were intending to take—it cut through the hill off the northern road and down into the desert. The village was tucked behind the ridge there, cutting off the view from the buildings.

He looked down at it. Clear, as far as he could tell. So far, so good.

And what of the nightmare for the soldiers on the ground? They had two great fears—their legitimate enemy, trying to kill them, and the innocents walking through the village.

If they *were* innocents. How could you even tell?

It was easier in the old days, when you just decided everyone was bad and rolled over the place.

The SAS troopers crossed the street near the mosque.

"We're going north on the street," reported Rodent. "We—"

He stopped talking. Turk heard gunfire in the background.

"We're under fire," said the Brit.

"Do you have a target?" called Grizzly.

"Negative," said Rodent. "We're in cover. We can't see the gunman."

"Rodent, is it the mosque?" Grizzly asked.

"Stand by."

"I can take the mosque out."

"Stand by."

"Turk, you see the gunfire?"

"Negative."

Turk, about a mile and a half behind Grizzly, zeroed into the area on his screen, using maximum resolution. He couldn't see any gunfire at all. Hitting the mosque would be easy enough, but without a positive ID that it was the target he couldn't take the shot. The helicopter, meanwhile, held short, about a mile and a half away.

"We need a target, Rodent," said Grizzly.

The ground unit replied with a curse.

"Rodent, can you beam them with your laser designator?" asked Turk.

"Negative. We're not sure where they are."

"Are you under fire?"

No answer.

"Rodent?"

"We're sorting it out, mate. We hear people moving east of us."

"East of you?"

"And north. Both."

"I'm going to try and get eyes on," Turk told Grizzly. "I'll come through, then maybe we can nail them."

"Roger that. Good."

"Rodent, can you try and get them to fire?" Turk told the ground unit.

"They don't bloody well handle requests, Yank. And if they did, that wouldn't be one I'd make."

The haze from the earlier smoke grenades had drifted across the eastern end of town, obscuring Turk's view as he came up from the south. As he cleared past it, he saw two quick flashes on the far right. They were coming from the roof of a building on the corner of the intersection. The location didn't seem to have an angle on Rodent's position, however.

"How close is that gunfire?" he asked the ground unit.

"Close enough to count."

He told the British soldiers about the building. They agreed it was the likely source, though from where they were they could see only a small corner of the roof.

"May be why they're missing," said Rodent.

"You sure that mosque is clear?" Grizzly asked Turk. "It has that whole road covered."

"I didn't see anything there. You?"

Grizzly didn't answer. He told the SAS troopers to keep their heads down, then dialed his Maverick into the building Turk had ID'ed as the sniper nest.

Ten seconds later the building exploded.

Rodent called in to say that they were moving.

More gunfire erupted on the street, coming from behind a parked car. This time the target was obvious. The Brits took cover, and Turk put a Maverick into the vehicle, setting it on fire and killing or wounding the two gunmen behind it.

"You sure that mosque is clean?" asked Grizzly.

Stop with the mosque, thought Turk. But he answered calmly. "I don't see anything there."

"We're moving," said Rodent.

There were a few more shots, but the pair made it to the northern fork and then ran down the hill. They were clear of the village.

"Helicopter is inbound," said the controller.

"Let's take a pass between the landing zone and the village," said Grizzly. "Make sure things are cool."

Turk got behind him. Grizzly told the controller and the helicopter what they were doing.

"You sure that mosque doesn't have anything?" asked Grizzly.

"Yeah."

"I'll bet that's where they came out of. Those places are nests."

Grizzly went across the top of the hill. Turk got his Hog a little lower. His airspeed kept declining; he was barely over a hundred knots, very close to getting a stall warning.

"Looking clear."

A large black bug appeared on the horizon. The SAS men ran toward it. As the Blackhawk swooped in, the two A–10s flew east to west across the village, between it and the SAS troopers.

"Something on my left," said Grizzly as he cleared west. "You see that?"

"I'll look for it."

"Two or three people."

Turk saw the figures on a small path at the side of the knoll. There were four—at least two were children.

"Just kids," he told Grizzly.

"You sure?"

Turk slid his aircraft left. He could have fired at them if he wanted.

But they were kids.

"Yeah. Just kids."

"You see a weapon?"

"Negative."

The helicopter touched down. Within thirty seconds it was back in the air, Brits aboard. Grizzly took another pass, running between the village and the Blackhawk. As he did, there was a puff of smoke from the hillside.

"Flares! Break right, break left!" called Turk, even before the missile launch warning began blaring. "Missile! Turn hard! Left! Flares! Flares!"

Something sparked in the sky. Turk looked to his left, where the other aircraft should be, but there was nothing there.

He jerked his head around, afraid. But Grizzly was there—he'd gone right.

Turned toward the damn missile.

There was a dot of red in the pale blue. Two dots.

Decoys, thought Turk. He's past.

"I'm hit," said Grizzly a moment later.

2

Southern Libya

DRIVING AWAY FROM THE RADAR COMPLEX, RUBEO zipped his jacket against the cold and considered something one of his professors had told him.

Only thought experiments fully succeed in science.

As a pimple-faced teenager extremely full of himself, he had considered that an exaggeration. He'd pulled off dozens of experiments that were one hundred percent successful. As time went on, however, he saw the truth in his professor's remark. And while he had come to appreciate that the failures were almost always more interesting than the successes, at this particular moment the limits of science were a challenge.

Even though the UAV gathering the electric data had been shot down before completing its survey, the map it provided of the devices at the complex was fairly complete. The aircraft's sensors had found the main generators and the trailers with the radar control units. The detail was good enough for an eighty-five percent certainty on the ID of the radars that detected planes and controlled the missiles.

Eighty-five percent was considered more than enough; the matching algorithms were extremely exacting. Additionally, the radars had already been identified by the receiving unit independent of the Mapper, so the match confirmed that the system was working properly.

The next stage was more difficult. The computers at Rubeo's headquarters compared the diagrams with known circuitry maps of the "stock" radars. They found them exactly the same. Since modifications would be needed to interfere with the UAVs, Rubeo could now be certain that hadn't happened.

Or rather, that those units hadn't done it. Because there was still a portion of the complex that had not been mapped. The section included a small shed and a trailer. The electronic map implied some sort of activity there—there were two power lines leading in—but the rest was open for interpretation.

Or imagination. Unable to rule anything out, most people tended to think of the worst. It was an interesting human prejudice, Rubeo knew, but one even he couldn't escape.

Would a jamming unit fit in the trailer?

Absolutely. The devices the Russians had deployed near the Georgian border to deter spying UAVs were about that size.

If they were there, wouldn't the Libyans have used them to deter the attack?

Perhaps. But that was just it—a guess, not definitive proof.

"Guys could use some rest," suggested Jons.

Rubeo turned to him. He'd been concentrating so fully on the problem that he forgot where he was.

"Halit up there keeps nodding off," added Jons. "If we stop out here, away from the town, we'll be a little more secure. Sleep until the afternoon. You wanted to see the place in the day."

"Yes," said Rubeo, coming back fully to the present. "Let's find a place."

3

Over southern Libya

GRIZZLY'S PLANE WAS AHEAD OF TURK, TO HIS RIGHT, just below eleven o'clock. It looked OK, rising in the sky.

He escaped.

He got lucky.

A black smudge appeared on the left side of the plane. It grew exponentially, surrounding the engine.

Flares floated below. Smoke trailed down to them, black and gray billowing in a mad stream.

"Grizzly! Get out!" Turk yelled over the radio.

"I have the plane," replied the other pilot.

"Your left engine—there's black smoke pouring out of it."

"Yeah, I got a problem there. You get those guys?"

"Negative." Turk was in no position to take a shot at them and wasn't about to leave the other pilot simply to get revenge.

"I told you to watch those people on the hill."

"They were kids. They weren't the problem."

"I'm coming through one thousand feet," said Grizzly. "Still climbing."

"Think about getting out," said Turk. "Are you sure you got it?"

"I got it."

Turk told the controller what was going on. He wanted the helicopter that had just made the pickup to stand by in case the Hog went down.

Grizzly jettisoned the last of his missiles, lightening his load. He was at 3,000 feet, still climbing, though slowly.

He had sky under his wings. Maybe he could make it.

He's going *to make it,* Turk told himself.

Besides the engine, the A–10 had been hit in the wing and tail. There was damage to its control surfaces. Grizzly reported a small leak in the hydraulic system. He'd also taken a few splinters to the side of his windscreen.

"Nice little spiderweb on the left side," he told Turk. "Almost artistic."

Turk plotted a course farther east that would get them away from most of the government forces. The trade-off was that it would increase the amount of time it would take to get home.

"I'd rather take my chances in a straight line," said Grizzly. "If we go too far east, I'm going to run out of fuel anyway."

"Be better if you could get higher," Turk told him.

"No shit. I'm trying."

Turk rode in and took a look at the left wing. He was stunned at what he saw—it looked like something had taken a bite out of the last five feet. The rest of the metal was ripped and gouged.

"You got a bunch of holes," was how he described it to Grizzly. "How's your fuel?"

"Gauge says I'm good."

"The tank on the left wing?"

"Full."

Turk doubted that the reading was correct. He hesitated to say anything, however—for all he knew, the aircraft itself didn't know, and saying something would break the spell.

"I think it's optimistic," he said finally.

"You see fuel coming out?"

"Negative."

"Bladders might have contained the damage." The A–10's tanks were equipped to stop leaks.

"Maybe. We're coming up toward the Castle," Turk added. "You're gonna have to cut east. There's no way you're going to make it. You're still way under ten thousand feet."

The Castle was a government-held town that had gained its nickname early in the conflict because it was so well armed. While the antiaircraft launchers stationed there had been bombed repeatedly, it was thought that the government still had a number hidden in the city. Besides those weapons, there were ZSU antiaircraft guns, which posed a serious threat to a low-flying aircraft.

The air boss had vectored a pair of Spanish F–16s south to provide cover. Turk checked in with them, giving them a rundown of the situation. They could deal with a major antiair site, but Turk was more worried about a MANPAD or even an overachieving triple-A battery. By the time one of those was spotted, it might be too late.

"You have to come more east," he told Grizzly.

"I'm working on it. Having a little trouble steering. It's really fighting me."

"Copy."

"I don't want to have to bail out," added Grizzly.

"I know. I'm with you."

"I don't like the idea of parachuting, Turk. The only times I've done it, I puked."

"It's better than the alternative."

"I don't know."

Turk realized that the other pilot was worried his plane would fall apart if he stressed it at all, even in a slight bank. While he sympathized, he couldn't see an alternative.

"We gotta turn, Grizzly. You aren't gonna make it otherwise."

"I should have some sort of wise-ass comeback here, shouldn't I?" asked Grizzly. He put the Hog into a gentle bank eastward.

Grizzly made the turn. The plane stuttered, but leveled off. A few minutes later, still south of the Castle, Turk noticed its rear tail surface was shaking up and down.

"Grizz?"

"I'm going to have to get out," answered the

other pilot. "I'm sorry. We just aren't going to do it today."

"It's cool."

"I'm going to try to get a little farther north."

"Don't hold it too long," said Turk.

"Yeah, yeah, I know."

The helicopter that had picked up the last SAS men was about ten miles farther east, and the AWACS controller had another SAR helicopter coming south. The F–16s had been joined by a flight of Eurofighters for air cover. And Shooters One and Two, having just completed their refuel, were heading in their direction as well.

Turk got a radar indication. Something at the Castle was beaming them.

"You see that?" he asked Grizzly.

"Yeah. Bitchin'."

The radar was a SURN 1S91 "Straight Flush" used for target acquisition by SA–6s—not particularly welcome under the circumstances.

The F–16s immediately went to work. But that didn't make the sweat factor any less for Grizzly or Turk. They flipped on ECMs, hoping to confuse any missile that might be launched.

But Grizzly had other problems.

"My other engine's ramping down," he said.

"I'm seeing smoke from the right side," said Turk, noticing a wisp near the wing root.

"Ah, shit, I got a lot of problems here," said Grizzly. "Panel looks like a goddamn Christmas tree. Controls not responding. Damn."

Something flew off the right wing.

"Grizzly—out! Now! Your wing's coming

apart," said Turk. He was shouting over the radio. "Time to get out. Go! Go!"

"Left engine failing. I think the fuel pump or something is going."

There was the understatement of the year, thought Turk. "Time to bail, damn you."

"I want a couple more miles."

"Get out now while you can. I'm seeing flames."

"Got another warning."

"I'm going to shoot you out if you don't pull that damn handle," cursed Turk.

The answer was a small explosion from the aircraft as Grizzly abandoned his plane. A second later the A–10E's right wing flew apart. The plane jerked hard to the left, then fell into a spin as flames enveloped the fuselage.

Turk banked, watching the parachute descend. As he took his first turn, he got a launch warning—a trio of SA–6s had been fired in his direction.

His first thought was to get away from the parachute—he didn't want Grizzly to be hurt by the missiles. It wasn't necessarily rational—the odds of the missile hitting the pilot were exceedingly small—but he nonetheless reacted automatically, pushing away from the falling canopy. He then turned to try and beam the missile's radar—putting the plane on a ninety degree angle to lessen the odds of it tracking him. He fired metal chaff, accelerating, and finally pushing down hard on his wing.

One of the missiles tanked, pushing down into the desert, where it blossomed in a mushroom of dirt and spent explosive. The other two sailed well past the Hog, losing it in the fog of electronic countermeasures.

Turk turned back in Grizzly's direction, hunting for the parachute. It wasn't where he thought it would be. His heart lurched and a hole opened in his stomach: Where the hell was his wingmate?

Finally he found the chute, farther east than he had thought. That was a good thing—it was farther from the city.

"I have a chute," he told the AWACS. "A good chute. He's looking good. I have him."

A fireball rose from the direction of the city. The missile battery that targeted him had just been hit by radiation-tracking missiles.

Turk settled into a wide orbit above the parachute. The AWACS vectored in more support aircraft; the SAR helicopter and the Blackhawk with the SAS soldiers both headed for a rescue.

Turk spotted a pair of pickup trucks coming from the direction of the city. He dropped low and accelerated, heading in their direction.

"I have two trucks approaching the landing area," he told the controller.

"Roger that. We're seeing them."

"I'm hitting them."

"Stand by," said the controller.

The ROEs directed that Turk could only shoot at the trucks if they took hostile action. But there was no question in his mind what he was going to do. He rolled toward them.

I should have hit the kids earlier.

But they were kids.

"Shooter Four, you are not authorized to engage."

"Give me a break," snapped Turk.

"Repeat?"

"I'm going to protect my guy."

"Shooter, you are not cleared to engage. We have them under surveillance."

Where the hell was your surveillance when he was hit? Turk thought. But he didn't say that. He forced himself to be logical—got back inside his calm pilot head.

"I'm going to check them out," he told the AWACS.

"Predator is overhead," said the controller. "We are looking at the truck. No hostile activity or indication at this time."

Turk tucked the A–10E toward the ground, riding up parallel to the road. The trucks were ahead.

"Shooter Four, this is Shooter One," said Ginella over the radio. Her voice was sharp. "Say your status."

"Checking out two trucks headed in Grizzly's direction, Colonel," responded Turk.

"Be advised, Big Eyes is telling us those are civilian trucks. You are not to engage. Repeat. Do not engage."

"Negative," said Turk, who was now close enough to see the vehicles. "Both have men in the back. Uniforms."

"Don't shoot them, Turk. You are not cleared."

He flashed by.

"Shooter Four, what's your status?" asked the controller.

Turk didn't respond. He pulled the Hog around, checked the air around him, looked at the ground, then put the A–10's nose directly over the road.

If he wanted, he could take both trucks with his gun in short order.

And maybe he should do that.

Was he compensating for having screwed up earlier? But he hadn't screwed up—he'd done the right thing. They had been kids. Surely.

He knew what he saw. And yet the other Hog had been hit by a missile. The facts were the facts.

"Turk, acknowledge," said Ginella. "Where are you and what are you doing?"

"I'm looking at them. The trucks. They're on the road. They're a mile from where Grizzly's coming down. Going in that direction."

He was sure they must be soldiers—rebels wouldn't be coming out from the Castle.

Maybe they'd shoot at him. He pressed the plane down, went over the trucks at barely fifty feet.

No flash, no launch warning. Not a peep.

By the time he banked away, the trucks had stopped dead in the road. Both made quick U-turns and headed back in the direction they'd come.

"Still think they're sightseers, huh?" said Turk.

"Not the point, Shooter Four," responded Ginella.

"I have helicopters inbound," said Turk, spotting the approaching birds. He could hear them calling Grizzly on the Guard or emergency band. Grizzly acknowledged, then waved.

"SAR assets in contact," reported Turk. "They're in contact."

"Let the choppers do their work," said Ginella.

"That's my plan."

SHOOTER SQUADRON ESCORTED THE HELICOPTER TO the coast, then split away as the chopper headed for the Italian carrier *Garibaldi*.

Turk got a fuel warning when he was still twenty miles from Sicily. He contacted the tower and the entire squadron was bumped up, allowing him to land right away.

He pulled himself out of the cockpit, feeling as if every part of his body had been pounded.

Ginella met him on the tarmac.

"What the hell happened?" she asked.

"We were north of the hamlet. They'd just made the pickup of the SAS guys." Turk held his hands wide, trying to sort it out in his head. It had been so vivid when it happened, yet now it seemed clouded. "There was a group of kids—"

"Start from the beginning. What happened with the SAS guys? Did they find the pilot?"

Turk realized he wasn't even sure, though in fact they had. As he recounted the story, he realized he had either blanked out or simply forgotten vast portions.

Given how much debriefing he'd been doing over the past few days, he ought to be getting better at this, but for some reason it seemed worse.

More details would occur to him as he went, and he had to backtrack and revise.

"How did you let him get hit?" she asked finally.

"I—I didn't let him get hit," said Turk. "He turned right. I told him to break left. He went into their path."

Would that have saved him, though? Turk wasn't sure.

She shook her head.

"The only people I saw on the ground were kids," added Turk.

"Kids with a launcher?"

"No. Absolutely not."

Ginella stared at him.

"You think I screwed up?" he said.

"You didn't see the missile on the ground?"

"I saw kids. That's what I saw."

She turned and walked away without saying anything else.

4

Tripoli

KHARON'S COLLABORATION WITH THE RUSSIANS HAD brought him any number of complications over the years, and he knew better than to trust them any more than absolutely necessary. And so while he could have asked Foma to arrange for access to

Russian satellite intelligence on the war, he decided it was much safer to simply steal it.

Russian hackers were arguably the best in the world at getting into secure systems, even better than the Chinese groups that tended to dominate news reports. But the security on the Russian government's own systems left much to be desired. The feed sent to certain Spetsnaz units in Chad and southern Libya used a common and easily defeated encryption. Getting past it was child's play.

Finding that out had taken a bit of work on Kharon's part, but now he enjoyed the benefits, looking at near real-time satellite images as they were relayed to the unit. He sat at the console in his university lair, flipping through the quadrants as they loaded.

Nothing much had changed in the past two weeks. The reinforced lines were still where they had been for days. The only exception was in the east, where a number of tanks were poised to strike near Sawknah, a small city liberated by the rebels early in the war. Wisps of black smoke drifted in the area.

Zooming in for detail, Kharon could see irregular troops lining the ruins at the southwest corner of the road. The buildings immediately behind them were badly battered. Many were heaps of rubble. The one three-story that remained intact on that side of the street had several men on the roof, obviously snipers.

It was impossible to predict the outcome of the battle from the image. But the fact that the government felt strong enough to fight back there surprised Kharon. Everything he had seen to this point had led him to think they were not only losing, but on their last legs. But launching an attack some two hundred miles from their strong point implied they were stronger than he believed.

The government leadership had just been shaken up as well. Maybe there was life left in them after all.

But Kharon was not really interested in the direction of the war; he was looking for Rubeo.

He delved into the Russian intelligence bulletins, searching out information. The name didn't jump out. Nor were there details about the UAV incident. The Russians seemed not to care about it—at least not tactically.

That made sense. It had little impact on anything the Russian special ops troops would be involved in.

One odd thing stood out—the government had fired antiair missiles overnight in the same area where the Sabre UAVs had operated. They had claimed they shot down two aircraft, but NATO had not acknowledged any losses.

A coincidence?

Kharon went back to the satellite imagery, examining the grids linked to the summary.

He spotted two large pickups parked well off the road behind a ridge of sand and rock. There were tents nearby.

He zoomed to the trucks. They were large American vehicles, unlike the small Japanese models common in the region.

Rubeo?

It had to be.

Damn, he thought. Right under my nose.

5

Sicily

"LOOKS LIKE DREAMLAND ISN'T THE SUPERHERO HE'S cracked up to be," said Paulson when Turk walked into the squadron's ready room.

"What the hell does that mean?" snapped Turk.

"It means what it means."

"That's enough," said Ginella. She was at the front of the room, poring over a paper map.

"Excuse me," said Paulson. "I didn't mean to insult teacher's pet."

"Knock it off, John." Ginella went to the coffeepot at the side of the room, walking between the two men. She poured herself a cup, even though the coffee was clearly cold. Everyone else took a seat.

They went through the squadron debrief mechanically. All of the squadron's pilots and a lot of the enlisted personnel, including Beast and the others who were still suffering from the flu, came in to hear what had happened.

Turk had always felt a bit like an outsider, but it was worse now, much worse. No one said anything, but he felt that they were all blaming him for Grizzly being shot down.

What could he say?

It wasn't his fault. But that sounded lame. Better to keep quiet.

He played the scene over and over in his head, trying to re-create what had happened. No matter how he tried, he couldn't see a missile, or any weapon for that matter—nor a shadow that looked like one.

The bastards had hidden it somehow.

"Grizzly will be back tomorrow," announced Ginella. "I spoke to him right after I landed. He claims he's going to steal a helicopter off the Italians if they don't let him go. I'm sure they will send him back—it sounds like he's eating them out of house and home."

The others began applauding. Somehow, that just made Turk feel worse. He slipped out the door, heading in the direction of his car.

He was already in the lot when his phone began to vibrate. Dreading talking to Ginella or anyone else, he hesitated before pulling it out.

It wasn't a call. It was his calendar, reminding him of the appointment he'd made to play soccer with the kids.

Dead tired, all he wanted to do was pour himself into the car and go home to the hotel. He walked to the car, unlocked it, and got in.

His key was almost in the ignition when he pulled it back, deciding he just couldn't blow off the kids. Ten minutes of running around—even twenty—weren't going to make him that much more tired than he was.

Hell, maybe he'd just call a taxi anyway. Get a ride to the hotel, grab a few beers and collapse.

Turk walked over to the day care center, where the children were just coming out for their recreation break. The boys' shouts cheered him up, and for the next half hour he forgot how tired he was, how depressed he was, how out of sorts he'd been. He laughed and joked with the children, lost in the game. When he was done, he told them he would be back, though this time he was smart enough not to make an exact appointment.

Turk went to the fence, preparing to hop over. Li was standing there, a big grin on her face.

"Playing soccer again?" she said.

"Uh, they're playing. I'm more of a spectator."

"You seemed to be holding your own."

"Thanks." He put one foot in the chain links, then lifted the other over the top bar. Tired but determined not to fall on his face in front of her, he lifted his body over, sliding down slowly.

"I'm sorry about what happened with Grizzly," said Li.

"Yeah."

In an instant his spirits sagged. Not only did his fatigue return, but he felt depressed and defensive.

"I heard Paulson talking," Li told him. "He was out of line. Everyone knows you did what you could."

"I guess everybody thinks I screwed up. That I missed the missile."

"No one thinks that," said Li. "We all know you would have done everything you could."

"I was—I flew right over that group, a couple of times," said Turk. "I was close to them—there was no weapon there. I was close enough to see that they were kids, you know? Older than these guys"—he gestured toward the children in the yard—"but still kids. And there wasn't a gun. Let alone a rocket launcher."

If he'd been in the Tigershark, the aircraft's AI sections would have ID'ed the weapon for him.

Maybe he'd grown lazy, relying on the machine to do his job.

"I really didn't see anything," he said.

Li's eyes seemed to have grown larger.

With disbelief, he thought.

"I gotta go," he said, turning in the direction of his car.

"Hey. Wait. Captain—" Li trotted after him.

"People are pissed because I took their slot, I guess," said Turk. "I'm sorry—if I thought those kids were a threat, believe me, I would have shot at them. With or with permission."

"You would have shot at children? Even with a launcher?"

Turk pressed his lips together. The truth was, he would have a hard time doing that, even with permission.

But if he'd seen a missile launcher, if he'd seen something capable of taking down a plane, he would have done it. Definitely. To protect a fellow pilot.

"I just . . . didn't see anything."

"You have kids?" Li asked.

"I'm not married."

"You don't have to be married to have kids," she said.

"Duh," he said sarcastically.

She frowned and started to turn away.

"Hey, no, I'm sorry." Turk reached out for her arm. She drew back, but stopped. "I didn't mean— I'm just—I'm tired and I guess— I'm just tired."

"I know." She nodded.

"This, and the village before. I had nothing to do with that. I—I shot down those planes. Nobody thinks about that."

"I think they do, Turk. I think you should lighten up on yourself."

She had an incredibly beautiful face.

"You want to get a drink or something?" he asked. "My car's in the lot. We can go and—"

"I'm on duty," she told him. "I was just taking a break to see what the day care center needed."

"Oh."

"Maybe later. You look like you could use some sleep."

"Yeah. OK. Later." He took a step toward the car.

"What time?" she asked.

"Time?"

"What time do you want to meet?"

"How's dinner?"

"Dinner would be nice."

"Can you get to my hotel? The restaurant

there's pretty nice. Or we could go into Catania. It's a nice little city. They look like they got a couple of restaurants and things."

"Oh, Catania would be great. I haven't been there yet. But how do we get there?"

"I can borrow a car," said Turk. "There's a bunch allotted to the personnel at the hotel, and there's always one or two open at night."

"That would be fantastic."

"I'll pick you up at your hotel around seven. OK?"

"That'd be great. Real great."

UP UNTIL THE MOMENT HE DROVE INTO THE PARKING lot of Li's hotel, Turk didn't give Ginella a thought at all. But as soon as he saw the lit lobby, he was filled with dread, worrying that he would run into her.

Would she be jealous?

Of course.

But maybe not. They were just having a flirty thing, nothing important.

Would she see it that way?

He pulled the car around to the far side of the lot, then took out his cell phone. He didn't have Li's phone number, but the hotel desk agreed to connect him to her room. She answered on the fourth ring, just as the call would have gone to voice mail.

"This is Turk," he told her. "Are we still on?"

"Of course." She sounded surprised that he would even ask.

"Are you ready?"

"I was just on my way down."

"I'll be at the front door in like, zero three minutes," he said.

"I'll meet you in the lobby."

He hesitated, thinking of Ginella.

"OK," he told her finally, deciding it was more important to keep Li happy. "I'll be there."

Even so, he waited a full ten minutes before getting out of the car. He could feel his heart starting to pound as he walked around to the driveway, and by the time the automatic door at the front swung open, his pulse was approaching a hundred beats per minute.

Ginella wasn't there. Li greeted him with a smile, and they went out quickly to the car.

THE SICILIAN CITY WAS EVEN NICER WITH SOMEONE TO share it with. They walked around for more than an hour, checking out the menus posted outside the restaurants. Never picky about food, Turk would have agreed to go into the very first place, a modest-priced *ristorante* promising "Roman style" cooking. But Li was more of a foodie, and insisted on checking as many places as possible. She didn't just look at the menus; she glanced inside, and eyeballed the diners as well.

"You can judge a lot about a restaurant by who eats there," she told him. "What we want is a place that the locals eat at."

"How do we know that they're local?"

"You can tell if they're Italian," she said. "Look at the clothes. The shoes, especially."

Once she had pointed it out, differences became very noticeable. A lot of people wore jeans, just as they did, but they had different hues and washes, and tended to be fairly new. The shoe styles were very different, and even the way people walked could give them away.

"I was a psych major in college," Li told him. "Reading people is more sociology—you can tell a lot by what they're wearing, and just the forms of how they interact."

"Can you tell that much about me?"

"I can figure out a few things," she said. "But it's no fair in your case—I already know you."

"What do you know?"

"I know you're a good pilot. And a good person."

"I could say the same about you."

"Could you?" Li laughed. It was a little girl laugh, innocent. Aside from the jeans, she was wearing a thick knit sweater that coddled her neck. She couldn't have looked prettier to him if she were wearing a flowing gown.

They circled through downtown, Li studying the menus, Turk studying her.

"How did you get from psychology to flying Hogs?" he asked.

"You don't think flying Warthogs takes a lot of psychology?"

"Seriously."

"I was in an ROTC program. That's how I paid for college. But I was always going to be a pilot."

"Or a psychologist?"

"Not at first. I was in engineering. You wouldn't believe the red tape switching." The corners of her mouth turned up with a quick smile. "But I was also thinking that maybe I would use it, if I didn't make it as a pilot. And maybe down the road."

"Are you going to psychoanalyze me?"

She laughed, a long, warm laugh. "I don't think so."

They settled on a small restaurant whose menu was entirely in Italian. The waiter tried explaining the dishes, patiently answering Li's questions. Turk ended up with a fish dish, even though he thought he had ordered beef. He barely tasted the food, completely entranced by the woman he was sharing the meal with. Everything Li said seemed interesting—she talked about her hometown in Minnesota, about the fact that she had been adopted, about the grudging acceptance of other pilots because she was a woman.

She could have talked about differential calculus and he still would have hung on every word.

His phone rang during dinner. He pulled it out, and not recognizing the number, decided to let it go to voice mail. Then he turned the phone off.

Driving back to her hotel, he searched for some reason to keep the night going. He asked if she wanted to hit the bar. She said she was tired and wanted to turn in.

He let that hang there—it wasn't an invitation, and in the end he simply said good night.

When she hesitated for a moment before reaching for the door handle, he wondered whether he should kiss her. But the moment passed.

He rolled the window down and called after her. "I'll see you tomorrow."

"I hope so," she told him, before turning and going inside.

BACK AT HIS HOTEL, TURK CHECKED HIS VOICE MAIL. He'd missed three calls—all from the same number. Belatedly, he realized it was Ginella's.

She'd left only one message.

"Where are you?" she said, her voice raspy and tired. "I thought I'd see you tonight."

Breaking things off wasn't going to be easy. He turned in, leaving it for another day.

6

al-Hayat, Libya

WHEN RAY RUBEO WAS EIGHT YEARS OLD, A COUSIN'S house had caught fire and burned to the ground. Rubeo visited the house the day after, as a bulldozer tore down what was left. A metallic smell hung in the air, mixing with the diesel exhaust of the Cat. His cousin's family stood around, eyes glassy as they watched the dozer work through what had been their home for more than a decade. There had not been time to rescue any of their belongings. Toys and clothes and furniture were jumbled in the flotsam.

The smell and the emptiness returned to him now as he walked through the ruins of the buildings hit by the Sabre's missiles. The ruins hadn't been touched since immediately after the attack, when the victims were pulled out. Now the bricks were being salvaged; two young boys were piling them on one side. Otherwise the area was deserted.

"Seen enough?" asked Jons.

"Not yet."

"I don't want to stay too long," said the bodyguard. "We stand out here."

"Understood."

Rubeo walked along the narrow street at the center of the attack, coordinating what he saw with what he remembered from the map. With the exception of a pair of buildings at the eastern end, where a fire had started and then spread, the rubble petered out at the edges of the street and three alleys that intersected the target area. That meant the computer had identified the buildings as targets.

Which he already knew.

Or did he? Because really, looking at the targeting information, they simply assumed that the computer had deliberately gone after a building. But it could just as easily have been looking at pure GPS coordinates.

It was a subtle, subtle distinction. Given the coordinates, the targeting section would look at the building, and go from there.

Significant?

Certainly this had not been a random act—the house was struck perfectly.

No, that didn't mean it wasn't random. That just meant the house was struck perfectly. Because in theory, to the machine there was no difference in the coordinates for an empty desert.

Not true—the machine took the coordinates and looked at them, deciding if it was a building or a tank or whatever. It then worked from there.

To an investigator coming in later, it would look purposeful. But that didn't mean it necessarily was.

If it had been given an empty desert, it wouldn't have attacked at all. But given a location with a house . . .

Rubeo played with his earring. The mission had been programmed in. Assuming there was no interference, what had happened could be explained by a change in the navigation system that made the Sabre think it was several miles away from its intended target, *and* by an override to the targeting computer that put the strike into dumb mode—in other words, turned off the target recognition feature. Two separate events that someone would have to beam in.

Dumb mode wasn't on. It hit the house—it was going to a target.

Maybe by accident. Or not accident exactly, but whoever had worked out the coordinates knew it would be close enough to look deliberate.

To reprogram it, you'd have to physically access the system. You'd need a fairly sophisticated knowledge of the Sabres as well as the computing system.

No. You could do it with a sophisticated knowledge of the Flighthawk GPS and backup system, which was the model for the Sabres. In fact, it was essentially the same, ported over with minor changes to account for the hardware.

How would you figure that?

Easy—look through the Air Force bids relating to the project. If you had access to different defense contractors.

So you're in. How do you get to dumb mode in the targeting section?

Easy—just flip a software switch. But you had to know it was there.

Hmmmph.

Interference, but an extremely sophisticated form.

Hard to get all of that data into the aircraft via the GPS channel. And then you had to erase it.

Rubeo worked the problem out in his mind, seeing the lines of code he would need to write if he were the one introducing the problem.

No, that was the wrong approach. Too complicated. It assumed too much knowledge.

Go back to the random theory. What if rather than playing with the software, which was always recorded, you attacked the hardware—if you changed the voltage to a particular circuit, you might be able to change the targeting mechanism. If you affected the GPS sensor for a short period of time, you could send the aircraft to a new location.

Was that all you needed?

He wasn't sure. He tried picturing the different circuitry in his mind. One thing he did know, however: when the system returned to normal, there would be no trace.

Who would go to that kind of trouble, though? With that much knowledge, wouldn't you just reprogram the unit to fly to wherever you wanted it? The Chinese would pay dearly for it.

Rubeo jerked his head around as he heard something fall nearby. The bricks had fallen on the two boys working on the wall.

He ran toward them, Jons right behind.

The Filipino who'd been watching that side of the perimeter got there first. One of the child's legs was pinned by the rubble. He scooped the material off and lifted the boy gently out. He put him down on the dirt nearby, then swung his rifle up and took a guard position a few feet away.

Rubeo found the second kid dazed but apparently unharmed. He lifted him by the shoulders and deposited him next to his friend.

"Are you hurt?" he asked the child.

The kid looked too shocked to talk.

Jons called over Halit, who had been back by the car with Lawson. The translator took a stern tone with two kids, immediately beginning to berate them for playing in the ruins.

"Don't yell at them," snapped Rubeo. "Find out if they're all right."

"They are fine. Look at them." Halit waved his hands as if he was an exasperated crossing guard. "These vermin are always wandering where they don't belong. They are worse than monkeys. Monkeys would have more manners."

"Ask them," said Rubeo.

Halit began to question them. Neither boy spoke, clearly intimidated. Rubeo went to the kid whose legs had been pinned under the rubble and helped him to his feet. There was a bit of blood near the right knee. Rubeo started to roll up the pants leg; the boy jerked back.

"Tell him we'll fix his leg," he told Halit.

"See? He is already OK. He moves around like a monkey. Faking."

"I have a first aid kit," said Lawson. "Let me see him."

Lawson rolled up the boy's pants, exposing some scrapes and minor scratches. A thick welt was already shaded purple on his shin. Lawson took out a bacteria wash and cleaned the cuts and scrapes. The boy barely reacted, even though the antiseptic must have stung.

"Let's see you walk a little, fella," said Lawson. When the child didn't react, the former Ranger began mimicking what he should do. He added a few words in Arabic, then pretended to be a toy soldier or robot—it wasn't clear to Rubeo which—bouncing around back and forth.

The child laughed. He took a few steps, apparently not greatly harmed.

"See, laughter is the best medicine," said Lawson.

"Let's take them home," said Rubeo.

"Good idea?" asked Jons, in a tone that suggested the exact opposite.

"Ask them where they live," Rubeo told Halit. "And say it in a way that gets us a correct answer, or you may find it difficult to walk yourself."

THE BOYS WERE COUSINS, BUT LIVED TOGETHER IN A small apartment complex a few blocks away. Five stories tall, with walls of large brown bricks and a stucco material, the buildings were not much different than what might be seen in Europe or even parts of America. The Gaddafi government had erected similar developments throughout the country, awarding them occasionally to the poor, but more often to families connected in some way to the power structure.

The interior hall of the building was clean, and smelled of some sort of disinfectant. But the disrepair was obvious as soon as they were through the door. The elevator, its door scratched and pockmarked with indentations, was out of order. The railing next to the stairs leaned at an angle, missing several supports. The floor tiles were cracked and pitted.

Lawson, with the two boys in tow, led the way up the stairs to the third floor, where they lived. By now he and the kids were great friends, so much so that they ran to the door and pushed it open, shouting to their family that they had found rich Americans. Halit was clearly nervous, hesitating near the door as Rubeo took off his shoes.

"You're coming in with us," Rubeo told him.

"Of course," said the man unhappily.

Lawson and the Filipino nicknamed Joker went first, followed by Jons, who stayed in the doorway until the other two had made sure the place was clear. Abas and the others stayed below.

Four girls and two women were crowded into the living room just off the small foyer. They were the only ones home; all the others were either out at school or work. From what Halit said, there were two families here, and a grandmother. The grandmother, who was in her early fifties, was in the living room and acted as the family spokesperson.

After the children had told their story, she went to the kitchen to prepare some food for the visitors. Rubeo had Halit tell her that they'd just been fed but would gladly like something to drink. Anything more, Rubeo realized, would undoubtedly mean the family wouldn't eat for a week.

The grandmother found two dusty bottles of an Italian soft drink, and served cups all around. Rubeo told Halit to find out what he could about the family, then to ask if the woman knew the people who had been killed in the bombing.

Halit balked.

"To ask this—it is difficult to know the reaction," said the translator.

"Tell her we want to help them."

"She won't believe you."

"Probably right, boss," said Jons.

"Then let's ask the kids," said Rubeo. "Have them take us to the families."

"There was a riot here the other day, Ray," said

Jons. "We've really pushed this far. Very far. I really don't think we should go any further."

"Fortunately, you're not the one making the decisions," said Rubeo.

7

Sicily

TURK WAS ON HIS WAY TO THE BASE WHEN DANNY Freah called him on his cell phone and told him to report to him ASAP.

"What's up, Colonel?" asked Turk.

"We'll discuss it when you get here."

Danny's tone made it clear that he should expect trouble, so when Turk walked into his office, he wasn't surprised by the colonel's stoic face—Freah's standard expression when things were going sour. The colonel wasn't a shouter—Turk couldn't remember him *ever* raising his voice. But in many ways his silent, unspoken disapproval was far worse.

"Have a seat, Captain," said Danny. He was sitting at a computer screen, and after giving Turk a brief but meaningful glare, turned back and resumed typing.

The wait was excruciating, but Turk knew the best thing to do was wait for the colonel to speak. Danny's keystrokes seemed to become harsher as he typed. Finally he was done. He sat back from the computer, crossed his arms, and swiveled in his seat.

"Half the NATO command thinks you are an irresponsible pilot willing to fire on civilians—" started Danny.

Turk cut him off. "No way."

"You had to be ordered several times not to open fire on civilian vehicles."

"I—I didn't shoot."

"And then there are people who think you withheld fire because you're afraid of hitting anything."

"What?"

Unfolding his arms, Danny reached across his desk for a piece of paper.

Turk took it and started to read. It was an e-mail detailing part of an after-action report about the A-10E "incident."

. . . despite having been cleared because of the earlier engagement, Captain Mako erroneously held fire. A few moments later there was a flash from the ground. The flash was the launch of an SA–14, fired from the group Captain Mako had passed. The missile or its shrapnel struck Shooter Three on the right side, disabling the engine and much of the control surfaces . . .

"That's bullshit," said Turk. "That's total bullshit. Who's saying this?"

"Check the heading."

The e-mail was from Colonel Ernesto.

"Ginella said this? No, no way. No way," sputtered Turk. "I couldn't assume that I was cleared to fire—that's totally missing the intent of the ROEs. Even if I saw a weapon—"

"Did you see a weapon?"

"No," Turk insisted. "No. If I had seen a weapon, then—"

He stopped short. If he *had* seen a weapon, he would have fired. Even if it was a kid.

He would have, wouldn't he?

"She's giving me a heads-up as a courtesy," said Danny. "She said there may be an explanation, and she's not putting anything in writing until she talks to you."

Turk felt as if he'd been punched in the stomach. He had a feeling this had nothing to do with the incident itself, but rather Li.

Damn.

"Colonel, I swear. No one in that group was armed. I would have seen a missile launcher. I looked. I really looked."

"How fast were you going?" Danny asked.

"I don't remember."

"Three hundred knots?"

"No." Turk shook his head. "It would have been a lot slower than that."

"A hundred?"

"That's stall speed. A little faster." Turk shook his head. "Colonel, I know what I saw."

Danny frowned.

"You can't let her say that. It makes me look like . . . a coward."

"It's not up to me what she says."

Turk knew the e-mail was meant as blackmail. But he couldn't tell Danny that.

"You have to believe me. That's not what happened," he said. "They're saying crap about me because I'm not a member of the squadron. And for the record—I told Grizzly to break the other way. He turned right into it. It was dumb, not his fault, but . . . I mean—"

Danny put up his hand. "She's the one you have to talk to."

Turk shook his head.

"Are you saying you don't want to talk to her?" asked Danny.

"No—I'll talk to her. I'll talk to her."

"You want me to come with you?"

That wasn't going to work.

"It's all right. Thanks."

"In the meantime, you're not flying for anybody but Whiplash. You understand?"

"Yes, sir. That's fine."

DANNY WATCHED TURK LEAVE THE OFFICE. HE FELT bad for the kid—Ginella's e-mail was extremely harsh, even without the very strict rules of engagement they were operating under.

Technically, she was within her rights to go through with a report criticizing Turk. If she did, Danny would make sure it was countered somehow.

Still, the damage would be done. Better for Turk to talk her out of it himself.

On the other hand, was her implication

correct—had Turk missed the weapon? Had he seen it and dismissed it? It couldn't have just appeared suddenly.

Between that and the incident with the trucks, which the air commander had mentioned to him earlier, it seemed like the pilot was unduly stressed.

Understandable, he thought. He'd been there himself.

PAULSON WAS STANDING IN THE OUTER OFFICE WHEN Turk came in.

"Here's the Dreamland hotshot who nearly got Grizzly killed," said Paulson when he saw Turk in the hall. "Thanks a lot."

"Fuck you," snapped Turk.

"You gonna slug me?" asked Paulson.

Turk was sorely tempted.

"Mr. Paulson, that will do," said Ginella, coming to the doorway.

"We're all grounded, you know," Paulson told Turk. "Nice going, hotshot."

Turk felt his face warm.

"We're taking a breather, Captain," Ginella told Paulson. "Captain Mako, why don't you step into my office?"

"Yes, ma'am."

Turk went to the chair quickly and sat down. He watched Ginella close her door, then walk over to her desk.

She was all business. That was a relief.

Or was it?

"I understand you were out with Captain Pike last night," said Ginella, sitting down.

"We went to dinner."

"Had a good meal?"

"Yes."

"I'm glad."

"Listen—"

"I just spoke to Colonel Freah on the phone," said Ginella. "He showed you the e-mail, I understand."

"Yes, and it's bullshit," said Turk.

"Is it, Captain?"

"Absolutely. I told you what happened."

"If you didn't miss the missile, where did it come from?"

"I don't know." Turk clenched his fists, then struggled to unknot them. "I—it wasn't on that hill when I passed. There's no way it came from that hill."

"No way?"

"No. Maybe somebody climbed up there after I passed," said Turk. "I don't think so—it wasn't with the kids."

"You don't think they might have hidden the missile launcher somewhere?"

She was pushing this ridiculously hard. Turk wondered when she would drop the charade.

And what would he do then?

"Well? Could it have been hidden?" she asked.

"Maybe," said Turk reluctantly.

"I see."

Ginella's eyes bored into him. Turk tried to hold her stare but found he just couldn't. He blinked, looked down at the floor, then back up.

"You're worried that if the report is written this way, it'll hurt your career," said Ginella.

"It's not the truth. That's my concern."

"Understood. You can go, Captain."

"Are you going to change it?"

"I'm not sure what I'm going to do."

"But—"

"Dismissed, Captain. I don't need you in the squadron anymore. Thank you for your help."

"Listen, this is all—"

Ginella stared at him. What was she thinking? Was she actually trying to blackmail him? Or was she just being a tough commander? Grizzly thought he'd screwed up—maybe she was just taking his word over his own.

Most squadron leaders would let it go. On the other hand, if she really thought he had messed up, she did have a duty to press him on it.

But . . .

"What is it you want to say, Turk?" Ginella asked.

"I—I just want to say that I know what I saw."

"I'll take it into consideration."

Unsure what else to do, Turk started to leave.

"One last thing, Turk," said Ginella as he opened the door. "It's always best to answer your phone."

It took every ounce of his self-control not to slam the door on the way out.

8

al-Hayat

RUBEO HADN'T KNOWN EXACTLY WHAT TO EXPECT from the families hurt in the attack, but he thought he would see some outer sign of grief or at least chaos; if not direct mourning, then some sadness or grim resolve. But the family the boys took him to see were cheerful, happy, and grateful to have visitors.

Which was strange, because there were eight of them crammed into what looked like a 1960s travel trailer, the sort that would be used back in the States only as a derelict hunting shack, if not the target on a shooting range.

Two of the family members—the mother and a girl about three years old—had been wounded in the bombing, which damaged one wall of their house. The mother had a cast on her arm and her head was bandaged. The little girl's leg was in a cast. They spoke freely about the accident, telling Lawson—he had instantly made friends, with the help of the boys—about the disaster.

Rubeo listened attentively, interested in every detail. The sudden explosion, the darkness from the cloud, the grit falling down, the surge of fire—listening somehow made the strike more scientific to him, more real. If it was real, it could be understood more readily.

Curious neighbors began gathering outside. Jons was getting more and more agitated. He'd posted Abas and the Filipinos a short distance away, with their guns out, but the team would be very easily overcome if a large crowd gathered and became hostile.

"What about the other day?" Rubeo asked the woman. He made Halit translate. "Ask her about the riot."

"Thieves hired by the government. Many of them soldiers," said Halit.

Rubeo looked at Lawson. "More or less, I think," he told him.

"Find out if they have a bank account," said Rubeo.

"I can tell you without asking, they don't," said Halit.

"Look around," said Jons. "These people don't have anything."

Rubeo dug into his pocket for his roll. He unfolded ten ten-euro notes.

"See if you can find some contact information," he told Halit. Then he bent toward the grandmother and slipped the money into her hand.

"I have to go," he said as she stared wide-eyed at the bills.

"WHAT ARE YOU GOING TO DO?" JONS ASKED A FEW minutes later in the truck as they left the village, heading west in the direction of the missile site.

"We'll find the people who were victims," said Rubeo, "and get them new homes."

"The allies will handle compensation."

"What I do is independent of the government."

"Ray, this is not a good place."

"I'm not going to stay here and do it myself, Levon. You needn't worry."

"Yeah, OK, good. It's not a horrible idea."

Jons, clearly relieved, checked his mirrors quickly. They were in the lead, their escorts a few dozen yards behind.

"It's just going to be tough to figure out who truly deserves it, you know?" added Jons. "Once word gets out. Especially here, with the government crumbling. Everybody's going to have their hand out."

"It doesn't look particularly endangered to me," said Rubeo.

"Don't fool yourself. They don't have much of a grip. Things can turn around in an instant."

Rubeo looked out at the countryside, a vast roll of undulating sand. The encounter with the families had taken his mind off the problem of the UAV and what had gone wrong.

He wondered why he hadn't thought of helping the people before. It was an obvious thing to do.

Dog was right. That was why he suggested I come. He didn't say it, because he knew I would only appreciate it if I reached the conclusion myself.

So good at giving others advice, at balancing their problems against the world's. But he couldn't overcome his own demon.

His loss was far greater than theirs.

"I want to go back to the radar site," Rubeo told Jons. "There are two other structures I need to look at. I want to see what's in there."

"Inside them?"

"Yes. I need to know if they have equipment in them."

Jons frowned.

"You think that's a problem?" asked Rubeo.

"It's a big problem. We'll never get inside there. I don't even want to go close—they'll be on their guard after finding the two UAVs. We can't, Ray. Absolutely not."

"I wasn't considering marching up to the gate and demanding access," Rubeo told him.

What he had in mind, however, was every bit as dangerous—they would sneak in from the south side of the facility, go to the building, and inspect it firsthand. Ten minutes inside each should be enough to eliminate the possibility of anything having been beamed from it. Once that was done, he could pursue what he saw as the more promising theory. But interference had to be ruled out first.

"You're not going in," said Jons. "If I have to physically hold you back, you're not going in."

"Of course not. And I'm not going to risk you either. I intend to send a pair of bots in," Rubeo told him. "All we need is someone to get them past the fence."

"I don't know."

"Please—there are dozens of people who live in that little hamlet. None of them can be bribed to change places with someone?"

"Well, that we might be able to arrange."

"Good." Rubeo took out his phone and called up a satellite map. "There's a road ahead to the right that gets lost in the desert about two hundred yards north. If you are careful, we can drive across the desert and completely miss the gate. It'll save us considerable time."

"I don't think we need to be in a hurry."

"I do. The plane with the bots will land in Tripoli in four hours. We don't need to be there, but I don't want to wait too long before we retrieve them. Besides, if we get there quickly, we can get back in time to finish the probe by first light tomorrow. I'm sure you'll agree that the sooner we're out of this hellhole the better."

9

al-Hayat

HE'D MISSED HIM.

Kharon thumped his fist against the dashboard. He was tempted to yell at Fezzan, who'd taken so long getting them here, but he held his anger in check, not least of all because the two men in the back of the SUV were the driver's friends. He barely trusted them with weapons under the best of circumstances.

Meanwhile, the boy who told him that the Americans had left stood trembling by the car window, frozen in place by Kharon's retort at hearing the news.

"Are they coming back?" Kharon managed to ask.

The boy quickly shook his head.

"Go," said Kharon, dropping a few coins in front of the boy. "Go."

He rolled up the window. Rubeo had moved much more quickly than he had expected. But of course—this wasn't a fantasy anymore, this was reality. And the reality was that Rubeo was very, very good. Kharon couldn't afford to be sloppy, to play the child. He was a man and needed to act and think that way.

"What should I do?" asked Fezzan. "Where are we to go?"

"Find a place for them to eat," said Kharon, jerking his thumb. "Not too expensive."

The car bumped along to the north end of town. Fezzan drove as if he knew exactly where he was going, but Kharon could never really tell with him. Like many of the people he dealt with, the Libyan was an excellent bluffer.

Kharon had hoped to catch Rubeo in the ruins—it would have been easy to separate him from his bodyguards, especially with the others to help. The plan to embarrass him had been abandoned. It was too ambitious, and he had lost his patience besides. At this point he wanted only to kill and be done with life completely.

His anger had grown exponentially since the chance meeting in the hotel. Why was that? What alchemy had caused his anger to become so insane?

He was capable of recognizing that it wasn't rational, yet powerless to do anything about it. He couldn't blame it on any fresh insults or indignities; nothing compared to the death of his mother.

The restaurant was located in the ground floor of a small office building. There was a small crowd of people outside, perhaps a dozen, waiting to get in.

"Very popular place," said Fezzan. "Come. We will get in."

"You know the owner?" Kharon asked.

"I know what he likes."

Yes, of course, thought Kharon. Money. For enough, the man would undoubtedly kick out his own mother.

Kharon's phone buzzed as he got out of the car. It was Foma.

"Go ahead," he told the others. "I have to take this."

Kharon handed Fezzan a few bills, then walked a few steps away and held the phone to his ear.

"This is Kharon."

"Where are you?" asked Foma.

"Running an errand in the south."

"Are you still interested in what we spoke of?"

"Yes."

"Good. It happens that I know where your man is going."

Kharon felt his throat catch. He hadn't mentioned Rubeo specifically. The Russian was a step ahead of him.

"Where?" asked Kharon.

"He has a cargo flight landing at Tripoli very shortly," said Foma. "I would imagine he or his people will be there."

"No. He doesn't do that sort of thing himself."

"I would imagine that whatever is landing will reach him eventually," said Foma. "So even if he is not there, it is a way to find him. Unless that is what you are already up to."

"You can't just follow him," said Kharon. "He's clever. He has surveillance gear."

"I'm sure he has many things. Do you want to get him or not?"

"How do you know I'm looking for him?"

"I should have realized it long ago," admitted Foma. "But only when I thought of whom your parents had been did it become obvious."

Kharon glanced up at the empty street. All these preparations, and still he was blindsided at every turn. To work with Foma—truly the Russian was the devil.

But this was devil's work.

"Do you want to get him, or not?" asked Foma.

"Tell me how."

10

Sicily

DANNY FREAH TURNED FROM THE CREDENZA AT THE side of his office and held out the fresh cup of coffee to Zen. The two men had been friends since their Dreamland days, through a variety of ups and downs. Something about serving in combat together made for a deep relationship despite surface differences.

"I get the sense there's something going on between Turk and Ginella," said Danny. "But the kid won't say."

Zen took the coffee. "You sure he's just not blaming himself for the shoot-down?"

"Well, he seems pretty convinced that he wasn't at fault."

"What's that saying, 'protest too much'?"

"Maybe. I don't know." Freah poured himself a cup. Boston had managed to commandeer all the comforts of home: a working coffee machine, a minifridge, and two padded desk chairs. The place was still cramped, but it was habitable. "He's had a pretty stressful few days."

"He shot down four enemy fighters," said Zen. "That oughta have earned him some time off."

"I know." Danny took a sip of his coffee, then sat down. "We had to keep him around to help test the aircraft systems—I should have sent him home. He wanted to fly."

"Pilots *always* want to fly, Danny."

"He seemed to do pretty well with the Hogs. Ginella loved him—until this."

"Want me to talk to him?"

"Don't you have to fly to Libya with Zongchen?"

"I have a little time."

"Well." Danny wasn't sure what good, if any, that would do. But maybe Turk would open up to another pilot. "If you want to take a shot—I might be making too much of it. He just seemed, bothered, you know?"

"Uncle Zen has his shingle out." He adopted a fake Viennese accent. "But sometimes, Colonel, a banana is just a banana."

"I don't get the joke."

"Never mind. Probably there's nothing there. I'll talk to him and see."

"Thanks."

A HALF HOUR LATER ZEN FOUND TURK AT THE TIGER-shark's hangar. He paused for a moment, sitting near the door, watching the young pilot gaze contemplatively at the aircraft. Zen thought of himself doing the same thing, though under vastly different circumstances.

"Pretty plane," he said loudly as he rolled forward. He still wasn't comfortable with the chair. It seemed to steer a little harshly and pulled to one side.

"Um, hi, Senator."

"Fly as sweetly as they say?" asked Zen.

"It's pretty smooth, yeah," said Turk. "Once you're used to it. It's very quick. Doesn't have the brute thrust of the F–22, but it's fast enough. Because it's so small and light."

"You like lying down to fly?"

"It's more a tilt, really," said Turk. "Closer to the F–16 than you'd think."

"Cockpit looks pretty tight," said Zen. "Almost an afterthought."

"It was, pretty much. Just there to help them test it."

"You think you could just sit on the ground and fly it?"

"No." Turk scowled, his brow furrowing. He was thinking about the plane, Zen realized, gathering his actual impressions. "It's different being in the air, you know?"

Zen knew very well. "It's not easy to explain, is it? People always asked me about flying the Flighthawks. It was . . . hard to tell them, actually. Because you don't think about it when you're doing it. You just do it."

"Yeah."

"And you're not really separated from the plane. You don't *think* of yourself as separated," added Zen, correcting himself. "Because if you thought of it that way, you'd have less control."

Turk nodded. Zen turned and looked at the aircraft. It was rounded and thin, a beauty queen or model.

"Big difference between this and the A–10," he said.

"Oh yeah."

"What's that like?" asked Zen. "I never flew one."

"Oh. Uh, well, it's a really steady aircraft. It, um, pretty much will go exactly where you want. Very physical—compared to the Tigershark. In a way, for me, it's kind of closer to flying the Texan."

"The T–6 trainer? The prop plane?"

"Yeah, I know. But for me, that's kind of the parallel."

"I learned on a Tweet—the T–37. Great aircraft."

They traded a few stories about flying the trainers, solid and sturdy aircraft, perfect for learning the basics of flight. The planes were more forgiving than the flight instructors.

"There's nothing like feeling the plane move where you want it to move," said Zen finally. "Truth is, I could never look at a Flighthawk without feeling just a little bit of anger."

"Because of the accident?"

"Yeah."

Zen wheeled toward the Tigershark. "Flying was different once I lost my legs," he said, talking more to himself than to Turk. "At first, I did it more or less out of spite—I had to prove to the Air Force, to everyone, that I was still worth something. They didn't want me to come back. But they couldn't exactly bar me. They could keep me out of a cockpit, obviously, because I couldn't fly an F–15 or an F–22, or any real fighter. But the Flighthawks were different. My hands were still good. And my reflexes."

"It must have been tough," said Turk.

Zen slid his chair back to look at Turk. "Truth is, I was really, really angry. That helped. It gave me something to overcome. I like a fight." He laughed gently, making fun of himself, though he wasn't sure Turk would realize that. "How about you?"

"Like to fight? Well, I shot down those airplanes."

"Not that kind of fighting."

Turk pressed his lips together. He knew what Zen meant—dealing with the bureaucracy, with your superiors when they were being unfair or stubborn or both.

"Whatever you say is between you and me." Zen nudged his wheelchair a little closer. "Doesn't go out of this hangar. Nothing to your superiors."

"You're investigating the Sabres—"

"But not what happened with Shooter Squadron. What did happen?"

"I didn't see anything on the hill," said Turk. The words started slowly, then picked up speed. "I came across the ridge, checking. I had a good view of the kids there—"

"Kids?" asked Zen.

"They were definitely kids. There were all sorts of references on the ground. I could tell they were short—there was a bush, some vegetation. They were definitely kids."

"You were moving at a hundred and fifty knots?"

"A little slower."

"But you know what you saw."

"It's burned in my brain. If it was the Tigershark . . ."

Turk's voice trailed off, but Zen knew what he was thinking: the Tigershark's sensors were far wider than the A–10E's, and would have captured a full 360 degrees. The computer would have examined the figures for weapons. There'd be no doubt.

Something else was bothering Turk. Zen didn't know him very well, but he knew pilots, and he knew test pilots especially.

They were always sure of themselves. Granted, Turk was still pretty young. And back-to-back incidents like the ones Turk had been involved in had a way of shaking even the steadiest personality. But Turk was pretty damn positive about what he had seen.

So what else was troubling him?

TURK LOOKED AT THE EXPRESSION ON THE OLDER MAN'S face. He was serious, contemplative, maybe playing the engagement over in his mind. The recorded images from the A–10 had been inconclusive. That didn't help Turk.

Still, he knew what he had seen.

Didn't he? He couldn't repicture it in his mind now. With all this talk . . . maybe they were right.

No. No, it was just Ginella undermining him, trying to get him back.

Or had he really missed it? Had his eyes and mind played tricks?

"You think they're right?" Turk asked Zen. "You think I chickened out?"

"Chickened out? Who said that?"

"It's implied. Like I was too scared to fire at

enemy soldiers because of everything else that had happened."

"I don't think that would be a fair assessment, do you?"

"It'd be bull."

Zen studied him. "What did Colonel Ernesto say?" he asked.

Turk frowned. "She . . ." He shrugged.

"She what?"

Turk shook his head.

"What's the personal thing going on here, Turk?" asked Zen sharply.

"What do you mean?"

"What is it with you and Ginella? One day she's singing your praises, now she's tossing you under the bus. What did you do to her?"

Zen couldn't have surprised him more if he'd risen from the wheelchair and begun to walk on his own.

"What do you mean?" asked Turk.

"It's written all over your face. There's something personal here. What exactly is going on?"

"It's nothing bad."

"Whole story." Zen had the tone of a father interrogating a child sent home from school by the principal. "Now."

Reluctantly, Turk told Zen everything that had happened between him and Ginella, including her reaction to Li.

"There was never a quid pro quo, or anything like that," he added. "But it was, uh, awkward."

"Is that what's really bothering you?"

"I did *not* see a missile on that hill. She can say anything she wants, but I didn't see it. And I wasn't affected by the Sabres. I mean, it was bad and everything—it's terrible, but that wasn't my fault either."

IF TURK HAD BEEN A WOMAN, THE AFFAIR WOULD clearly be a problem for Ginella. A commanding officer couldn't have an affair with a subordinate, even one temporarily assigned.

But the role reversal blurred everything. Maybe it shouldn't—from a purely theoretical sense, a colonel was a colonel, and a captain was a captain. But in real life, old prejudices died hard. A man simply wasn't viewed as a victim of sexual harassment, no matter what the circumstances.

And in truth, that wasn't necessarily the case—not legally, at least. Ginella hadn't explicitly threatened Turk's career.

The real problem wasn't Ginella, it was Turk. Maybe he hadn't blamed himself for the Sabre accident, but Zen remembered him being troubled when he landed. Maybe he'd just missed the missile on the hill—at that speed and height, it wouldn't be surprising at all. But whatever had happened, he was definitely second guessing himself now.

Fighter pilots couldn't have that. In the darkest moment, you needed to know you could trust yourself. You needed to be able to just *do*, not think.

"Are you afraid Colonel Ernesto's going to screw up your career?" Zen asked.

"I don't know," admitted Turk. "I guess what I'm really—what really bugs me is somebody saying I'm a coward."

"If you missed a missile, that wouldn't make you a coward. That idea shouldn't even enter your mind."

"Well."

"Seriously. It's bull. And I don't think you missed it."

"Thanks."

"Don't worry about Ginella," Zen told the pilot.

"You're not going to say anything to her, are you?"

"Nothing that doesn't need to be said."

11

Tripoli

THE MACHINE CALLED ARACHNE STOOD BARELY HALF A foot tall with its six legs fully extended, and could easily hide behind a crumpled piece of newspaper. The work module on top was smaller than a watch face, but its interchangeable sensors were more powerful than even the most advanced timepiece. One provided a 360-degree IR image, another an optical image in 10^{-4} lux.

In the rarefied world of advanced robots, Arachne was a superstar—or would have been, had anyone been allowed to boast of her prowess. The "bot," as Rubeo and his people referred to her, was a hand-built terrestrial spy, able to do things that human spies could only dream of. Developed privately, she was still undergoing testing before being offered for sale to the CIA.

Where better to give her a realistic test than in Libya?

Rubeo finished the bench calibration on the third and final sensor, more critical in this application than the others—a magnetometer that mapped currents. The device had to be carefully calibrated, then gingerly handled until it was locked on the unit. The procedure was relatively straightforward for the techies who worked with it routinely, but unusual enough that the man who invented the device had to proceed extremely slowly.

Rubeo finished his checks, locked out the options panel, and then killed the power to the unit. He unscrewed it gingerly and brought it over to the bot, which was sitting on the bench in the hangar across from the larger transport bot, Diomedes.

Also invented by Rubeo's company, a version of Diomedes was already in operation with Whiplash and the U.S. military. The Greek name was used only by Rubeo; the versions delivered to the military had extremely mundane designations like "gun bot 34MRU" and "WGR46Transport-Assist," which alluded to their ultimate use.

Diomedes was about half the size of a gas-powered lawn mower, with a squat, rounded hull that featured a flat payload area about twelve by eighteen inches in the back, and a broad mast area that looked a bit like the bridge superstructure from a modern destroyer. The skin was made of a thick, webbed resin composite, sturdy yet light. The motor, powered by hydrogen fuel cells, was extremely quiet. Diomedes could operate at full speed for sixteen hours without being refueled; in combat under normal operation, it might last a good week before needing a new fuel cell.

Unlike the smaller bot, Diomedes had two tank-like treads on either side of its rectangular body. Fore and aft of the tread systems were wheels that extended from large shafts. Ordinarily, the wheels remained retracted next to the transport bot's hull, but when meeting an obstruction or if needed for balance or quick maneuvering, the bot extended them. This helped get the machine over small obstacles or balance on very difficult terrain. There were two armlike extensions at the front, and a miniature arm with a crane hook in the flat rear compartment.

Rubeo slid the sensor atop to the plastic holder, making sure the metal shielding was properly in place. The system was designed to ignore the fields generated by the bot, but he considered the shielding an important safeguard nonetheless.

Lawson was hovering nearby, watching. He was excited about the bots, which he called "little creatures." He wasn't actually in the way, but his lurking presence would have been annoying if he hadn't been so enthusiastic.

Actually, it was annoying, but Rubeo let him stay anyway. The others were seeing to last minute details or guarding the area outside. Uncharacteristically, Rubeo felt the need for human company tonight.

He glanced at his watch as he snapped the last prong in place on Arachne. Clearly, they wouldn't be able to get south before dawn—it was almost 5:00 P.M. now. The process had taken far longer than he thought it would.

His fault, really. He should have had more of his people here to help. He needn't have done all the prep work himself.

Should he go to the hotel rooms they'd rented and get some sleep? Or sleep in the desert?

He'd ask Jons what he thought.

"So the spider creature walks right in to where we want it to go?" asked Lawson.

"When told to." Rubeo went to the bench and took the control unit—a modified laptop—and brought it over to finish orienting Arachne. The unit had to be told what sensors it was carrying; once that was done, the process was fully automated and quick.

"How does it get in?"

"It will depend. If necessary, Diomedes will cut a hole through the wall," said Rubeo. "Or do whatever is necessary."

"Oh. I thought maybe it would, like, crawl up the drain spout or something."

"It could, if there was a drain spout," said Rubeo. "We haven't seen an easy access. Diomedes will check the external perimeter, and if there is an easy access, we'll use it. Cutting into the building is the last resort."

"Because of the noise?"

"The saw is relatively quiet," said Rubeo. "But because of that it works very slowly."

"Are you a better weaver than Minerva?" Lawson asked the bot.

"I'm impressed," said Rubeo. In Roman myth, Arachne was a weaver who was turned into a spider after her work outshone Minerva's in a contest. Jealous, Minerva took revenge by changing her into a spider. "I didn't know you knew the story."

"Oh, I know my myths. That of course is the Latin version. There's a parallel in Greek. Minerva would be Athena. Of course, this is all coming from Ovid, so who the hell knows what the real myth was."

"You don't trust Ovid?"

"Do I trust *any* poet? Hell, they lie for a living, right? For all I know, he was working for an extermination company when he came up with the tale."

Rubeo laughed, unexpectedly amused by the mercenary soldier. He finished his work, unhooked the laptop, and placed the small robot inside a delivery compartment at the base of Diomedes. Then he keyed his access code into the larger computer, waking it up.

"Follow me," he told the machine.

It did so, moving out to the pickups. One of

the Filipinos had set up a ramp; Rubeo directed the machine to drive up it, into the back. Once there, he deactivated it and covered it with a tarp. Lawson helped tie it down.

Jons was in a parking area about three hundred yards away, talking with their helicopter pilot. Rubeo called him, telling him they were ready to leave. They discussed whether to go right away or not. For Jons, it was a no-brainer—better to move out as quickly as possible.

Lawson gathered the Filipinos. Halit had been dismissed. Abas was to stay with Kimmy, the helicopter pilot, in case they needed backup.

Jons suggested they tell the alliance what they were up to. Rubeo rejected the idea out of hand.

"They'll only tell us not to," he said.

Rubeo went to the front seat of the truck, brooding. He was fairly sure now that the Sabres hadn't been interfered with from the ground, so why even bother going back?

Was the risk worth it for fifteen percent of doubt?

If that wasn't the cause, though, what was? The sabotage theory seemed even more improbable.

His sat phone rang. Rubeo looked at the number, and at first he didn't recognize it. But then the last name came up.

It was Kharon.

"This is Rubeo."

"Ray, hi, say, um, I kind of need a little help."

"What is it, Neil? What can I do?"

"Well . . . I kind of flew in to Tripoli and I got into a little problem at the airport. I was wondering if you could call one of your connections and maybe talk to them to get me sprung."

"You're in Tripoli?"

"Actually, I'm at passport control in the airport. I should be able to just go—it's an open city, right? But they're questioning my stamp from Italy. I guess the guy who stamped it there didn't stamp it right."

"Where are you?" asked Rubeo, still not quite believing what he had heard.

"Passport control. In the terminal. Tripoli. Maybe if, like, you could get one of the officials or somebody you work with—"

"Wait there. I'll be there in a few minutes."

"You? Here?"

"Just sit tight."

KHARON HUNG UP THE PHONE. IT HAD BEEN EASIER than he thought.

"He's on his way," he told the passport officer. "You know what to say?"

"Of course."

Kharon held up the one hundred euro note. The man eyed it greedily.

"Soon," promised Kharon. "When you release me, I slip you the passport to stamp. It'll be between the back pages."

The man nodded. Bribing your way through customs was a time-honored practice in Tripoli.

A few minutes later Kharon spotted a dark-haired American strutting through the hallway as if he owned the place. He stopped and asked someone near the lobby for directions. The man pointed toward the small desk where Kharon and the customs agent were standing.

He sent one of his people, rather than coming himself. I should have known that.

"You Neil?" asked the man, spotting him. His voice was very loud, as he was shouting across the hall.

"It's me," said Kharon.

The man walked over, grinning. "Name's Lawson. What's the trouble?"

"Passport, this not correct," said the customs agent quickly. His English was actually quite good, as Kharon had learned earlier; he used fractured grammar for effect.

"Well we can fix that, can't we?" asked Lawson. He winked at Kharon. He switched to Arabic. It was a little stiff, but grammatically correct. "I have heard that the paperwork can be corrected on the spot by the proper authority," Lawson said. "Naturally, there are fees involved."

"This is true," said the passport officer softly.

"Perhaps we could do that in this situation."

"Very well."

"What is the fee?" asked Lawson.

"One hundred euro."

Lawson didn't bother trying to talk the man down. He reached into his pocket and pulled out two fifties. The customs man's face fell—he realized he could have gotten more.

The rest of the transaction was completed swiftly. Kharon handed over his passport, and got it back stamped—and a hundred euros lighter.

"Not that I think he'll change his mind," Lawson said, starting away. "But let's not give him a chance."

"Is Dr. Rubeo in Tripoli?"

"He's waiting for us outside."

RUBEO SAW THE YOUNG MAN TRAILING ALONG AFTER Lawson, looking a bit sheepish. He was smart, undoubtedly, but a bit naive. Surely a simple bribe would have gotten him out of trouble immediately.

But perhaps he didn't have the money.

"Neil, I didn't think you were coming to Africa," said Rubeo, opening his window as he approached. "What brings you here?"

"I thought, since I was so close, I should see what was going on," said Kharon. "You actually inspired me."

"How is that?"

"I thought if a famous scientist like you was going to visit the country, then I should, too. An adventure."

"This is hardly the place for an adventure. We'll take you into town. Do you have a hotel?" Rubeo asked.

"The Majesty, in the old section."

"I'm sure we can do a little better than that," said Rubeo. He turned to Jons. "What about the Citadel?"

"Yeah, something along those lines." The foreign hotels in the new sections had much better security.

"I, uh, really can't afford that—"

"You're my guest. Think of it as part of the interview travel. Unfortunately, I have to do some more traveling, but I'll be back by tomorrow, and then we can talk. Some of my men will come with us and you can see the city, and have your little adventure."

KHARON SLID INTO THE TRUCK. A DARK-SKINNED FILIPINO sat next to him. The man was silent, but had an AR–15 between his legs, pointed at the floor.

The closed space of the unfamiliar SUV began to bother him. He felt the first tingle of fear rising along the back of his neck. He turned toward the window.

"I need some fresh air," he told the others, and opened the window.

They weren't paying attention. In front of him, Rubeo adjusted his ear set and told the men in the second car that they would meet them on the highway south. The driver, Jons, was clearly unhappy.

"I'd rather they rode behind us."

"I don't want the bots exposed," said Rubeo. "The less they're seen, the better."

"They're tarped. It just looks like equipment in the back."

"And that won't raise questions?"

Jons didn't argue. Rubeo was the boss.

They drove away from the terminal, heading toward the Al Amrus Highway.

"I don't want the truck driving all through the

city," Rubeo told Jon as they reached the highway.

"I don't like splitting up."

"It's only for a few minutes. The bots are safer at the airport."

The traffic was light. The truck sped around the circle and onto the highway.

Kharon sat back, waiting.

RUBEO REALIZED HE WAS GETTING TESTY, AND THAT was affecting his judgment. He ought to let Jons do his job.

"I'm sorry," he told him. "Call them to catch up."

"Good," said the driver. He took his foot off the gas and reached for the mike button on his ear set.

A moment later there was a sharp pop at the front of the truck. Jons gripped the wheel tightly, holding the truck steady as it jerked to the right.

"Blowout," muttered someone.

There was a flash. Rubeo felt himself lifted into the air, then spinning.

"Damn," he said, cursing for one of the very few times in his life. Then everything went black.

PRISONER OF CONSCIENCE

1

Tripoli

THIS ISN'T THE WAY IT'S SUPPOSED TO GO!

The voice screaming in Kharon's head refused to be quiet. He pressed his arms over his head, trying to run away, even though he was held tight in his seat as the SUV tumbled over.

It was the closet, cramped and dark, the hiding place he had run to years before.

No. I'm not a child anymore!

The truck's engine revved. There was another explosion nearby.

Time to get out! Get out! Go!

He was upside down. Kharon managed to undo his seat belt and push to the right. His window was still open and he half fell, half crawled out.

This isn't the way it's supposed to go!

The fresh air relieved his claustrophobia and his head began to clear. He went back to the SUV and struggled with the front door, finally pulling it open. Rubeo dropped out of the truck. The scientist was coughing, only semiconscious. Kharon took hold of him under his arms and pulled him away from the wreck.

For a few seconds his animosity disappeared. In the confusion and chaos, Kharon sought to get them both to safety.

Guns were firing. Cars screeched. Something had gone wrong, completely wrong—the kidnapping was supposed to take place after he gave the signal at the hotel.

Why the hell had they tried to blow them up?

RUBEO CRAWLED UP THE SIDE OF THE ROAD, AWAY from the SUV. He tried to fight through the mental fog, focusing his thoughts on what he saw before him.

Dirt. Sky.

Kharon pulling him away.

Rubeo coughed. Jons was back by the vehicle, firing his weapon.

Rubeo pushed at Kharon. The young man released him and Rubeo got to his feet, pulling his gun out from under his jacket. Two men were running toward him. They had rifles.

On his side?

They were wearing brown fatigues. His men wore Western clothes.

Rubeo pointed and fired twice. Both fell.

"Neil—Neil stay with me!" Rubeo shouted. He rose to his feet. A dozen men swarmed from the other side of the road. Jons was firing ferociously.

Rubeo spun around. There was no one nearby.

He could see a wall with houses behind it some forty or fifty yards away.

"We can retreat to cover!" he yelled to Jons. "Let's go!"

A fusillade of bullets sent him diving for cover. Kharon crawled next to him.

"Stay near me," said Rubeo. He began to run. He sensed Kharon near him, but temporarily lost track of Jons. He threw himself down as he reached the wall.

Jons ran to him. "Over the wall, over the wall!" yelled the bodyguard. As he yelled, he picked Rubeo up and boosted him over the wall. Rubeo tried to land on his feet but stumbled, his legs giving way. He fell onto his back, momentarily stunned.

Kharon scrambled over the wall next to him.

"Guns!" yelled Kharon.

Rubeo pushed over, trying to get up. He couldn't see what Kharon was pointing at, but raised his weapon anyway. Then he turned back to see Jons jumping over the wall.

"Our other SUV is coming," yelled the bodyguard. "Go right."

Rubeo started in that direction, then realized that Kharon was still behind him. "Come on."

They began running toward a dirt alleyway twenty yards away. They cut up it to the left, Jons trailing behind to watch their backs. Rubeo ran toward a cemetery filled with mausoleums and surrounded by a low wall. Winded, he collapsed against the wall.

Kharon helped him to his feet. Clambering

over the wall, Rubeo steadied himself against a nearby tomb, taking stock.

I'm a scientist, not a soldier. Can I do this?

You can do anything you need to, to survive.

Jons came over after them.

"If we go up this way there's another street," he told them. "Our other truck will meet us there. I have the helicopter coming in case."

"Who attacked us?" asked Rubeo.

"I don't know."

"Were we hit by a missile?"

"May have been a grenade. Or maybe an IED," said Jons. "God damn place is going all to shit."

"What about Joker?" asked Rubeo. The Filipino had been in the back with Kharon.

Jons shook his head. "Can you run?" he asked Rubeo.

"Yes."

Jons turned to Kharon. "You?"

"Yup."

They sprinted for a hundred yards or so, running up the hill to the knoll at the center of the cemetery. But once more Rubeo began to tire, and after another ten yards his pace was nearly a walk.

"The helo is coming," Jons told him. "Come on. We'll wait out by the street."

They ran under a row of trees and stopped at the edge of a walled yard. Rubeo dropped to his knees, holding the gun. Kharon moved back next to him. He wore an angry expression.

"It's all right," Rubeo told him.

"Truck is coming up," said Jons. "Let's move to it. Helo can shadow us."

They rose together and began running toward the road. As they did, there was more gunfire. Rubeo ducked back and turned. A gunman wielding a pistol jumped over a low wall in the alley behind them. Rubeo zeroed his pistol and fired.

The man fell. Kharon took off, running to him despite Rubeo's shout. The young man scooped up the gun and returned. Rubeo pushed his legs in the direction of the helicopter's heavy beat. After he'd gone about twenty yards, he looked behind him, but couldn't see Jons.

Kharon caught up. He pointed his gun at Rubeo.

"Careful where you're pointing that," Rubeo told him. He took a step back against the wall. There was a flash above—Rubeo glanced toward the sky in time to see a red fireball flash and turn into a black fist above him. Then metal began raining down.

The helicopter had just been shot down.

"You're mine," Kharon said, jumping on him.

Stunned, Rubeo raised his gun. Kharon hit him in the temple, then stepped on his wrist. Rubeo squirmed to get away, but Kharon hit him again. This time Rubeo's eyes closed for a moment.

When they opened, two men were next to him, AK–47s in their hands.

2

Sicily

BEING A SENATOR HAD A NUMBER OF ADVANTAGES, and one of them was immediate access to any military officer who had even the faintest dream of making general—by law and long tradition, promotion to the star rank required approval by the Senate.

Colonels tended to be very aware of this. So when Ginella's aide in the outer office told Zen that he didn't think the colonel was available, Zen told him to pick up the phone and try anyway.

The colonel appeared so quickly Zen wondered if she had even bothered to hang up.

"Senator, I'm pleased that you're interested in our squadron," she told him. "Won't you come in?"

"Glad to."

Zen couldn't remember meeting Ginella when he was in the service, but he nodded agreeably as she mentioned several generals he knew, deciding he had nothing to lose by letting her drop names.

"Would you like to see the aircraft?" she said finally, running out of names.

"I'd like to, but unfortunately I'm pressed for time tonight," said Zen. "I have to catch a flight in ten minutes."

"I see."

"I'm interested in the incident yesterday, when

your squadron was covering the retrieval of the allied commando unit."

"Yes, the SAS troops. We were up for quite a while," said Ginella.

"And then you lost one of your planes."

Ginella's face clouded. "I did."

"Why was Captain Mako flying in your squadron?"

"Captain Mako? He was a substitute pilot," she said defensively. "He . . . came to the squadron at my request."

"That's a little unusual, isn't it?"

"Not if you're undermanned. I think he was an excellent pilot. He had experience in the A–10E before any of my pilots, or myself. And I think he's clearly a good combat pilot."

"So do I," said Zen. "So what happened on the mission?"

"Are you here in an official capacity, Senator? Your tone seems a little formal."

"I'm interested in knowing what happened," said Zen. "I'm interested in making sure that Captain Mako gets a fair shake."

"He's not in any trouble that I know of," said Ginella.

"Good."

"I assume you're referring to the fact that he passed over the area the missile was fired from just prior to the shoot-down," said Ginella.

"I understand he did."

"He missed the missile launcher. Whether he would have seen it in time or not, I don't know."

"You're sure he missed it?"

"I have to tell you, Senator, it's difficult to believe the missile wasn't launched from that point. So by definition, if he didn't see it—"

"What do the reconnaissance videos show?"

"Unfortunately, the closest UAV was not in a position to capture that portion of the battlefield. The others show just the general area. And the images from his plane are inclusive as well."

"I think any account of the incident should indicate that," said Zen. "But it should also indicate what he said."

"I'm sure it will."

"None of your other pilots saw the missile."

"We weren't close enough."

Zen nodded. "As for personal feelings, I hope none will enter into any of your reports, or actions. One way or another."

Ginella stared at him but said nothing.

"Great," said Zen finally. "I'm glad that will be the case."

He started to wheel away.

"Personal feelings have no place in battle," said Ginella.

"Agreed, Colonel," said Zen, not bothering to look back. "Though in my experience, they often seem to intrude."

3

Tripoli

KHARON KICKED THE GUN AWAY FROM RUBEO, THEN pulled the scientist to his feet. His arms were shaking.

The revenge he'd dreamed about since he was a child was in front of him now. The only question was how to take it.

The two thugs who'd run up from the highway shouted at him in Arabic to put the gun down.

"You idiots. I hired you," Kharon answered. "Fezzan works for me."

"But they don't work for Fezzan," said a voice from up on the hill, back in the cemetery. He was speaking English, with a Russian accent.

Foma Mitreski.

"You are a foolish young man. Put the gun down or they will shoot you," said Foma.

"What are you doing?"

"Gun down," said Foma. He told the others to take aim.

Kharon thought of pointing the gun at the Russian, then, dejected, he let it drop.

AS THE GUN FELL, RUBEO SAW HIS CHANCE. HE DOVE after it, planning to grab it and shoot the man who'd come down the hill—he was sure Jons would be up the alley and take care of the men with rifles. But as his fingers touched the cold metal, the butt stock of one of the guns smacked him in the side of the head.

He felt the air rushing through his mouth, then slid forward in the dirt, scraping his chin as he lost consciousness.

I'm a scientist, not a soldier . . .

"WHAT ARE YOU DOING? WHY DID YOU BLOW UP THE truck?" Kharon asked Foma as the goons trussed Rubeo.

"Ah, the idiot Libyans are too enthusiastic. But, eh, things happen. We have what we want."

"You're lucky he's alive."

"I want the robot and the sensors," said Foma. "The scientist is a bonus. But I don't know. Maybe we kill him anyway."

"Let me."

Foma laughed. "You are an idiot. You should be begging for your life."

"Why?"

"You think that I was such a fool that I didn't know your plan? Do you think that I would let you use my operation for some petty goal? You think the SVR is stupid? Something to be used by a child whom we employ? You are clever, Kharon, but not experienced. We have helped you many times, and you didn't even know—how do you think you found the shelter under the university? Do you think you could have broken into the computer systems there without our help?"

"I did that myself."

"Yes, yes, of course you did. You are a very brilliant man. You have an IQ of one hundred and eighty, almost twice as much as mine, eh? But I am the one with the guns."

"Bullshit." Kharon raised his fist to swing at the fat Russian. As he did, something hit him across the back of the head and he fell forward, limp.

4

Sicily

DANNY FREAH WAS NOT PARTICULARLY SUPERSTITIOUS, but a second before the phone rang he had a premonition that it was about something bad. It was a vague and inexact feeling, but as soon as he heard Breanna Stockard's voice, he knew he was right.

"Something has happened to Ray," she told him. "We have an alert on our system—the computer is tracking him moving south of Tripoli, but he hasn't answered his sat phone."

"Tripoli?" Danny stifled a flood of curses. "I told him not to go to Africa. Did you approve that?"

"Ray is not under my command," said Breanna. "This isn't Dreamland anymore, Danny. We can't tell him what to do."

"Damn it." It was all he could say. "We talked about it—I talked to him, I told him not to go. His people here haven't said a word—they claimed he was busy. Damn."

"We're tracking him on the MY-PID system," she told him. "There was a spike in his heartbeat that alerted the system monitor. His people tried to get ahold of him, and then the security team with him. It looks like his bodyguards were killed. There's apparently some high-tech equipment that may have been taken as well. We're still getting details—this all only happened a few minutes ago."

"We'll get him back."

"Obviously, this has top priority."

"Damn." Danny didn't know what else to say.

"What the hell was he thinking?" Breanna asked. "You told him not to go to Africa? What was he thinking?"

"That he's omnipotent. The arrogant SOB."

NOT MORE THAN A MINUTE LATER A MAN NAMED CLINTON Chase sent a message to Danny on the MY-PID system's secure line, asking for a video conference. Danny flicked the laptop screen and opened the com window. The round, slightly reddish face of a man in his late fifties appeared, practically filling the entire square.

Chase, a former CIA agent, was the security director for one of Rubeo's European companies, Intelligence Appliquée. Danny had never heard of Intelligence Appliquée, though he knew Rubeo operated through a veritable spiderweb of companies and partnerships.

"I'm assuming you're tracking his whereabouts on the system," said Chase.

"He's ten miles south of Tripoli," said Danny.

"When are you launching the assault?"

"Hold your horses," said Danny. "I literally just found out about this. I can't just snap my fingers and charge across three hundred miles of water and another hundred miles of sand without a plan in place. I'm not even sure what resources I have yet."

"You're Whiplash," said Chase. "You're supposed to be able to deal with things like this."

"I was here in a different capacity," said Danny, practically grating his teeth. "I have team members, but we're not prepared for a rescue at a moment's notice."

"Well who is?"

Danny decided it was better not to answer. Chase might prove useful, and it was best to avoid alienating him to the extent possible.

"I'll be in Tripoli by noon," added Chase. "If you care to coordinate with me, contact me."

"I don't want you doing anything that's going to jeopardize our getting him back," said Danny.

"That makes two of us," said Chase sarcastically. He killed his connection.

"What's up with that asshole?" asked Boston, who'd come into the office during the conversation.

"Don't you knock, Chief?"

"I did and you didn't hear." Boston smirked. "Chief's knock."

Boston's expression changed quickly as Danny explained what had happened.

"We've got Shorty and we got Flash," said the Air Force chief master sergeant. "That's it on personnel. Unless you want to start borrowing Eye-tralians. Two Ospreys for transport and firepower. That's not a lot if they were able to grab Rubeo in broad daylight. What the hell was he thinking?"

Danny shook his head. Arrogance was a difficult thing to explain.

"How soon can you get the Ospreys airborne?" he asked.

"Gotta talk to the maintainers," said Boston. "Probably pretty quick, though. Half hour? Twenty minutes? Whatever it takes to get fuel into them."

"All right, let's get moving. We'll do this on the fly."

"Say, Cap?"

Danny winced at the old nickname.

"Sorry—Colonel," Boston corrected himself. "What about having the Tigershark fly cover? Come in pretty handy."

"I don't know."

"The aircraft's all checked out."

"I wish I could say the same for the pilot."

But it was a good idea. Danny picked up his phone and dialed Turk's cell.

5

South of Tripoli

RUBEO REGAINED CONSCIOUSNESS ON THE FLOOR OF a panel truck, his arms and legs bound. It was dark, but he could tell he wasn't alone. He pushed to the side, rolling over halfway until he hit something.

Another body.

Jons, maybe.

Whoever it was, he didn't move or speak. His shallow breaths sounded like groans.

Rubeo pushed in the opposite direction, moving a foot and a half until he got to the wall. He maneuvered himself upright and sat, back to the wall of the truck.

As his eyes adjusted to the darkness, he examined the other person in the truck with him. He looked too thin to be Jons.

Lawson? He'd been in the second vehicle.

Rubeo scooted over and leaned close.

It was Kharon, tied as he was.

Rubeo pushed back to the wall.

Kharon's animosity had shocked him. But Rubeo understood exactly where it must be coming from—Kharon blamed him for his mother's death.

"Neil. Neil?"

"What?" groaned Kharon. "What happened?"

"I believe you are in a far better position to explain than I am."

Kharon, apparently realizing where he was, struggled to free himself. He jerked and rolled, but it was no use—the bonds were strong and well-tied. He flopped around like a prize brook trout confined to a canoe.

"You're only going to hurt yourself," Rubeo told him.

"I hate you," said Kharon. "I hate you."

"Why?"

"My mother." Short on breath, Kharon began to choke, then wheezed and finally cried. He screamed, and banged his head on the floor of the van.

Rubeo closed his eyes. The manic display of grief continued for more than a minute, until finally Kharon collapsed, completely spent.

"I've blamed myself as well," said Rubeo softly when the other man was still. "I told her not to work that night, but I should have made her go home. I shouldn't have let her work. I am tremendously sorry for it."

"I don't believe you," whispered Kharon. The words were barely audible.

"It wasn't an accident," said Rubeo. "I know they didn't tell you the whole story. It's still classified."

Kharon didn't react.

"The accident was actually sabotage," Rubeo continued. "We had a Russian agent at the base. It was the tail end of the Cold War."

"You're lying."

"No." Rubeo closed his eyes, remembering Dreamland. Kharon's mother's death was just one of several incidents that had eventually led to the shake-up, the threats of closing, and finally the coming of Tecumseh Bastian.

So good did come of it. Though it was impossible to explain that to Kharon. Nothing would ever compensate the ten-year-old who had lost his mother.

"I don't blame you for not believing me." Rubeo leaned his head forward, trying to undo the terrible muscle knot forming at the back of his neck. "I think if you ask Breanna Stockard, she'll tell you. She knew your mother."

Kharon didn't answer. Rubeo wondered if he had passed out again, until finally he realized the young man was crying uncontrollably.

6

Sicily

DANNY JUMPED FROM THE HUMMER AND TROTTED toward the waiting Osprey. Boston was hanging out the door, waving him on.

The huge propellers, which rotated on their nacelles at the wingtips, whipped overhead, anxious to pull the craft into the air. Danny ran behind the wing to the door, shading his eyes against the dust kicked up by the rotors. Boston grabbed him by the forearm and helped him up. Not a half second later, the Osprey leapt forward, pushing into the stiff Sicilian wind.

"Body armor over there," said Boston, pointing to the side bench as the hatchway closed behind them. "Gear and weapons."

"Thanks," said Danny, going over to suit up.

ACROSS THE TARMAC FROM THE OSPREY, TURK SAT AT the controls of the Tigershark II, waiting as a long queue of NATO fighter-bombers moved up the taxi ramp to the runway. The com section bleeped; he cleared it, and the image of Danny Freah appeared in front of him.

"Turk?"

"I'm here, Colonel. Just waiting for clearance to take off."

"Thank you for getting ready so quickly."

"My pleasure," said Turk. He meant it—he wanted nothing better than a chance to get back in the air and prove himself.

Again. Which he shouldn't have to do.

"Dr. Rubeo wears a locating device that tracks his location continually," said Danny. "The information has been tied into MY-PID, and we're uploading into your connection now."

Turk was sitting behind a transport and a tanker, waiting for clearance. As the aircraft in front of him moved forward, he nudged the Tigershark to follow.

The tower gave clearances and directions to a pair of other planes, the controller's voice drowning out Danny's.

"You got that?" asked Danny.

"Stand by. I'm queuing to take off," Turk told

him. He reached his arm up and touched the virtual switch to open the map panel. "MY-PID interface." The computer blinked. "Find Rubeo," he told his computer.

The map panel flickered. Turk used his fingers to zoom out a bit, getting some perspective—the indicator dot was some eighty miles south of Tripoli. According to the computer, the vehicle was moving at roughly fifty miles an hour on a paved highway toward the city of Mizdah.

"Plot intercept at maximum speed," he told the computer.

"Nineteen minutes, twenty-eight seconds from takeoff," said the flight computer. The distance was a little over four hundred miles.

"We can do better than that," Turk told it.

"Command not recognized."

"You're a slowpoke."

"Command not recognized."

"Turk?"

"I see it. It's going to take me about twenty minutes to get there."

The plane in front of him jerked forward. He was now next in line.

"I need you to get there as fast as you can," Danny told.

"Yeah, roger that, Colonel." That was the funny thing about ground officers—they always assumed jets could simply get to where they needed instantly. "ROEs?"

"Avoid contact with the enemy. You're just scouting."

"What if they come for me?"

"Let's play it by ear. We're authorized to use deadly force to get Rubeo back, if it comes to that."

"Roger that. Understood."

The space in front of him was empty. It was his turn to fly.

"Whiplash, I'm clear for takeoff—talk to you in a few."

ABOARD THE OSPREY, DANNY STUDIED THE SAME MAP that Turk was viewing, using a portable touch computer that accessed MY-PID. It was hard to like anything that he saw. Rubeo was being taken toward a city ostensibly still held by the government.

There was a small army base to the west. A large number of soldiers there had deserted, and the latest intelligence estimated that no more than three thousand were still in uniform and willing to fight. But three thousand was still far more than the Whiplash team was prepared to deal with.

Danny didn't have enough people to take down a well-guarded house in the city—and guarantee that Rubeo would be alive. If he went into the city, he would have to call for backup. He'd already alerted the U.S. Special Operations Command, or SOCCOM, which had placed a platoon of SEALs at his disposal. They were on a carrier in the Mediterranean; he could send one of the Ospreys back to pick them up if necessary.

Turk would get there in twenty minutes. That

would put the truck just outside the city. The Osprey would be roughly an hour away.

He went up to the cockpit.

"Tell Whiplash Osprey Two to double back and rendezvous with the SEAL platoon," Danny told the copilot. "I'll talk to the SEALs."

"We're still heading south?" asked the pilot.

"As fast you can."

7

Libya

RUBEO KNEW HIS PEOPLE WOULD BE TRACKING THEM by now. The best thing to do was to stay alive until they were rescued.

But that was far too passive.

It was true, he wasn't a soldier. But he wasn't a wimp either.

Searching the back of the van for something to cut the ropes, he hit on the idea of using the hinge edge. It wasn't quite sharp enough to cut the rope, but by wiggling the rope against it, he was able to stretch the strands. The pressure on his wrists hurt, cutting off his circulation to the point where his fingers felt numb, but when he stopped, the restraints were loosened. He worked them back and forth, finally getting one free.

He pulled the other out, then went over to Kharon, facedown on the floor.

"Are you all right?" he asked, reaching to the young man's hands, which were tied behind his back.

"What are you doing?"

"I'm going to untie you."

"Why?"

"So we can get the hell out of here."

"I still hate you."

"Should I just leave you?"

Kharon didn't answer. The knot was difficult, but Rubeo kept at it. Finally it came undone. Rubeo slid back, unsure what the other man would do.

KHARON'S ARMS FELT AS IF THEY WERE PARALYZED. They'd been behind his back so long that the muscles were stiff and his nerves were tingling, making them feel almost limp. He flexed them, trying to get some circulation back, trying to get control of them.

The strange thing was, he believed Rubeo.

But he still hated him.

He had so much anger and emotion, it needed to focus on someone. He hated that his mother had died, that her death had destroyed his father, that he had been left on his own, abandoned.

Angry at his mother? How could he be mad at her?

The faceless saboteur? Even if that was true, how could he hate someone he didn't know?

"Come on," said Rubeo, standing up. He had to duck so he wouldn't hit his head. "Undo your legs."

"We can't just jump out of the truck," said Kharon.

"Why not?"

"They'll kill us."

"I doubt staying in the vehicle will decrease those chances," said Rubeo. "We can roll out. It should be dark by now. They may not see us. My people will rescue us soon."

"We need weapons."

"If you find any, let me know."

Rubeo went to the back door. The truck rattled, but it was impossible to judge even their speed from what he heard or felt.

Surely they were in the desert somewhere. Getting out made more sense—it would be easier in the open space than in a city. Rubeo knew that from Dreamland.

"They'll kill us," said Kharon as Rubeo felt around for the lock. It was in a small pocket at the door and impossible to see in the dim light.

"Are you coming or what?" asked Rubeo.

"I don't know."

Rubeo went back to him.

"I wear a device that lets the people who work for me track me. They won't be far behind. Come on. We just have to get a little way in the dark."

He reached down and began undoing Kharon's feet. Kharon pushed him away and then started untying them himself.

"Who helped you do this?" Rubeo asked.

"A Russian spy."

"Name?"

"Like you'll know him?"

"I might."

"Foma Mitreski," said Kharon. "He was interested in the technology you flew in. And in the transmission from your aircraft. As soon as your aircraft arrived, they contacted me and asked me to help them. We cooperated. I—"

Kharon suddenly felt ashamed and stopped speaking. He'd been wrong—so wrong he could never make it right.

"The Sabres?" asked Rubeo. "How did you track—"

"No, the other one. The manned plane. The Tigershark. We recorded them. They wanted the transmission in different circumstances—they wanted to try and look at the data flow under circumstances they knew. If a radar came on—"

"You recorded them—or you interfered with them?" asked Rubeo.

"We didn't interfere. The encryption and failsafes are too good. You know yourself—if you can start to see patterns, known reactions—"

"Then how did you order the Sabre attack?"

Kharon felt his throat clutching.

"You were behind the attack, weren't you? Why did the Russians want that?"

"I wanted it," he mumbled. "To discredit you. To ruin you."

Rubeo stayed silent for a moment. "You killed innocent people to ruin me?" he asked finally, his throat dry.

Tears flooded from Kharon's eyes.

"Yes!" Kharon yelled. "Yes. Yes, damn it. Yes. It was easy to insert the virus in the hangars. As soon as the aircraft were located there, I knew it would be easy."

"Come on," Rubeo said. "Let's get out of here. You'll tell me what you did later."

HAND ON THE LATCH, RUBEO PRESSED HIS EAR against the door and strained to listen. But it was useless. He couldn't hear anything beyond the low hum of the motor and the rattle of the truck.

He glanced back at Kharon. He should have felt anger at what Kharon had done, but instead he felt something closer to relief—he wasn't the one responsible for the deaths.

He also felt an odd compassion. Kharon was a tormented and twisted soul, worthy of pity.

"Come on," Rubeo told him. "Get up and let's go."

Kharon got to his feet. Rubeo took a deep breath, then pushed himself out the door.

8

Over Libya

TURK SPOTTED THE TWO TRUCKS MOVING THROUGH the desert foothills north of Mizdah just fifteen minutes after lifting off the runway in Sicily. They were nondescript cargo vans, heavy duty extended versions. He zoomed the optical camera, then uploaded the image to Danny aboard the Osprey.

"Whiplash, this is Tigershark," said Turk. "I have our trucks."

"Roger that. Seeing them now," responded Danny.

"How do you want me to proceed?" he asked. He started cutting back on his throttle, preparing to set up in a wide orbit around the vehicles—the Tigershark couldn't cut back its speed slow enough to stay directly above the vehicles.

"Just stay with them for now," responded Danny. "We are about forty-five minutes from your location."

"Gonna reach the city by then," said Turk. "Want me to slow them down?"

"Negative. We want no chance of harming our package."

"Acknowledged."

"Check the city and the army base. See if there's activity."

"On it."

Turk moved west, gliding over the hills at roughly 20,000 feet. He nudged the plane into an easy circle, banking over Mizdah. There were no air defenses there that could threaten him, but the computer did spot and mark out a pair of ancient ZSU–23–4 antiaircraft weapons parked near the soccer field at the center of town.

A pair of helicopters sat in a field adjacent to a compound at the southern end of the city. They were an odd pair—an Mi–35V Hind, Russian attack/transport, and an American-made CH–47C Chinook.

The 47 was a powerful aircraft whose speed and cargo carrying capability belied the fact that she had been built some forty years before; her sisters were still mainstays in the U.S. armed forces. The Hind wasn't as big, but it could carry guns and missiles, combining attack with transport.

Turk assumed they were government aircraft, though the computer couldn't link them with an existing unit. The computer identified the compound where they were parked as the home of a regional governor. There was no further data.

He guessed that a small contingent was in the compound. The building wasn't particularly large; it might hold a dozen troops.

"Observe helicopters in grid D–3," he told the computer. "Alert me if they power up."

"Observing helicopters in grid D–3. Helicopters are inert."

More ominous than the city were the army barracks Danny had mentioned. These were located several miles to the west, in an open area separated from the city by another group of low hills and open desert.

Turk glanced at the threat indicator. Technically this was unnecessary since the computer would warn him verbally, but there were certain things that no self-respecting pilot could completely trust the machine to do—even if the source of the information was exactly the same set of sensors.

The scope was clear.

He had the camera zoom as he approached. The complex of low-slung buildings looked deserted.

"Computer, how many individuals at the complex in grid A–6?" Turk asked.

"Scanning." The system took a few seconds to analyze infrared data, comparing it to information from the normal and ground-penetrating radar.

"Complex includes Class One shelter system," said the computer, telling Turk in advance that its estimate might not be accurate—though far better than anything aboard most aircraft, the radar aboard the Tigershark could not penetrate bunkers designed to withstand nuclear strikes. "Infrared scan determines 319 bodies within complex area. Size of underground shelter would indicate possibility of two hundred additional at nominal capacity."

"Three hundred is good enough for government work," Turk told the machine.

"Rephrase."

"Ignore," Turk told the machine. The estimate was lower than the intel he'd gotten earlier, a good sign—the troops were deserting.

He turned his attention to a large area of shelters to the northwest of the complex. These looked like long tents, half buried in the sand.

"Identify military complex in grid B–1," he told the computer.

"Missile storage complex," said the computer immediately. "NATO Scud B variant. One hundred seventy-three units identified in bunkers. Do you require technical information?"

"Negative. Are there launch vehicles?"

"Missiles are stored on TEL erectors. No activity noted."

"Personnel?"

"No personnel in Missile Storage Complex."

"No guards?"

"No personnel in Missile Storage Complex."

"That's great," said Turk. Enough missiles sitting out in the desert to destroy a dozen small cities, and no one was watching them.

Turk told the computer to identify other large weapons in the general area. There was an abandoned antiaircraft facility about two miles northeast of the missile storage area, back in the direction of the highway that led to the city. Though defunct since the 1990s, six tanks were parked there, along with a number of tents and enough personnel to crew the vehicles.

"Vehicles are identified as T–72, Libyan export variants," said the computer. "Vehicles had moved within the last seventy-two hours."

"Observe tanks," Turk told the computer. "If they move, alert me."

"Tanks will be observed."

Turk swung back over the hills, moving toward

the trucks carrying Rubeo. The scientist was in the lead truck.

"Zoom on target truck one," directed Turk.

Flying the Tigershark and Hogs was like night and day. He loved both, but the tools here—you couldn't knock the computer's help.

As he pulled to within two miles, Turk saw something flapping at the back of the vehicle. Dust flew up and something fell at the side of the road.

"Focus on object," said Turk. "Identify."

"Two males. Subject One is Dr. Rubeo."

"Son of a bitch," muttered Turk, flicking onto the Whiplash channel to tell Danny.

9

Libya, north of Mizdah

RUBEO HAD CALCULATED THAT HIS ARMORED VEST would absorb some of the impact as he fell. But whatever buffer it provided was negligible at best. The ground poked his ribs so hard he lost his breath. Rolling and wheezing, he scrambled desperately to get up and get to the side of the road.

It was lighter than he thought, still daytime. Things had happened much faster than he'd realized. He'd counted on it being night, and now saw there were hours before the sun would set.

He caught a glimpse of another vehicle—the one with the bots, he guessed.

His only goal was to get far away before whoever was in the truck could react.

Go! Go!

Rubeo struggled to his knees. His breath came back in a spurt. He pushed forward, head down, then remembered Kharon.

"Neil?" he grunted.

The young man was on the ground nearby. Rubeo went and grabbed his shirt. He tugged. Kharon bolted to his feet and began running. Rubeo followed.

"That hill," yelled Rubeo, pointing westward. "We'll get behind it."

Something flew up near him, a puff of dirt.

It was a miniature volcano.

A gunshot.

"They're firing at us!" yelled Kharon.

10

Tripoli

ZEN'S NOSE REBELLED AT THE HEAVY WHIFF OF MOroccan hashish he smelled as they entered the hotel suite. He glanced at Zongchen, who seemed puzzled by the odor.

"Hashish," whispered Zen.

The Chinese general didn't understand, and there was no time to explain. One of Princess Idris al-Nussoi's aides came out to welcome them.

"The princess is expecting you," said the aide, with a hint of annoyance. They were about an hour late, though given the conditions in the city, that should have been expected.

"We're glad she could see us," said Zongchen diplomatically. They were using English, as it was a common language for most of the people on the committee, and the rebel leader knew it as well.

A thick bump loomed at the doorway. Zen grit his teeth and blustered his way over it. He was glad to get through—despite everything he'd accomplished in his life, an inch and a half of wood could still stop him cold.

Even though they were in territory that at worst could be deemed neutral, Zongchen had taken three times as many security people as before. Besides the plainclothes UN team, he had two dozen British SAS commandos. To a man, they looked ready to snap necks and eat livers; Zen was a little scared of them himself. A good portion crowded into the suite with the committee members; there was hardly room for the rebels to move, let alone attack.

"Gentlemen—so many of you," said Idris al-Nussoi. She was lounging on a couch, her head leaning back on a pile of pillows, an iPad in her hand. She waved them to the chairs with her free hand. "I just have to send this message, if you don't mind."

"Of course," said Zongchen.

Zen glanced around. The princess's suite was a mess, with jackets flung across the furniture, newspapers on the floor, a pair of suitcases on their sides. Pushed against the wall were trays of half-eaten room service food.

Not to mention the light scent of hash, still wafting from the hall.

This was the most powerful leader in the rebel movement?

"Senator Stockard. It is my pleasure to meet you, sir." A portly man with a South American accent approached Zen and held out his hand. Zen shook it.

"I am Oscar Sifontes, a friend and advisor to the princess. We have heard very much about you, Senator, and your exploits with Dreamland."

"Long time ago," said Zen.

"Very important. We honor you even in my country. Venezuela," added Sifontes, guessing correctly that Zen had no idea where he was from. "And you are General Zong."

"Zongchen," said the committee chairman, bending his head.

The princess finished what she was doing. Introductions were made all around.

"So, you have come with a message?" said the princess.

"We have come with something that may be of great interest to you," said Zongchen. "We have an offer from the government to negotiate peace. One of their ministers will meet with you, and some other representative of the movement, personally. The aim would be to have new elections—"

"We have won!" The princess leapt from the couch. "If they are suing for peace—"

"They are not," said Zongchen carefully. "They wish to talk. They have offered discussions only."

"Oh, don't be naive, General. They have refused to talk all this time. Now, obviously, we have them where we want them."

Sifontes was beaming by her side.

Zen tried hard to keep a neutral face.

"So you are open to talks?" asked Zongchen.

"I will have to discuss this with my supporters."

"Why talk when they are ready to surrender?" asked Sifontes. "They must be on their last legs to be making an offer like this. There's no more fight left in them."

"I wouldn't overreach," said Zen. "I wouldn't underestimate the force they have left."

"I will take this under advisement," said the princess firmly. "Thank you, General. Thank you all. This is very important news."

Wheeling out of the suite, Zen couldn't help but wonder if the allies had supported the wrong side. The government had certainly been horrible, but if Idris al-Nussoi was an example, the rebels didn't look like they would turn out much better.

The other members of the committee appeared to have similar feelings, chattering among themselves as soon as they got into the elevator.

"Best to withhold judgment," said Zongchen as they started downward. "Peace has many handmaidens."

"Or something like that," muttered Zen under his breath.

11

Over Libya

"VEHICLES HAVE STOPPED," TURK TOLD DANNY, watching from above. "We have two guys getting out of the second truck—they're armed. Request permission to—"

"Fry them," said Danny before he could complete the sentence.

"Gladly."

Turk leaned the Tigershark on her right wing, lining up the rail gun. The targeting computer did the math—the pipper glowed red and hot on the two men.

He pushed down on the trigger control, firing a single slug at ultrahigh speed.

"Slug" made the round sound like a brick, but in fact it was a highly engineered and aerodynamically shaped piece of metal. The tail end looked somewhat like a stubby magnet. It contained the electronics to propel the projectile, and was discarded as the round came out of the gun. The payload holder was a cylinder with a pair of four-fingered arms that rode the bullet down the rail. Friction from the air forced it to drop away as the rocket-shaped bullet sped toward its target at over Mach 5. Fins stabilized the projectile.

None of this was visible to the naked eye, and even the sophisticated sensors aboard the Tigershark would have had a hard time focusing on the crisply moving arrow. The slug obliterated the gunman it had been aimed at, slicing through his weapon and his chest.

A half a second later Turk fired again. The force of the bullet disintegrated the target's skull before burying itself deep into the earth.

Turk pulled up, sailing past Rubeo and whoever was with him on the ground. Meanwhile, the rail gun's enormous heat—the most problematic part of the weapon—was dissipated by the air and liquid cooling system.

"Rubeo and a second individual are running in the hills," Turk reported. "I have two more guys, back by the first truck. They're examining the rear of the vehicle. Can I engage?"

"Are they showing weapons?" asked Danny.

"Negative." Turk glanced to the right, where information on the two figures had been compiled by the computer.

NO WEAPONS flashed in the legend. The computer didn't detect any.

"Hold off. Can you disable the vehicles?"

"Yeah, roger, OK. Stand by."

Piece of cake, Turk thought to himself, swinging around to line up his shots.

WATCHING THE FEED FROM THE TIGERSHARK, DANNY saw the stopped trucks and the men near the rear of the first vehicle. The Tigershark pivoted above, then seemed to settle over the front of the second truck. It was descending almost straight down.

There was a burst of steam from the vehicle. The truck jerked backward, propelled by the impact of the rail gun's shell striking into the ground. Dirt flew upward, obscuring the van.

The view rotated, Turk slowly turning the aircraft to take the second shot. Danny selected the global ground-facing view—an image caught by a camera back on the belly of the Tigershark with a wide angle lens.

The image was a curved panorama some 160 degrees wide. Nothing happened for a moment. Then the truck jerked backward and to the side, a puff of smoke engulfing the front.

The men who'd been behind the first truck started to run along the highway south, undoubtedly for their lives.

"Splash two trucks," reported Turk. "Uh, two runners on the ground, going up the road, away from the vehicles."

"I see them," answered Danny. "They any danger to Rubeo?"

"No weapons."

Danny clicked into the interphone circuit, connecting with the pilots. "How long to the target area?"

"Thirty-five minutes, Colonel. We've got the pedals to the metal."

"Keep them there."

12

Libya, north of Mizdah

THE EARTH SHOOK A SECOND TIME AS THE SKY CRACKED behind them. Rubeo recognized the distinctive sound immediately—the Tigershark had fired its rail gun. Whiplash was nearby.

Action was *always* the best alternative.

But they weren't in the clear yet.

"Up over there, onto the peak of that hill," Rubeo told Kharon, pointing to the left. "Come on, come on."

But it was Rubeo who lagged, tiring after only a few steps. While he was in reasonable shape for his age, he had never been an athlete, and on the far side of fifty he wasn't about to win any sprints, let alone a marathon. He went down to his knees as he reached the peak, struggling for breath.

"The trucks blew up," said Kharon.

"It's the Tigershark—it's a Whiplash—aircraft. We're going to be—rescued," said Rubeo, hunting for his breath. "It's just a matter—of time."

"There are two men, running up the road," said Kharon.

"Let them go."

Rubeo pushed up to his feet, steadying himself. They'd run about four hundred yards, not quite a quarter mile.

If the Tigershark was above them, a rescue

team wouldn't be too far off. All they had to do now was sit and wait.

KHARON LOOKED ACROSS THE SANDY HILLTOPS, ORIenting himself in the landscape. There was a town or city to the south, on his right. Behind them, to the west, were more hills. The ground was dry, but small trees and shrubs grew in rows in the valleys. These were the few spots where water remained from the wet season. While the area was not quite as barren and inhospitable as western Libya, where the Sahara's dunes and moonlike extremes ruled, it was neither a breadbasket nor vacation spot.

Should he stay with Rubeo and be rescued? There was no alternative—even if he reached whatever city was to the south, it was a good bet that Foma would find him there.

But surely he couldn't return with Rubeo—he'd be prosecuted for the murder of the villagers. And while he hadn't told Rubeo everything about his work with the Russians, he'd certainly told him enough to warrant an arrest.

Just the sabotage alone would condemn him.

The men with the guns had been killed. Maybe he could get their guns, arm himself, and get to the city. At least then he would have a chance.

He looked at Rubeo. The scientist was thin, older, not frail but certainly not the tall and powerful man in his imagination. Not the monster.

If he could be believed. If what he had said were true?

Kharon, to his shame, sensed it was.

"I forgive you," he told Rubeo. "I was wrong about you." And then he set out on a dead run toward the trucks.

13

Over Libya

DANNY FREAH TAPPED HIS HELMET TO LET THE INCOMing communication pass through to his screen.

It was Chase, the security director of Rubeo's European company.

"Colonel Freah, I see that you have located Dr. Rubeo," said Chase. He sounded as huffy as ever.

"You see that, huh?"

"We've just a few minutes ago intercepted telephone communications between a Russian individual in Tripoli and the Libyan government. He has asked them to scramble forces to retrieve Dr. Rubeo, or kill him if necessary." Chase cleared his throat so loudly that the antinoise dampers in Danny's helmet—designed to filter out the sound of an explosion over the radio—kicked in. "They are also intending to retrieve two items that we have in the second van. Those items are our property, and we want them back."

"What are they?"

"Robots."

"What type?"

"I do not have the details. Both are experimental and highly valuable."

Danny doubted that Chase didn't have the details, but let it pass. "I'll take that into consideration."

"Colonel, I would greatly prefer that the items are recovered intact," said Chase quickly. "I'm sure Dr. Rubeo would agree. However, if that is not possible, one of the items contains equipment that is extremely sensitive. If the situation warrants, you may have to blow it up."

"You don't know what they are, but you think we should destroy them?"

"An ounce of prevention—wouldn't you agree?"

"How exactly do you know about the communication?" asked Danny. "Are you bugging their telephones?"

"We have taken steps to protect Dr. Rubeo," said Chase smugly. "Some of those are not available to you, for a number of reasons."

"Who is the individual?"

"He's a Russian officer with the SVR. I will transfer the information to you anonymously."

"Thanks," said Danny.

THE TIGERSHARK'S COMPUTER WARNED TURK THAT four aircraft were coming off the runway at Ghat.

"Identify."

"Aircraft are MiG–25 NATO reporting code name 'Foxbat,' variant unidentified."

The MiGs were rocket fast—and about as

maneuverable as a refrigerator. They were no match for the Tigershark: easier prey than the Mirages, though they could certainly run away faster.

Their airfield was some four hundred miles south. Assuming they went to their afterburners, they could be in firing range within twenty minutes, perhaps even sooner. That didn't make them an immediate threat, but it could potentially complicate the pickup, as the Osprey would be easy prey.

"Danny, I have four government aircraft getting airborne in a hurry," he radioed. "Not sure yet where they're headed. They could be a threat."

"I doubt they're heading in your direction," said Danny.

"Acknowledged. If they do, can I engage?"

"Hold your present position, Tigershark. I have to sort this out."

Turk understood that getting clearance would be a problem—the aircraft were not yet considered hostile. And in fact they might not be until the Osprey was in serious danger.

"I say we warn them off," suggested Turk. "Tell them to stay clear."

"I'd rather not advertise the fact that we're in the middle of a rescue operation," said Danny. "My pilot says we're about fifteen minutes from touchdown."

"That's still going to cut it close," said Turk. "Your aircraft will be in range of their missiles if they go all out." He pointed at the detail panel, showing what the computer interpreted the MiGs were carrying.

"Computer says they have an Apex variety, R27 missiles. That's a decent medium range missile, Colonel," Turk reported. "Could take out your aircraft."

"Stand by," Danny told him.

"Yeah, roger that," said Turk. He recalculated an orbit that would take him south, putting him in a better position to intercept the planes. As he did, the computer gave him a fresh warning—the Mi-35V Hind and the Chinook in town were revving their rotors.

14

Libya, north of Mizdah

RUBEO STARED AFTER KHARON IN DISBELIEF AS THE other man ran down the hill.

What the hell was he doing?

"Neil!" yelled Rubeo. "Neil!"

There was no answer or acknowledgment. Cursing, he followed.

"Where are you going?" yelled Rubeo. "We have to wait—we'll be rescued shortly. I'm sure of it. Stop. Just stop!"

Kharon either didn't hear him or didn't want

to pay attention. He kept running toward the trucks.

"Damn," muttered Rubeo, his pace slowing to a walk. "Stop!"

KHARON RAN TOWARD THE TRUCK THEY'D BEEN IN. From the rear, it looked undamaged, and he began to hope that he might actually be able to escape—he could drive into the city and find someone, anyone in charge. Eventually, he'd find a way to sell his services in exchange for passage out of the country.

To where? Not to Russia, obviously, as Foma would easily find him there. And there was no going to the States.

Venezuela—the fat bastard Sifontes might actually be useful. But Sifontes was in Tripoli, or somewhere with the rebels. This was government territory.

Just barely.

He could buy his way out to freedom. Maybe South Africa.

Kharon collapsed against the side of the truck. He pushed himself up, then worked his way over to the front with a sideways shuffle, aiming to get in on the passenger side and jump over.

As he reached the door, he saw that the hood had a large hole in it. He stared at it, unsure what he was seeing—something had blown clear through the sheet metal and the engine, and plunged deep into the earth.

The engine had been destroyed. He wasn't going anywhere.

Desperate, he ran to the other vehicle.

RUBEO WALKED THE LAST TWO HUNDRED YARDS, HIS legs drained, his lungs heaving. By the time he got to the trucks, Kharon had collapsed between them.

"Stay away!" he yelled at Rubeo, getting up when Rubeo was only a few feet away. "I don't want to hurt you."

"What are you doing?" asked Rubeo.

"I'm getting the hell out of here. I'm going to the city."

"It's miles from here."

"I have no choice."

"Neil—"

"What do you think? You think they'll let me go when they find out what I did? Do you really think I should hang around to be rescued by the allies?"

Rubeo realized that he was right—surely the allies would treat him harshly once they realized what he had done.

Kharon had tried to ruin him and kill him. There was no way in the world that he should feel anything but disgust and hatred toward him, Rubeo thought.

And yet it seemed he had to do something to help Kharon. Was it the fact that he had loved Kharon's mother? Did he in fact still feel guilty over her death?

It was a death he had no fault in. And yet he did feel remorse—guilt. There was no other way to express it.

Why should he feel guilty for something a criminal had done?

And why did he feel bad, terribly bad, for Kharon, another victim of the crime?

Most people would say that Ray Rubeo was the last person on the face of the earth who would feel an *emotion* toward someone, let alone toward someone who had tried to harm him so badly. And yet, he felt emotion, a deep emotion, as if he had to save a son.

As if he could, if only he could think of something. If only he could find the right equation to solve things.

"Neil, if you go into that town, the Russian agent is going to be looking for you. Your only hope is to stay with me."

"No." Kharon shook his head. "Listen—they're already coming."

Rubeo did hear the sound—a pair of helicopters in the distance. He strained for a moment, trying to identify them. They weren't Ospreys, which would be what Whiplash would use. But perhaps they were other allied aircraft.

Then he realized something else was wrong.

"They're coming from the city," he told Kharon. "Come on. We better take cover."

15

Over Libya

THE ALLIED NO-FLY ZONE EXTENDED ONLY OVER NORTHern Libya, and under the standing rules of engagement, jets elsewhere could be shot down without prior approval from the alliance command only if they were a direct threat to civilians or allied aircraft. Danny had been instructed to notify the allies "if reasonable" before engaging any aircraft, and he dutifully did so, talking directly to the air commander aboard the AWACS aircraft surveying the airspace.

The commander had already vectored two French jets south, and was in the process of alerting another flight as backup.

"Your aircraft is clear to engage if necessary," said the air commander. "We're establishing direct coms now."

"I'd like to keep him over my operation area," said Danny.

"That's all right with us. Colonel—we're seeing two helicopters taking off nearby. We're not sure if they're hostile."

"Can we shoot them down?"

"Have they taken hostile action?"

"I'd rather not wait for that."

"Stand by."

Danny clicked into Turk's frequency.

"I'm talking to the allied command about the helicopters," he told him. "Stand by and be ready."

"They're getting close."

"Are they armed?"

"The Hind has a chin gun," said Turk.

"Understood. Anything hostile, take them out. We're a few minutes away."

"Yup," snapped Turk, clearly irritated that he had to wait. The helicopters could get right next to Rubeo without doing anything hostile, and then shoot. Turk knew there would be no way to protect him.

"Whiplash, be advised, those helicopters are part of the rebel alliance," said the air commander, coming back on the line.

"They came out of a government city," said Danny.

"City leadership has gone over to the rebels."

"When?"

"It's in progress," said the controller. "The helicopters are not hostile. We have spoken to one of their ground commanders."

"You're sure of this?"

"Affirmative."

"They're moving into an area where my guy on the ground may be threatened," answered Danny. "Tell them to get the hell out of there."

"We're working on it. Do not engage."

"Tell them to change course," Danny said.

"I am not in direct communications with them at this time. We're trying to establish a direct link. Suggest your aircraft attempt to contact them as well on Guard."

"If they continue, they will be shot down," Danny warned. He went back to Turk. "Turk, command is saying the aircraft are considered friendly. Try contacting them directly. If they look like a threat, nail them."

"I want them to stay back."

"Understood and agreed. Warn them off. Don't fire unless you have to, but keep Rubeo safe."

"What about the MiGs?"

"Air command allegedly is taking care of them," said Danny. "But same thing there."

"Yeah, roger, I got it. Easier if we were just running this on our own."

"But we're not."

"Tigershark copies."

16

Libya, north of Mizdah

KHARON HESITATED, UNSURE WHAT TO DO. FINALLY HE decided to follow Rubeo, who was heading back up to the hills where they had been. After the first tentative steps, he put his head down and began running in earnest.

Whatever happens, I'll stay with him. I'm as good as dead now anyway.

He caught up with Rubeo and trotted alongside him for a few steps. Then he decided to go ahead.

"I'm going to see if I can see anything from the top of the hill," said Kharon.

"OK," wheezed Rubeo.

Kharon started to run again. He cut left, up the steep side of the hill. Several large rocks blocked his way. He veered right, then felt the side of his foot giving way in the loose dirt. The next thing he knew, he was on the ground, the left side of his face burning.

RUBEO WAS ABOUT TEN YARDS FROM KHARON WHEN he went down. He changed direction, huffing with every step.

The young man lay curled up, in obvious pain. His face had hit the rocks and blood streamed down the side to his chin and the ground. As Rubeo started to inspect the wounds, he saw that Kharon's pants leg was soaked red as well. He reached over and started to examine it.

Kharon yelped as Rubeo touched the leg. His bone had punctured the surface; he had a compound fracture.

"H-Help me," muttered Kharon.

"You're going to be OK," said Rubeo.

"I'm cold."

"You're going into shock," said Rubeo. "You broke your bone. It's a compound fracture."

"What's going to happen?"

"We're going to be OK. My people are coming for me."

The helicopters were getting very loud. They were exposed here, easily seen.

"I'm going to get one of the guns from the van,"

Rubeo told him. "Just in case we have to hold out for a few minutes."

"Don't leave me alone."

"I'll be right back. I promise."

17

Tripoli

THE THREE VANS CARRYING GENERAL ZONGCHEN'S committee and their security team were met at the airport by a pair of NATO armored personnel carriers that had just arrived. The alliance had also added more ground troops—two companies' worth of Spanish infantrymen, who fanned out around the far section of the airport.

Another ring of security had been established near the hangar where they were to meet the Libyan defense minister. Here, members of GROM—roughly the Polish equivalent of American SEALs—stood guard. The committee's own security team was instructed to stay outside the building; no guns were to be allowed inside the walls.

Zongchen looked at Zen as the Polish GROM commander, through a translator, informed him of the ground rules, which he seemed uncomfortable with.

Zen shrugged. "I don't think we're in any more

danger here than anywhere else," he told the general. "Assuming you trust the minister."

"I trust no one," said Zongchen. "But let us proceed."

The minister's presence at the airport was supposed to be a secret, but with all these troops, it was obvious to even the dullest human being that something important was going on. It wouldn't take much to guess what that was.

Zongchen's energy level had increased during the short trip to the airport; he practically sprang ahead toward the terminal. Even Zen, with his powered wheelchair, had trouble keeping up.

The interior of the hangar was empty except for a ring of Polish guards around the walls. A pair of folding tables had been placed end to end near the center of the large space. There were a dozen chairs arranged somewhat haphazardly around them. Three were occupied—one by the new Libyan defense minister, one by his translator, and one by an army general.

Zongchen greeted them enthusiastically. The bearing of the Libyan delegation was clearly more to his liking than that of the rebels, and he seemed more relaxed than he had been in the city. Introductions were made, and as the committee members began sorting themselves into seats, Zongchen began saying that he had just come from a meeting with one of the rebel leaders and they were very eager for a settlement.

"They will have to lay their weapons aside," said the defense minister. "When they have done that, then we will have a talk."

"That wasn't the impression you had given us earlier," said Zen.

"There is much eagerness," added Zongchen. "But it might behoove the government to make a sufficient gesture—perhaps a public announcement of a cease-fire."

The defense minister turned to the general. The two spoke in quick but soft Arabic.

"We need something from the alliance," said the defense minister. "A sign that you will cooperate with us. A temporary cease-fire. From the alliance, and the rebels."

Technically, the alliance wasn't at war with the government, merely enforcing the no-fly zone and protecting interests declared "international" by the UN. So agreeing to a mutual cease-fire was not a big deal. Zongchen told the minister that an agreement might be reached quickly for a cease-fire.

"And from the rebels?"

"They would have to take their own action. But if you had declared the cease-fire, then they would respond to that, I'm sure. Within a matter of—"

"It cannot be unilateral! We cannot just declare the cease-fire ourselves. They won't observe it. You see what dogs we deal with. They lie and cheat at every turn."

We're off to a great start, thought Zen.

18

Over Libya

IT SEEMED AS IF ALL LIBYA WAS DESCENDING ON THE two wrecked vans. Not only were the helicopters only a few minutes away, but now trucks were heading out from the city as well. A small group of people—apparently civilians, though a few had AKs—had left a hamlet about a half mile to the east of the road and were coming up, probably to see what the commotion was about. Meanwhile, the four MiGs were flying northeast on afterburners, taking no heed of the two French Mirages coming in their direction.

The computer calculated that the Mirages had about a sixty-forty percent chance of shooting down the MiGs if they engaged within the next sixty seconds.

Turk didn't particularly like those odds. He had a good opinion of the French pilots, but they were still pretty far north, and since they had to contact the MiGs to warn them off, no chance of surprising the enemy.

"Whiplash, what's your ETA?" Turk asked Danny.

"We'll be overhead in ten minutes."

"I have people on the ground who are going to get there first."

"Hostile?"

"Unknown. They look mostly like civilians, but a couple have rifles. Hard here to tell the difference sometimes." Many people carried rifles for self-protection; Turk certainly would have.

"See if you can scare them off," said Danny.

"You want me to buzz them?" asked Turk.

"Yes, but don't use your weapons if you don't have to. If you're in danger, screw the ROEs. I'll take the heat."

"Roger that."

It was nice to say, but Turk knew he would be court-martialed along with Danny. Still, better to go to prison than live with the death of his guys on his conscience.

"Helicopters have not responded to my hails," Turk answered. "What about them?"

"We'll try raising them on the radio."

"They're getting awful close. I'll buzz them, too," added Turk.

"Copy."

Turk banked to get closer to the people. He wanted to do a loud run to show them he was there.

The problem would be judging their reaction—if they kept coming, did that mean they were on his side?

"Tanks are moving," said the computer as he came out of the turn.

"Computer—which tanks?" asked Turk.

"Tanks in Grid A–3." The area flashed on his sitrep map. "Additional vehicles are under way."

"Why not," muttered Turk. "Just one frickin' open house picnic in beautiful suburban Libya."

19

Libya, north of Mizdah

RUBEO WALKED BACK TOWARD THE TRUCKS, CONserving his energy. His leg muscles had tightened, but adrenaline was surging through his body, and he knew if he could just pace himself, he'd last the ten minutes or so until his people arrived.

He was sure they were close. *Ten minutes*, he told himself.

About fifty yards from the first truck the sky exploded above him. He threw himself down, sure that a missile was streaking at his head.

Gradually he realized it wasn't a missile but the Tigershark, descending at high speed in the direction of the helicopters.

Rubeo got up and continued toward the van, half running, half trotting. One of his dead captors lay in the dirt about thirty feet away. He saw the rifle nearby and ran to grab it. Winded, he paused to catch his breath and examine the gun, making sure it was loaded and ready to fire.

The helicopters were directly south along the road. One was a large Chinook, the other a Russian-made Hind. The Tigershark flew across their path twice, apparently trying to warn them off, but neither helicopter changed direction.

Rubeo thought about the bots, sitting in the back of the nearby van. Diomedes wasn't particularly exotic; it was basically a personalized version of robots Rubeo's company sold to the government. But Arachne was at least a generation and a half beyond what anyone else in the world was using, including the U.S.

He went over to the back of the van, thinking he would put a few bullets through the bots' sensors and intelligence sections. But as he opened the door to the vehicle, he realized he might be able to use the larger bot to get Kharon to safety. And if he was going to save that bot, he might just as well save the other, especially since Arachne was still attached to Diomedes.

He climbed up into the truck. Deciding the laptop-sized controller would be awkward to run with, he removed the smaller handheld mobility controller attached to Diomedes that worked on voice commands. This was a transmitter about the size of a television remote, intended as an aid to workers when moving the bot. Its limited command set could not control any sensors, but that wasn't important now.

Rubeo took the controller and unwound the small headset, which looked like a slightly heavier-duty version than the stereo and microphone headsets used for many mobile phones. The machine took a few moments to boot itself up, checking subsystems and sending current to its motors and limbs. The bot then authenticated Rubeo's voice, checking it against the patterns stored in its memory.

"Exit truck," Rubeo told it as soon as it was ready.

The machine began backing from the vehicle.

Six small video and IR cameras and a sonar suite allowed the bot to orient itself.

"External imagery unavailable," declared the machine, telling Rubeo that there was no feed from an overhead source such as a UAV. This was actually an artifact of the combat control program, which was configured to assume that a full combat situation awareness suite was present. The machine also had a GPS locator and could download area data into its temporary memory if necessary.

"Understood. Proceed."

As Diomedes came to the edge of the truck bed, the sonar unit detected the drop-off. It measured the terrain and decided it could handle the drop. It pushed off quickly, adjusting its arms to balance its weight; it looked almost human, if something with the profile of a sawed-off vacuum cleaner could be said to resemble a person.

It landed flat and drove itself toward Rubeo.

"Follow me," he said, and as he did, something whizzed over his head.

"Gunfire detected," warned the bot. The warning was another attribute of the combat program.

"Move faster," yelled Rubeo, scrambling for the rocks.

20

Above Libya

"GROUND FIRE DETECTED," THE COMPUTER TOLD Turk.

"Locate."

"Highlighted."

"From that group of civilians?"

"Rephrase."

"Disregard." Turk clicked into the Whiplash circuit. "Danny, I have gunfire on the ground. Rubeo is under attack. Somebody in that group of people is firing."

"See if you can scatter the group and isolate the people with guns," said Danny. "Take them down."

Turk turned the plane northeast so he could swing down and attempt to scatter the group.

From his perspective, the gunners were using women and children to shield themselves, making it difficult for them to be attacked without killing innocent lives. Of course, that was the idea. They figured they couldn't lose: if he didn't shoot, they'd get Rubeo. If they were shot at, the odds were the civilians would be hurt as well, undoubtedly giving them some sort of propaganda victory.

Had something like that happened with the kids? Were they actually trained to use MANPADs? Was one hidden somewhere nearby?

But if so, what could he have done?

As Turk approached the group, he lit off IR decoy flares, showering the area. At the same time, he pulled the Tigershark onto her back and hit the throttle full blast, jerking the aircraft upward. The noise was deafening—not quite a sonic boom, but more than a little distracting. One or two of the people began to run, then everyone started to follow, fleeing to the east.

He tilted on his wing, trying to get back into a position to find the people who had fired. But they'd thrown down their weapons in panic, and when he asked the computer to identify them, it responded that none of the people were armed.

"Who threw the guns down?" said Turk.

"Rephrase."

Turk decided to concentrate on the helicopters instead. They were almost at the trucks.

He fell back toward the earth, spinning the wings level and sending off another shower of flares, this time directly in the helicopters' path. They diverted east.

Turk zoomed out the map and took a look at the tanks, which were now moving on a road in the direction of the highway and Rubeo.

"People ran. Helicopters going east. Tanks are still moving," he told Danny. "Can I take them out?"

"Stand by."

"They're close enough to fire," warned Turk.

"I know—hold on. I have allied command."

Danny's tone made it clear that he wasn't happy about what he was hearing on the line.

"I HAVE PEOPLE UNDER FIRE," DANNY REPEATED FOR the French colonel who'd contacted him directly from the command staff. "I have to be permitted to protect them. We're in the middle of a rescue operation."

"We have been told that there is active negotiation between forces, and all forces require an immediate cease-fire," said the colonel, whose English was so-so. "I have these orders, which have come from the general himself to me. All allied aircraft and forces are to stand back."

"Listen, Colonel, with all due respect, I am going to protect my people."

"You must follow the order."

"Yup, that's what I'm doing," snapped Danny, closing the line. A few seconds later the combat air controller came back on.

"We're seeing those tanks moving," said the controller. "You want some help to watch them?"

"I want clearance to blow them up."

"I can't give that to you," said the colonel. He spoke quickly. "I have a flight of A–10Es that I'm going to divert south."

"Are they cleared hot on the tanks?" Danny asked.

"Negative at this time."

The controller gave Danny the contact frequency and call sign—it was Ginella's squadron, which of course made sense, since they were the only Hogs in the theater. Danny quickly made contact with Ginella, who was leading the flight.

"We are en route to you," she told him, without the slightest hint in her voice that they had ever spoken or met. "We should be there in about zero-six minutes."

"Appreciate your help."

"Be advised, I have been ordered to restrain from using weapons at this time," added Ginella.

"Copy that."

"Colonel, just so you know: I do not intend on allowing any American to be harmed in this operation."

"You and I agree one hundred and ten percent," said Danny.

21

Libya

BY THE TIME RUBEO REACHED THE FIRST ROCK AND started up the incline, the bot had caught up. It moved to the right of him and began trudging up the hill, moving at a slow but steady pace. The gunfire had stopped, and the helicopters appeared to have moved off.

Rubeo told the bot to pause as it crested the summit of the second hilltop. He reached it a few moments later, caught his breath, and then had it follow as he climbed over the last hill separating him and Kharon.

The young man blinked at him as he came down the slope. Pain lined his face.

"They'll be here any minute," said Rubeo.

"Don't shoot me."

"I'm not going to. Don't worry," said Rubeo. He glanced self-consciously at the gun, which was pointed at the ground.

"What's going to happen to me?"

"You'll go to the hospital."

"Then what?"

"I don't know." Rubeo shook his head. "I'll help you."

"Why?"

Rubeo couldn't answer the question, not even for himself. He had only a sense that it was the right thing to do—not because of logic, but because of emotion. And even that was vague.

Something shrieked overhead. Rubeo turned his eyes upward, sure it must be the Tigershark. Then there was a loud clap nearby, and the ground seemed to shatter.

"Something is firing at us," he told Kharon.

A second shell whistled nearby. This one was even closer; dirt and debris rained across his back.

"We have to get out of here."

"TANKS ARE FIRING!" TURK TOLD DANNY.

"Take them."

"Yeah. I'm on it."

He was already on a direct line for one of the tanks, roughly three miles to the west. He zeroed it in his targeting screen, corrected slightly, and fired.

A slug sped from the aircraft, hurtling into the fat turret of the tank. Unsure of the result, Turk fired twice more, then pulled off.

The bullets put three large holes in the top of the tank, disabling its main gun and the engine. The T–72 jerked to an abrupt stop, disabled though not in fact destroyed. The almost surgical gunfire had left the crew hatches undamaged, and within a few seconds the three men who had been manning the tank scrambled away from it, undoubtedly stunned and unsure what would happen next.

"Tigershark, this is Shooter One. Are you engaging the tanks?"

"Affirmative Shooter. They have commenced firing."

The sitrep map showed Turk all four Hogs, IDing them by their call signs and squadron identifications. Ginella was flying lead.

Her wingman was Li.

"We can engage," said Ginella. "We're just coming into range."

"I have the one to the north, that one leading on the road," said Turk. "You can have the rest."

"Roger, Tigershark, we copy. We're going to take the others."

"Copy."

Turk swung north to line up his shot. As he did, the RWR began to sound—the MiGs that were supposed to be intercepted by the French planes had turned in his direction. But it wasn't him they were targeting; it was the A–10s.

DANNY FREAH TOOK A LONG, SLOW BREATH, IGNORING the cacophony of protests in his headset. He leaned forward between the two Osprey pilots, trying to spot the trucks in the distance.

"I'm being told to turn back north," the pilot told him. "The air commander is trying to reach you."

"You're under my direct orders," Danny told him calmly. "You have no responsibility."

"Sir, I'm going to save our guys, too. Screw everything else."

"Let's do it, then."

"We have more vehicles coming up the road," he told Danny. "Looks like a scout car, and a couple of pickups. Those pickups usually have fifty cals on the back. I'd like to engage them."

Even without the allied order to stand down and avoid combat, engaging the vehicles was highly questionable. They had not fired at either the Osprey or Rubeo, and in fact had done nothing overtly threatening. But the situation now was simply too chaotic, and their mere presence was a threat. The Osprey couldn't land close to a fifty caliber, let alone three of them.

"Fire some warning shots and see if they stop," Danny told the pilot.

"If they don't?"

"Then splash them."

RUBEO HEARD THE ROAR OF THE OSPREY'S ENGINES IN the distance, but the shells were still raining down, passing overhead. He guessed they were being aimed at the road, but that was hardly a consolation—any second now he expected one to land short and wipe them out.

"I can't carry you," he told Kharon.

"Leave me!"

"That's not what I meant. Come on." Rubeo hooked his arms under the other man's shoulder's. "I have to get you on the bot."

Kharon screamed in anguish. Rubeo hesitated, but the whistle of another shell going overhead convinced him to continue. He half lifted, half dragged Kharon to the nearby bot, cringing as the younger man howled in pain.

"We're getting out of here," Rubeo told him, putting him down as gently as he could manage on the rear bed of the bot. Kharon twisted, grabbing hold of the spar.

"Diomedes, follow me," Rubeo told the bot, starting out of the small hollow where he'd taken shelter.

He'd taken exactly three steps when he felt himself pushed from behind, thrown forward by a force he couldn't fathom.

22

Over Libya

TURK ZEROED HIS GUN ON THE TANK AND FIRED SIX bursts, the bolts leaping from the gun in a sharp, staccato rhythm that seemed to suspend the Tigershark in midair. The line of his bullets was tighter this time, and there was no escape for the men inside—the first slug ignited one of the tank's shells, and secondary explosions ripped through the tight quarters of the armored vehicle, mincing its occupants. The rest of the bullets simply sliced through the fireballs.

As soon as he let off the trigger, Turk turned his attention to the MiGs. They had separated into two groups, one duo diverting toward the French interceptors and the other coming at the Hogs.

The A–10s were easy targets for the MiGs, but to their credit they remained in their attack patterns, closing in on the tanks.

"Shooter, I'm on those MiGs," Turk told Ginella. "I have them."

"We appreciate it."

There was a launch warning—the MiGs were firing.

"Four missiles," reported the computer. "AA–10 Alamo. Semiactive radar."

"Plot an intercept to missiles," said Turk. He could line up and shoot at the missiles with the rail gun.

"Impossible to intercept all four."

"Best solution."

A plot flashed up on the screen.

Three targets. Two were heading for Ginella's aircraft, Shooter One. The other was going for Beast in Shooter Three.

"Identify target of remaining missile," Turk said.

"Missile is targeted at Shooter Four."

Li's plane, on Ginella's wing.

"Recalculate to include missile targeting Shooter Four."

The computer presented a new solution, striking one of the missiles on Ginella as well as Li's sole missile. But Beast was completely unprotected. Before Turk could decide what to do, four more missiles launched. The computer began running a variety of solutions, but Turk realized that none were going to completely protect the Hogs.

"Choose Solution One," he said, moving to the course queue as it snapped into his heads-up. "Shooter squadron, you have missiles inbound."

"We're aware of that, Tigershark."

"I can get some, not all."

"Whatever you can do for us," said Ginella. Her voice was cold and flat, without effect. "Tanks will be down in a second."

23

Libya

DANNY FREAH GRABBED FOR A HANDHOLD AS THE Osprey pirouetted above the road, the chain gun in its nose tearing up the road in front of the approaching vehicles. The two trucks veered off to the side but the armored car kept moving forward.

"Stop the bastard," said Danny.

The Osprey spun back quickly. The gun under its chin swiveled, and a steady *rat-rat-rat* followed. Danny leaned forward, watching through the windscreen as the gun's bullets chewed through the rear quarter of the lightly armored vehicle. Steam shot up from the armored car. The right rear wheel seemed to fall away, sliding from the cloud of smoke and disintegrating metal. The rest of the vehicle morphed into a red oblong, fire consuming it in an unnaturally symmetrical shape. The red flared, then changed to black as the symmetry dissolved in a rage.

"People on the ground, coming up along the road," said the copilot.

"Where are our guys?" asked Danny.

"Going for them now."

RUBEO FELL FACE-FIRST INTO THE SIDE OF THE HILL. His face felt as if it had caught fire and had been ripped downward at the same time; his head pounded with pain. He pushed back with his hand, then fell to the side, exhausted and spent.

What had Bastian's advice been? What was his old colonel telling him?

Find out why it happened. For yourself.

He'd done that—Kharon had caused it, with the help of the Russians. He'd closed the circle of a crime committed years before. A crime Rubeo knew he had been completely innocent of, yet one he'd always felt guilty about.

How did he benefit from knowing that?

He should feel relief knowing he wasn't responsible for the accident, and more important, for the civilian deaths. And yet he didn't. He should feel horror at Kharon's crime—he'd committed murder. Anger. Rage. But all he felt was pity, pity and sorrow. Useless emotions.

Was that what knowledge brought you? Impotent sadness?

The man who had built his life around the idea that intelligence could solve every problem lay in the dirt and rubble, body battered and exhausted. He knew many things, but what he knew most of all now was pain.

Up, he told himself. *Up.*

You know what happened. And what of it? Knowledge itself is useless. It's how it's put to use, if it can be used at all.

Diomedes idled behind him. He could feel the soft vibration of its engine.

Time to get up. Time to move on.

"Follow me," he said, starting to move on his hands and knees.

The bot moved behind him, carrying Kharon and nipping at Rubeo's heels.

His ears pounded. Rubeo realized belatedly that he couldn't hear properly. The ground vibrated with something, but whether it was far or close, he had no idea.

Gradually his strength returned. He pushed up to his knees, then to his feet, walking unsteadily up the slope. The world had shaded yellow, blurring at the edges. Rubeo pushed himself forward, trudging across the side of a hill, then down to his right, in the direction of the road. The loose dirt and sand moved under the soles of his feet, and he felt himself sliding. He began to glide down the hill, legs bent slightly and arms out for balance; a snowboarder couldn't have done it better.

The bot followed. Rubeo glanced at it, making sure Kharon was still on the back. Then he began moving parallel to the road. He passed the disabled trucks, continuing toward a flat area he remembered from earlier.

KHARON'S LEG HAD GONE NUMB, BUT HE ACTUALLY felt better. The shock had passed; his head was clear. He felt stronger—still injured, of course, but no longer paralyzed.

He clung to the crane arm of the bot as they rumbled across the terrain, the vehicle bobbing and weaving like a canoe shooting rapids. It settled somewhat as it moved off the hill onto the level shoulder alongside the road.

An Osprey, black and loud, approached from the south. Kharon stared as it grew larger. His eyes, irritated by the grit in the wind, seemed to burn with the image. The ground shook. The wings seemed to move upward, the control surfaces sliding down as the rotors at the tips tilted. Dirt flew everywhere.

The world began to close around him, becoming dark. He was a child, trapped in the closet, waiting for something that would never happen.

All these years, and he had never really moved beyond those long, terrible moments. Everything he had done, his achievements, his studies, paled compared to that dreadful time. Life had failed to lift him beyond the sinkhole he'd crawled into that night.

Such a failure. Such a waste. Even the one thing I lived for, revenge, proved unreachable. Rubeo wasn't even the culprit. Rubeo wasn't even the villain. The people who helped me were. They probably knew it from the start.

Nothing is left.

DANNY MOVED TO THE DOOR AS THE OSPREY STARTED to settle toward the earth. Boston was already there, gun in hand, ready to leap out. They had to move quickly; the Osprey was extremely vulnerable when landing and taking off.

Not to mention on the ground.

Something shrieked. The aircraft jerked upward.

"Incoming shells," said the pilot over the interphone. "Evading—hang on."

RUBEO SAW THE AIRCRAFT AS IT SWEPT OVERHEAD. Dirt swirled from the wash of the propellers spinning. He put his head down, shielding it with his hands.

"Into the aircraft," he said, speaking into the microphone for the bot. He still couldn't hear; his voice in his head sounded hollow and strange. "Go to the ramp at the rear."

The wind increased. Rubeo bent almost double and stopped moving forward. All he had to do now was wait.

They were out of this damn hellhole.

Diomedes poked him in the back. Rubeo turned, then fell as the wind peaked. He rolled onto his back, eyes and face covered by his hands. He spread his fingers hesitantly, then saw something black fleeing above.

The Osprey was scooting away.

"What the hell?" he yelled in anguish.

The ground shook. Rubeo jerked back to his feet and began shouting at the aircraft. A geyser of sand and dirt rose from the road about a hundred yards away.

"We're being fired at," Rubeo yelled to Kharon. He turned and saw Diomedes, which had stopped about twenty yards away, waiting in the spot where the Osprey would have landed. A fresh geyser rose just beyond the bot.

The explosions were smaller than before—a mortar or maybe two or three.

"This way," Rubeo told the bot. He fingered the microphone cord and started south. The bot quickly followed. He heard something, a growl in the air—his hearing was returning.

"MORTAR TEAM BEHIND THOSE TWO TRUCKS," THE pilot told Danny.

"Eliminate it."

"With pleasure."

The Osprey's tail rose, tilting the gun in its nose toward the trucks. A chain of bullets began spitting from the aircraft, chewing the ground just behind the vehicle. The Osprey danced right. The bullets disappeared in a stream of debris. A cloud rose where they landed, growing quickly until it mushroomed over the trucks and everything within fifty yards.

The mortar fire stopped. But there were more vehicles coming out from the city. And the people who had come from the village were gathering along the road about two miles away. Whiplash had blundered into the middle of an uprising—troops who had deserted earlier interpreted the military action as an attack from the loyal troops, and were coming out to fight. The government forces, meanwhile, had seen the action as a rebel attack. And in the middle was the scientist they were trying to rescue.

"Colonel, the air commander is reporting that there's activity at that army base to the west," said the Osprey pilot. "This place is getting damn busy."

"I thought these bastards were negotiating a cease-fire," cursed Danny.

24

Tripoli

THE DEFENSE MINISTER'S AIDE LEANED OVER AND WHISpered something in his boss's ear. The two spoke quickly.

"I have a report that I must hear," the minister told Zongchen and the others. "There is a confrontation—American aircraft are involved."

"Which American aircraft?" asked Zen.

"Several. A black aircraft like a helicopter. And A–10 fighters—"

"You mean an Osprey?" said Zen.

"There is a major fight with rebels," said the minister. "A rebellion in Mizdah. I must take this call."

The aide handed him a phone. Zongchen looked at Zen.

"Excuse me a second." Zen wheeled backward from the table. There was only one unit operating a black Osprey in Libya—Whiplash. He took out his satellite phone, hesitated a moment, then hit the quick dial for Danny.

Instead of getting Danny directly, the call was rerouted through the Whiplash system to a desk operative at Whiplash's headquarters in the U.S. on the CIA campus. The officer was assigned to monitor and assist Danny and the team during operations; he was in effect a secretary, though no one would ever call him that. "Colonel Freah's line."

"This is Zen Stockard. I need to talk to Danny right now."

"Senator, he is in Libya right now, in the middle of a firefight."

"I know exactly where he is. I have battle information for him," said Zen.

"Stand by, Senator."

The line cleared, seemingly empty. Then Danny came on, as loud and clear as if he were in the same room.

"Zen, we're in the middle of heavy shit here. Rubeo is on the ground and we're trying to get to him. I got government and rebel forces on both sides."

"I have the Libyan government minister here. I'm going to get a cease-fire."

"That would be damn timely."

"Give me your location. Then keep the line to me open if you can."

"Near Mizdah."

Zen put the phone in his lap and wheeled back to the table.

"If you want a negotiated peace," he told the minister loudly, "call your forces off the Osprey at Mizdah they're telling you about."

Zen turned to Zongchen. "We need to tell the princess to get her people down there to stop as well."

25

Libya

THE OSPREY ROARED OVERHEAD. RUBEO COULD HEAR almost perfectly now—the engines sounded like a pair of diesel trucks that had lost their mufflers.

The aircraft circled around, checking the nearby terrain as it came down to land.

"Follow," Rubeo told Diomedes. He looked at Kharon, still gripping the crane spar. Kharon looked haunted, shocked into another dimension. "It'll be all right," Rubeo yelled at him. "We're getting out this time."

The aircraft settled down thirty yards away. Troopers leapt from the door at the side. Rubeo tried to run toward them but his legs wouldn't carry him any faster than a walk.

Someone grabbed him. It was Sergeant Rockland—Boston.

"Come on, Doc," yelled the sergeant, hooking his arm around so he supported Rubeo on one side. "Let's get you the hell out of here."

"The bot."

"Yeah, yeah, the mechanical marvel."

"Kharon, get Kharon."

"We're getting him," said Boston. "Let's go, let's go. There are all sorts of people heading this way."

KHARON CURLED HIS BODY DOWN AS THE WIND swirled around him and the robot rolled to the rear of the Osprey. One of the troopers ran beside him, gave him a thumbs-up, then turned and waved his gun back and forth, making sure there was no one there.

God, help me.

The bot continued inside the hull of the aircraft, moving forward. The side door was open, a trooper leaning through the open space, a safety belt holding him as the aircraft pitched upward. Kharon was a foot or two away.

The roar began to quiet. For a moment Kharon felt safe, untouchable. But then he noticed the darkness around him, the walls close by.

The closet.

Someone was yelling outside.

"Neil! Neil!"

His mother.

Kharon unfolded his fingers and then his arm. He took a tentative step. Someone grabbed for him. He pushed away.

Leave me alone!

Leave me!

"Neil!"

The sides closed in. He couldn't breathe. He was going to be smothered.

The door was open in front of him.

With all his strength, he leapt for safety, ignoring the surge of pain in his leg, ignoring all the pain, ducking his head and driving ahead for the light.

BY THE TIME RUBEO REALIZED WHAT KHARON WAS doing it was too late. The Whiplash trooper at the door dove at him, but Kharon moved too fast: He leapt through the open hatchway at the side of the aircraft, tumbling down some one hundred feet to the rocks.

"Damn," muttered Rubeo, sinking back onto the web bench at the side of the aircraft. "Oh damn."

26

Over Libya

THE TIGERSHARK SPIT ITS SLUGS IN A COMPUTER-controlled spurt, current and metal flashing in a dance of force and counterforce.

The rail gun had originally been conceived as an antiballistic missile weapon, and the computer program controlling it still bore that DNA, able to handle the complicated coefficients of speed, mass, and trajectory with quick ease. From a mathematical point of view, the fact that the warheads it was aiming at were comparatively small did not present a great difficulty; the formula always aimed at a single point in space, and as with any point, it had no dimension whatsoever. It was simply there.

But on the practical level, the predictable margin of error increased dramatically in an inverse proportion to the suitable target area; in other words, the smaller the target, the more likely the slug was to miss. To compensate, the computer spit out more slugs as Turk fired. While he could override this, it wasn't advisable in an engagement with missiles, especially given that each individual encounter lasted only a few seconds at most.

But this did mean that the gun needed additional time to cool down between engagements, and even if the time was measured in fractions of seconds, each delay meant he might not reach Li in time. For the pilot stubbornly insisted to himself that he would in fact save her; that he would finally end in position to shoot down the last missile before it got her.

The Hogs completed their attacks and ducked away, firing chaff and working their electronic countermeasures. The Russian missiles were sticky beasts, staying tight to the trail of the planes they had targeted.

To the west, one of the MiGs had already been shot down, but that didn't change anything for Turk—there were eight missiles in the air, and every one of them was homing in on the back of someone he needed to protect.

Danny's voice came out of the buzz around his head. "Whiplash is away."

Turk didn't bother acknowledging. The only thing that mattered now were these eight missiles.

A tone sounded in Turk's headset and his screen's pipper flashed black—the computer had calculated that the first target was "dead." There was no time to linger over the kill, or even watch the missile explode; Turk immediately turned to the next course, following the line laid out in his virtual HUD.

By the time the computer reported "Target destroyed," he was already firing at the nose of the second missile, pushing the plane down at the last instant to keep with the missile's sudden lurch. The maneuver probably meant that the missile had been sucked off by one of the countermeasures, but Turk was too intent on his mission to break at that moment. Once again he got a kill tone; once again he came to a new course.

He saw Li's plane out of the corner of his eye. Had she gotten away? Would she?

Tempted to make sure, he started to fire too soon. The computer tacitly scolded him, elevating the course icon and flashing its pipper yellow, indicating he was no longer on target. He willed himself back to course as he continued to fire, pressing the attack until the tone. Then he pushed hard right, looking for the last missile, looking for Li.

He saw her plane, then saw the missile closing.

God, why didn't I save her instead of Ginella?

The computer set up solutions for the remaining missiles, but all Turk could see was Li's plane.

He turned hard, still with her, then saw something flashing next to her.

By the time he cringed, it had passed. The Hog went on its wing to the left; the missile exploded right.

She was OK. Her ECMs had managed to bluff the missile away.

Turk turned hard to the computer's suggested course, aiming for the next missile.

27

Over Libya

AS FAR AS DANNY FREAH WAS CONCERNED, NEIL Kharon's body wasn't important enough to risk going back for.

It was a cold decision, but one he had no trouble making. There was still sporadic fire in the area, and he had Rubeo and the robots aboard.

"We'll get him if things calm down," Danny told Rubeo, kneeling on the deck of the Osprey as the aircraft sped northward. "Zen is working on it."

"It doesn't matter, really," said Rubeo blankly. "It doesn't really matter."

"Antiair battery to the east activating radar," warned the copilot. "Radar—we have a lot of radars. Everything they got."

Danny got up and grabbed his phone. He was still dialed into Zen's private line.

"Zen, are you there?"

"I'm here, Danny."

"We could really use that cease-fire you promised," he said as the aircraft tucked down toward the ground. They would attempt to bypass the radar by staying close to the earth, where it would have trouble seeing them.

"The defense minister is on the phone with the air force right now," Zen told him.

"There's an antiair battery north of us. It—"

"All right, hold on." Zen said something Danny couldn't hear, then came back on the line. "Give me a GPS reading."

"Every goddamn radar in the country is lighting up," said Danny. "Get them all."

Zen didn't answer. Danny could hear someone speaking sharply on the other side of the line but couldn't make out what they were saying.

"Radars are turning off," said the pilot.

Danny waited. Zen came on the line a few minutes later.

"Danny?"

"I'm here. The radars are off. Thanks."

"Not a problem."

"What'd you tell him?"

"I said we'd blow them up if they weren't off in sixty seconds," said Zen. "I wish every negotiation was that easy."

28

Over Libya

THOROUGHLY CONFUSED BY THE ELECTRONIC COUNtermeasures and now at the far end of their range, the last two missiles blew themselves up several miles from their targets, destroying themselves in a futile hope that their shrapnel might take out something nearby.

Turk pulled the Tigershark higher as he got his bearings. The A–10s were forming up to the north, taking stock and preparing for the flight back home.

All except Shooter One, which was climbing to the east.

At first Turk assumed that Ginella was checking on the tanks, making sure they had been destroyed. He left her, and checked in with Danny, who said they had recovered Rubeo and his gear and were on their way back to Sicily. Then he talked to the air controller, who said frostily that there were no longer any Libyan aircraft in the skies.

"State your intentions," added the controller, sounding as if he were challenging a potentially hostile aircraft.

"I'm going to escort Whiplash Osprey back to Sicily," said Turk, setting up a course.

"Acknowledged."

I bet you'll be testifying at my court-martial, thought Turk.

He radioed the Osprey pilot. With the Libyan radars now silent, the aircraft was climbing, aiming to get high enough to escape any stray ground fire.

"Stay on your present course and I'll be with you in zero-five," said Turk.

The computer estimated he would catch up in two minutes. He checked his instruments, working systematically as he took stock.

The Tigershark had performed well, and according to her indicators was in prime condition, none the worse for having fired more slugs in anger in five minutes than in her entire life.

They could say or do what they wanted about Turk; the aircraft had passed every real-life test thrown at it. As for the Sabres—once whatever had screwed them up was fixed, they too were ready for front-line duty.

He'd proven himself. Whatever he had missed the other day with Grizzly—if he'd missed anything—it wasn't because he was afraid to fire. He wasn't a coward or a shirker or anything else.

He was sure he hadn't missed the weapon. But one way or another, he was sure of his ability to fly and fight.

Turk felt himself start to relax. He tried to resist—it was dangerous to ease up before you landed.

He checked the sitrep map. The French Mirages had shot down one MiG and now, ironically, were helping guide an allied rescue helicopter in. The other government planes had fled south—not to their base, but to Chad.

The pilots were getting out while the getting out was good, Turk thought.

He zoomed the sitrep to check on the Hogs. They had separated. Shooter Two and Three were flying north, heading on a straight line back toward Sicily. Four, meanwhile, was flying west toward Shooter One, which was climbing to the east.

Which seemed odd to Turk.

Given his history with Ginella, he hesitated to ask what was going on. Still, her flight path was almost directly across the Osprey's.

"Shooter One, this is Tigershark. Wondering if you're setting up on a threat in Whiplash Osprey's direction," he said lightly.

There was no response. Turk tried again.

OK, he thought when she didn't answer. Be that way. He checked his location; he was about a minute and a half behind the Osprey, catching up fast. Ginella was going to pass just to the north, but would clear the MV–22 by a good distance—she was at 30,000 feet and climbing.

Turk remembered an old joke about the Hogs, to the effect that the pilots climbing to altitude packed a lunch. The new engines took a lot of the punch out of the joke.

He told the Osprey he was coming up on his six. The Osprey pilot asked him what was up with the A–10; there had been no communication from Shooter One.

"I'm adjusting course to the west just to widen the distance," said the pilot, giving himself an even wider margin for error. "Are you in contact?"

"Negative."

Not acknowledging his hails was one thing, but not acknowledging the Osprey pilot's was, at best, extremely unprofessional—so much so that Turk realized something must be wrong with Ginella. He was just about to try hailing her again when Li called on his frequency.

"Tigershark, this is Shooter Four. Are you in contact with Shooter One?"

"Negative, Shooter Four. I have been trying to hail her."

"Same here. There's got to be some sort of problem with her aircraft," added Li. "Can you assist?"

"Stand by."

Turk talked to Danny and the Osprey pilot, telling them that he thought the Hog was having some sort of emergency. Both assured him that the flight could get back on its own if necessary. A few moments later the flight controller came on, requesting that he help make contact with the Hog.

Turk acknowledged and changed course, accelerating to catch up quickly with the A–10. The aircraft had continued to climb, and was now at nearly 35,000 feet.

"Was Shooter One damaged in the fight?" Turk asked Li.

"She said she got a shrapnel hit but that it wasn't much. Her last transmission said she was in good shape and going to check on the tanks."

"Sound giddy?"

"Hard to say. You think she's OK?"

"I'd say no. I'm guessing hypoxia."

"Yeah. Or worse."

Hypoxia was the medical term for lack of oxygen. There was a whole range of symptoms, the most critical in this case being loss of consciousness. Turk suspected that Ginella's plane was flying itself. With no one at the controls, it would keep going until it crashed.

She might in fact already be dead.

He tried hailing her several times, using both her squadron frequency and the international emergency channel. A pair of F/A–18s were coming southwest from a carrier in the eastern Mediterranean, but Turk was much closer, and within a minute saw the distinctive tail of the aircraft dead ahead.

"Shooter Four, I'm coming up on her six."

"Four acknowledges."

Turk backed off the throttle, easing the Tigershark into position over the Hog's right wing. He zoomed the camera covering that direction so he could look into the bubble canopy of the A–10E. At first glance there seemed to be nothing wrong beyond a few shrapnel nicks in the aircraft's skin. But when he zoomed on Ginella, he saw her helmet slumped to the side.

Turk radioed Li and the controller, giving his position and heading, then telling them what he saw.

"She's gotta be out of it," he added. "Autopilot has to be flying the plane. I don't know if we can rouse her."

"Maybe if you buzz nearby," suggested Li. "Maybe the buffet will wake her up."

It was a long shot, but worth a try. Turk took a deep breath, then moved his hand forward on the simulated throttle.

SOME TWENTY MILES WEST, DANNY FREAH LISTENED to the pilots as they attempted to rouse the Hog squadron commander. He'd heard of some similar incidents in the past, including one that had involved an A–10A that was lost over the U.S.

Any pilot flying above 12,000 or so could easily succumb to hypoxia, even in an ostensibly pressurized aircraft, if he wasn't receiving the proper mix of oxygen, or if something otherwise impeded the body's absorption of that oxygen.

How ironic, he thought, for a pilot to survive combat only to succumb to a run-of-the-mill problem.

"I knew his mother," said Rubeo, who was sitting on the bench next to him.

"Who?" Danny lifted the visor on his helmet and turned to Rubeo. "Who are you talking about?"

"Neil Kharon. The man who jumped. His mother worked at Dreamland. It was before your time."

"I'm sorry."

Rubeo nodded.

"I was listening to a transmission," said Danny. "One of the aircraft that was helping us is having a flight emergency. They can't raise the pilot."

"I see."

"Turk thinks she lost oxygen."

Rubeo stared at him. Danny was about to turn away when the scientist asked what type of airplane it was.

"An A–10E. One of the Hogs I mentioned earlier."

"Have the Tigershark take it over," suggested Rubeo.

"How?"

"Give me your com set."

"It's in the helmet."

"Then give me the helmet."

TURK PULLED THE TIGERSHARK BACK PARALLEL TO THE A–10, this time on its left side. Three swoops and Ginella had not woken.

The plane, however, had moved into a circular pattern, apparently responding to a slight shift of pressure on the controls.

"She's going to be bingo fuel soon," said Li, begging the question of how her own fuel was.

"I'm not sure what else we can do," Turk said. "Maybe as she starts to run out of fuel the plane will descend. Once she's below twelve thousand feet, she'll regain consciousness and she can bail."

Li didn't answer. The odds of that scenario coming true, let alone having a good outcome, were incalculable.

"Tigershark, this is Ray Rubeo." The transmission came from Danny's helmet, but Rubeo's ID flashed on the screen, the Whiplash system automatically recognizing his voice. "Are you on the line?"

"Affirmative, Dr. Rubeo."

"You are following an A–10E. Am I correct?"

"Yes, sir. The plane is flying in a circular pattern. I'm guessing she has a very slight input on the stick because—"

"No response from the pilot?"

"Copy that. No response."

"The A–10E is equipped with a remote suite that can be controlled from your aircraft by tuning to the proper frequency and using the coded command sequence, just as if it was Flighthawk or Sabre."

"Yeah, roger," said Turk. "I did some of the testing. But the pilots told me the circuitry is inactive in these planes."

"Inactive but not nonexistent, Captain. Stand by, please. I need to consult one of my people."

THE DILEMMA INVIGORATED RUBEO, GIVING HIM SOMEthing to focus on other than Neil Kharon and his horrendously wasted talent and life.

The A–10E system had been adopted from one of the control setups developed for the early Flighthawks. It wasn't quite cutting edge, but that was by design, since the Air Force specs called for a system that was both "compact and robust"—service-ese for a small but well-proven unit.

One of the primary requirements—and one of the things that had caused the main contractor on the project serious headaches—was the need to make the remote flight system entirely secondary to the "ordinary" pilot system. Unlike the Tigershark, which had been built from the ground up as a remote aircraft, the A–10E had to include legacy systems, most significantly in this case the autopilot, which had only been added to the plane in the A–10C conversions. Because of that, one of Rubeo's companies had worked closely with the main contractor, developing a system that allowed both to coexist in the aircraft.

The head of that project was Rick Terci, an engineer based in Seattle. Rubeo's call woke him up.

"The system won't dead start in the air if it's been under human control," said Terci when Rubeo explained what was happening. "Not without her permission. The only way I can think of to get the remote on would be to turn the autopilot on first. Then you could cut in with the command. That would work. But you have to get the autopilot on."

"Yes." Rubeo saw the unit in his head, a black box located at the right side of the fuselage just in front of the canopy. For a normal aircraft, the shot would be almost impossible. But the Tigershark's rail gun could hit the spot with precision.

How, then, would they get the remote control to engage?

"I'm thinking if we could jolt the plane electronically," Rubeo told Terci. "If we could surge the power, and the computer would reset. At that point we can contact it and take over."

"You mean reboot the entire electrical system? In the air? Sure, but how do we do that? And still have something left?"

"Well how *would* you do it?" Rubeo asked. He let his mind wander, trying to visualize the system.

"Can't think of a way," said Terci. "Not while it's flying. Not and still have the plane able to fly."

"If we shoot out the generators?"

"Then you have no power at all. Not going to work." Terci made a strange sound with his mouth. Rubeo realized the engineer was biting his thumbnail.

A good sign; he only did that when he was on the verge of an idea.

"No, it's simpler," said Terci. "Just have a flight condition where the autopilot takes over. Then sign in from there. But you have to get the autopilot on . . . Say there's a sudden dip so the airplane loses altitude."

"The safety protocol won't allow the system to take over if it went into autopilot while under pilot control," said Rubeo. "We still need to have the system reboot somehow."

"Yes," said Terci, repeating Rubeo's point. "You need an electric shock to delete what was originally programmed, or it will just return to the pilot. It just has to reboot—no, wait—you could just delete that part of the memory. No, just make the computer think there's an anomaly. You don't need a massive event, just a reset."

"How?"

"Hmmph."

"What if we overload a data collector circuit so the computer reads it as a fault and has to reset? If the circuit no longer exists, it will reset into test mode."

"Yes. You take over in retest. Sure, because it's resetting the program registers."

"Will that work?"

"Maybe. I'm not sure. But what circuit would be the right one to blow out?"

"There must be a dozen. Can you access the schematics?"

"I don't know if my computer is on. Then I have to get into the company mainframes."

"You have less than ten minutes to discover the proper circuit," said Rubeo. "Please do not waste them by saying how difficult the task is."

TURK HEARD LI CONTACT THE TANKER. HE COULD TELL from the tone in her voice that she thought Ginella was gone.

And maybe he did, too.

There was no reason for him to want to save her. On the contrary, he was sure his life would be easier if she were dead.

But it was his duty to try.

"Captain Mako, this is Ray Rubeo."

"Go ahead, Doc."

"I have a sequence of events that I believe if followed very minutely will result in the aircraft's remote control apparatus starting up. At that point, you will be able to issue the proper commands and fly the plane from the Tigershark."

"Really?"

"There is an element of doubt," added Rubeo. "But I am of the mind that it is better than nothing. I think it does have a chance of working."

"I'm game."

"I am going to add one of my specialists to the line. Your first shot must be very precise. The second even more so."

Turk listened as the engineer described the locations on the Hog that had to be struck. Fortunately, the engineer was able to upload the targeting data to him through the Whiplash system, and within a few seconds the Tigershark's computer marked the location.

Making the first shot was simply a matter of climbing 5,000 feet, then ramming straight down to an intercept course at exactly 632 knots and firing.

That was tough, but the second shot involved an even more difficult problem. It had to be made at a box housed near the plane's right wing root within thirty seconds of the first.

"Thirty seconds?" Turk asked.

"Has to do with the monitors that control the emergency system check-in," replied Terci. "The battery will—"

"All right, all right," said Turk. "Getting into position for the first shot."

Turk hit his mark 5,000 feet over the Hog and pushed down so he would be on the intercept point. As he reached the target speed, the computer gave him the shooting cue and he fired.

Perfect shot.

But as he swung into position for the second shot, the A–10E turned on its wing and began to dive straight down.

"There's a problem," he told Rubeo. He pushed his plane to follow. "I think we're going to lose her."

SINCE THE HELMET WAS TIED INTO THE WHIPLASH system, Rubeo could command the screen to show him what the Tigershark saw. He did so, then immediately began to regret it—the A–10A was in what looked like a slow motion downward spiral, heading for the ground.

They had not calculated this possibility.

Why?

"The pilot must be semiconscious," said Terci. "She's fighting the controls."

"Yes."

"If she can level off at ten thousand feet or so, she'll be fine."

"What about the second shot?"

"You won't get it now. Get her to level off."

"I doubt that will be easy for her to do. How else can we override that system?"

"That's the only circuit possible, and even that's iffy."

Turk looked at the airplane. He had to strike a glancing blow on a plane that was very close to entering a spin. Even lining up to get to the right parameter for the computer to calculate the shot was going to be tough.

There was no other choice.

"I DON'T KNOW THAT I CAN MAKE THE SHOT, EVEN WITH the computer's help," said Turk.

They were now at 25,000 feet, moving downward in a large but gradually tightening circle. If Ginella was trying to regain control—a theory Turk was dubious about—she wasn't having any particular success.

The computer's solution was for the Tigershark to exactly duplicate the Hog's flight. It was the sort of solution a computer would propose—it saw nothing out of the ordinary, since the impossibility of doing that hadn't been programmed.

"I can't follow this course and keep my plane," Turk told Rubeo. "She's going to end up in a spin. It'll get faster and faster. I have to try to stop it, then take the shot."

"How exactly do you propose to do that?"

"I come in along the wing and tap it. It'll knock the plane out of the course she's on."

"Will it stabilize it?"

"No way—but if I can just get the flight path to straighten out a little, I can take that shot."

"How do you propose to do this?" said Rubeo sarcastically. "Are you going to reach your hands out?"

"No. I use my wings. It'll work if I'm careful. I just have to do enough to disrupt the plane."

"You're sure?"

It was as much of a long shot as Rubeo's original solution, even more so. It was very possible he might throw it into an even worse situation. But it was the only thing he could think of to save her. And he knew he had to try.

"Yes," he told Rubeo, trying to put steel in his voice. "It will work."

Turk dropped the Tigershark closer to the Hog, ignoring the proximity warning.

Every novice flier has to demonstrate that he or she can recover from an incipient spin before being allowed to do anything very fancy in an airplane. The first few times, the experience is fairly scary, as the sensation of vertigo—and worse, the feeling that you aren't moving at all—tends to completely unnerve someone new to the cockpit. There is actually considerable time to correct the problem, but only if you go about things methodically, with a clear mind.

Mastering this and other emergency situations isn't important just because of the danger they represent. Being able to control the aircraft through them instills a critical level of confidence in a novice pilot.

Turk felt like a newbie now. He remembered the leading edge of his first incipient spin. He'd almost panicked—almost, *almost*, lost it.

The trick had been to let go. Not literally, but mentally—to let go of his fear and self-doubt and trust himself, what he had been taught, what he knew he had to do.

To trust the plane.

It was an important lesson—one you always needed to relearn, especially in the face of mistakes.

But did that lesson really apply here? This was something very different. He trusted himself and his plane—but the A–10E wasn't his to trust.

Instinct told him to try. There was no other choice.

"Tigershark, we don't think that's going to work," said Rubeo.

"Too late, Doc. I'm already on it."

He nudged the aircraft closer, trying to merge with the other plane. Turk told the computer to stop its proximity warnings, but his own sense of space held him back. He had to fight against his instincts as he lifted the wing to the left, coming up against the Hog's.

The Tigershark jerked down as the force of slipstream off the other plane's wing pushed it away. Turk struggled to control the plane but lost altitude too quickly to stay close. He saw the Hog moving overhead and tried to adjust, shifting to the right for another try.

Do it, he told himself. *Do it.*

Tap the wing. Throw it off course. Take your shot.

"What?" asked a disembodied voice. "What?"

A woman's voice . . . Ginella's, as if coming out of a dream.

"You're going into a spin," he said over the radio, trying to push the Tigershark closer.

"What?" asked the other pilot.

"You need to recover," said Turk. "You're at twelve thousand feet and dropping."

"I . . . can't."

"You can," said Turk. He backed the Tigershark off. "Your O-two is screwed up."

"My . . . oxygen."

"Recover!"

"I—"

"Do it!"

Turk started to move back, desperate now—he had done so much, to the point of sacrificing his own plane in a desperate attempt to save her.

He had to succeed.

He started to come back.

"Where are you?" Ginella asked.

"I'm nearby. Can you eject?"

"I . . . eject."

"Eject."

"I . . . I have it. I have it."

The Hog's wing steadied. The plane was still moving in a circle, but the flight was sturdier, more under control. Turk took the Tigershark out wider.

"I'm at—I have control," said Ginella. "I have . . . control."

The A–10 recovered, pulling out ahead, then swooping straight and level.

"Do you think you can handle a refuel?" Turk asked. "If we set a course to the tanker?"

"Yes." Ginella's voice was still a little shaky.

"You sure?"

"I am not walking home from here, Captain," she snapped, her voice nasty.

Good, thought Turk. She's back.

"I need a vector to the tanker," said Turk, talking to the controller. "I need a vector and a tanker. And get rescue assets."

The Hog began to climb.

"Stay under eight thousand feet," he told Ginella. "The lower the better."

"Copy that. You can rejoin your flight. I have it from here."

"Just follow me," Turk told her. "We're going home."

THE TINT OF SUCCESS

1

Sicily

RAY RUBEO FELT HIS LEGS START TO GIVE WAY AS HE reached the tarmac. He reached out and grabbed Danny Freah's side, taking him by surprise and nearly knocking him over.

"Sorry," the scientist said.

"It's all right, Ray. You all right?"

"I will be."

They walked together to the waiting Hummer, Rubeo steadying himself against Danny's shoulder for a few more steps before his balance was back.

"Hell of an adventure," said Danny.

"I owe you an apology," Rubeo said, stopping before the truck. "I shouldn't have gone to Africa."

"No, you shouldn't have."

"I had to, though."

Danny frowned.

"I had to know why the aircraft had made that attack. Kharon had arranged it. He was working with a Russian spy. They had someone insert a virus to infiltrate the system. I've worked it out in my head—they put it into the computer that we used to make sure the GPS system was properly calibrated before takeoff. They must have used one of our memory keys. I suspect the base maintenance crew was infiltrated."

"We can look into that."

"It wasn't a mistake we made. I had to know."

"We would have found out eventually."

"I don't know that we would have. Frankly, if Kharon hadn't explained it, I wouldn't have been able to puzzle it out."

"Don't you always say the science will provide the answer? Doesn't everything work logically?"

"It doesn't always."

Rubeo realized that he had just made an enormous admission—not to Danny, but to himself.

He'd lived more than fifty years, and he was only realizing that now.

Science, logic, were still critical. Emotion was a messy thing. It couldn't necessarily be trusted—it had ruined Kharon's life, and the lives of the people on the ground the plane had attacked. And yet, it had been necessary, it *was* necessary. Because science wasn't everything.

"We're going to have to answer a lot of questions," said Danny.

"I take full responsibility."

"Right."

"I don't blame you for being angry. You're right to be angry. I was foolish. But thank you—thank you for saving me."

Danny nodded. "Let's get some rest."

2

Tripoli

HAVING FORCED THE LIBYAN GOVERNMENT TO DEclare a "temporary cease-fire for humanitarian purposes," Zongchen's committee had accomplished something the UN and allies had been seeking for months. They immediately exerted pressure on the rebels to follow suit.

They were reluctant, until told explicitly that their aid would be immediately cut off.

An hour later the princess and the other rebel leaders issued a statement that they were "putting hostilities aside for now" and were prepared to "join fruitful negotiations."

The Libyan defense minister boarded a plane for "consultations" with the rest of his government. Zen, Zongchen, and the others were left alone in the giant hangar, considering what might be the next step.

"The scientist who worked on the Sabres believes they were sabotaged," Zen told the Chinese general. "I think he'll be able to show the committee exactly what happened."

"That would be optimal."

Zen next spoke to the allied force commander. He wasn't very happy with Danny or any of the rest of the Whiplash team. But given the outcome and the importance of Rubeo's companies to NATO, the allies couldn't afford to make a big deal about the incidents. Not that anyone, Danny or Turk especially, would be praised.

Danny was at a point in his career where this might hurt him, Zen realized; politics at the star level was intense. But he also knew that Danny was the sort of officer who didn't care about politics—he cared about getting the job done.

Which was why Danny was so effective. And one reason they were friends.

As for Rubeo—he was simply too important a person in the scheme of things to be penalized in any way. But if Zen ever got his legs back, Rubeo would be on the list of people to get a kick in the butt.

Fortunately for Rubeo, it was a long list.

With his career as a peace negotiator now officially over, Zen mingled with the other committee members. Soon he and Zongchen found themselves alone, talking about aircraft. The Chinese general had many questions about the Hogs. Zen answered the few that he could, then told him that further answers would have to wait until he got an expert.

"How does it feel to be a peacemaker?" Zen asked, changing the subject.

"Very odd," admitted Zongchen. He smiled. "I am reminded of a proverb to the effect that making war is easier."

"Messier, though."

"Yes. Should we return to the hotel? I believe a round of very stiff drinks are in order."

"That's an excellent idea."

3

Sicily

BY THE TIME TURK AND GINELLA LANDED, THEY HAD A veritable armada of escorts flying around them, including Li, who was fully fueled and had resumed her position on Ginella's wing.

Turk circled the field until the others landed. As he taxied in, every muscle in his body stiffened. He'd been so tense for so long, his legs and arms and neck were virtually frozen into place. He was tempted to have the Tigershark's computer take over and taxi the aircraft to the hangar parking area. But after all that had happened, he felt it was wiser if he stayed on the stick, following the truck that had come out to escort him back.

Night had fallen. As he powered down and prepared to pop the top, he wondered what he would say to Ginella.

He didn't hate her. If anything, he had more respect for her—she had fought through an incredibly difficult situation. She was a hell of a pilot and in truth an excellent flight leader in combat.

Her personal life was something else.

He taxied into his parking area, popped the top and powered down.

"Look what you did to my wing," groused a familiar voice as he poked his head over the side.

It was Chief Al "Greasy Hands" Parsons. The head of the technical operations for Special Projects, he'd arrived in Sicily while Turk was on his sortie.

"Hey, Chief." Turk climbed onto the rollout ladder and started down.

"What were you trying to do? Break it? You know how much this costs, mister?"

"I—uh—"

The older man shook his head, then burst into a loud fit of laughter.

"I was briefed on the whole thing. After the fact." He shook his head, and helped Turk off the ladder. "You know what you were trying to do wouldn't have worked, don't you?"

"Sure it would have."

"Pilots." Greasy Hands laughed.

The veteran crew chief walked all the way with Turk to the flight changing area set up inside the hangar, where the specialists were waiting to help him out of his flight gear.

"Hey," said Beast, who was there with most of the rest of the squadron pilots. "There he is."

Turk braced himself, not sure what to expect. But the other pilots began applauding.

He stopped, unsure of what to do. He'd never had a reaction like that before.

"You really showed a set of balls trying to get the colonel home," said Beast, acting as de facto spokesman. "Thank you."

Even Paulson was, if not actively enthusiastic, at least not antagonistic.

"It wouldn't have worked, Dreamland," said the squadron's executive officer. "But it's the attempt that counts. A hell of a try."

"Thanks," said Turk, as graciously as he could manage.

He looked around, expecting to see Ginella somewhere. Instead, he saw Li beaming at him—a much more welcome sight.

"You were great," she said, eyes wide. "You were really great."

"Thanks."

She squeezed his hand in a way that made him flush.

"Where's the colonel?" he asked.

Beast snorted. "Medical people grabbed her. She didn't want to go. Practically had to knock her out to get her into the ambulance."

"I heard she decked half of them," said Paulson.

"Don't expect a thank-you," added Beast. "Not from the Dominatrix."

"I wouldn't expect anything," Turk said. "Not a thing."

New York Times Bestseller

DALE BROWN
AND
JIM DEFELICE

THE DREAMLAND THRILLERS

REVOLUTION

978-0-06-218817-5

The Dreamland team must stop a dangerous revolution in the making in Eastern Europe.

WHIPLASH

978-0-06-218818-2

On the African continent, one man holds the power to unleash terror and global chaos. But the covert strike force Whiplash is armed and ready to spring into action.

BLACK WOLF

978-0-06-171301-9

Powerful elements within a newly resurgent Russia want to stop an alliance with NATO. Can Whiplash stand up to a covert army of genetically enhanced assassins?

RAVEN STRIKE

978-0-06-171302-6

In the blistering heat of the Sudan, the CIA has gone rogue. And now the ultimate weapon has fallen into the wrong hands.

COLLATERAL DAMAGE

978-0-06-171303-3

Something has gone terribly wrong with a "foolproof" new superweapon, resulting in the deaths of innocents.